Fossils, Ferals and Flies

Carolyn Lang

Illustrated by
Alice Taylor

ISBN: 978-0-646-85441-0

Published by Geosed Consulting and Editing Services

January 2022

❀ Created with Vellum

Preface

The following fictional account was inspired by my experience as a cook in a geological field camp in North Queensland during the eighties. Like Cynthia, the narrator, I had no experience that could possibly have prepared me for that job. These days I would reject such a proposition immediately, more accurately assessing my chances of success as poor, and therefore likely to be too stressful to be bothered with. But such is the optimism of youth, I went ahead regardless and never regretted my decision (at least not in the long term). Yes, there were failures and flops and steep learning curves, but there were other things too. Living in the bush plunged me into a different culture, a whole new world, one I'd been largely unaware of during my Brisbane upbringing. It also introduced me to the world of geology, a science which deals with such vast dimensions of time, it can make human concerns seem as inconsequential as the trail marks of a long-extinct species of worm, etched and preserved on a rock.

Writing this story was like taking a cauldron and tossing in an assortment of ingredients. Into the mix went memories from field camp days, impressions of the people I encountered and the stories and gossip I picked up along the way. A few ring-ins from completely different contexts found their way into the pot along with a few pinches of seasoning for added flavour. The mixture was stirred and simmered. What emerged from this process was obviously not a completely accurate representation of the field camps I had experienced. It's more like a parallel version where much is familiar, but much is not quite the same, a slightly skewed version of reality. In other words, it is a fiction-alised rendition of that world.

For a start, Burkes Hill, Blue Ridge, Bogarilla, Wallaby Gorge and the Black Bream River are fictional, although they are based on real places. As for the characters, while it would be misleading to suggest that 'any resemblance to any known person is purely coincidental', it would be just as misleading to suggest that any one of the characters presented here is a real-istic portrait of any one person I encountered during those years. They have come out of the cauldron transformed. There were too many people involved in the field camps to include them all, so a smaller group of characters represent the whole. A bit of mixing and matching went on. As a result these characters have had to do some heavy lifting and have developed their own separate identities as they took on other characteristics and roles.

Names have been changed, except in the case of Paul, Grasshopper and Hendo, all of whom in their younger years expressed the desire to appear in a book. They may have a different opinion on this matter now they are pushing through advanced middle age; however I have remained true to their youthful selves and indulged this request. But they too, if they ever get round to reading this, will be surprised by some of the things their characters do and say.

Some of my own memories from those times seem far-fetched nowadays, although I wrote the first version of this narrative decades ago when my memories were still fresh and sharp. But memory can be tricky, even in the short term. It's selective, focussing on some things and overlooking others. For example, I have depicted the occupants of the sister field camp of Bogarilla as a bunch of carousing drunks, and yet not so long ago at a dinner, I sat next to a person who had been stationed at the real-life version of that camp, who assured me most sincerely that he had drunk only tea and had gone to church each weekend. It goes to show that you're much more likely to recall the wild guy shooting shaving cream over his party hosts than you are the quiet one sipping tea in the corner and disappearing off to church.

If memory is selectively unreliable, then the stories I have included that were told to me by others are probably every bit as unsound. My informants could spin a good yarn but their object was never accuracy. The telling of stories, particularly those focussing on the misadventures of others, was part of the atmosphere, and was probably cathartic. There was some mischief making in this—we all enjoy being entertained at the expense of others. But there is also something humanising in telling funny stories about each other. They remind us that no individual is better than any other. At heart we are all equally as foolish in our own ways, and equally as valuable.

In today's raw and imperfect human world there is a tendency to present curated and perfect images of our lives, with the flaws erased or kept firmly beyond the edges of a photograph, and yet how tedious that becomes after a while. It begins to numb the mind. It gets boring. Real people have spots and scars and sagging skin. They can be heroic and brilliant, also belligerent, kind, creative, maddeningly inconsistent, generous, argumentative and illogical.

In this story, if Cynthia had been utterly capable and arrived in the north to a camp of impeccable people who treated one another with unvarying courtesy, it would make for dull reading indeed. There's freedom to be had in embracing our flaws and foibles and accepting that absurdity is part of the human condition. Those colourful people whose antics pepper our lives with interest should be celebrated. They keep us amused and remind us that there are times when life should not be taken so seriously. They can also prick through our individual and collective bubbles of self-importance.

I met many people like this in North Queensland, but the place itself was even more effective at deflating any sense of self-consequence. It's hard to be superior with a fly in your nostril. All the creatures in that wilderness – the kangaroos, the emus, the gentle rock wallabies, the turtles, the birdlife, even the wild pigs – were reminders that there are many other entities that make up this world. And the landscape, the rocks that the geologists studied, had a deeper message still. They tell a story in which humankind is nothing but a speck in the grand drama of the earth's history.

This is a planet of constant tumultuous and wondrous change, in which continents clash and mountain ranges rise and fall, where ice caps form, spread then melt, where strings of volcanoes appear to migrate as the crust moves across a hot spot. The fossils in the rocks remind us that whole orders of life come and go, just as the ice ages come and go. We can respect and love this planet; we can live sustainably for the benefit of ourselves and the flora and fauna we share this world with, but we can't save the planet. It will get on perfectly well, with or without us, just as it has for most of its cataclysmic existence.

But if any of us in those field camps were impervious to the message to be read in the landscape or in the rock samples that were littered about the camps like trash, then we only had to glance above at the sky each night. Far away from the city lights, the cosmos blazed and sparkled in the darkness, so it was impossible not to be aware that the earth itself is just a speck on the edge of a galaxy that sits among a host of other galaxies swirling into infinite space. And if that observation was terrifying, it was also somehow soothing.

It seems that Cynthia is about to embark on quite a journey...

Chapter 1

Burnt potatoes

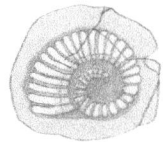

ONCE, on a starry night back in the eighties, in a more innocent and less fettered time, I watched a man sprint around an old mine site in the dusty old town of Burkes Hill in North Queensland. He was wearing nothing but a pair of running shoes that had been smeared with toothpaste.

The human world was not then so encumbered with committee meetings, ideologies, and the entanglements of social media. The word *inappropriate* was not heard so often, and the finger pointing that people enjoy so much these days didn't happen as frequently. This man was breathing freer air as he leapt from mullock heap to mullock heap. If his soul compelled him to run naked through the night smelling of dental hygiene, there wasn't much that would urge him to rethink his choice, especially when a bunch of his friends were cheering him on from the roof of a nearby caravan.

All inhibitions had been cast aside. Only a few moments earlier, these guys had been screaming out their frustrated sexual yearnings in a ghastly booming chant that had echoed across the neighbourhood. The neighbours, disturbed by the rumpus, assumed there had been a breakout from the institution on the other side of town. It seemed the most likely explanation. It didn't immediately occur to them that members of the visiting geological team had caused the disturbance.

Geologists often passed through town—an amiable bunch of outdoorsy nerds with a morbid interest in extinct animals. They occasionally turned up to community social events where they would help the kids with their rock collections and drink a beer or two before retiring to bed, tired out from all that hearty outdoor work. They were not known for carousing through the streets in the early hours of the morning or for shouting out their most personal problems for the whole community to hear.

But these particular geologists and their field hands had been based for too long at the camp known as the Compound, a dismal place built amongst the mullock heaps on the edge of town—a vista of ditches and dust and broken-down dongas, with non-functioning facilities and a complete lack of homely comforts. The place had eventually got them down, eaten into their souls and dislodged their minds. What had begun as a recreational evening down at the pub to listen to a local band had got out of hand. It was understandable; they'd been marooned at the Compound with their colleagues for months.

Those colleagues were part of the problem. There was no getting away from them. They chobbled breakfast cereal at the table each morning and snored nearby each night. And they weren't a cohesive group of kindred spirits either. There were women with strong feminist leanings and blokes whose aims in life never went beyond shooting feral pigs and watching the State of Origin matches. There were philosophers and hedonists, tea-drinkers and drunks, churchgoers and atheists.

At the beginning of a field season the novelty of the situation, as well as an abundance of good will and good manners, smooth these differences. But as the weeks go by, things change. Tensions build. Not because of anything significant, more usually the provocations are slight: a jarring laugh; a joke told too many times; an overheard whisper, misconstrued. But just as a volcano will not remain forever dormant no matter how peaceful the forested slopes appear, trouble will come. Sooner or later.

* * *

My involvement with the field camps began a few years before the naked-man-with-toothpaste-on-his shoes episode when I was offered the cook's job at the GIU (Geological Investigations Unit) Blue Ridge Base Camp. I had no qualifications for the job and limited experience, but the employers were so desperate they couldn't care less. Cooks had a bad reputation at the GIU. There had been a recent run of bad luck with cooks, a succession of sour-tempered miseries, troublemaking drunks, jailbirds and thugs. Perhaps, the logic went, it would be better to engage a non-cook. And that's when I got the phone call from Eddie, who was based at the field camp, telling me that the potatoes had burned three times in a row.

'I thought you had a cook up there,' I said.

'Well, no actually. We don't. That's just what I want to talk to you about.'

I was married to Eddie. He had been gone for several weeks at this point and I was missing him, a factor that distorted my judgment. There was no reason whatsoever for me to go charging north to Blue Ridge, an obscure mining town so small you could walk across it in less than five minutes. I didn't need the work and I was in the second trimester of pregnancy. This was no time to be throwing in a good job, uprooting myself, and galloping off to the middle of nowhere. His suggestion was flattering but ridiculous.

'I'm not a cook, Eddie,' I said.

'Precisely,' Eddie replied. 'That's just the point. We don't want a real cook up here. They're way too much trouble. They get drunk on the lemon essence. They sulk. They roll the camp vehicles. They have to be bailed out of jail. No, what we need is somebody entirely different, somebody sensible and good-tempered and tolerant.'

'Somebody who can cook?'

'You can cook Cynthia. You've done dinner parties. Cooking for a geological party shouldn't be any different. Bring a few recipe books and follow the instructions. Besides, I'd love you to come. You haven't lived till you've seen Wallaby Gorge and the Black Bream River. You've got to see the ripple marks, the fossilised wormholes, the oolites, the adhesion warts ...'

'What?'

'Yes ... well ... um ... Look, there's other things you'd like up here—wallabies and birds and the starriest skies you'll ever see. You can count the shooting stars at night. And we can be together again. Just imagine, you and me sleeping under the stars, listening to the crackle of the campfire, night creatures rustling. At least think about it. And why not give Gerald Drake a call?'

Gerald Drake was the director of the GIU, an overweight and amiable middle-aged man, soft from too much airconditioning, fat from too many free lunches, and prone to fantasy. He was notorious for the wild stories he told at Christmas parties, when, with the help of a few beers, he forgot that he was the manager of the outfit, forgot that his office chair had the thickest padding and the highest back, and remembered only the good old days when he was the most heroic of field geologists searching for outcrop in the far-flung regions of Queensland.

Back in those mythical days enormous crocodiles with t-rex habits lurked on the riverbanks in gangs and venomous snakes were frequently found in swags. Gun-wielding landowners with a grudge against geologists prowled through the bush and the camp cooks were often insane.

I can't explain now why I even bothered to call Gerald Drake about the job at Blue Ridge, but whatever was whispering to my soul and luring me on was not rational thought.

'God's Own Country!' Gerald Drake enthused over the phone. 'Wind in the trees, dew on the grass, dingoes howling in the night ... nothing like the taste of billy tea first thing in the morning ... the smell of eucalypt leaves on the fire ...'

'Gerald, I was asking about the cooking job?'

'Yes, I know, and I'm delighted to hear from you. Come and join our big happy family. And have we got a deal for you. We pay the cooks a full-time wage for part-time work. Sounds good, doesn't it? You're only needed at weekends. Everyone's in the field all week and there's nobody in camp. You can do what you like. Go out in the field with Eddie. Discover God's Own Country for yourself. Expand your soul.'

I was too naïve then to realise that a casual cook on weekend penalty rates would earn far more than the full-time pay I was offered. But Gerald had a tone of irrepressible enthusiasm in his voice that made this seem like an unmissable opportunity, as if there was something far more enchanting waiting for me than just a drudge job peeling thousands of potatoes in the north Queensland heat.

Before I had fully grasped what I had agreed to (if I had agreed to it at all), I was packing, shoving aprons and recipe books into a bag. There seemed to have been a general assumption in Blue Ridge that I would turn up sometime soon and take up the cooking job, but there was no formal agreement. I felt as if I had stumbled inadvertently onto an express train that was hurtling me to a far destination I hadn't bargained on. And yet this wasn't a failure of will either. I could have refused to go along with the plan at any point, but there was a part of me that didn't want to. Baby coming or not, rational decision or not, the wilder pathway was so much more alluring than the well-paved road of routine existence.

Just as my mind was swirling in that surreal way that happens when life suddenly changes its trajectory, a total stranger bowled up to my door and knocked loudly. When I opened the door, there he stood on the doorstep waving a large, vicious weapon in my direction. This was disconcerting, but there was not a shred of aggression in his demeanour and a pleasant expression was plastered on his face. It was as if he imagined I had been hoping all day he would drop by with the thing. That surreal vibe escalated as he plunged into conversation in the friendliest manner. Anyone listening would have thought we'd known each other for years and were taking up where we had left off.

This was all very confusing, but I somehow managed to glean the following facts:

1. He had a son called Paul who was a field hand based at Blue Ridge.
2. Blue Ridge was overrun by feral pigs.
3. Paul needed the crossbow so he could exterminate them.
4. I had promised to take the crossbow to Paul.
5. He and Paul were very grateful.

I had never heard of Paul and didn't care much for his mission. Intellectually, I could appreciate the need to control feral animal populations. Personally, I wanted nothing to do with it. However, I must have stood there in stunned silence because before I knew it I was in possession of the thing, apparently having made a commitment to transport it all the way to Blue Ridge.

To be honest, being seen in public with a large animal-exterminating implement was not part of my self-image. It was mortifying. The next day I crept into the airport, trying to look inconspicuous. In these modern security-ridden times such an object wouldn't be permitted anywhere near an airport, but in those days nobody even blinked. It was as if pregnant women in maternity smocks strolled into the place every day lugging crossbows along with their luggage.

There I was in the departures queue, clutching the crossbow, feeling like a jerk, and wondering what the hell I was doing there. What had I been thinking? Eddie and Gerald Drake had spoken of starlight, campfires and dingoes. God's Own Country. But as I watched that crossbow vanish into the black hole beyond the departures desk, I had an ominous feeling that I may have been misled.

Chapter 2

Vogue for men

God's Own Country was not impressive at first sight.

Eddie collected us at the airport, the crossbow and I, and we drove west to Burkes Hill, a town that had once thrived in the goldrush days but hadn't thrived much since. Eddie wasn't keen to drive further although we could have easily made Blue Ridge that day. He claimed the road was dangerous after dark and we were better off staying where we were. The possibility of cattle on the road or the odd suicidal roo would not usually deter him, so I suspect he was trying to put off the moment when I would actually see the field camp. We stayed in a run-down old pub in the main street of Burkes Hill and delayed reality until morning.

Leaving early, we continued north along a bleached-bones highway, through an interminable tract of ironbarks, past crows and wedge-tailed eagles pecking at the roadkill. Eventually, Eddie pulled the vehicle off the highway, which stretched on in a straight line towards eternity, and headed into Blue Ridge.

Blue Ridge was a tiny snippet of suburbia flung out amidst the ironbarks, a tidy town, managed by the local mine, with lawns and gardens and well-kept homes. But the vehicle sailed past these and came to a halt outside the two most dilapidated houses in town. The lawns were dissolving to dust and were littered with battered billycans, odd tarpaulins and rock samples. A man approached us through this scatter of objects. He looked like a youthful Santa Claus dressed for a bush picnic.

'Hey Slanger!' he called out. 'Thank God you've arrived.'

Eddie leapt from the car. 'Cynthia, meet Christopher Craddock, our party leader.'

Christopher extended his hand and muttered something polite about a cup of tea. But he stared at me with a cautious stare, as if I was an animal about to break loose into wild and unpredictable behaviour. I suppose he couldn't help himself. All those past cooks must have left a mark upon his soul. He brightened up soon enough, recalling that I was a non-cook cook.

'It's time to get this show back on the road. Grab a cup of tea and we'll all get out of here. And Cynthia, get Eddie to show you the kitchen. You'll have the mechanic in tonight,' he said.

What! What was this about the mechanic? And shoving me straight into the kitchen? Didn't he know I was employed just for weekend work? Today was Tuesday. According to Gerald Drake, I was free. Free to settle in, or go into the field with Eddie, or explore God's Own Country. I could ballet dance or write poetry. Or walk across the town. Anything but hang about in the kitchen and cook dinner for a grease-splattered mechanic.

'But Gerald Drake said ...'

'You don't want to take any notice of what Gerald says,' said Christopher. A peculiar expression flitted across his face. His eyeballs darted about their sockets and his nose twitched like a rabbit's. The conversation was making him nervous.

'Why not? He's the boss.'

'Well, yes. Theoretically,' said Christopher.

'Theoretically?'

'Theoretically,' said Eddie. 'Because he's a long way away

and he can't always be abreast of everything that's going on up here.'

I had not even gone through the doorway yet and I already regretted my arrival. The urge to run away and leave them all to their burnt potatoes was strong, but there was nowhere to go and no means of getting there. I was trapped like a fly in a cobweb.

'Cheer up Cynthia,' said Eddie. 'The mechanic won't be here long and then you can come with me to see the ripple marks and so on. They're not going anywhere. Already been there 450 million years. They can wait a week or two.'

With that irritating bit of wisdom, I left him to the luggage and headed into the house. I was desperate for that cup of tea. The inside of the house was as shabby as the outside. There was grime on the windows and dust on the floors. In the living area a few plastic chairs were arranged around a rickety table on which had been placed an old metallic teapot, a tin of biscuits and a collection of enamel mugs. Seated on those plastic chairs were several slovenly creeps. At least that's how they appeared to me at that moment, and I felt as alien as if I'd blundered in on a baboon troop.

I smiled at them feebly and they smiled back equally as feebly and went on slurping at their tea and munching on biscuits. None of us knew what to say to each other, so we said nothing. I had been hoping this cup of tea would put some heart and soul into me, but it didn't have the soothing effect I expected. The teapot, almost too hot to touch, sizzled, spat and hissed, as if it had been made in a school metal-working class by a kid with a grudge against the world. I scalded my hand when I poured the tea and the apemen looked on silently.

Eventually a guy who looked more like a yowie than a man broke the ice. He pointed to my belly and said, 'You gonna give us another little field hand, hey?'

'Shut up, Wally. You don't say things like that.' The speaker, wiry and sunburnt, looked like he had recently given himself a haircut without bothering to look in a mirror. It was only when he glanced into the hallway and saw the crossbow Eddie had dumped there that the conversation really got going.

'Pigs ... pigs,' he whispered in a sudden rapture.

'Ah,' I said, 'You must be Paul.'

'Pigs,' he replied.

I changed the subject. 'So, does Gerald Drake ever come and visit these field camps?'

'Yeah, occasionally. Sort of,' he responded.

'And stays to sleep under the stars and listen to the dingoes howl?'

'Nah. Not that. He stays around long enough to gorge himself on the cook's scones then pisses off. He probably told you that crap about God's Own Country, wind in the trees blah blah blah. It's pathetic. Thinks it's motivating.'

'Yeah. But we're motivated by pigs,' said Wally.

'Yeah!' Paul agreed, and they thrust their fists in the air with a gesture of masculine idiocy.

I averted my eyes, looked through the window at the sun pouring over a rampant bougainvillea vine. There was a hammock swinging over a small porch. Below it was an ashtray crammed with cigarette butts.

'I don't know that Gerald could fit into a swag anymore,' said Paul thoughtfully. 'Besides he told me last Christmas that coming out into the field at his age causes constipation.'

'Ah, but you'll like it here, luv,' said Wally kindly. 'It's great. You can shoot pigs, fish the water holes, go to the pub ... Yeah. It's the best job.'

'It only looks like the arse end of world,' Paul added.

At this point Eddie and Christopher joined our little gang. They were obviously in great haste because they poured themselves tea and gulped it down without bothering to sit. The formalities involved in my arrival had delayed the fieldwork for a day and they were keen get back to it. Not that those formalities had been great. I had been collected from the airport, told to ignore the manager and informed the mechanic would be in for dinner. Apart from that I would have to work it out for myself.

But the orientation did continue after morning tea, when Christopher and Eddie showed me the bedroom I would share with Eddie whenever he was back from the field. It was a bare little room with a ceiling fan, a very peculiar bed and a steel box that functioned as a bedside table. Eddie and Christopher looked smug as if they were showing me a palatial room with a feather bed, designer linen, and handmade chocolates on the pillowslip.

'We know it's not right for a pregnant woman to sleep on the floor,' said Eddie. 'So, Christopher and me, well we built this bed. Specially for you.'

I wasn't sure whether to be touched or afraid.

Christopher said, 'I have one more bit of good news for you. I have just this morning managed to engage an assistant cook. It took quite a bit of persuasion, but she finally agreed. She's the draftsman's wife and she'll be along later to help out.' And with a sigh of relief at having completed all formalities, he gathered his troops. 'Come on. Time to get back to the glorious pursuit of outcrop!'

Before I knew it they were gone, driving out towards the highway with their baboon assistants. They would not be back till Friday. I confess to a moment of panic. I suppressed an urge to shriek abuse at them for abandoning me here with strangers. That mechanic would almost certainly be a grubbier version of Paul and Wally and that draftsman's wife, the assistant Christopher was so pleased about, was probably a bad-tempered old bag. Not much to look forward to. But it was no use screaming at the honeyeaters twittering in the trees above or the dog down the road, tongue out, lying in the shade of an orange tree. I went into the kitchen.

Right or wrong, like it or loathe it, I had a new job and I would have to make the best of it. I could begin by surveying the equipment and the stores. That would be a start. Three cockroaches played dead in the sink, but the kitchen was otherwise tidy and I felt a tiny flicker of motivation. After all, for all I knew, this could be the beginning of a new and brilliant career.

If it was the beginning of a brilliant career, it didn't start well. When I tried to open the door of the nearest cupboard, it leapt at out at me with unnatural aggression and clattered onto the floor with a reverberating clang. This seemed a very bad sign. I couldn't even enter the kitchen without the place falling apart. As the clang echoed through the house, I could feel that draftsman's wife glaring with disapproval into the kitchen. Actually, there was nobody there at all, but it was still humiliating.

I retired to my bedroom to sulk. Just like all those past GIU cooks, I'd been told about, the ones who would sulk for days, serving foul slops and not speaking all the while. Not that I sulked for long. It was impossible. The bed made a grating noise when I flung myself upon it and did not yield to my contours as beds usually do. It was so uncomfortable I wondered if the mattress was stuffed with pumpkins. Sulking in comfort was not going to work, and as for sleeping ...

Eddie and Christopher were good geologists, but they lacked talent in bed design. They had scrounged an ancient mattress from an old shed, plonked it onto an arrangement of old paint tins, and congratulated themselves on a job well done. It was a failure. I kicked those paint tins out from beneath the mattress and immediately felt better, as if I had discarded the burdens of negativity and joined the world of positive action.

With a fleeting burst of energy, I grasped at reality. Eddie was expanding his soul in God's Own Country, probably watching birds in flight and feeling the wind on his face. I was stuck in a dusty broken-down house in a half-dead town. I was the cook and the mechanic was on his way, expecting dinner.

If only Eddie and Christopher had bothered to describe this mechanic, I doubt I would have been so depressed at having to stay behind to feed him. He arrived in the afternoon and wandered into the house, pausing to gaze at his reflection in the mirror that was suspended on the hallway wall.

'Hi there,' he said, 'I'm Jeremy Leech. And you, I'm guessing, are Cynthia Slanger. I've heard all about you. Good of you to sacrifice yourself like this in a good cause.'

I stared. This man was nothing like a grubby version of Wally. He had good looks and style. Impossible to think that he'd just been driving for hours along dusty outback roads. It was more likely that he had just popped in from a classy photo shoot where he had been gazing seductively at the camera from beside an expensive vehicle. Jeremy was bronzed, blue-eyed, fair-haired, and he possessed a quality of refinement completely lacking in anybody else I had so far encountered at the Blue Ridge field camp. He wore a pink shirt with *Vogue for Men* written on it, and his hands were clean and smelled of hand lotion. I couldn't imagine him ever lying in the dirt beneath a vehicle and wondered what twist of fate had caused him to end up miles from anywhere as the GIU mechanic.

'So, why are you here in Blue Ridge, then?' I asked.

'Purely for the money,' he replied. 'This is a lucrative gig for me. You know—weekend overtime, penalty rates and so on. And I get around a bit, can take days off down at the coast, unwind with a spot of deep-sea fishing or scuba diving over the reef. Not like you, underpaid and confined to Blue Ridge.'

'I thought I might go out into the field with Eddie when you're not around.'

'Why? There's nothing there, just rocks and miles of emptiness. There's more action here in Blue Ridge, and that's saying a lot. Don't worry. I'll be here sometimes, and I can keep you amused.'

His face contorted and he perambulated about the house like an overexcited chimpanzee. He came to a halt on the porch where he kicked the ashtray into the garden bed, plunged into the hammock, and shut his eyes.

'I'm exhausted. I've come all the way from Bogarilla. It's a long, boring drive and I need some refreshment. Could you fix me a cup of tea please? I have it white with six sugars, but don't stir it, I don't like it sweet.'

Chapter 3

The golden age

I was at ease with the world by the time I nestled onto the mattress that night and fell asleep to the chirrup of cane toads. The evening hadn't been nearly as bad as I had imagined it would be when I first stepped over the threshold that morning and glimpsed the grey walls and bare-boned furniture. Sure, I had probably made a terrible mistake in disrupting my life to come to such a dump. And yet ...

This change of attitude began when the new assistant cook, Janey Smith, the 'draftsman's wife', turned up in the afternoon. Just one look and all visions of that grumpy old bag dissolved immediately. Janey was cheerfully pushing an infant in a stroller, a nappy flung over her shoulder, baby vomit on her tee-shirt. It was all so refreshingly human. Nobody had heard of yummy mummies in those days. We must have had lower standards back then.

The Smiths lived together in an old bus parked in the field at the back of the GIU houses. This field was right on the edge of town and as the bus faced the ironbark wilderness that started just metres from their doorstep, they must have felt all alone out there and miles away from the rest of the field party. Janey said this wasn't because they were antisocial or because they liked to watch the wallabies creep out from the trees each evening to graze in the field; it was because their baby wasn't keen on sleeping at night and preferred to yell at the top his lungs. It was only civil to keep separate.

Eric Smith, the draftsman, looked as if he had just stepped out of an old black and white photograph dating from the time of Australia's federation. It was the mixture of whiskers, beard, composure and tidiness that did it. He could have been one of those venerable characters whose images are splashed on our paper currency. But unlike those men who stood so stiff and solemn when they were photographed, as if life was too serious and weighty a matter to allow for any levity, Eric knew how to crack a smile and relax. He was one of those guys who billow good will into the atmosphere almost biologically, and who think nothing of telling a few corny jokes if they think it will improve somebody's day.

Eric spent his days drafting in the silver caravan parked out near the bus in the field at the back while Janey pottered about Blue Ridge with a feeling of permanent jet lag. If she had not been so tired she would have been the perfect candidate for the non-cook cook the camp was seeking, but she was far too sensible to mix responsibility with exhaustion. Multiplying the stresses would be bad for everybody, she said. There was no point. Much better just to put up with burnt potatoes and scorched saucepans.

'Assistant cook', she said, 'Now that's another matter. I see it as a flexible arrangement where I escape the burden of it all. If something goes wrong it will be your responsibility. But don't worry, nothing will go wrong as long as we take care not to burn any more potatoes.'

Meanwhile the mechanic, who had been dozing in the hammock, awoke and wandered into the house to sing arias in the shower. He emerged sometime later in a velvet gown of midnight blue with a white bunny embroidered on it. He was enveloped in a cloud of powdery floral perfume and strode directly into the kitchen where he bent to inspect the beef and potatoes sizzling in the oven.

'Fab!' he said. 'And what shall we have with it?'

Jeremy, it turned out, loved to cook. In fact, he was a much more enthusiastic cook than he was a mechanic. Mechanics got tedious after a while, he said. It involved getting one's hands dirty and he detested dirty hands.

'Perhaps I should have applied for your job,' he said. 'But it doesn't pay well, and I wouldn't get much of a suntan cooped up in a kitchen ... hey look, cooking sherry, a whole carton of the stuff. Bet that was ordered by last year's cook and I bet she didn't cook with it either. Let's do sherried carrots.'

* * *

The next day the house didn't seem anywhere near as grim as it had the day before. Of course, it was just as shabby, but I didn't bother looking at it much. There were other things to take up my attention. Eddie could go ahead and revel in the delights of the fossils along the Black Bream River without me. I would be okay.

This state of mind lasted for the remainder of the week. Every morning as the sun rose over the ironbarks, Jeremy discarded his velvet dressing gown to reveal a fine body clad only in a pair of exceptionally brief, bright yellow bathers. In this garment he intended to work on the vehicles parked out in the yard and sunbathe as he went about it. The fabric was so thin that the sun shone straight through with no protection at all.

'Tan through,' said Jeremy. 'I like an even colour. None of those white patches where the pants have been. Not a cool look.'

He turned up for breakfast each morning with a bottle of coconut oil and wanted it massaged into his back before he started work. In return he pretended to be a gorilla defending his family on a mountaintop or would share a few recipes. These were unexpected and novel circumstances and I enjoyed them.

Conditions were favourable that first week in Blue Ridge. Jeremy gleamed with oil and smelled like a beach. Eric cracked a series of jokes so pathetic we had to laugh. And Janey and I baked cakes for the freezer and told each other our life stories, all the while becoming infused with what I now realise was totally unrealistic optimism. We thought we had set the bar too low by imagining that success meant not burning the dinner. We could do far better than that. We could instigate a new era for the GIU cooks. A golden age.

We could already smell the delectable aromas of finely cooked food that would greet the workers as they returned from the field each Friday afternoon. There would be intelligent smiling faces behind the benches, not the boozed up, angry, or sulking wretches of the past. No longer would the Anzac biscuits burn in the oven while the cook tried to seduce the mechanic in the dark beneath the mulberry tree. It wasn't that we lost complete touch with reality. We didn't imagine we were celebrity chefs or anything. We just thought that the good-tempered delivery of wholesome food was a perfectly reasonable goal.

Friday was the real beginning of our career as camp cooks. On Friday morning Jeremy flung out words of encouragement as he slowly fried in the sun while he bent over a motor in the yard. We swept out the dining room, covered the trestle tables with checked cloths, and tried to improve the ambience with neatly placed cutlery and arrangements of decorative weeds from the garden.

By late afternoon everything was in order when the first vehicle arrived. Within seconds an extremely filthy man bolted into the kitchen as if he had been catapulted from the car. He collapsed like a cowering animal against the pantry door and shut his eyes. The sight of us working in the kitchen must have been too overwhelming for his shattered nervous system to bear.

'He doesn't shut up,' he muttered. 'Talk, talk, talk, all week without stopping. And he drives like a bloody maniac. It's a bloody miracle we're still alive.'

'Hey, James McCracken!' I said, recognising him beneath the layers of grime. 'How are you doing? Are you okay?'

He opened his eyes.

'Cynthia, you've arrived. Don't think I'm not pleased to see you. I am. I really am. I would have had a nervous breakdown if you hadn't come and I had to eat one more burnt potato. And I think you'll do well here, even if you are a bit hormonal and peculiar right now. Much better than the emotionally disturbed ratbags they usually send ...'

He suddenly abandoned the conversation and hurled himself out the back door with all the frenzy of a pursued rabbit.

'What's going on?' asked Janey. 'And what's with the "hormonal and peculiar" bit?'

But there was no time to discuss it. We heard the sound of bare feet slapping along the hallway vinyl and our next visitor arrived. This was another familiar face, Eddie's brother, Sebastian, who had just finished his first week of work with the GIU. Apparently, he had turned up unexpectedly a couple of weeks before, riding a motorbike, with a small bag and guitar strapped to the back. He was looking for work. Sebastian was a wild man with wild hair and missing teeth and had never bothered much with conventions. But none of this deterred Christopher Craddock from appointing him as a field hand. Personal presentation wasn't big on the list of job criteria for field hands and Christopher probably felt he'd fit right in.

'Hey Cynthia, welcome to the place that God forgot. Shouldn't complain. It's work,' said Sebastian, leaning towards me and kissing my cheek.

I was immediately engulfed by the smell of campfire smoke and sweat, a smell that mingled unpleasantly with another odour that had begun to drift from the oven.

'Where's James gone?' he asked. 'Jumpy fella. I've got his gear here. Jeez Cynthia, what the hell are you cooking in that oven? Stinks something severe.'

Right at that moment the new golden age began. Most of the geologists and field hands arrived all at once and poured into the house. But there was no appetising aroma to meet them as we had hoped, only a nauseating and pervasive stink. There were no smiling faces either. How could we smile when something had gone hideously wrong with our meal plan? We ignored the newcomers, leaving them to congregate in the lounge room and make faces at each other in communal dread of the meal to come. I guess they were wishing they had gone for the only real cook available, a promiscuous troublemaker with a drinking problem.

Meanwhile, I scrabbled in the oven to find what was amiss. The casserole and the upside-down puddings were fine, almost perfect, but a pile of muck bubbled on the base of the oven. This spillage may have appeared inconsequential, but it not only pumped out the horrendous stench, it also caught alight. By the time Christopher crept into the kitchen to check on us, flames were leaping from the oven.

He was not a man normally given to shrieking, but on this occasion he shrieked—'Fire, fire, fire!'

This helped neither our morale nor our plummeting reputation. Janey glared at him, snatched up a saucepan lid and smothered the flames with it.

'Stop panicking!' she said. 'Anybody would think the whole house was on fire! It's only a bit of muck on the bottom of the oven. Easy to deal with. No need to cause a riot.'

'But ... but ... what about the meal?'

'There's no problem with your dinner! It will be ready in precisely half an hour.' I was feeling so edgy I snapped at the man.

'Good,' he replied as his eyes fell on the bottle of cooking sherry we'd left on the bench. 'Aha!' he continued in a voice that combined revelation with insinuation, as if he imagined he had just discovered the root cause of the problem. 'Cooks and the cooking sherry, hey ... Oh well, I'd better go and have a shower.'

'For heaven's sake,' said Janey. 'You'd think we'd been guzzling the stuff. All we did was put a tablespoon in the carrots.'

We had wanted to make a good first impression, or, at the very least, be accepted as pleasant, capable women. Instead, we were exposed as a couple of irritable incompetents who couldn't even cook a meal without setting fire to the oven. And the cooking sherry on the bench was taken as a sign we were on some slippery slope to hopeless alcoholism. Not a great beginning.

Our personal cheer squad wasn't available to help right then, either. Jeremy was busy in his bedroom applying moisturisers to his skin and Eric was bathing the baby. But at least Eddie turned up to give us some support—'Hey, Cynthia, Janey, how are you doing? What's that smell? Have you two been trying to burn the house down or did you just overcook our dinner? I saw some great ripple marks this week.'

Chapter 4

The pony club

THE MEAL BEGAN. This was our chance to redeem ourselves. Janey and I laid the dishes on the table and hovered in the doorway to watch the reaction. A hairy intimidating mass filled the dining room, although I noticed a small group of women sitting together at the end of a table—two geologists, Priscilla and Michelle, and a field hand, Jen. Jeremy Leech stood out much as a zebra would if it was grazing with a flock of dirty sheep.

The meal went over well except for an awkward moment when a geologist mistook the bowl of rice for a bowl of mashed potatoes. This was Bugsy, a kindly soul, nicknamed because of prominent teeth and wide cheeks, not out of rudeness, I was told, but as a mark of respect and affection. When Bugsy became aware of his mistake he apologised profusely, blaming his poor eyesight. He shovelled a forkful of rice into his mouth and proclaimed it excellent.

'Shut up Bugsy. You're making it worse,' said Paul. 'The rice is gluggy but it's okay. They probably followed the instructions on the packet. That never works.'

After that things settled down to a pleasant buzz. There was a cask of wine, a fridge of beer, and plenty of chitchat. James McCracken was completely recovered from the frazzled state that Sebastian's driving had caused. A shower and a beer can do wonders. He even told a funny story at his own expense about an amorous emu that had chased him about a paddock during the week.

'How's that for a blow to my self-esteem? I mean do I resemble a female emu in any way at all?'

'Pheromones probably,' said Jeremy.

'You must have some kind of animal magnetism,' said Janey.

'Really? Do you think the girl from the grocery store will notice?'

Things could have gone on harmoniously like this all evening, if only Paul could have restrained himself from mentioning the pig subject. But he turned to Wally and just had to ask, 'So how many pigs did you blast off the face of the earth this week?'

Wally shook his head. 'Nah mate, not a pig did I see all week. Not one. But mate, I'll tell you what I got. I got one of them plains turkeys, you know, a bustard, and I stuffed him with tinned peaches, and I roasted him on a bed of coals and ...'

Something had gone very wrong.

I had never heard anybody make such a social blunder quite so nonchalantly. He could have been casually confessing to a murder, which in a way I guess he was.

Something like a bolt of lightning flashed out from the corner and rent the atmosphere. The pleasant buzz ceased. The most insensitive could not have missed the flood of emotion that followed, which emanated from the women on the other table. The place may as well have been hit by a freak wave.

Priscilla, the dominant force in the group, rose to her feet and glared at Wally with such fury I thought he would spontaneously combust. She cut a striking figure that evening, reminding me of a snow queen about to dispense with a naughty boy. Priscilla had a certain quality about her and managed to maintain an aura of glamour even when wearing khaki clothes and army boots.

'What did you just say?' she asked in a voice remarkable for its freezing quality.

'What a delicious meal,' broke in Bugsy, unable to bear the rising tension. 'Especially the rice. Quite a marvellous texture.'

But nothing was going to divert the wrath of Priscilla.

'You despicable numbskull!' she yelled. 'You can't shoot those birds. You can't eat those birds. They're protected by the law. You've committed a crime.'

Jen, a large woman with spiky hair, also rose to her feet. She was tense with aggression and for a moment I thought she was going to leap across the table to clobber him.

'You're in deep shit buddy! I'll report you. Worst case, jail. Best case, you'll be fined something awful. No more trips to the pub for you. The beers off,' she said. 'Pigs are one thing. But bustards? What did it do to deserve that?'

Wally looked dazed. His mouth hung open. He could have been a hunter gatherer from ancient times suddenly confronted with agricultural society and confused by the new social order and morality that came with it.

'But Priscilla, I get a bit fed up with beef. It's all we ever get to eat out here,' he muttered.

Right then I saw a guy wriggle his brows at me from across the table. He had a thatch of stiff sun-bleached hair and greenish eyes and he whispered, 'If I were you, I'd serve dessert now.'

It seemed a wise idea. Priscilla was screeching, 'And you scumbags think the pigs are feral!'

Where it all would have gone without the distraction of those glistening upside-down puddings, I don't know. The peacemaker was a field hand known as Grasshopper for reasons I never did figure out. He seemed to be in with the pig-shooting crowd, but he was much more often to be found sitting under a tree playing the harmonica. Grasshopper was one of those people the world barely notices who quietly smooth out life's wrinkles and then slip away.

* * *

The next day everything seemed calm. I doubt Wally had forgotten that he had been called a despicable numbskull in front of everyone, but he didn't seem a vengeful type. It's likely the events later were just random, but you wonder sometimes about cause and effect.

Still, early in the day all was well. The only troubled person in the camp was Sebastian who helped me with the dishes after breakfast. Getting a job at Blue Ridge, he said, was all very well and he needed the money, but if it meant having to share a room with that mechanic much longer ....

Jeremy had asked Sebastian the night before if he thought his hair would look good in a perm. Clearly the wrong person to ask.

'What the fuck? What's a bloody perm anyway? Isn't it something old ladies do?' asked Sebastian. 'And then he pulled out a pot of muck and asked me to smear it on his back. I told him to fuck off.'

'Don't be mean to Jeremy. He's the light of my life at the moment.'

'Light of your life! You've got to be kidding. Why? He's a prick. Look at him out there prancing about in those yellow pants. What's he here for anyway?'

But if Sebastian was in a mood, Priscilla, at least, had recovered her cool and was out in the yard with Jen. She had not yet joined the other geologists who were cooped together in the shadows of the second house, doing something with aerial photos and maps. She had other business out in the yard, which that morning was as busy as a beehive.

Field hands milled about with hoses, dustpans and rubbish bins. The yard was packed full of vehicles, all open with their contents spewed over the ground. Surrounding the vehicles was a circle of bedding, unrolled for airing. In the corner, Jeremy was bent over a motor as the sun beat obligingly on his back. Music blared out from a hidden source, an unpleasant song about a squashed rabbit crackling forth from a local radio station.

Through this scene wandered Priscilla. She was dressed brightly in pink and she circled the vehicles with an air that was strangely reminiscent of both a flitting butterfly and a cruising shark. Eyes alight, she came to a halt opposite Paul, who was replenishing the dwindling stocks in his tucker box, counting tuna tins and cereal boxes. She could have been a different person to the one I saw sizzling with outrage the previous evening.

A few seconds later she was strolling away clutching a tin of strawberries. Paul was shouting after her. 'Hey, Priscilla! Come back. I didn't say you could have those.'

She turned to him with a glittering smile, 'Oh but you did. Remember, when I bent over the box. It was very sweet of you.'

By lunchtime she was in an excellent mood having helped Jen fill her tucker box with the most delectable titbits available in Blue Ridge, all ready for their next week's traverse. Now she turned her attention to her recreational life, announcing at the table that she would like the occasional Sunday morning ride. Did anybody know where she could borrow a horse?

Wally emitted a crude snort at this request, but when Priscilla stabbed a sharp glance down the table, the sound rapidly subsided, transformed into a munching noise as he stuffed a lettuce leaf between his teeth.

'I want to join the pony club,' she said.

'Shouldn't be a problem at all,' said Eric. 'Horses all over the place here. They come into the field out the back to graze when I'm drafting. Janey's seen them wandering down the main street and raiding people's gardens. They eat the flowers. Must belong to someone.'

'You need to go down to the pub, luv,' said Wally with a coarse laugh, 'Plenty down there on a Saturday afternoon who could fix you up with a ride pretty bloody quick.'

Eric was horrified. 'No, no Priscilla. Don't listen to Wally.'

But Paul interjected, 'Yeah, Priscilla. Pub's the centre of social life in Blue Ridge. You want to find out something? Go to the pub.'

It was a wonder that Priscilla actually heeded their advice, if you could call it advice. They weren't people whose ideas she would usually pay any attention to at all. And I doubt Wally was trying to help; he was just being rude. But she wanted to join the pony club as soon as possible and their suggestion seemed reasonable. It was true that the pub was the centre of social life in Blue Ridge.

Wally and Paul smirked behind Priscilla's back when she left for the pub that afternoon. They knew who would be there at that hour: a bunch of bored blokes, warming the bar stools, downing pots of beer, whingeing about the emptiness of their lives. Here they were stuck in a hole of a town where nothing ever happened. And although they earned good money, there was nothing to spend it on but beer. That force which sets the world spinning and the heart singing was completely absent from their lives, as they returned each night to the single mens quarters across the highway.

Life had become more troubling after Wally first arrived on

the scene. He appeared to have all the sex appeal of a mangy ape and yet he had bragged to them that he lived with several gorgeous women. When Jen pitched up at the pub the following week, they concluded that Wally was a liar. Jen was good fun and fond of a beer on a Friday night, but she was built like a brick and did not remotely match Wally's descriptions.

On that Saturday afternoon, these men were in the beer garden gazing out at the sun-drenched ironbarks, wishing they were somewhere else and getting slowly pissed. And along strolled Priscilla with her long brown legs and her long blond plait, dressed in pink. This was a potent mix.

'Those guys won't know what's hit them when she walks in,' said Paul, shaking his head as he imagined the scene. 'They'll think they're dreaming. Do you suppose she'll tell them she needs a pony ride? God knows how they'll respond to that one. I hate to think.'

* * *

Priscilla's trip to the pub was far more successful than she ever would have envisaged. It was also unpleasant and confirmed her opinion that the males of Blue Ridge were worthless scum, somewhere far below earthworms and slime moulds on the biological scale. Never a woman to be easily overcome, she extricated herself from the riot of enthusiasm she had caused and fled back to the GIU base camp.

'Where's Wally? Where's Paul? Wait till I get my hands on them! They must have known that bunch of drunks was down there. The entire mob of them should be done in for sexual harassment.'

She stormed across the mess of vehicles and camping trash. The busy morning had degenerated into a drowsy and passive afternoon. Paul was suspended in the hammock reading a

Phantom comic. James and Grasshopper were sprawled on swag mattresses that had been dragged into the sun beside the porch. Wally had conveniently disappeared.

James sat up drowsily and watched her for a second or two before launching into a speech almost as provocative as Wally's had been the previous night. 'No, no, no,' he said. 'You've got it all wrong. You just don't understand men, that's all. Those guys had no intention of harassing you. Nothing would have been further from their thoughts. It's called appreciation. They were paying you a compliment.'

'It was not a compliment. It was harassment.'

'But you've only got to picture the lives of these guys,' said James. 'There's hardly any women around here and then you pitch up. You can't blame the fellas for getting a bit excited. I mean the most thrilling thing that happens in this town is the annual cane toad races. And you suddenly materialise in your pink hotpants and all.'

He was silenced by an immense wall of negative energy that beamed at him from her eyes. For a moment it looked as if she was about to obliterate him for the audacity of his wrong-headed thinking by the mere strength of her facial expression.

'What is wrong with pink?' she asked, slowly pronouncing each word in a tone that could promote the advance of the world's glaciers. 'If I feel like wearing pink, I'm going to wear pink. And I'm not going to adjust my wardrobe to suit you or any other thick-headed drunken thugs at a hotel. It's pathetic when grown men have less control over their impulses than a bunch of toddlers running round a kindergarten. It's not me that should be looking to the state of my dress, it's you lot that should be looking to develop some self-discipline!'

The velocity and warmth of this speech increased as she went on, until she conveyed the extraordinary impression that she was freezing James with fire, but he seemed unfazed by this approach. He must have been accustomed to it.

'Ah, maybe,' he replied reasonably, 'You could be right about that ... Anyway, you said you wanted a horse. Well, Princess, you'll get one, probably the finest horse in the district. Wait and see.'

He wasn't wrong. The first one arrived during breakfast the next day, a beautiful, dappled animal led by a young man with combed hair and a perfectly ironed Hawaiian shirt. Priscilla was eating muesli in the dining room. When he pounded on the door she gestured to me violently, eyes flashing. I was compelled to answer the door and put the bloke off. She might have wanted the horse, but she didn't want anything to do with the man.

He was the first of many. The only person unaware of the stream of rejects pouring from the premises that day was Eddie. He had been in the office dreaming of Devonian fish. If he noticed the horse manure scattered over the front yard, it didn't occur to him to ponder its meaning. So, in the late afternoon, he was convinced that Priscilla would be delighted to see the bloke who stuttered her name as he wandered into the yard with a white horse. Eddie thought he had heard Priscilla mention yesterday that she wanted a horse to ride.

'Ah, yes, you must be from the pony club,' he said kindly. 'Priscilla will be so pleased you've come. Jeremy here will look after your horse, a fine beast, and I'll take you inside.'

But Priscilla was *not* pleased.

There are swings and there are roundabouts. The beneficiary of that weekend was the local pony club, a small organisation, struggling for existence. But to everyone's surprise it suddenly achieved record membership from a most unlikely sector of the community. Men, who had done nothing with their spare time but drink beer at the pub, took up cantering with the children down at the pony club on weekends, hoping for a glimpse of those elusive female geologists. It was good for everyone involved.

As for Eddie, James, Wally and Paul, they were all subjected to what Priscilla considered was a well-deserved dose of the Freezer Treatment.

Chapter 5

Roast beef

TIME WENT ON. The potatoes didn't burn; the cakes didn't stick to the tins. We may have nearly burnt the place down when we first started, but now we were doing okay. What had been wrong with those troublemaking cooks of the past? This wasn't a stressful job. Cooking was just a matter of paying attention and following a few basic rules. Or so we thought for a brief interval until the day the Sapshorts came to dinner.

If I had known I was about to make a jerk of myself that day I doubt I would have bothered getting out of bed. But as I baked the scones for morning tea I was relaxed and confident. A few minor successes and it all goes to your head, makes you forget that old saying about pride coming before a fall.

That morning Priscilla had encouraged the local horses to cram into our backyard to graze. I was enjoying the spectacle through the window above the kitchen sink until I realised that one of horses was a nonconformist who preferred garbage to withered grass. When he was dissatisfied with the quality of the garbage in the bin, he tossed it about the yard in disgust, before plunging his head back in to search for something more delectable. This had to stop. It already looked as if we lived in the middle of a garbage dump and it was getting worse by the second. I went outside to confront the creature. He had huge teeth and huge hooves, an obvious physical advantage. A little daunted, I grabbed the lid of the rubbish bin and clanged it back in place.

'Stop that!' I said, looking at the horse eye to eye. He might have been bigger than me, but I was in charge.

He paused, gazed at me thoughtfully for a moment, and having sized me up as irrelevant, put his mouth back to the lid, tossed it off, and continued to rummage through the bin.

'Hey!' I said, ineffectually.

The horse lifted his head, turned, and stared at me with the same expression a person would use if they were rudely laughing in your face. He may have lacked the vocal equipment, but his attitude was clear enough. I was powerless; that horse was going to do whatever it wanted regardless of how inconvenient to me. After the horse gang had stripped the yard of grass and trashed the place, they moved on to devastate another garden and I was left to rake up fragments of stinking rubbish. I should have seen it as an omen.

'Adorable!' said Priscilla at morning tea, 'Specially clever boy Charlie, finding all that rubbish.' And as she got carried away on the subject of horse personality, she forgot to tell us that she had organised an evening out and we would need to adjust the meal hour. When it eventually dawned on her that if she wanted to eat earlier that night she would need to inform the cooks, she popped her head round the kitchen door. But it was well after lunch by then.

'Hi,' she said, 'I've got a favour to ask. We're all going to the movies tonight. Is it cool if we eat an hour earlier? You'd both be welcome to join us, if you'd like.'

'Where's the cinema?' asked Janey, looking at Priscilla as if she had gone nuts.

'No cinema,' said Priscilla. 'But they show movies every Sunday evening up at the mine. It's usually crap. Sex and violence must be all those drongos can comprehend. But they're showing *A Man for All Seasons* tonight and I've heard it's excellent.'

'Will the roast be ready in time?' asked Janey.

'I'll just go and turn the oven up full blast. That should do the trick.'

I didn't doubt this strategy, even though I wanted everything to be perfect for the Sapshorts. My limited experience suggested that if you shoved something in the oven, a more or less favourable result emerged sometime later. It never even occurred to me to ask Jeremy for advice.

Bill Sapshort was a regional geologist who planned to visit with his wife, stay overnight and then move on. The Sapshorts had already arrived when I went across to the other house where the meat was roasting. Bill was in the office chatting to James about mineral prospects. He was a bespectacled man with bulging knees, who wore his shorts with sandals and long socks, and he greeted me politely, thanking me for inviting him and his wife to dinner. Not that I had anything to do with the invitation. I told him about the movies at the mine and he replied that the meat smelled great and they were looking forward to dinner. I checked the meat, prodded it, basted it, and turned the oven up. It really did smell good. Very appetising indeed.

* * *

When the sun was low in the sky, the hungry hoards paced restlessly about the yard, like lions in a zoo prior to feeding time. They were scrubbed up unusually well, ready for the movies. Bill conversed with Christopher near the rose bushes while his wife examined a bloom. The aroma of roasting beef drifted across the yard.

Working to the timetable with superb precision, I removed the beef from the oven. It was flavoured with garlic and herbs and had developed a coating that smelled fantastic, that fragrance of crisped fat, so relished by the gods of old. I had no inkling at all that anything could possibly be wrong. In fact, I heard murmurs of appreciation as I cut through the waiting throng with the tray of beef.

I brought it into the kitchen, laid it on the board on the bench and immediately began to carve. I had no idea in those days that you're supposed to rest meat after cooking, but I doubt it would have made any difference, even if I had. It dawned on me straight away that something wasn't quite right. I wasn't carving meat; I was carving pink, quivering blubber. The word 'rare' didn't even begin to apply to the stuff that was filling the serving dish. This was something revolting, raw and fatty.

Meanwhile the dining room had filled. A rowdy group clamoured for food and banged their cutlery on the table in an irritating rhythm. The Sapshorts accepted this behaviour as part of the cultural experience. Hilda Sapshort had helped herself to the wine cask and clinked her glass with her husband's beer can.

'Bon appétit,' I heard her say.

In the kitchen, Janey and I gazed with horror at the tray of raw meat and broke into hysterical laughter. There was a brief, blessed moment of mindless pleasure in which tears ran from our eyes as we appreciated how funny this predicament would be if it was happening to somebody else. But, alas, it was not happening to somebody else; it was happening to us, and the clamour in the dining room had reached a crescendo.

'What are we going to do?' asked Janey.

'We could drench the blubber slices with gravy and sprinkle

them with dried parsley flakes,' I suggested. 'Do you think anyone would notice?'

'Yes, I think they will,' said Janey flatly. 'You'll have to go and announce the meal is er... delayed until further notice. You could say it's due to some ghastly circumstance beyond our control. Better get it over with.'

'Hang on. I'm not going to expose myself like that straight up. And they're all set to go to the movies. There must be something we can do. Why don't we just grill the bits and disguise them with gravy. That might work.'

Unfortunately, we never got an opportunity to try this scheme, because the mob, sensing a problem and anxious that they would miss the opening lines of the film, suddenly filled the kitchen and sized the situation up in an instant. There was such a rush of confusion that only a few disjointed images remain in my mind of what followed. Paul's voice echoed through to the visitors in the dining room— 'The vegetables look excellent, but the meat's bloody raw.'

I was quick enough to reserve the choicest piece of meat for Hilda Sapshort. As I placed the meal before her she gave me a glance in which pity mingled with disappointment and amusement. It was excruciating. What Bill Sapshort ate I don't recall.

'If you're kind enough to cook for me, then I'm kind enough to eat it,' said Grasshopper, shoving a lump of blubber between his teeth.

Bugsy tried to do the same but wasn't equal to it. Jeremy was in the corner, helpless with laughter. He was probably noting every detail of our failure so he could tell it as a funny story to the cook at Bogarilla when he returned. Christopher ate two slices, but the rest of the mob ignored the raw meat, shoved the cooks aside, and descended on the remaining food like a school of piranha fish. Within minutes everything had been demolished: pumpkin, potatoes, beans, carrots, apple pies and cream, and they all vanished to the mine for the movies.

A pile of blubber and three beans were left for the cooks.

'Well! This looks a nourishing and satisfying meal for a pregnant woman and a nursing mother,' I said.

Eddie opened a tin of spaghetti, so we didn't starve. I can't recall whether we laughed or cried after such a humiliating experience, but I do know we were never so smug about the failures of those other cooks again. However badly some of them may have behaved I never heard that any of them had ever served a raw roast to visitors.

Christopher didn't go to the movies that night. He was very kind to us, soothing our wounded pride by blaming the butcher for the debacle, and asking what else could be expected from a man who was also the town undertaker, as well as the agent for hardware goods. 'Look at this!' he said, pointing to the meat left congealing on the board. 'He sold us lumps of fat and called them rolled roasts. Nobody on the planet could have cooked this. Doomed to failure from the start!' And he plunged his hands into the blubber, placing the fat on the scales as if he was conducting a scientific experiment.

'Ratio's all wrong. And the meat in this is far too fatty. It's all about the insulating qualities of the fat you see,' he remarked, as if he knew as much about the principles of roasting meat as he did about the geology of Queensland.

I learnt that day to blame the supplier of the ingredients whenever I failed. It was a good technique that protected my self-esteem. But whatever Christopher said, deep inside I knew I had failed miserably. I just didn't want to have to remember it. Ever. It should have been possible to forget all about such an embarrassing incident, to lay it aside in some dusty, cobwebbed junkyard of the mind. But I couldn't, not with Bill Sapshort in the world.

My preference would have been never to see Bill or his wife ever again in my entire life. But no. Bill made it his mission to remind me of my past mistakes. He would suddenly materialise at the oddest moments, his eyes gleaming behind his spectacles, his face suffused with pleasure. I was never allowed to forget I had once served a raw roast for dinner. Sometimes he didn't even bother to say hello, just smirked and asked if I remembered that meal I cooked once in Blue Ridge.

'You know—that roast?'

Chapter 6

Bowerbirds

'I BLAME THE BOWERBIRDS,' said James McCracken, lingering over lunch, and speaking in a voice that expressed a mood somewhere between exasperation and depression.

'Bowerbirds!' snorted Paul.

'Do you think it's my fault I lost those tracks? Nope! It's the flagging tape. It just vanished. It's gone. Three tracks in three weeks. What else could be taking it?'

'It's happened to me too,' said Bugsy. 'I found the most awesome cave. Thought we might all go out some weekend and check it out ... but I ... I'm afraid I lost it. I left a very clear trail but when I went back, the trail had disappeared. Not a sign of it anywhere. Something very strange is going on.'

'Yeah, it's called bowerbirds. It's only logical. Must be the time of year. Those birds are stealing our tape to adorn their nests. We're being inconvenienced to benefit a bunch of horny birds.'

'Can bowerbirds undo knots?' asked Grasshopper.

'Sure they can. Very intelligent creatures, birds. They know how to use those nifty beaks and claws all right. But we can outsmart them. We'll go down to the library and do some research. Those birds must have a thing about bright pink. If we use a colour they don't like, the problem's solved,' said James.

Paul came into the kitchen and slammed his dirty plate on the sink. 'I've heard everything now! You'd be just as likely to see a phoenix in these parts as a bunch of bowerbirds, but never mind that. Who are they trying to kid? I know a moron when I see one.'

It didn't occur to me then that I would eventually solve the mystery of the missing flagging tape. It didn't even seem so interesting a problem at the time. But that was the week that Jeremy packed his coconut oil and moisturising creams, fastened his box of tools and left. His departure back to Bogarilla meant I could at last escape the kitchen and scrub from my mind the memory of the raw roast disaster. I could now go into the field with Eddie to discover God's Own Country for myself.

Bowerbirds were the last thing on my mind that first morning of freedom when I sat in the back of the vehicle as it belted down the highway. Sebastian was driving and Eddie sat beside him in the front, his head bent over a clipboard of aerial photographs. Out the window magpies swooped through the trees in the early sunlight. It would have been peaceful but for the firecracker monologue that Sebastian indulged in as he drove. With dizzying rapidity he discussed the damaging impact of materialism, the health benefits of cannabis, the hypocrisy of most Christians, the evils of alcohol, and the psychological problems of Aunty Nancy, who had ruined his life when she insisted on his first haircut at age three.

There seemed no expectation that we actually participate in this conversation; in fact, there wasn't much opportunity to. I'm not even sure he expected us to listen. Eddie paid no attention to him at all, and probably hadn't heard a word. All his attention was devoted to the aerial photographs in his lap. Eddie didn't even notice all those times when Sebastian flung his hands from the steering wheel and flapped them about the cabin like a propeller.

The road was long and straight but it wasn't empty. Several times we encountered those monstrous, multi-segmented cattle trucks called road trains that hogged the whole highway and forced oncoming traffic to pull aside and shudder in the roadside dust as they thundered by. It would have been better if the driver kept his hands on the wheel.

And it wasn't just Sebastian's hands that were a worry. It was also his head. He was impressively loose jointed and every so often his head swivelled around to check on me in the back. His eyes were anxious as if he thought something might go wrong at any moment. Left to himself, I imagine he would have been just as relaxed about driving a pregnant woman through the bush as he was about belting down the highway towards a road train with his hands flapping about the cabin. But he had listened to some worrying talk back in Blue Ridge and it gave him the jitters.

Gerald Drake and Eddie were the only ones who thought it was a good idea that I come out into the field. There was nothing but disapproval from everyone else. This stemmed from an unusual and never-to-be-repeated alliance between Wally and Priscilla. Wally had seen some B-grade movie that gave him the impression that pregnancy was a state of precarious delicacy. He thought that rough roads and pregnant women were a catastrophic combination. It would all lead, he claimed, to a blood and guts scenario and the field party would be traumatised from cleaning up the mess. Particularly those unfortunate enough to be sent out with me. Sebastian for instance.

Priscilla's argument was more reasonable. She said that I would be more comfortable if I stayed in Blue Ridge and had a hot shower every day. This was true if comfort was my goal. But what I would have missed! And James and Bugsy would never have found out what had become of their missing pink flagging tape if I had taken this advice.

Despite the opinion of the rest of the field party and despite Sebastian's nerve-racking driving technique, I enjoyed myself hugely that first day in the field. At lunchtime we sat on the bed of a dried-out river beneath the paperbark trees and ate corned beef sandwiches while black cockatoos screeched in the boughs overhead. This was life. Much better than being stuck in a kitchen watching the cakes rise in the oven.

After lunch the road became rough and rambled across a row of rocky ridges. Progress was slow, but eventually we stopped on the highest ridge and got out to stretch our legs. Bugsy and Paul had been following us, lagging behind at some distance to avoid our dust, but they soon caught up. When they arrived, Eddie and Bugsy took off with their geopicks towards a distant rocky outcrop. They had planned to collaborate for a couple of days. Paul shook his head as he watched them vanish.

'Don't worry about anything Cynthia. Flying Doctor Service is available at the end of my fingertips. A simple radio call, a few map coordinates, a billy full of boiling water ....'

He made a fire, set the billy on to boil, chucked a few dry twigs onto the flames, and considered the landscape. 'Nowhere round here that a plane could land though. They'd have to send a chopper.'

There was a superb view from the ridge, far horizons in all directions, a vast sea of trees and undulations, with not a sign of civilisation anywhere.

'Since when did it dawn on you that Wally was an expert in obstetrics?' I asked.

'Yeah, well, Wal sure can put a bullet through a pig! But, you're right, he's not the sharpest card in the pack, poor Wal. But still ... thought you'd like to know there's a system out here. You know ... if needed.'

'Listen, both of you, if pregnancy is as fragile as Wally makes out, the human species would have died out by now, like the dinosaurs. So just relax.'

And we tried to relax, hunched in the dirt, staring at the ants, as we waited for Eddie and Bugsy to come back. But Paul was irritable because there were no medical emergencies to solve and no pigs to kill. He hadn't seen the faintest trace of a pig all day, and if I had seen any, I wasn't saying.

Sebastian pulled his guitar from the back of the vehicle and was strumming restlessly at its strings when Paul, surveying the pigless landscape once more, said: 'What say I give you a run down on the art of being a field hand. I mean I bet nobody bothered giving you any sort of guidelines or anything. They never do round here. They just chuck you in at the deep end and expect you to manage without being told a bloody thing.'

'All I know is I'm supposed to assist on these camping trips with the vehicle and food and all that,' said Sebastian.

'Some camping trip! Look, the official line is we're on traverse to map the outcrop. But we're also exterminating the feral pigs. Unofficially. They forgot to fill you in on the whole point of the bloody exercise. That's typical.'

Sebastian shrugged and said nothing. He must have strained his vocal cords during the morning drive.

'No, seriously,' Paul continued. 'You're right, you gotta manage the vehicle and the food. But, more important, you gotta manage the geos. Fact is, those guys wouldn't even make it into the next paddock if it weren't for us fieldies. You've seen it— chased by emus, losing flagging tape, losing tracks. I mean, how can you lose a bloody track? Bugsy's even lost an entire cave system. Bloody hopeless!'

'They can't help it if birds pinch the tape,' I said.

'Oh Cynthia! Bowerbirds live in the rainforest. Does this look like rainforest to you? There aren't any birds out here taking the flagging tape. They've lost it. That's all. There's no mystery about it!'

Paul addressed me as if I was a child who had failed the simplest of counting tasks. And I didn't like it very much. Right then I wanted to prove him wrong. I wanted to find that tape and those bowerbirds. He was far too cocky.

In the distance we could see Eddie and Bugsy legging their way back towards us through the trees. 'About bloody time!' said Paul. 'Yeah well, we've had it easy today. Some days are like this and you can drive to most of the outcrop. Might have to do a bit of bush bashing, but that's okay. Then you amuse yourself killing pigs while the geologist looks at the rocks.'

'Too easy,' said Sebastian.

'Yeah, but it's not always like this. Some days you gotta trudge after them with a pack full of water and rock samples. They'll go for miles. When you get back you feel like shit. You're hot. You're tired. You just want to collapse under a tree or plunge your bare feet in a creek.'

Paul was cranking the fire back up, setting the billy back on the flames.

'But no,' he continued. 'You gotta go and light a bloody fire in the blazing heat and make a mug of tea. Anyone else on the planet knows that beer is the only drink for a time like that. But not these guys! They want tea. It's refreshing, they say. It has a cooling effect, they say. Well, I've never noticed.'

'Tea?' said Sebastian. 'It's a drug. Full of caffeine. Bad for you!'

'Yeah, but you can't tell them anything ... Hey watch me and I'll show you how to make the best bush tea. It's all in the swing of the billy.'

By nightfall the world had transformed. Reality encompassed just the warmth and glow of the campfire and the few feet surrounding it. We sat transfixed within this small world, talking of stars, sipping hot chocolate and eating Paul's damper with butter and honey. The immeasurable cosmos beyond the perimeter of firelight had become as elusive and impenetrable as the dream world. But when we stepped beyond the circle of firelight and contemplated that cosmos, we could see that we were on the edge of a galaxy of vast whirling spaces. It dawned on me that missing flagging tape was of no importance at all, and neither was petty one-upmanship. I forgot about the bowerbirds for a while.

But perspective changes with the daylight. When the sky is blue, the brilliance of the sun blinds us to the immense, alive, infinity of the spaces beyond this world, and then the small things come back into focus. After the sun had risen, I thought again of Paul and his assumption that the geologists were all a bunch of shambling incompetents, crippled with stupidity, and I still wanted to prove him wrong.

I looked about at the birdlife, saw many birds, some travelling with strands of grass or other nesting materials, but none at all with ribbons of bright pink flagging tape in their beaks. Paul was right, none looked remotely like bowerbirds. But just as I was beginning to think it was hopeless, I found them.

It took a while though.

* * *

On the first day of my second trip into God's Own Country, towards late afternoon, Sebastian said: 'Fuck! Check the sky out! It's awesome!'

It was. Extravagantly awesome. Purple, red, orange, even green were splashed overhead. It looked like the gods were throwing a party. There was something timeless about that sky, even though the shifting colours were ephemeral, only likely to last moments. Here we were, miles and miles from the thin line of bitumen that linked town with town, in a cosmos that seemed untouched by anything that had gone before. We could have been at the beginning of the world, before humankind and civilisations, before religion and weapons and wars, before art and music and urban squalor. But we weren't at the beginning of time; we were in north Queensland in the twentieth century and a large dirty swag was blocking our path.

'Must have fallen off the back of a truck,' said Eddie, leaping from the vehicle to retrieve it. 'There's a ringers' camp around here somewhere; must belong to them.'

If the sky was magical, so was the ringers camp when we found it at the interface of sunset and stars. Maybe it was the glow of sunset, but I was entranced. The ringers were relaxing in hammocks strung out amongst the eucalypt trees, gazing at the fading sky, while a pot bubbled on the fire and the horses grazed beneath the trees. This was life at its purest and best, lived beneath the sky, beneath the stars, in the presence of fire.

At that same hour, far to the south in the capital cities, trains snaked their way through suburbs, with a load of blank-faced commuters, all buried in the newspaper or in the gloss of a magazine, just as today they would be mesmerised by their devices, but every bit as oblivious to the real world that spins by out the window. And at that moment I was very glad I was not on a commuter train but was there under the trees in what could have been another world.

The ringers did not have much to say for themselves, but they waved at us as we heaved the swag at them, and we went on our way to set up camp. That night I longed for a hammock, so I could lie suspended and dream about the timeless things of this world. Bowerbirds were far from my mind, although I was closing in on them.

The next morning the colours were bleached from the landscape by the glare of the sun. I sat with a book by a dried-out gully, while Eddie and Sebastian trudged off with backpacks and geopicks. It was not a picturesque place, but some magic remained, because the ringers we had met last night were nearby on horses. They were slumped in their saddles, rolling cigarettes and watching a few scrappy beasts lurking in the scrub. But to me, for a short while, those men seemed full of dash and glamour, like the outback heroes in beer and cigarette advertisements, working up a thirst in the dusky golden light while a symphony plays in the background.

It didn't take long, however, to realise that they were actually just ordinary blokes doing a boring job. Their task involved staring passively at a bunch of cattle that stared passively back. Occasionally a beast would bolt away from the group and one of the ringers would dash after him while the others smoked their rolled cigarettes and looked on. Then they would all get back to staring at each other.

However, something more exciting was happening that day, something stirring, something impending, something that was felt by every fragment of life sharing that dried-out gully. Every blade of grass, every leaf on every tree, every ant scuttling through the dirt, every fly that hovered about my face could sense it. Change was coming. The bright blue sky of yesterday was gone. It was a different tone today, a steely blue, and it seemed closer. There was a smell of earth and dried grass, and a faint suggestion of moisture. It was also hot.

Down in the gully the ringers mopped their brows. A couple of kilometres further along, Eddie and Sebastian quarrelled on the dry creek bed. They hadn't expected that it would turn from mild to blistering hot in the course of an hour and they hadn't brought enough water. Sebastian blamed himself for this but was infuriated at the injustice of his own self-accusation.

'How the hell was I to know the heat wave was due to strike

precisely now?' he yelled. 'All I've heard since I arrived up here is how bloody cold it's been. I've even heard the pawpaw trees have been complaining. Frostbitten— that's what I was told!'

'It's no big deal. We're on a creek bed. I saw a few pools of water on the way up. We're not going to die of thirst,' said Eddie, and they began to stride back along the gully towards the oasis of the vehicle with its water tank and car fridge.

Meanwhile, I was getting to know the ringers better. Whatever they were doing in that gully was boring work. To break the monotony, they abandoned the cattle for a few minutes to ride up and exchange a few words with me as I sat in a camp chair beneath a tree near the vehicle. We had now been aware of each other's presence for about three hours, and it was about time to develop the relationship.

There were three of them, all wearing dusty old hats. The first in the group, a stocky man with a dusky face and bright dark eyes, began the conversation in the usual way.

'Bloody hot, hey?'

'Yeah, it is,' I said.

'Watchya doin' here with them fellas?'

I told him I was the cook.

'Well, I reckon that's a stroke of luck for the lot of us,' said the man in the middle. He was long and lanky and his words came out with slow ease. 'We're in need of a new cook ourselves. Ever since that bastard ran off. And I reckon you could do better than workin' for that mob. If you want my opinion, they're not all there in the head.'

The third man laughed, crossed his eyes, circled his index finger around his ear, and said, 'Crazy.'

The man in the middle resumed, 'That tall skinny guy with the moustache. What's his name?'

'You mean James?'

'Yeah, him. We ran into him a couple of weeks back. He was

with that huge, hefty sheila with the spiky hair. They were runnin' round in circles scratching their heads. Didn't seem to know where the hell they were.'

'You don't wanna be involved with clowns like that. Not when there's work over this way,' said the guy with the dusky face.

If a dreamy image of horses, hammocks and firelight flickered across my mind, it didn't last long. The bloke continued, 'That fella you're with, he scared the living crap out of us this morning.'

What! How? Eddie had gone to see them in the morning to tell them where he planned to work that day. Thought it was polite. What could possibly have been intimidating about that? I loved Eddie, for all his fascination with fossilised worm holes, but I could see at a glance he was no match physically for these men. They were of the rugged type, broad shouldered, full of brute strength.

'Yeah, we thought he'd shoot us!' he said with a casual laugh.

'Eddie's harmless.'

'Oh yeah! Why's a pistol hanging from his belt then?'

'You mean that old pouch? You won't find anything that shoots bullets in there. Probably just a tape measure and a compass. Maybe a notebook and pencil.'

'If you say so,' said the long lanky one, 'Even so, couldn't blame the fella if he was pissed off. There has to be some reason those blokes were tyin' ribbon to the trees. It's not Christmas, is it?'

Aha!

Here were the bowerbirds that Paul did not believe existed and here was the missing flagging tape. Why hadn't I noticed it earlier? Their battered hats all had new braided hatbands and although the colour was obscured by the dust, it was unmistakably pink.

'So that's what happened to the flagging tape!'

'Yep', said the third man, removing his hat and chucking it in the air. 'We reckon they're pretty snazzy.'

'Yeah, they are. They all thought it was bowerbirds taking the tape.'

'Bloody big bowerbirds!' said the long lanky man.

'Bowerbirds?' said the first guy. 'Nah, you won't find them in these parts. Back a bit towards the tablelands maybe ... Hey you fellas, better get back to it. Boss'll pitch up soon.'

And, with a wave and a final message, they rode back to the cattle. 'We'll be hangin' round this way for another two weeks. If you get sick of those fellas, give us a yell and we'll fix you up with a job.'

'Thanks guys.' I settled back to my book, rather pleased with myself.

By this time, Eddie and Sebastian were over halfway back. They had come across one of those pools that Eddie had predicted, a relic from when the stream last flowed, a pool of murky green depths with a strange earthy, vaguely unpleasant aroma. But they were very thirsty, so it seemed to them, in that instant, as attractive as if they had stumbled upon a pool of crystal clarity surrounded by wildflowers. That pool was so attractive there could have been one of those alluring but wicked water fairies sitting by, weaving spells and beckoning. 'Come touch, come taste.'

They plunged their hands in and splashed the water over their faces, tasting the drops as they fell on their lips. For a moment or two it was very sweet indeed, and then feeling more chilled, Sebastian lifted his head and began to laugh. 'Hey, look at that boulder there in the middle of the pool. You could call that Boar Rock. It looks just like .... oh shit ....'

In some other dimension that water fairy cackled with laughter as she transformed from a beautiful and alluring fairy to a nasty old crone. In this dimension all that could be seen was the decomposing corpse of a big old boar, right there in the water in front of them.

'Hey, Eddie, mate, you look kind of greenish,' said Sebastian.

'Of course, I look green. It's just the reflection of the water. Let's get out of here.'

The interlude at the pool had lent them energy and their pace increased. They hadn't gone far before they heard a distant roar that got louder and louder, and which materialised in seconds as a helicopter flying so low it was just above the treetops.

'Jeez, that looks like it's about to land over near the vehicle! What the hell's going on?' said Eddie. They picked up their pace even more, but there was no need for concern. The arrival of the helicopter was spectacular, accompanied by a blast of wind and a mighty swirl of dust and flying leaves, but after the blades had settled it was all a bit of an anticlimax. The ringers' boss stepped out carrying packets of sandwiches, bananas and a flask of cordial and strolled down to the gully for a picnic.

His departure after lunch was just as impressive. The ringers galloped off soon after, leaving the cattle grazing about the gully as they had been all morning. What it was all about, I don't know. Perhaps I had just seen a tiny fragment of a massive counting exercise. They reminded me once more to come and see them if I wanted a new job and galloped off towards the blue haze in the west.

They rode into a storm. They had only been gone minutes before that haze transformed into clouds that billowed out across the sky like giant mushrooms. By the time Eddie and Sebastian staggered back up the gully the light had diminished, thunder rumbled, and the first raindrops were falling. The first storm of a season always feels like a celebration. We didn't dance in the rain, but we felt like it. Instead, we ate our sandwiches out in the weather and let the raindrops fall on our skin. We could smell the moisture as it hit the dry earth and released fragrances from the plants. Soon the creek in the gully would be running again and that pool Eddie had described would be recharged and transformed.

'Not much of a place, this,' said Eddie, looking about him. 'Even in the rain. Must have been dull for you being stuck here all morning.'

'Not at all,' I said. 'Far from dull. I've been offered another job. And a a helicopter dropped from the sky, just over there. Oh, and by the way, I also found out what happened to all that missing flagging tape. Not bad for a morning's work. You can tell James that the breeding season is over. Those bowerbirds won't take any more tape.'

The storm moved on, gathering its clouds and drifting across the sky towards the coast. Sunlight persisted as the clouds raced away, sparkling on the wet earth and shining on the storm, now dark and distant on the horizon. 'Hey look at that!' said Sebastian. 'Have you noticed? There's always a white bird in front of every storm cloud.'

Chapter 7

The bloody awful nature of life

ONE NIGHT the Smiths had a particularly bad time in their old bus in the paddock out the back. The baby woke up hourly and as the night wore drearily on, Janey and Eric blamed each other. They knew this wasn't helpful, but nobody functions well at 2.00 in the morning. Eventually the sun rose and they stumbled out to face another day, while the baby kicked out his legs and looked upon the world with the contentment of a young creature without worries.

'You two look terrible!' said James, when he saw them come in with the bub in the stroller. 'Go back to bed and get some more sleep. I'll look after young Freddie. I'm an uncle. Heaps of experience.'

Janey and Eric looked at him blankly for a moment before a ray of hope dawned. They were so exhausted they would have agreed if clever boy Charlie and his horse gang had offered to babysit. James told them that he would take Freddie for a walk to the golf club. Everybody else was already there that morning.

'Tar greens, ironbarks and kangaroos. It's an excuse for a golf course if you ask me,' he said. 'But Freddie won't know any better. He'll enjoy watching Jen swinging that club and missing the ball. Should keep him entertained for a while.'

He put a hat on the baby's head, checked that he was secure in the stroller and suggested that I come along as well. 'It would do you good to leave the kitchen grease behind for a while and get out into the open air,' he said.

He was right. It was good to be out. Blue Ridge was a fine place if the squalor of the GIU establishment was overlooked. The sun shone and the grass was green. Most of the native shrubs were in bloom; there was a profusion of scarlet bottle-brush, white melaleuca and grevillea of all colours. The breeze was scented with honey and lorikeets flashed through the air.

As James pushed the stroller along, he told me a story about a night he had spent in the field with Bugsy a couple of weeks earlier. The moon had been full and the dingoes were howling. The campsite was perfect – flat ground, waterhole, lots of fire-wood – but, even so, they kept feeling something wasn't right and it wasn't just the eerie blue light.

'We kept feeling that we weren't alone. That something was watching us. It was creepy, real creepy,' he said. 'And then, and then ... we heard this noise—'

He broke off and produced a sound that would have been blood curdling at night in the middle of the bush when you were already freaked out, but sounded highly comical in Blue Ridge on a sunny morning with the honeyeaters twittering in the trees above.

'Bugsy shoots from his swag, trips flat on his face, and then leaps into my swag. Terrified he was, poor bugger. I reckon he thought the place was haunted by those bad spirits you hear about. And it sure sounded like it. But you know, we're scientists and we don't really believe in that crap. There's always a rational explanation. So ... I checked that sound out.'

He paused for a moment as if he was expecting me to

commend him on his courage and logical approach, but when I said nothing he continued, 'You know what it was? Possums. Bloody possums. I don't know what they were up to that night, fighting or breeding or what, but they were sure making one hell of a weird racket.'

This story amused me mainly because I had heard a different version from Bugsy the week before, with the interesting variation that it had been James who had leapt in fright from his swag and fallen flat on his face. In that version, Bugsy was the heroic one who kept his head. I never discovered the truth of the matter, but I imagined them both clutching at one another and stumbling about in blind fear. I only wish I had seen it.

'Oh my God!' said James abruptly as we continued to amble along towards the golf course.

I could see nothing in the vista ahead to cause any alarm at all, nothing but a small-town street with trees and houses and gardens. But James shoved his hat way down over his face, abandoned the stroller and the baby in the middle of the footpath and ran for his life. Maybe he had seen a possum dozing in one of the trees, but all I could see was the girl from the grocery store hosing her garden. I waved at her as I collected the stroller and continued on my way. At least I could meet up with Eddie as he was finishing his golf game.

When we returned to the house, James was slouched in the hammock with his hat still pulled over his eyes. 'Well, James McCracken, what happened to you?'

'Didn't you see her?' asked James with a biting fury, as if the reason for his behaviour was blindingly obvious.

'Who?'

'Her! The girl from the grocery store! Didn't you see her hosing the garden?'

I must have been thick because I failed to see how the sight of this girl should make him about face and gallop off.

'She gets more attractive every day.'

'Yeah,' said Paul, who was hovering about. 'I've noticed that. Prettier every day.'

'I don't see why that should make you run away in terror. Anyway, I've got to get lunch, and you're supposed to be looking after Freddie. He needs a clean nappy.'

'Wake up Cynthia! If I'd been seen pushing a stroller beside a pregnant woman, I would have ruined all my chances. She never would have looked at me again.'

'Probably wouldn't have looked at you anyway. The clean nappies are over there.'

'Oh no! I said I would look after the infant, not change his nappies. Eddie can do that. He needs practice.'

* * *

That afternoon Janey was refreshed and functional again. We were in the kitchen following a recipe for Anzac biscuits out of an old book we had discovered lying in a corner amongst a pile of cheap magazines and Phantom comics. It was called *Easy Cookery for Single Men*. We had been very diligent in cooking cakes and scones for morning and afternoon teas, but the mechanic was back in town and he said that the cook at Bogarilla was an angelic soul who kept a constantly full cookie jar. Wouldn't it be good, he suggested, while scratching his underarms and making intermittent hooting sounds, if we did that too?

Jeremy had disgraced himself that week by getting his eyelids severely sunburnt. This was painful, and, worse (for him) disfiguring, but the field hands had no sympathy for him at all. They sneered that there was only one way to get sunburnt eyelids and it never happened to them. They were inclined to dislike Jeremy, not just because he wasn't into exterminating pigs and drinking beer, or because he wore pink shirts and considered getting his hair permed, but because he earned way more money than they did. This would have been barely tolerable even if there was evidence that he worked hard for it. But sun-tanned skin and sunburnt eyelids? It seemed he had so little to do he spent the weeks basking in the sun with his eyes closed.

But Janey and I didn't care. We liked to have Jeremy in the kitchen entertaining us with gossip about people from Bogarilla and giving us ideas for menus. Not that he stayed long that day, not after James arrived. But if James had come to apologise for running away that morning, Jeremy put him off completely.

'What are you doing in here? I thought you were supposed to be out there fixing the tojo. And what the hell happened to your eyes? Did you know the skin's peeling off your eyelids?' he asked, glaring at him.

Jeremy hunched over like a chimpanzee, emitted a few wild squeaks, and fled out the back door. James stared after him in bewilderment. 'What's wrong with the guy? What the hell is he doing that for?'

'Just for fun,' I said.

'For fun? What a jerk! The things I have to put up with in this place. It's bloody awful!'

He cast a black look towards us as if we were yet another facet of the bloody awful nature of the place and began to complain at length. There was too much dust. The bathroom was too shabby. There was no bath and not enough hot water. There was no opera company in Blue Ridge, no seafood to be had, and no women.

'What do you mean? No women?' I asked. 'There's us for a start. And then there's ...'

'Huh!' replied James with a not very flattering emphasis. 'For my purposes, there are no women.'

'I see,' said Janey. 'And those purposes are?'

'Don't get me wrong!' he replied hastily. 'I'm not trying to be crude here. I'm actually just a romantic soul.'

'And you're after a bit of light romance?' I asked.

'Precisely!' said James.

Janey had missed the morning's events and didn't know about his growing interest in the girl from the grocery store. 'But James you're missing what's right beneath your own nose. Right this very minute in that house next door sit two of your colleagues, bored and knitting jumpers. They're attractive women and they're smart.'

'Haven't you been listening?' he asked, disgusted by the suggestion. 'I said I was after romance and you suggest Michelle or Priscilla. Hell, I was at uni with those girls. I know them too damn well.'

Apparently, in his world, knowing a woman well instantly eliminated any potential for romantic involvement. He would prefer to fantasise about the unnamed girl who presided so mysteriously behind the checkout counter down at the grocery store.

'Besides,' he said thoughtfully. 'I want an equal relationship with a woman. I don't want to be completely dominated, walked all over and ground into the dust.'

'Oh James!' I said, 'Really!'

'Yes really. If you haven't noticed by now who really runs this outfit, then you're not very observant. It's bloody awful! You say the wrong thing and you get the Freezer Treatment. We can't even see a movie without them approving it as suitable viewing. I bet they even dictate what you're going to cook for dinner.'

He seemed to have forgotten all about his romantic soul.

Life was full of injustices, he declared, predicting a day when Michelle and Priscilla would complain to Gerald Drake that fieldwork was destroying their social life. 'And I know exactly what will happen. They will be sent to map the Whitsunday Islands where they can stay in resorts with their boyfriends, and I will be sent off to some god-awful hole worse than Blue Ridge. It's just the bloody awful nature of life.'

Meanwhile, we continued to mix the batter according to the instructions in *Easy Cookery for Single Men* and two trays of Anzac biscuits were ready for the oven.

Cooking is supposed to be a predictable art. You mix precise quantities of ingredients together and bake them at a predetermined temperature to get consistent results. That's the theory. But it doesn't always work like that. A butterfly's wings flutter here and a typhoon forms across the world. Chaos, the missing factor not mentioned in the cookbooks.

The first tray of biscuits we pulled from the oven resembled a tray of vomit superglued to the tin. Who knows why? Was there a misprint in the recipe book? Too many distractions in the kitchen? Or just the random impact of chaos at work? Did James breathe dissatisfaction into the batter? Does emotion change chemistry? Or did we just forget to grease the trays?

When Jeremy re-appeared in the kitchen he bent double with laughter at the sight of them and suggested we contact the cook from Bogarilla. Her biscuits never failed. But Sebastian had also turned up in the kitchen, hoping for a snack. He volunteered to take the tray into the backyard where he scraped it clean with his tongue and the remains of his teeth, managing to ingest the entire batch. He said they tasted bloody good considering how disgusting they looked.

The second batch also stuck to the tray. A complete flop. And yet there was a quality in that chaotic splattered arrangement of oats and coconut that answered a deep echo in James' soul. It was a work of art, a reflection of some cosmic pulse. He offered to drill a hole in the tray and hang it on the dining room wall, entitling the piece *The bloody awful nature of life.*

Janey developed an attachment for this artwork and took it home with her at the end of the season. Before she had time to hang it on the wall, her dog somehow managed to gobble enough of it to entirely ruin the artistic effect. *The bloody awful nature of life* went in the bin and the dog was sick.

Chapter 8

A pleasant spring phenomenon

Hot, drowsy, Thursday afternoon and we were jolting through God's Own Country. It was hot, dry and dusty. A harsh light beat down from the blue burning sky. The silver-leaved iron-barks were stunted and spindly and cast little shade. A mob of huge wallaroos lounged at the edge of the road. They couldn't be bothered moving and stared at us with languid, unafraid insolence as the vehicle crept past within inches of their noses. The road had been washed out in the last wet season and was in bad condition. The surrounding landscape bent and undulated in waves.

Outside the flies made pests of themselves, settling upon our clothes in black swarms and flying into our nostrils whenever we stopped. The vehicle was a haven of relative peace. Sebastian was driving, and he expanded on his usual conversational themes as we progressed, but neither Eddie nor I paid much attention that day. Eddie stared silently out the window, lost in a vision of ancient Devonian landscapes and primitive fishes. An unreliable cassette player, plugged into an obscure spot on the dashboard, rattled out music from a concert hall in Europe. Music and landscape blended together strangely. This music had been created in a country where a landscape like this would have been almost beyond imagination. In this setting it rippled out oddly, whispering of the infinite possibilities that lie hidden throughout the universe.

Sebastian's question penetrated the music. 'What's that burning smell?'

'That's no burning smell. That's just some aromatic plant that grows around here,' replied Eddie.

I looked out the window and saw only withered grasses and stunted ironbarks crisping in the sun. But when we drove around the next bend the whole world was on fire with both sides of the road alight.

'Shit!' Sebastian panicked. 'This is my fault! I must have forgotten to put out the campfire.'

'Don't be a dick,' said Eddie. 'I put the fire out this morning. This is nothing to do with us.'

But there was little point wasting time figuring out what had caused the fire. What we were to do about it was a far more crucial question. The only way out from this location was along the road ahead. If we waited around on the off chance the wind might change we could be cornered. The afternoon breeze was due to kick in sometime soon and that would only make everything worse. We turned the music off and began to drive further along the road, tentatively, as if we were entering the borders of hell. The fire remained some distance from the vehicle, and, as if in a dream, I was just becoming accustomed to the fiery visions out the window, when Sebastian announced the vehicle was just about out of petrol. He would have to stop to refuel.

'You've got to be kidding,' said Eddie, 'You can't stop and pull out a bloody big jerry can of fuel here. You'll blow us all up! Just put your foot down and let's get to hell out of here!'

A minute further down the road and the vehicle spluttered to a halt. 'Shit!' said Sebastian.

Eddie glanced about uneasily. We seemed to be on an island of relative safety. The nearest flames were some distance away. Perhaps there was no better chance to refuel than here, if we were to survive at all. 'Be as quick as you can,' he muttered.

We all got out of the car. Sebastian pulled the jerry can out, took the petrol cap off and was poised to refuel when the afternoon breeze sprung up and thrust its weight behind the wall of flames. The fire came charging towards us. There was a sound like a train rushing by at full speed. Sebastian turned around at the sound and gaped as flames twice as tall belted towards him as he hugged his tin of fuel. He would explode any second and we would all be annihilated. One moment I had been staring dreamily out the window with no greater worry than what to serve for dinner the following night. Now I faced death with a blast from the afternoon breeze. I stood rooted to the road and waited for this unexpected end while my baby turned somersaults inside.

But Eddie refused to acquiesce to the elemental forces. 'Let's get to hell out of here!' he yelled.

And fast, faster than the flames, Sebastian thrust the petrol cap back on and threw the jerry can in the back. We all leapt into the vehicle. Sebastian turned the key, pulled the choke, and slammed his foot onto the accelerator until the vehicle coughed and lurched forward, having located the last meagre drop of fuel.

In stunned silence we fled through the flames until we reached the front of the fire. And still we went forward as far away as possible until again the vehicle ground to a halt. No one said a word. We just sat there breathing in and out, in and out.

'Fuck!' said Sebastian, finally breaking the silence.

He refuelled the car and I said, 'We may as well go back to Blue Ridge. I don't want to stick around here and get burnt to death.'

But Eddie could see no logic in this response. 'Look Cynthia, I'm not paid to skulk about Blue Ridge every time we encounter a few problems. I'm paid to map the rocks and I'm going to map the rocks.'

'In the middle of a raging bush fire?'

'Well, yes, I know it makes life a bit complicated. I'll have a talk to Christopher on the blower at six and get his advice.'

To my everlasting astonishment Christopher thought the fire was no big deal at all. 'Yes, you do get the odd grass fire about at this time of the year,' his voice crackled through the radio in the most nonchalant tone you could imagine. 'Nothing to worry about,' he continued. And signed off.

'Nothing to worry about? Nothing to worry about!' I screeched. (I was not feeling calm.) 'We just about all get blown up and it's nothing to worry about. I think we should go back to Blue Ridge.'

'You heard what Christopher just said. We're not going back to Blue Ridge. We'll just go and map somewhere else. Anyway, we're not in any immediate danger now,' said Eddie, gazing back at the clouds of smoke drifting across the landscape. The air was thick with the scent of burning vegetation.

Health and Safety was in its infancy back then. Rules and regulations were much less prolific and Christopher could make whatever judgement call he thought best. Assessment of risk was more a matter of gut feeling and trust in good luck than focusing on potential calamity. Christopher would have gone to bed that night completely satisfied that no harm would come to us. I was not so convinced.

'But we could be burned alive in our swags tonight,' I said.

'You're over-reacting Cynthia,' said Sebastian. 'We don't want to look like a mob of wimps.'

'I don't care if we look like wimps as long as we're alive. I don't get it. We were nearly killed back there and you're both acting as if we're just dealing with some harmless little spring phenomenon. Just because Christopher – who isn't even here – says it's nothing!'

'Relax Cynthia,' said Eddie, having never understood how much I detested being instructed to relax when I wasn't in the mood. 'I'll tell you what we'll do. We'll camp by the road on top of the ridge tonight. We'll be able to see for miles. If the fire comes our way, we're already on the road to Blue Ridge and we'll get out. If not, I check out the outcrop along the fence line in the morning'.

We retired to the ridge and everything seemed a lot better after a mug of tea and a grilled steak. Sure, the flames still burned in the distant darkness and crept towards us bit by bit, but against the backdrop of night they seemed as innocuous as a transient fireworks display. They stopped being a threat and became beautiful instead. So beautiful that Eddie and Sebastian became complacent and fell asleep, flat on their backs with loud snores and dropped jaws. Nothing was going to disturb them, not even flames licking the canvas on their swags.

There would be no heroics from them in the middle of the night. I lay on my swag, facing the flames, not daring to close my eyes. I could feel currents of air swirl above my head, could hear leaves twitching in the trees above, while the fire continued to steadily burn, and I wondered how these elements would blend as the night wore on. If I lapsed into sleep then the flames could be at my feet in minutes. I imagined myself stumbling down the road towards Blue Ridge in a wild panic while the snores of Eddie and Sebastian faded behind me. I awoke towards morning in terror, but the fire had died away. Only the ashes glowed.

The sun rose but I didn't roll my swag. I wanted to go back to sleep while the others traversed the fence line. Impossible. The heat was building and there were swarms of flies. All I could do was whack at them and wish I was somewhere else.

In the afternoon we were on our way back to Blue Ridge when we came across Bugsy and Paul, also returning from their week together in the limestone country. They were resting beneath a tree. Bugsy was taking gulps from a foully dirty water bottle.

'Am I glad to see you people,' he said, removing his hat and tipping the last of the water over his head. 'We've been worried sick about you. Saw that fire and knew you'd be in the thick of it. Don't know why you didn't go back to Blue Ridge. That's what I would have done.'

Paul munched on an orange by the roadside. 'Bugsy was worried. Not me. I wasn't worried about you at all.' He spat out a seed.

'Well you should have been worried! Sebastian nearly blew us all up with a great tin of petrol, and I had to stay awake all night just in case we got burned alive while they snored beside me. I didn't get any sleep at all. Don't expect a gourmet meal tonight, because you won't be getting one.'

'We never get gourmet meals anyway, so what's the difference?' asked Paul. 'By the way, in case you're wondering, I know how that fire started. Those friends of Cynthia's were entirely responsible.'

'What friends?' I asked.

'You know. Those ringers. The ones with the pink flagging tape wrapped around their hats. They were belting along Deadman's Gully Road in an old white ute. Time of the year they do a bit of burning off they said. They'd already started that fire. Didn't know you lot were camped down towards Wallaby Gorge of course.'

Just because we survived a bushfire and nearly blew ourselves up with a tin of fuel that week, didn't mean we impressed anybody back in Blue Ridge. Christopher Craddock, the leader of the troop, had seen many field seasons come and go. He had seen snakes in swags, he had seen floods and he had seen fires, and although I had heard him screech in panic when he thought we had set fire to the Blue Ridge house, nothing that happened out in the field alarmed him much. When, over our meal that night, we retold our story with only the most minor of embellishments, how Sebastian had hugged the jerry can of fuel with one-hundred-foot flames bearing down on him, he waved his hand dismissively.

'You think that's bad?' he asked. 'I heard from Murray Crow up at Bogarilla today. Jimmy Keen needs a new set of boots.'

Christopher was a man generally moderate in his habits, but he must have had way too much beer that evening. Jimmy Keen's boot problem was of minor significance compared to our brush with death, and yet he spoke as if this bit of news blew our story right out of the water.

'Yeah, and so what?' asked Wally. 'I need new boots too.'

'But your boots are worn out with too much walking. Jimmy's probably burnt his off his feet,' James remarked.

'Too right,' said Christopher. 'Fire got to his boots, melted the soles.'

'It was bound to happen sooner or later,' said James. 'I've been in the field with Jimmy. He's mad. Collects empty spray-paint tins and chucks them on the fire. Does it all the time, just to watch the explosions.'

'That's what he did this week apparently. Threw the tin on just after the billy boiled at lunchtime. Not a good idea. A willy-willy blew through the paddock at the exact moment. Well, you can imagine ...'

'Jeez. What happened?' asked Wally.

They were all much more interested in what happened to the guy with his empty spray-paint tin and the fire and the willy-willy than they were in what didn't happen to Sebastian and us when he hugged the petrol tin in the bush fire.

'He ended up in a ring of fire, with the circle getting smaller by the second. Would have been a disaster but they were doing the helicopter survey this week. Helicopter got him just in time. Couldn't save his boots though.'

'Jeez,' said Wally.

'Willy-willies and grassfires,' said Christopher contemplatively. 'Just some of nature's delightful springtime phenomena.'

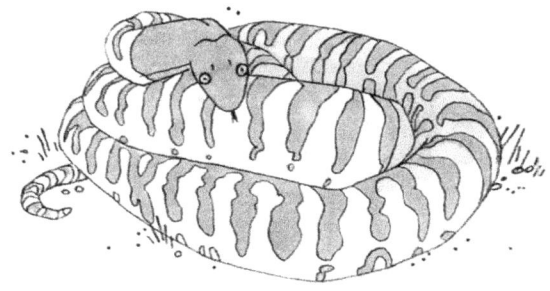

Chapter 9

Bogarilla

THERE WAS a place close to Blue Ridge where the river flowed. It was a place of green light and rushing water, and it was cool beneath the drooping paperbark trees when it was hot everywhere else. It was a place to escape to on Sundays for an hour or two between clearing up the lunch mess and peeling the vegetables for the next meal.

One Sunday, I lay in the river, feeling the water swirl past. Eddie had vanished amongst the rocks to lie in the rapids. Beside the river, Grasshopper, sodden, sat hunched on a rock like a tired baboon, smoking a pensive cigarette. James McCracken, dressed in board shorts, hovered on the water's edge and cautiously stuck his big toe in. Christopher sat on the sandy bank with his back propped against a paperbark tree, quietly watching the river flow.

'You can have a break next week, Cynthia,' he said. 'We've all been invited to a birthday party at Bogarilla. Donny Potts is turning twenty-one.'

'Yippee!' yelled Grasshopper.

'Isn't Bogarilla a bit far to go for a party?'

'Nowhere is too far for a party,' said Grasshopper.

'Bogarilla's about five hundred clicks away. Just an afternoon drive,' said Christopher.

'Who's Donny Potts?'

'Field hand. Great fella!' replied Christopher.

'If you're not shut up in a vehicle with him for several hours,' muttered James, still skirting on the edge of the water. 'There's something wrong with his insides.'

'But I'm paid to cook at weekends, not go to parties.'

'Yes, but there won't be anyone left here to cook for. We're all going. Just what we need to boost our morale.'

'Speak for yourself,' said Janey, who was sprawled with Eric on a blanket, watching as Freddie shoved fists full of sand into his mouth. 'Five hundred kilometres just to go to a party, then all the way back the next day. I couldn't think of anything worse.'

Why didn't I listen? The following Saturday I was squashed into an overloaded vehicle heading north along the thin strip of highway. Beside me James was pressed up against the window, staring gloomily out at the sunlight streaming down through the ironbarks.

'Here we go again,' he muttered.

He looked depressed, more like a convict facing transportation than a young man on his way to a party. We drove past kangaroos dozing beneath the trees, scarlet bottlebrush bending over creeks of shimmering water, past lorikeets and cockatoos and eagles, but he was unmoved by it all. A family of emus strutting along a fence made him shudder.

'Huh, I get this bloody stuff all week and now I've got to look at it all weekend.'

I wondered why he had bothered to come along at all. It would have been more comfortable without him in the back. 'So why have you come? It's not compulsory.'

'I ask myself the same question,' he responded. 'They're a

bunch of drunks up at Bogarilla. You know that, don't you? Has
Slanger warned you? You're in for a revolting spectacle. And
just you wait, tomorrow we'll feel so rotten we'll want to shoot
ourselves and we'll have to stuff back into this car like sardines
and drive all day through this rubbish again.'

Time went on and we hit the Ninety Mile Scrub. The drive
became long and straight and hot and dusty and flat. The road
had a surreal quality of never-ending monotony and it felt as if
we had been driving forever, stuck in a time warp. But eventually the road curved and we were out of the scrub, climbing
above the flatland. Suddenly it was green. There were rich
sloping fields, jersey cows, patches of rainforest.

'I think I can see a break coming up,' said Christopher, who
was driving.

Yes, a break. Just what we needed. A picnic ground near a
rainforest would be ideal. But we drove past the rainforest and
on through a road cutting where the rock walls rose up on both
sides of the road. Christopher slammed his foot on the brake
and we were all flung forward like sacks of potatoes. The vehicles travelling behind us did exactly the same and everybody
poured out onto the road.

This was the place Christopher had selected for the break.
Not a rainforest— a road cutting. There was no shelter from the
blazing sun and barely any space between the tar of the road
and the dull rock wall that rose above. If a semitrailer happened
to drive by at that point we would have all been mown down
and hurtled off into the next world. But nobody was trained
back then to consider the dangers hidden in the simplest of
actions. There was nobody likely to ruin the spontaneity of the
moment by insisting we all wear reflective vests and prop
witches hats about. So, with unaccountable joy the geologists
strolled along the road cutting. James had perked up consider-

ably and he urinated on the rock wall so he and anyone else interested could better see the detail in the rocks.

The field hands weren't so thrilled. They rolled their eyes, lit cigarettes and sneered. When Eddie, looking in appreciation at the rocks, remarked that he had just seen another nice dike, Jen took it badly, taking it as a personal comment on her sexuality. 'Watch your mouth Buster. What's it to you?'

Eddie looked at her in confusion. He had never given any thought whatsoever to her personal life. 'Look Jen, up there. Another volcanic dike. Nice one,' he explained.

But she just told him he was nuts.

Then a driver in a small red car joined us, a victim of herd mentality. In his view, if there were people clustered in the road cutting there was obviously something worth stopping for. He galloped across to the field hands.

'You've found it then, hey?' he asked, inexplicably.

'Found what mate?' asked Grasshopper.

'You know,' said the man, and in reverent tones named a species of endangered rock wallaby, as if it was perfectly plausible that such a creature would be sitting in a barren road cutting passively accepting the admiration of the accumulating passers-by.

'There's no rock wallabies around here,' said Jen. 'This is a road cutting.'

'What are you all here for then?' he asked.

'Good bloody question,' said Jen.

'We're just lookin' at the rocks, mate,' said Grasshopper.

'Why?'

'Another good bloody question,' said Jen.

An hour later we were amongst the tobacco fields of Bogarilla. Stella, the Bogarilla cook, ran out from the small farmhouse at the centre of the GIU camp, greeting me as if I was a long lost relative. 'You must be exhausted!' she said. And before a minute had gone by, I was resting on a bed, sipping from an enormous mug of tea.

The party was to be held on a neighbouring property that belonged to a couple called Jock and Betsey, who also owned the place the GIU leased at Bogarilla. Their parties were legendary. When Eddie and I arrived, the orange sunset glow was merging with darkness and the stars of the Milky Way gleamed in a velvet sky. There were open fires and roasting chickens and huge pots of pasta bubbling amongst the smoke. Betsey welcomed everybody enthusiastically, waved a lipstick carved in the shape of a penis at all newcomers, then ushered us all into a large shed where quite a crowd had gathered.

Donny Potts couldn't be missed. He was clad in a voluminous yellow raincoat which bore a sign reading X *Juvenile Delinquent*. An absurd hat made from birthday paper, ribbons and fluorescent condoms was on his head. A condom dangled from his ear. He was swigging beer with the local cop, while Micky Wren, one of the Bogarilla field hands, flitted about them waving a crisp, absolutely pristine, one hundred-dollar note.

'Hey Potts, see this. It's yours, mate. Yours! A birthday present.'

'Jeez Mick, that's real good of you. Wouldn't have thought ...'

Micky snatched the note away and stroked it like a pet, enjoying its untarnished purity. 'As I said mate, it's yours. On condition ... On condition you shave all your hair off right now.'

A tin of shaving cream and a razor appeared, and Potts didn't hesitate, not for a moment. 'You're on!' he said, ripping off his hat and untying the ponytail hidden beneath.

The Bogarilla crowd roared. They had been drinking as if it was a competition to see who would get wiped out first. James was with them and was leading the pack. I tried to join in with the festivities by pouring myself a small glass of wine, but I wasn't allowed to enjoy it. Sebastian loomed up like a disapproving schoolmaster. 'What are you doing Cynthia? You can't have that. You'll ruin the life of my nephew.'

'Surely not with just one.'

'Not even one. Alcohol—filthy stuff, full of impurities and preservatives. It does terrible things to the liver and it turns people into idiots. You've only got to look at them.' He pointed in disgust to Potts and the Bogarilla crowd.

Dinner was being served. Guests were coming into the shed with plates of pasta, chicken and salad, while Potts and his friends were doing their best to ruin the ambience of the meal with a mess of shaving cream and clumps of greasy hair. Not that Betsey was at all disturbed. She had put away her penis lipstick and watched Potts with glowing eyes. When at last his pink scalp shone bare in the farm-shed light, a cheer erupted from the party guests. Potts grabbed the money from Micky and rammed it in his pocket.

'Bravo!' yelled the cop, reaching for another beer. 'This one's for you, Potts.'

That was the cop's last beer. Having discharged his social obligations, he now had other matters to attend to. He was well-liked in Bogarilla for his fine community spirit and he waved at the party guests like a celebrity as he left, lurching out towards his police car.

'Do you reckon he should be driving?' asked Sebastian. 'He's as pissed as a bloody newt.'

Within seconds the sound of a deep thud reverberated through the shed and the party guests poured outside, gabbling with excitement. If Potts shaving his head had been great entertainment, this could be even better.

Outside, the policeman stood in the darkness contemplating Jock's damaged fence and his own crumpled car. He waved at the assembled revellers who showed their support with wild cheering.

'Ah, it's nothing,' he said. 'Just those bloody roos again.'

* * *

Morning came. Sunlight dappled the tobacco fields, lit up dams of shining water, shone on the farmhouse and green tents of the GIU camp, and illuminated several swags where bodies lay inert, shutting eyes against intrusive light. Grasshopper was crouched beneath a tree, green and queasy. Nearby, James McCracken, who looked like a corpse, was stretched out on a lump of corrugated iron. Some obscure impulse from the reptilian part of his brain had urged him to seek repose there in the depths of the night. Christopher, who was not afflicted by any overindulgence, was in the farmhouse enjoying tea and toast in the company of Stella, the cook, who said she rarely bothered cooking breakfast on Sunday mornings as nobody ever seemed to want it.

When Eddie and I got to the farmhouse, Potts was slumped over the kitchen table, his head buried in his hands. He was mumbling in incoherent misery. We walked across the tattered vinyl floor towards the teapot on the bench.

'Would you shut the bloody door!' he screeched. 'All that horrible glaring light. Why did the sun have to rise?'

Eddie slammed the door shut. 'Hungover again?' he asked.

'A hangover is nothing,' muttered Potts. 'I've just gone and made a complete dick of myself.'

'What's new?' asked Eddie, pouring tea and pushing a cup towards me.

Potts looked up with bleary eyes and caught his reflection in a mirror suspended on the opposite wall. 'Oh Christ! I look like a bloody dugong! I'm fucking ruined!' He flung his head back down onto his arms.

'Dugongs are rather cute animals and very popular with

conservationists,' commented Priscilla brightly. She was far too disciplined to ever suffer from a hangover.

But Potts just groaned.

'Don't worry Potts. Your hair will grow back in no time and just think how much more attractive you'll look,' said Stella. 'Girls prefer tidy men.'

'Nah, it's not that. That was just a bit of fun. I can put up with looking like an imbecile dugong and I can do without the girls, at least for a while. Too much bloody trouble most of them, anyway. But I don't like stuffing up my life before it's really got going. Bloody depressing that.'

'You're not making much sense, son,' said Christopher, munching on toast and vegemite in the corner.

'No? It's just that I was going to make something of myself. Go to Uni. Do geology. You know – a future, a real career – but I've blown it now. I'm expecting Jock to pitch up soon and chuck us all off his property. I'll get the blame and the GIU will sack me, and I'll be forever marked as the dickhead who wrecked an entire field season. Unemployable, that'll be me. And I haven't even enrolled for the bloody course yet.'

'Oh Potts,' said Stella. 'Don't blame yourself. It's not your fault the copper had one too many and knocked the fence over.'

'No,' said Priscilla. 'You did make rather a jerk of yourself last night, and it was foul eating dinner surrounded by greasy clods of hair, but quite honestly, Jock and Betsey didn't seem to mind at all.'

'Yes,' agreed Michelle, 'I thought they looked like they were thoroughly enjoying it.'

'Stop trying to be kind,' said Potts. 'You can't help me. You don't know what I did after.'

'Let's hear it then' said Eddie. 'Mightn't be as bad as you think.'

'Nah mate, it's bad,' said Potts. 'Memory's a bit fuzzy, but I know I broke into Jock's house after the party. They'd already crashed. Were lying on the bed. Not a stitch on either of them, I can remember that. And I was standing there with a tin of shaving cream in my hands, thinking it would be bloody funny if I sprayed it all over them. It was Mick's fault. He was egging me on. Don't know what happened next. Can't remember.'

'Well, I wouldn't worry about it,' said Stella. 'You probably had the sense to think better of it and went quietly off to bed.'

'Nah, woke up this morning with an empty tin of shaving cream beside me, feeling like I'd been busted up in the night.'

Micky Wren wobbled into the kitchen. His faced was tinged with green.

'Here comes trouble,' he said. 'Betsey's on her way up the driveway.'

'Put a paper bag over my head somebody,' said Potts. 'I'll pretend I don't exist.'

And there was Betsey beaming in the doorway, not remotely troubled about anything. 'Good morning everybody! What a fabulous party last night, hey?'

Potts had slumped back over the table and tried his best to disappear by covering his head with a sheet of newspaper.

'There you are Potts. Stop trying to hide. I can see you. You're a very naughty boy. Jock sent me across to get some helpers. Bit of a mess over our way this morning. Somebody went mad with shaving cream at our place last night. We could do with some help to clean up.'

'Sure thing,' quavered Potts. 'We'll do whatever you like.'

After breakfast Potts and his band of sickly helpers trudged off to Jock's farm with Betsey spurring them onwards as if they were a gaggle of geese. 'What's the point in life if you can't have a bit of fun now and again?' she asked.

And as they began to clean the mess, we all piled back into the vehicles for the long journey back to Blue Ridge. It was a quiet drive. Nobody even suggested stopping at any road cuttings. James had blindfolded himself and was suffering from headache. Sebastian was pale and mumbled about his poor weak liver, so I guessed he had been tempted by that filthy stuff alcohol.

'Never again,' said Grasshopper, looking at me with bloodshot eyes, but I knew they would be doing it all over again as soon as the next opportunity arose.

Chapter 10

Peeping toms, oolites & worms teeth

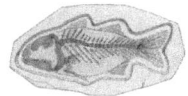

A SEETHING mass of uncontrolled lust—this was the vibe that Priscilla and Michelle picked up from the single mens quarters across the highway. It never occurred to them that these men were real people with personal histories and a whole suite of human emotions apart from sexual desire. From their point of view they had about as much charm as the bush flies and about as much reason for existing. When the rumours began about miners roaming the streets at night, peering through windows into family houses to watch women undress, they were unsurprised. But there were always rumours in Blue Ridge. They were needed like chilli sauce on a bland meal. They added an exciting edge to existence, a salacious kick, as the residents gazed out each evening onto the empty streets. They weren't necessarily true.

'Those guys should be locked away at night. Thickheads like them don't deserve rights. They don't have the self-control,' Priscilla said callously.

'I reckon you're a bit harsh,' replied Jen. 'I know these guys ... drink with them every Friday and I tell you they're no different from any other bunch of blokes you'll find in any other

Queensland pub. You've stirred them up a bit, that's all. But hey, they're bloody harmless.'

Priscilla and Michelle remained unconvinced. They were also unaware right then that there would be no escape for them from the pressures of sex and civilisation, not even out in the scrub on traverse, because the ringers had gone to the Blue Ridge pub on a binge and heard a different rumour. This one was about female geologists so beautiful they had to be seen to be believed.

'What? You mean it's just our rotten luck that all we've seen so far is you blokes, a couple of nerds, a pregnant cook and that huge, hefty sheila?' they asked.

'Yeah,' said Paul and Wally, feeding their fantasies, not bothering much with the truth.

They didn't mention that Priscilla and Michelle had discerning minds, were sharp-tongued and could be brutal to a delicate male ego. There was nothing about the freezer treatment. And they had no intention of expressing their true opinion, that these women were control freaks unlikely to ever appreciate true masculinity and would probably never go anywhere near any male within the remote vicinity of Blue Ridge.

Who wants the reality of cold, hard facts when fantasy is so much more attractive? Certainly not these three ringers who were romantic enough to weave hatbands from the bright pink flagging tape they had found blowing in the breeze.

'Not bad blokes really,' said Paul, afterwards.

'Yeah,' said Wally. 'But don't you think they seemed a bit too interested in where those girls are based? Do you reckon I blurted out too much?'

'Well Wal, you probably have, but who cares?' replied Paul. 'Shame though. I did hear Priscilla saying yesterday that the traverses are a … what did she call it? Yeah, I remember – "a welcome retreat from the town freaks" – yeah, that was it!'

Monday came around and everybody returned to the field. I was staying in town to catch up on cooking for the freezer and to see the doctor who flew into Blue Ridge once a fortnight to run a clinic. It was time for an antenatal check. Jeremy was at Bogarilla and I had the house to myself.

One evening midweek, when the Smiths had retired early to their bus, I stepped out of the shower and stood for a moment in the hallway, dripping and naked, thinking that everybody else on the planet was a million miles away. And there they were, those peeping toms I didn't believe in, gaping at me through the window. They had arrived at precisely the wrong moment.

I would have expected peeping toms to be gratified by the sight of a naked woman, even if pregnant, but this pair looked stricken with embarrassed horror. It was almost comical. Even so, overwhelmed by a feeling of sick panic, I bundled the towel around me and fled down the hallway to my room where I dressed in record time. I did not want men lurking in the hibiscus bushes all night and I resolved to get rid of them as soon as possible. It disturbed me that one of the faces had seemed oddly familiar, although that was hardly surprising in a town the size of Blue Ridge. I had probably seen him buying chocolate bars at the grocery store.

I grabbed a broom for self-defense, but exactly what I intended to do with it I can't recall. Perhaps I thought I could sweep them away. I would have expected peeping toms to be skulking about in the bushes but to my surprise they had made no attempt to hide. One was strolling about the garden while the other was banging on the glass door of the adjacent GIU house, staring into the dark and empty office.

'Hey! What do you think you're doing?' I yelled so loudly

and aggressively that Eric and Janey heard me from the bus. I waved my broom at them as Eric came galloping across the field.

The man at the door turned around and I realised that he was not a lurking peeping tom at all. I knew him. It was no wonder he had seemed familiar and no wonder he had been horrified when he had peered through the window. This was Oscar Feeney, a geology professor from the University of Queensland. I had no idea what he was doing in Blue Ridge at this hour of the night, but I needed to quickly adjust my attitude and forget embarrassment. I invited him and his friend in for coffee which he accepted in a voice so slurred I was convinced he had spent the preceding five hours drinking with the miners down at the pub.

'Are you crazy?' whispered Eric. 'There's no need to be charitable to these losers. I can get rid of them. They obviously got lost on the way back from the pub. I'll take them back to their quarters; somebody there can look after them.'

'But Eric, I actually know this guy. He's from the Uni,' I whispered back, as Oscar ignored our whispering and dragged his companion into the house where they both collapsed on chairs.

'Looks like you're stuck with them,' said Eric. 'I'll get Janey to come and help. Looks like they need a meal ... and a bed.'

We fed them four bowls of soup, three plates of stew and four cups of coffee. They revived after this nourishment like clockwork toys do after somebody winds the key, and Oscar found the energy to introduce his companion. Chen was a visiting scholar from China. They had been on the road all day on their way to the Black Bream River to join a group of students, but when they pulled into the Blue Ridge pub for a counter meal, they discovered the cook had knocked off early. The barman had said he was in bed with a bad back, poor man. All that was on offer were peanuts and beer.

'I wouldn't waste any sympathy on him. Bad back is code for the cook is pissed again and incapable of cooking. Happens a lot,' said Janey.

'A bit harsh on travellers. Lucky for us you're both in town. But we would have dropped in anyway. Christopher is lending us some gear. He said he'd leave it in the office. If you can help us find it, we can be on our way,' said Oscar.

'But you're both exhausted and you're hours away from the Black Bream River yet. And the road is terrible, covered in potholes and kangaroos. Why don't you wait till morning? There are plenty of empty rooms here and in the house next door. You can take your pick,' I said.

Chen perked up considerably at the thought of a nearby bed, but Oscar had no intention of giving in to fatigue. The night was still young, he said. He intended to wake up at the gorge in the morning. As for the road to the Black Bream River, he knew every twist and turn. It was a highway. He'd been going there for thirty years. They would be perfectly safe. As he propelled the reluctant Chen out the door, he assured him that in the morning he would be mightily glad they had made this effort. They disappeared into the night and I did not expect to see them again until their fieldwork was over, and they returned the equipment.

The following week I went with Eddie to Wallaby Gorge, also on the Black Bream River, upstream from the students' camp. Rainbow bee-eaters flashed about the trees above as I buried my feet in the warm sand by the waterhole and I thought there was no finer place to be on the entire planet. Opal colours flitted across the surface of the water and rock wallabies lived among the red rocks and cliffs of the gorge.

'I'm heading towards the Black Bream Gorge today. You should come and check out the oolites,' said Eddie.

I doubted that oolites, whatever they were, would be worth

the trouble.

'No really, you must see the oolites,' said Eddie. 'They're really interesting. It all starts with shell fragments or maybe sand grains that get tossed about the seafloor for a long, long time in the currents of bygone ages. Calcium carbonate precipitates about them and you end up with something that looks like fish eggs in the limestone.'

I stared at him, amazed. How could my partner in life so mistake my personal interests to think that I would rather see a petrified, fish-egg structure in some rock, than spend the day watching the acrobatics of the bee-eaters?

'Right ...' I said.

'If I dropped you off at the student's camp, you'd have some company,' he continued.

'Eddie, the wallabies and bee-eaters are good enough company for me.'

'But it's not just the oolites. There are other great rocks there. Devonian corals for example. The Coral Gardens we call it. Very special. Scenic. Not to be missed.'

'Well, okay. I'll come,' I said reluctantly.

On the way I told him about my encounter with Oscar and Chen the previous week.

'Chen? Yes, I've heard of him. The conodont specialist from China.'

'The what?'

'He specialises in a type of fossilised worms teeth.'

'Worms teeth? Don't be ridiculous Eddie. Nobody would devote their lives to worms teeth.'

'Well, they do, actually.'

And he swept into a monologue about these microworms with rapidly evolving teeth lining their alimentary tracts. There was probably some deep lesson in it somewhere about biological adaptation and environmental change, but what he said as he dumped me on the banks of the Black Bream River was this. 'The master of conodonts is the master of geological time. Conodonts date rocks, within certain boundaries anyway.'

The students' camp was deserted. Tents were open for airing and breakfast pots soaked in the sunlight, but there was not a soul in sight.

The river below the campsite was broken into a series of deep green pools and thin channels along a sandy bed and was lined with large sheets of polished limestone. I ignored the oolites, but wandered along the sandy riverbed, keeping company with the long-legged wading birds that were strolling on the sand.

Turning from the river, I walked up a slope and stumbled upon the ancient coral reef, now turned to stone through the eons of time. Brown blades of grass pushed through the earth and ants crawled between the heads of coral where once fish had swum. The river, the trees, the dried landscape seemed so permanent, so eternal, but there had once been a sea here. It was unsettling, almost thrilling, to see this evidence of the earth's great changes over a time scale too massive for me to comprehend. For one dizzy moment I grasped the fact that the earth was a place of fluid change and that time held dimensions I had never suspected.

I came to rest on the riverbank and sank into the sand. In the green depths below, fish swam with hypnotic movement and gazing at them, I fell asleep.

I awoke to see a trail of students trudging across the sand like a group of explorers who had been in the desert wilderness for months and were on the point of expiring. They came so close I could hear the grains of sand dislodging beneath their feet as they made footprints along the riverbed.

Strangely, the students ignored me completely even when I tried to capture their interest by mentioning the oolites. A troubled glance was all I got before they averted their eyes. I could read their thoughts. Why was there a strange pregnant woman on the riverbank, miles from anywhere, asking about oolites? There was no way they were going to communicate with an apparition. They'd been warned about what dehydration does to the brain, and it was happening to them already, threatening their very sanity after one simple hike up the gorge in hot weather. I had never before been regarded as a figment of a disordered mind, and I was feeling very awkward when Oscar Feeney came striding along at the rear of the group.

'Hi Cynthia. Great to see you here! Isn't this the most fantastic spot?' he asked jovially, not at all surprised to see me. He considered it only natural that anybody with a sense of real quality living would eventually materialise at the Black Bream River to take in its unique atmosphere. He waved his arm in the direction of the outcrop lining the river. 'It would take days to take all this in. Have you had a close look at the oolites?'

'Well ...' I began, as I watched Chen approach across the sandbank.

He had his own research program and had not been with the student group that morning. 'Hi Chen. How are you? I've heard you're here studying conodonts.'

'Yes, I have collected many samples,' he replied. His face glowed with pleasure. This was a man in a million, one who was truly inspired by the possibilities within the tooth of a worm.

Before we could continue the conversation we were distracted by the sound of a vehicle approaching, the motor humming monotonously through the silence of the bush.

'Eddie must be on his way back already,' I said.

But it wasn't Eddie at all. To our astonishment Michelle and Priscilla emerged from the vehicle and joined us on the sandbank.

'What a surprise!' said Oscar. 'I guess you've come to review the oolites. Who can stay away?'

Priscilla ignored this comment. 'Actually, we've come to camp here for the night. We're being followed about by a bunch of creeps on horseback, but they can't hassle us if we're down here with your crowd.'

'You wouldn't believe it,' added Michelle. 'All the empty space in the world out here and we have to run into these guys. They've been following us about all day, shouting at us. As fast as we jump in the car and drive off, they pitch up again. It's impossible to get any work done.'

'Has it occurred to you they're just some local lads with a message for you?' suggested Oscar, but Michelle and Priscilla snorted in disbelief and said they looked like thugs.

Meanwhile, my friends the ringers, in pursuit of Priscilla and Michelle, were heading down the track towards the Black Bream River when Eddie intercepted them. They all paused for a moment to exchange a few words. After a few comments about the weather, the long lanky guy made a complaint.

'Hey, we've been looking for them sheilas that work with you mob for the past two days, but every time we get close, they vanish like a bloody desert mirage.'

He pulled a pair of sunglasses from his pocket, delicately dusting the lens with the corner of his shirt. 'We found these along the track a bit, yesterday. We reckon they must belong to that girl, the one we heard about at the pub. Real beautiful they said. Priscilla, I think her name is. You'd think she'd want them back, but every time we get close they disappear like bloody rabbits down a hole.'

'I'll pass them on for you,' Eddie offered.

'Gee thanks mate, but we kinda wanna do it ourselves. Seems, you know ... more neighbourly.'

'You're probably wasting your time, though,' said Eddie. 'They look like Jen's sunnies, the ones she lost last week. She'll be real pleased to get them back. She's not far away either, over *Three Trees* way with James McCracken.'

The ringer laughed, 'Well, that explains a lot. No wonder them sheilas kept scurrying off. Probably thought we were up to no good, hey? We'll go look for Jen.'

They charged off with the air of olden-day knights on the brink of rescuing a damsel from a dragon. When they reached the outstation at *Three Trees,* they saw that Jen was not one of the fantasy figures they had believed in, that had come directly from Wally's imagination. She was the 'huge, hefty sheila' they already knew. But these ringers were men who could bend with the wind, who could adjust to the reality of a passing moment, who were well-disposed to the world. If disappointment registered at all, it was gone in a flash, as insubstantial as a wisp of cloud in a blue, blue sky. They grinned and waved the sunglasses at Jen.

'Gee, thanks lads, thanks a million,' she said. 'Hey, James, I reckon we've got enough beer in the car fridge. Why don't you fellas stick round for a bit and have a drink with us. Getting onto beer o'clock.'

'Yeah. Yeah, sure,' they said, and they all sat beneath the gum trees as the afternoon slowly faded, chatting of this and that.

Back at the Black Bream Gorge, Oscar asked if Michelle and Priscilla would give a talk to the students on their work. After all, they had been disrupted that day, and as they were spending the night at the camp, it was too good an opportunity to waste, particularly now that their anxieties had been allayed. As soon as Eddie arrived at the gorge he had informed them that those thugs they feared were currently galloping in the opposite direction towards *Three Trees* to return Jen's missing sunglasses.

Eddie and I never heard the talk they prepared. We returned to Wallaby Gorge.

Chapter 11

The radio shadow

'WELCOME TO THE WALLABY GORGE RESORT,' said Eddie.

Another Monday had come and we were back at Wallaby Gorge. Eddie suspended a hammock between two trees on the edge of the waterhole. This was a gift for my birthday later in the week. How he had come by such a thing in Blue Ridge was a mystery, shopping opportunities being limited to the grocery store and the butcher shop. But he had managed it somehow and life this week at Wallaby Gorge was going to be more comfortable and indulgent (I hoped).

There was nothing to do now for the next few days but laze in the hammock, watch the world, and swim in the waterhole if it got too hot. The facilities were basic, but I guess it wasn't a bad approximation of resort living.

Eddie had embarked on a detailed study of the outcrop down the river. He had begun this the previous week, assisted by Paul, who soon discovered that fishing the waterholes along the river was almost as good as hunting pigs. This varied our diet, which was great. But not so great when he emptied his haversack of flapping, fading fish onto the table amongst the sandwiches at lunchtime and demanded that I gut them before dinner.

That Monday he stashed his fishing line into his haversack as he prepared to hike down the river with Eddie. But he caught no fish, and in the evening decided to cook his Monday night special, the meal he called 'spag bog'. He had just got started when Eddie went across to the vehicle for the routine six o'clock radio session.

We could hear him trying to contact his colleagues but could hear nothing else beyond the crackle of the fire, no shred of radio static, no other voices, nothing. After a while he shrugged and wandered back to the fire.

'How odd. Couldn't get through at all. There's nothing there. Do you think we're in a radio shadow?'

Paul nodded as he browned the mince over the fire. 'Definite radio shadow.'

'But we were here last week, and we weren't in a radio shadow then,' I said.

They looked at me as if I had said something stupid and Eddie muttered indecipherable words about airwaves and complicated factors. He went to the car fridge and pulled out beer and chocolate, and we forgot about it until Tuesday evening when exactly the same thing happened.

The men nodded their heads wisely. 'Radio shadow,' they said.

The next morning we were woken at dawn, just before sunrise, by the sound of scuffling and grunting down by the waterhole. Eddie instantly leapt to his feet and kicked the inert shape in the swag on the other side of the fireplace.

'Paul! Quick! Pigs! A whole bunch of them down by the river. Quick!'

Paul sprang from his swag like a jack-in-the-box, shoved his feet into his boots, grabbed the crossbow and careered down the slope in his underwear, bootlaces untied and flapping. It was far too early for such enthusiasm, but he could barely suppress a triumphant whoop of joy as he charged towards the waterhole. Any pigs lurking down there would have heard him coming and galloped off as quick as their legs could carry them. Or maybe not. It wasn't long before we heard Paul call out, his voice alarmed and plaintive.

'What do you suppose is happening?' I asked. 'Sounds like he's negotiating with the pig before it proceeds with some horrible plan. Do you think he's okay?'

'Paul can look after himself,' said Eddie complacently. 'But hey. Look! There he is on the hill. Looks like he's running for his life. Oh well. He'll be okay.'

'You shouldn't have encouraged him,' I said.

Paul trudged back up the slope as we laid the breakfast foods out on the table. Not a shred of enthusiasm remained. He slumped heavily onto a campstool.

'Well?' asked Eddie.

'Well what?' replied Paul, with a touch of belligerence.

'What happened to the pigs?'

'What bloody pigs?'

'Plenty down there when we woke.'

'Oh yeah. Well, you made a mistake didn't you? Those were no pigs down there making that racket. It was kangaroos having some sort of orgy thing.'

'Sounded like pigs,' said Eddie.

'Well, it wasn't. The old man kangaroo, the alpha guy, had just finished making mincemeat of the young buck. And he seemed to think I was the next contender. You're bloody lucky I'm still alive. Bloody thing tried to disembowel me with its feet. They're bloody vicious buggers, not at all as cute as they look.'

'Have some cornflakes Paul,' I said.

But he waved them away. 'Look at all these scratches. I didn't even have time to put a shirt on.'

'I've warned you before about tearing off in your underwear,' said Eddie. 'I'm not surprised that poor old roo got confused about your intentions, turning up in your jocks like that.'

Paul wouldn't even have noticed a pig sauntering by at that moment.

'Bloody thankless job this,' he said despondently. 'Follow you about all day. Make you bloody tea. Cook you dinner. And what do I get? Sent on a wild goose chase after nonexistent pigs at the crack of dawn. And if that isn't enough of a disappointment, I get attacked by a bloody rampaging giant marsupial. And you just laugh! Huh.'

But the day beckoned regardless of mood. He picked up his canvas haversack and plodded back up the river with Eddie for another day of fishing the waterholes and hunting for pigs while Eddie measured the outcrop. I was not expecting to see them again before the days end.

That afternoon I lay long in my hammock down in Wallaby Gorge watching the slow bubbling rhythms of the turtles. The wallabies leapt about the boulders on the cliffs as the fiery tones cast by the setting sun diminished and the gorge lost its colour to the gathering dusk. And still I had not heard Eddie and Paul call out as they usually did when they were on their way back up the river.

I returned to the campsite. Paced about. Where were they? Why were they so late? The time for the radio calls had already come and gone. Something dreadful must have happened. Had Paul provoked a wild boar and been skewered? Eddie probably tried to help. The boar skewered him too. They were both bleeding to death somewhere.

No. That was ridiculous. They couldn't be that stupid. I

just needed to settle my mind somehow. Do something practical. There was a strip of deep dark blue on the horizon that marked the edge of the night sky. It would be dark soon; it was time to get the fire going. That would help. Then I could get a billy boiling. Make a cup of tea. Just what I needed to soothe my nerves.

Soon the fire was crackling and the billy was boiling. I went to the tuckerbox to get the tea, but there was none, not a solitary teabag, not even a tea-leaf. Paul had taken it all in his haversack and had left me alone without resources. In a split-second, anxiety turned to rage. What had happened to Eddie and Paul anyway? It was almost completely dark now and there was still no sign of them. They must have been bitten by taipans or fallen from a cliff. Soon I would have to stumble down the riverbed with a torch looking for them. And what would I do when I found them? The radio wasn't even working.

I needed some crutch to help me through this ordeal. It was then that I thought of the beer in the car fridge. If they could pinch my tea, I could pinch their beer. I didn't actually like beer, but other people did, and it was possible that it had similar soothing qualities to tea. Taking a tin from the fridge, I settled into a camp chair to try it. After a sip or two, I realised that I couldn't stomach the stuff at all. But I didn't return it to the fridge so Eddie or Paul could benefit from the remainder, I tipped the tin upside down and let the fluid dribble out onto the earth. Beer was in very short supply and this was a mean and childish thing to do. I know. But I was in a fury.

As soon as the last drop had sunk into the dust, I heard voices. Jubilant, happy voices, full of the joy of life. Yes, I was relieved, but no, my fury did not abate. It increased. By the time they were scrambling over the rocks that lined the waterhole I was screeching abuse at them. They just smirked.

'When you're finished, Cynthia,' said Paul, still smirking. 'Happy Birthday for tomorrow!' And they both began to sing with uproarious joy.

'Have we got a treat lined up for you,' said Eddie. 'Paul's going to cook you a birthday dinner.'

I was beginning to feel like a worm. But a justified worm. After all, they had taken all the tea.

'Yeah, yeah, I know we're a bit late,' said Paul. 'Yeah, and you were probably a bit worried, but I had to catch your dinner, right? You see we're having fresh black bream almondine, camp oven vegetables with lemon and garlic, and Paul's damper special.'

'Well, you are late. Very late,' I said.

'Radio's not working anyway,' said Eddie. 'And look what I've been hiding for you, cooling off in a pool down in the river.' He fished a bottle of white wine out of his backpack.

'Yeah, I won't tell Sebastian if you have a glass or two. Just what you need I reckon, after the way you were shouting at us back there,' said Paul.

'It'll do you good,' said Eddie. 'And tonight we'll crank up the music and we'll dance under the stars.'

'Great fire you've got going here Cynthia,' said Paul. 'I'll need those hot coals. You can give me a hand. How about you clean the fish. But check 'em. They could be full of worms. Eddie can do the potatoes and I'll do the rest.'

Eddie went to get beers from the fridge. 'What the hell? There's a beer missing. Now I know you wouldn't be drinking it, Cynthia. And it's not the kangaroos raiding the fridge. What's going on? Have you been giving our beer to those ringers?'

'Er, no.'

Slight communication breakdown. But overhead the stars swirled in a black never-ending sky, dinner was cooking over the fire, and life was too good to be bothered with minor squabbles. Even the rock wallabies danced to the music outside the ring of firelight that night.

* * *

The next morning we were breakfasting on cereal and fruit, bacon and eggs, and toast and vegemite, when we heard the hum of a distant vehicle chugging over the ridges. We always seemed completely alone at Wallaby Gorge and never heard or saw any other vehicles out this way. Eddie spluttered into his tea. Paul refilled the billy and put it back on the fire.

'Just as well we didn't eat all the bacon,' he said.

'What's going on?' I asked.

'I would hazard a guess that will be Bugsy or James coming to visit us on this fine sunny morning,' said Eddie.

'Why?'

'Oh, to say happy birthday to you of course,' he said. 'No, seriously, nobody's heard from us in three days. They're probably wondering what's happened.'

'Yeah,' said Paul. 'They're coming to rescue us. And I reckon they've gone without their breakfast to come and check that we haven't been abducted by aliens. Or whatever else they imagine has gone on. And I reckon they might be a bit touchy when they find us without a problem in the world, stuffing our faces with bacon and eggs.'

He was half right. When Bugsy and Sebastian turned up, Bugsy was relieved to find us safe and sound, but Sebastian was so outraged his eyes bulged. He would have been less disturbed if he had found that we'd been stampeded by wild bulls in the night. I recognised the emotion, the anxiety turning to rage thing, and I understood completely when he abused us, although I won't repeat what he said.

'All right, all right. Calm down,' said Paul. 'Here, I've got a feed of bacon and eggs ready for you. And a cuppa tea. You'll feel better soon.'

The breakfast worked like a magic formula. Soon Sebastian let go of any resentment he felt about the anxiety that had raked his soul and had been so pointless. Eddie explained that there had been a problem with the radio all week.

'Yeah, radio shadow, I reckon,' said Paul.

But when Bugsy tried his own radio, there was no problem at all.

'It's not a radio shadow,' he said, leaping into our vehicle. He pulled out the mouthpiece, twiddled with the knobs for a minute or two and shrugged, 'The thing's stuffed.'

'Yep,' said Eddie. 'Oh well, you can let everyone know we're okay and we'll see you all back in Blue Ridge tomorrow.'

Bugsy and Sebastian drove back to the limestone country, Eddie and Paul headed back to work down the river, and I hung out with the rock wallabies. They were accustomed to me by now and never scuttled away when I sat on their rock. They accepted me as if I was a boulder or another weirder form of wallaby and got on with wallaby life. Some of them were so curious they crept close and peered into my face. When the rock got too hard to sit on anymore, I left the wallabies and moved down to the hammock over the waterhole to watch the rainbow bee-eaters dart about the cliffs.

A slight flicker of a breeze arose and twitched the leaves above, and with that faint flow of air I sensed how this place had been beloved before, by generations of others, who in times past had come by this way and lived and loved and left scant trace. Not so long ago, when measured against the vast reaches of geological time. They would have slept beneath this same starry sky, traced meanings in the constellations and in the dark, velvety spaces between and told stories. We were in this place by the grace of a road, a vehicle, a car fridge full of food, and would struggle to survive out here without these props. But they would have made a good living along these riverbanks for many an age, until disrupted by the coming of people in boats bringing with them a devastating cargo of western diseases and ideas.

The breeze stirred again, just a whisper, and a leaf dropped from the tree above onto the surface of the waterhole, where softly it drifted. Nothing endures unchanged forever, not a people or a planet or a leaf, not a species or a rock. The rocks of the magnificent red cliffs that lined this river would erode to sand in the fullness of time and in the deep future perhaps build up to rock again. Even this gem of a continent is ephemeral, a passing thing. Those first people who came, maybe on boats, long, long ago, caught this continent as it drifted slowly north (like that leaf on the water). They rode the land like a raft on the sea, as year by year, centimetre by centimetre, it continued its northward journey. And saw on the way the end of an ice age, the drowning of coastal homelands as the ice sheets melted, and the demise of the megafauna. Nothing stays the same, not from moment to moment or age to age.

And If Eddie is right, then this continent, presently called Australia, will one day cease to be a great southern land as the continental plate pushes beyond the equator, eventually colliding with other lands to form a mighty mountain range somewhere in the northern hemisphere. By then all humans will be long gone, along with the gentle rock wallaby, and yet the sun will have barely aged at all. Perhaps Nature will have dreamed up new orders of fauna to grace the earth and ponder the meaning of existence.

Even galaxies collide. Our own Milky Way is heading inex-orably towards this fate. And what then? Do worlds upon worlds dissolve to dust? Will there be a mighty re-creation as dust and fragments swirl slowly into some other shapes? Or will it all be as inconsequential as our skin shedding a cell?

A family of pigs crossed the river on the far sandbank. Jauntily. And I was back. Away from the past and the dazzling probabilities of the future, away from voyaging continents and colliding galaxies. I was swinging in a hammock on a riverbank on a sunny day, cocooned in the present moment. And perhaps there is no better place to be in a universe where galaxies collide, than absorbed in the now of the passing moment and the gifts it brings— a pig, a bee-eater, a leaf adrift on the water.

* * *

The next day was Friday; the week was over. We jolted along on our way back to Blue Ridge, over hills, down gullies, over rocks, past the wallaroos and the trees burned in the fire. And as the vehicle lurched this way and that, I noticed a black cord dangling from the radio, swinging with the movement of the vehicle.

'What's that thing?' I asked.

Paul shot a glance at Eddie, who was gazing with interest out at the landscape, not remotely interested in anything dangling in the car, and plugged the cord in behind the radio, jamming it with force.

'It's nothing, nothing at all,' he muttered vaguely. 'But it's pissing me off. Distracting my vision.'

He was silent for some time, intent on the road ahead and humming along to the music on the cassette player. But an hour later when we were back on the tar, speeding along the highway towards Blue Ridge, he spoke again.

'Listen Cynthia, if anyone asks about our radio problem, don't mention that dangling cord. It would give the wrong impression. But it's not relevant. No connection whatsoever.'

'Of course not, Paul,' I said. 'It was some weird intermittent radio shadow effect. You know complicated factors, airwaves and so on. Some strange trick of the weather. Who knows what goes on in this universe?'

No fault was ever found in that radio and it worked perfectly from then on.

Chapter 12

Hormones

GRASSHOPPER AND PAUL bent over a map of Queensland, pointing out alternative routes to Brisbane and debating which town to stay in on the way back. Bugsy told me they took exactly the same route and stayed in exactly the same town year after year, but one look at the map and they felt the end of the season was finally within reach. It was a ritual, symbolic of a change of heart. They were fed up with heat, dust and flies; satiated with feral pigs and rocks. They wanted to go home.

A series of pink envelopes sealed with teddy bear stickers began to arrive for Christopher. They were from his wife, who was approaching the end of her pregnancy and wanted him home. Christopher had already organised a replacement to take over for the last weeks of the season. His timing was based on the expected delivery date he'd been given, which for him represented the best advice science could buy. I could have lent him a book that would have informed him that pregnancy was naturally variable and that 90% of babies do not arrive on the expected date, but he didn't really want to know.

It had been hot for so long now that any enthusiasm had long gone. We struggled to get up in the morning and we all wanted to be somewhere else. Dinner conversations had lost all vitality and although we tried our best to put up with one another, a barely suppressed sense of irritation flowed beneath the surface.

Priscilla tried her best to lift everybody's spirits by organ-ising a weekend excursion, returning early from the field on Friday afternoon for just that purpose.

'Great, I've caught you just in time,' she said breezily, coming through the door as we were starting dinner. 'I have good news. You can drop that for today. We're all going out this evening.'

I was astonished. 'What? Surely you're not going to risk the pub, not on a Friday night?'

'Of course not. I've just made a call from the post office and booked rooms in the best motel in Burkes Hill. When everyone's back we'll drive down. We can dress up and dine out at a restau-rant. And maybe by tomorrow we'll feel like real human beings again. As if we have a real life.'

'You mean everybody?' asked Janey sceptically.

'Well, everybody could do with a change, that's for sure,' said Priscilla. 'It feels like a century since I last dressed up. There's one dress hanging up in my room and I haven't touched it for over three months.'

I doubted that Burkes Hill would offer the sophisticated dining options she had in mind. There were a few pubs and a Chinese take-away. The best motel was the only motel and had a dining room that offered customers something fried from the deep-freeze cabinet, although it probably also had stiff linen tablecloths, plastic flowers in vases, and airconditioning. Was this enough to go driving hundreds of miles into the night for?

'I don't think Wally will want to go,' said Janey. 'He likes his Friday night binge at the pub too much.'

'Not sure about Sebastian either. I've got a feeling he won't want to fork out for a meal and a motel room. I guess we'd better prepare something,' I said.

'Suit yourselves,' said Priscilla. 'Wally and Sebastian aren't likely to add much to the ambience or the conversation in any case. And neither of them will have a decent shirt to wear anyway. But I think everyone else will come.'

As she expected, all the others went along with this plan, turned on by the novelty of the scheme. Only a few of us remained back in Blue Ridge. Wally wiped himself out at the pub, Sebastian played his guitar, and it was the most relaxing Friday evening we had so far experienced at the base camp. But it mustn't have been as relaxing for those who had rushed down to Burkes Hill for a night on the town. When they arrived back just before lunch the next day, they shuffled into the house looking as if they were all wishing they hadn't gone at all. After all the road was long and they had been driving all week.

'Whose brilliant idea was that?' I heard James say irritably as he approached the house. 'What was it all about? Was it supposed to make us feel good or something?'

'Stop whining,' Priscilla replied. 'You're getting on my nerves. You sound like a diseased sheep.'

'Yeah, but driving all that way to eat a pile of muck served by a mentally deficient waiter. It doesn't make sense.'

'Would you shut up!'

'And the motel. I reckon the cleaners there think it's okay just to spray the place with the aroma of fake new car. No need to get rid of the cockroaches in the sink or pick up the used knickers lying in the corner.'

'Would you shut up you blithering dick brain. No one imagined they would be staying at the Ritz, that wasn't the point. The point was ...'

'What's the point of anything?' James interrupted. 'But it's okay Priscilla. I know what's up. Saw it in a magazine. Your mind goes fuzzy, you can't think rationally, the world seems bleak, and you can't control your temper. Blame the hormones. Apparently a woman is just like a bag of unstable chemicals. Must be terrible.'

Priscilla replied with not a word, but she changed the orientation of her facial muscles into a prolonged, withering glare that was much worse than words and stalked off.

Back in the kitchen, Grasshopper slouched against the bench, bleary eyed. 'Some advice for you Cynthia. Never order seafood if you eat out in Burkes Hill. Dunno what I was thinking. I reckon I'll feel better after lunch. What is for lunch?'

'Salmon mousse and salad.'

'Oh jeez no. You'd better do me some dry toast and vegemite.'

* * *

There was no improvement in spirits as the weekend went by. Even Wally, who had avoided the long drive to disappointment on Friday evening, was fed up. On Sunday I heard his voice waft into the kitchen with the afternoon breeze. 'Yeah, bloody awful not getting any. But hey, if you sort of squint up your eyes that tree over there looks a bit like a sheila.'

No, maybe I hadn't heard that at all. Hopefully I had it all wrong. But I could hear squeals of laughter and when I glanced out the window I wished I hadn't. Wally, tongue dangling in a most revolting manner, was thrusting his pelvis at the tree.

James, however, did not join the laughter. He just murmured something wistful about the girl from the grocery store.

Human nature can be puzzling. Some of the miners from the single men's quarters would find reason to saunter down our street and casually hover about, hoping to run into Priscilla or

Michelle, plainly besotted by the very thought of these young women. Meanwhile the men in the GIU houses, viewed these same women as they would a pair of bossy aunts who cramped their style and forced them to standards of behaviour they would rather ignore. Likeable, but irritating, and certainly not sexually intriguing. Instead, they cast their eyes towards the girl from the grocery store. As a result, several of the GIU men frequented the grocery store at weekends, ruining their appetites with soft drinks, ice-creams and other rubbish. They also became aware, quite suddenly, that they looked like a mob of dishevelled slobs.

Grasshopper looked into the hallway mirror.

Jeez, I look terrible. You could mop the floor with my hair. Hey, Cynthia, do you reckon you could give me a haircut?'

'God no,' I said. 'I'd be hopeless.'

'Have some faith in yourself, Cynthia,' said Paul. 'It's a cinch. You just go snip, snip, snip and it's done.'

Ignoring my protests completely, and with ridiculous optimism, they dragged a chair into the backyard to serve as a barber's seat and a queue had formed, all eager to try my nonexistent haircutting expertise. It was like being appointed as the non-cook cook all over again, but with a much greater chance of failure this time round. It was only fair to trial Eddie first. He had less to lose as he wasn't expecting his hairdo to help him captivate the girl at the shop. Off I went – snip here, snip there – as guided by Paul, who actually had less of a clue than I did.

It was amazing how quickly that haircut queue disintegrated when Eddie rose from the chair.

'Jeez mate, you look bloody awful!' said Sebastian.

'Yeah, you're right, Cynthia. You are hopeless,' sniggered Paul.

Day by day, bit by bit, as several of the men grew slowly sillier, James continued to maintain that males were governed solely by the rational mind, unlike women, who were so unfortunately afflicted by the hormonal tides. Frankly, in the GIU house at that time, there wasn't much evidence to back this opinion up.

* * *

The day after Eddie's terrible haircut we went back out to Wallaby Gorge for the week. On our return on Friday afternoon, as we cruised slowly back towards the GIU houses, we saw Janey standing on the footpath, gazing anxiously up the street.

'I was hoping you were Christopher,' she said. 'I hope he turns up soon. His wife has gone into labor. The neighbours have just taken the phone call.'

'What?'

This was a slap of reality. A wake-up call. A reminder that babies don't stay conveniently tucked away in the uterus forever.

'Eric is down at the post office now, booking a flight. Next flight out of Townsville is six in the morning and Christopher's got to be on it.'

'But I thought the baby wasn't due till next month,' said Eddie.

'It's nearly next month now,' replied Janey. 'And as you'll discover yourselves very soon, babies hardly ever do what you expect. They come along to remind us that any control we think we have over our lives is purely imaginary. Adorable, but classic disrupters of order.'

Dinner was more animated than it had been for some time, as if we were all suddenly exposed to a vibrant current of life. This news of an impending birth cheered up everybody. We weren't living in a stagnant backwater, forgotten by the rest of the world after all. Conversation became exuberant and there were many jokes at Christopher's expense. Not that he joined in this mirth; he just sat at the head of the table, pale and stunned, as if he hadn't quite grasped what was going on.

Then he turned to Eddie and said, 'I can't leave till I've packed my rocks.'

That evening nobody went to the pub and nobody turned on the television. The whole party milled about in the fresh air at the front of the houses in festival mood. James was in such high spirits I thought he must have made headway in his relationship with the girl from the grocery store. Along with Grasshopper he offered to wake up at two in the morning to drive Christopher to Townsville, but he showed no inclination to go to bed early. Neither could Christopher get any rest. He was feverishly ramming rock samples into drums with the assistance of Eddie, who worked steadily beside him, both of them oblivious to surrounding activity.

James was the life of the party, circulating about with a pouch of coins and a clipboard folder.

'Hey Cynthia! You haven't placed your bet yet.'

'What?'

'You can have sex and weight, or time of arrival. Two dollars a bet. You can try as many times as you like. Winner gets a carton of grog and some cash. You've got a good chance. You'd have to beat Wally. He bet the baby will weigh 12.2 kilograms. I mean that would split the woman apart wouldn't it?'

I thought of the pink envelopes and the teddy bear stickers, and the woman who sent them alone in Brisbane.

'Don't be disgusting!' I snapped, flouncing off, refusing to play.

'What's wrong with her?' I heard Bugsy ask.

'It's her hormones, poor thing,' James responded.

Chapter 13

Cricket

MURRAY CROW WAS COMING from Bogarilla to replace Christopher.

'Oh no. Not him!' said Jen. 'Not Murray. I've known him for years. I've seen him walk in his sleep, I've heard him talk in his sleep and I've watched him grow a beard. And I can tell you he's mean. Real mean. This is the end of bacon for breakfast. Just as well we're going home.'

'Oh my god! Murray?' said Michelle. 'He'll drive everyone nuts with his economising. Remember that time he wouldn't let the cook buy cream to serve with the apple pies?'

'Yeah,' said Jen. 'He forced her to make custard with the out-of-date milk powder instead.'

'I can't understand why he takes it so far,' said Michelle. 'It's not as if he lived through the Great Depression and was forced to eke out an existence on edible weeds and the dregs from the pantry like Grandma.'

The Friday after I heard this conversation I lay in the hammock, waiting with dread for this control freak to arrive. These were probably my last moments of peace. Once Murray was here I would be told to scrub the ceiling fans when the cooking was under control. No bludging in the hammock while the casserole simmered on the hotplate. To make matters worse, he was bringing the entire Bogarilla crowd with him for a weekend cricket match. This was supposed to be a team-building exercise, but surely a weekend of cricket would be the last straw, enough to plunge us all into the depths of paralytic despair.

I had already formed a mental picture of Murray Crow – a short pugnacious man with slitty eyes and a sour mouth – so I didn't recognise him at all when he turned up with Jeremy Leech. The man who said his name was Murray had a fresh face and a pleasant manner and did not demand I get out of the hammock to scrub the fans. Instead, he waved a hand at me and positively told me not to get up as he was sure I needed the rest. And as I continued to lie there in the hammock he said it was scandalous how the GIU abused the goodwill of the cooks by not paying them properly.

'I should be able to swing some overtime payments for you while I'm here. This weekend, for instance, when you've got both camps to feed,' said Murray. 'Stella's coming down. But she's here for a break.'

What was going on? Where was the sleep-talking, sleep-walking mean man I had been led to expect? Had there been some miraculous character transformation or were Jen and Michelle confused and thinking of the wrong guy? Was it mischief-making or were we all living in parallel universes with perceptions that would never, could never correlate?

Meanwhile, Jeremy had leapt from the vehicle with his usual style, immaculately naked, fragrant of coconut, skin glistening. He never neglected any opportunity to improve his suntan and he refused to wear a shirt when he drove. He also refused to wear a seat belt, preferring to risk his life than to disrupt the even tone of his skin. He watched us chatting for a moment or two, before interjecting: 'Hey, I hear Christopher's wife had a little boy! Hooray!'

'Yes,' I said. 'He must have been a complete wreck when he got there, but apparently all went well. Mother and baby thriving and all that.'

They disappeared into the house and I settled back into the hammock. I probably only had seconds of relaxation left. Even if Murray was not going to be a problem, I still had the entire Bogarilla crowd to contend with. They would be here any minute now.

The visitors arrived gradually throughout the afternoon, along with the returning Blue Ridge field party. As each group arrived, they pulled out camp chairs from the vehicles, arranged them in the yard about a large blue Esky, and began to hurl beer down their throats. The exception was Stella, who kissed me drowsily, staggered into a bedroom and instantly fell asleep.

Janey and I had gone to some trouble for these guests. Jen had recommended we entertain them with a barbecue down at the park and we had prepared platters of salad and platters of meat, pavlovas and mulberry pies, all laid out upon the bench and ready to go. It had seemed a terrific idea at the time, but these visitors showed no interest at all in strolling down to the park for a picnic. They were interested only in the contents of the Esky and, once seated, looked as if they weren't going anywhere. Jen was throwing beer down with the best of them, having forgotten all about the park idea. Nobody seemed particularly hungry, and I could have saved myself a lot of effort if I had just thrown some salted peanuts in a bowl and sent it their way.

Eric had gone ahead to the park, armed with tables, boxes of gear and the first batch of food, to begin setting up and to commandeer a barbecue. He must have been wondering where in hell we all were. Even Priscilla, who could usually be relied upon to motivate a group to action, was completely unconcerned. She was giggling with Michelle in the lounge room. I couldn't blame them. This was their last weekend in Blue Ridge. I'd be giggling too if this was my last weekend.

'I'm not surprised nobody is interested,' said Eddie in a tired voice, after he arrived back from the field and found us in the kitchen staring blankly at the neglected feast.

There was something deflated about him that afternoon. He reminded me of a once jolly teddy bear that had lost its stuffing. Eddie's unquenchable enthusiasm had quenched. He had reached a point of exhaustion and with it came a realisation that no matter how brilliant the outcrop, fieldwork was not all it was cracked up to be when one has been doing nothing much else for weeks on end. Even the most enthusiastic have limits.

'I suppose it didn't occur to you that we've all been barbecuing and picnicking for the past four months and the charm has rather gone out of the thing,' he said, and went off for a soothing shower. After all, he had been in the field all week and he was filthy and unshaven.

The stars were already shining, the laughter growing louder and sillier by the minute, and still nobody wanted to move to the park. Any suggestion we made fell on deaf ears. Poor Eric, waiting down in the darkening park, had no company but plates and cutlery, and an overheated barbecue.

'They won't be capable of going at all if we don't shift them soon,' muttered Janey.

We packed the food, stashed it in a vehicle, and carried out a folding table. I was naïve enough to imagine that the sight of a pregnant woman heaving furniture would inspire a rush of assistance. I planned to propel them to the park as soon as they were on their feet. But there was no chivalry in them that evening and they watched us shift the tables as if they were watching the Sunday football. They just went right on drinking beer.

'Don't you people want to eat tonight?' I shrieked.

'No rush,' said Potts.

James and Sebastian ambled over; Sebastian to reprimand me for lifting furniture in my condition, and James to helpfully advise us that it was hopeless expecting anybody to get to the park that evening. It had been a bad idea in the first place because everybody was fed up with barbecues.

We eventually got the mob going thanks to Eddie. He was in no mood for a party but was highly motivated by hunger and had the wisdom to realise that the key to the operation lay in the large blue Esky. The mob would follow that Esky wherever it went. Eddie calmly loaded it into the vehicle despite the protests and instructed us to drive it to the park. After that it wasn't too much trouble to get the gang on their feet and stumbling parkwards, although Eddie still had to adopt the manner of a belligerent sheep dog rounding up a flock of particularly stupid sheep.

And so, the first ghastly meal of this ghastly weekend passed, and passed with reasonable success considering the unpopularity of barbecues. The mob, having got to the park, now showed no sign of wanting to leave, but that wasn't my problem, and I didn't care if they stayed out all night. It also wasn't my problem if they weren't in any fit state to play cricket the next day.

Eric and Eddie helped pack up the remains of the feast and when we left the picnic grounds the rest of the group were sitting cross-legged in the grass in a circle around the blue Esky. It could have been a sacred object about to be used in a primitive ritual. They were rubbing their heads and twirling their elbows and reciting some gibberish nursery rhyme. Eddie said it was a drinking game and if we were lucky it would keep them occupied for hours and we could all get some sleep.

The time of peace did not last long. Our heads had just touched the pillows and we were drifting towards oblivion when an onslaught of insects arrived at the picnic grounds and drove the crowd back to the house. They squeezed themselves into Jen's canvas tent, which was pitched not that far from our bedroom window, all set to continue the party. Disturbing sounds wafted into our window along with the night air. Unruly laughter. Snippets of silly conversation in overloud voices. Wally bellowing out a chorus, a song about catching yellowbelly in the old Barcoo.

Jen switched the lights on and inspired by Wally's singing, loaded her deck with a Slim Dusty tape and turned it up full blast. Eddie, jerked awake by the noise, lost all patience and yelled out the window, but his voice was as effective as the squeak of a mouse against that racket. Plan B worked much better. He simply pulled the plug from the power point beside our mattress, an action that abruptly silenced the music and plunged the tent in darkness. In the hush that followed Eddie screamed a torrent of abuse into the night. A roar of laughter could be heard in response, but the party was over.

* * *

I never would have imagined that the prospect of a game of cricket could generate so much excitement. The next morning our visitors were up early, so eager for the game that they jostled about the kitchen doorway, tripping over each other, clutching empty plates. I wondered if this was their usual behaviour at mealtimes, but their cook was not available for consultation. Murray Crow was feeding her tea and toast in bed. I was shocked by the enormity of their morning appetites. Janey and I seemed to be on a relentless breakfast-production conveyor belt.

'Do you suppose we've got enough?' she asked anxiously. There were beads of sweat on her brow.

'Hope so,' I replied doubtfully, just as James thrust an empty plate beneath my nose.

'Don't be so greedy,' I snapped. 'You can't have extra until everybody else has been fed first.'

'Why not?' he asked, outraged. 'I've only just got out of bloody bed! I'm entitled to my breakfast.'

'Oh, sorry James. Sorry. Didn't I only just give you two pieces of toast, six sausages, three eggs, two tomatoes and ...'

'That was Potts!'

'Look everything's a bit of a blur this morning. You're all starting to look the same.'

'My God!' said James. 'You'd better have a lie down after breakfast; you can't be well. Look at us! Potts has prickles, I have hair. He's fat, I'm thin. He looks like a dugong, I don't. I've got style, he has none. Where, exactly, is the resemblance?'

I handed him his breakfast and said sweetly, 'I'm sure the girl from the grocery store would notice the difference.'

Outside, a beautiful Blue Ridge morning had dawned, full of honeyed blossom and sunshine and chirruping birds, perfect for a day of sport. After dealing with the breakfast mess, I sauntered down to the park, to take in the cricket match. The players were spread out in a relaxed manner across the field while the sun beat down upon their heads. The large blue Esky was present once again, and the action seemed to be centred on it, although a couple of players held bats and occasionally a ball was tossed about. The fielders clasped tins of beer from which they took frequent swigs, an activity that was evidently of more importance than pursuing the ball. Nobody had a clue what the score was, and as far as I could see, the real object of the game was to get sloshed before the opposing team did.

I sat down near Potts, who was waiting to bat. He gestured to his neighbour and said, 'Hey Owen, do you know Cynthia?'

'Do I know Cynthia? Of course I know Cynthia. I've eaten her food,' said Owen, speaking as if eating my food immediately established a relationship of intimacy.

He moved closer and said, 'You're wonderful people, you cooks. Where would we be without you? Lost, miserable, malnourished, bad tempered! I must admit there was a time when I thought that all cooks were pathetic losers, but then I met Stella, and now I'm a changed man.' He sighed mournfully. 'You know Stella, our cook, well you needn't tell her this ... I'll get round to it myself one day, but ... But ... I love her! I'd marry her tomorrow if I could! When I taste one of her roast dinners, I just ... I just ...'

The poor fellow could barely articulate his feelings, but he made some primitive vocal noise suggestive of ecstasy. I instantly wished I was not serving roast beef for dinner. I had no hope at all as a cook against such competition as this. Nobody had ever groaned with ecstasy over one of my meals.

Stella didn't bother coming down to the cricket field that morning, and by the afternoon she was well rested. Janey and I invited her into the kitchen for a glass of cooking sherry. Although there was nothing at all intimidating about Stella, we felt under pressure. As a cook this woman was off the scale, her meals reducing recipients to a state of ecstatic incoherence. We were plodding no-hopers in contrast.

We abandoned common sense, which should have told us that after the version of cricket we saw played that day, nobody would notice what they ate, and with muddled motives aspired to elevate the basic roast to a slightly fancier version of itself by serving wine sauce instead of gravy. This turned out to be a terrible mistake, not just because there's nothing wrong with basic gravy and everybody likes it, but because Wally thought it would be fun to sabotage the wine cask. I don't know how he did it or why he chose that particular moment, I just know that when I touched that cask, it erupted like the Old Faithful Geyser, sending a plume of wine billowing upwards until it splattered over the ceiling and across the walls and cupboards, forming a red river which snaked over the kitchen floor and out beyond the kitchen to where there was a crowd of drunken hungry cricketers. The optics created by Wally's joke were most unfortunate.

In the lounge room Stella was involved in a deep and meaningful conversation with Owen, probably about gourmet food. Janey had nipped out to feed her baby. I was alone with the wine. For a second or two I stared in horrified fascination at the spectacle, then I threw the cask on its side into the sink. The torrent became a trickle that flowed harmlessly down the plughole. But the damage had been done and I could hear shrieks through the doorway.

'Oh my God. What's happened?' cried Jen, pale and swaying. She had consumed several too many down at the cricket field that day.

'Don't worry, Jen,' replied Eddie with warped and irresponsible humour. 'A haemorrhage probably. I'll go and mop it up. I'm sure dinner won't be delayed long.'

Jen may have had a tough exterior, but at heart she was a delicate creature. She sank onto Grasshopper who somehow got her into a bedroom to recover. The drunken cricketers made jokes at my expense and Eddie produced a mop, swirling it across the floor and pushing the puddles beneath the fridge.

'It's okay, Cynthia,' said Janey, sliding in the wine as she entered the kitchen. 'This is as bad as it's going to get. Half this lot will be gone tomorrow, and more will leave the next day, and it's not going to be this bad ever again.'

She was wrong. The next morning the Bogarilla crowd announced that they intended to stay another night. It was Paul's fault. He told them that if they left after Sunday lunch as originally planned, then they would miss the Blue Ridge Sunday movies.

Was this weekend never, ever going to end?

I felt like a mouse on a treadmill stuck in a cage where time moved incredibly slowly. Things could have been worse. I could have been a male emperor penguin trying to keep an egg warm during a blizzard in the middle of the Antarctic winter. But the thought was not consoling. I was not a penguin and that crowd of noisy beer-swillers with their perpetual need for a succession of substantial meals was not going to suddenly evaporate.

At least there was some respite at the close of the day when they all went to the movies. Exhausted, I collapsed on the mattress in my room and stared vacantly at the ceiling fan as it rotated round and round. Eddie lay beside me reading a riveting publication entitled *Allocyclic Controls on Volcaniclastic Oolitic Sequences*.

I heard the next day that the movie session had been disturbed by a patron with a gut problem. Disagreeable odours had drifted heavily through the hall and detracted somewhat from the movie experience. Potts was blamed for this and he blamed the cook.

'Don't mind me, just call me Fartman,' he said the next morning at breakfast. 'It's Cynthia's fault. She put something in the food.'

'You're just an animal, Potts!' said Priscilla. 'And don't blame Cynthia! It's all your own fault. Just accept it; your problem is beer. You drink far too much of the stuff. It makes you fart and it makes you fat!'

After breakfast Owen came to the kitchen and thanked me for a weekend of food, all the while gazing passionately at Stella, who didn't notice him at all. Perhaps she was accustomed to adoration. He managed to include her in his vehicle for the long trip back to Bogarilla, but as Potts was also in their company I doubted that any romance was possible.

I stood out on the footpath and watched every single vehicle as it turned the corner and headed for the highway. When I was sure they had all departed I walked back towards the house, suppressing an urge to dance, such relief did I feel.

'They've all gone,' I said.

Janey, Eric, baby Freddie and Jeremy were all that remained. We were back where we had been at the beginning of my term as non-cook cook, but I was now fed up and expended. Eric disappeared into his silver caravan for a day of drafting and Jeremy impersonated a baboon and tried to pick fleas off Janey. He said he was sick of mechanics and would prefer to spend the day in the kitchen.

'Go for it!' I said, 'It's all yours.'

I flung myself in the hammock, picked up a novel and listened to the lorikeets ripping mulberries off the trees. At lunchtime Jeremy came out to the porch with a tray of gourmet treats. Or was I dreaming?

Chapter 14

A romantic interlude

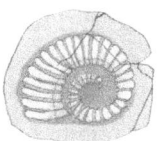

THE SEASON WAS ALMOST FINISHED. There was nothing left now but to pack, day and night, stopping only for meals and sleep. Day by day, people were driving off with loaded trailers. Janey and Eric had gone the week before, creeping into my bedroom in the dim morning light to whisper goodbye. There was no company in the kitchen now as I struggled to use up the dwindling supplies in the store cupboard. I would have preferred not to be among the small group left for the final few days of packing and cleaning. But Murray had not been persuaded by the words *impending birth, nappies,* or *medical attention* that I used to express my intention of leaving Blue Ridge at the earliest convenient opportunity.

'Having a baby is no big deal,' he shrugged. 'You just get a few pains and the thing pops out.' He managed to convey the impression that he had personally given birth several times.

'But I don't have any nappies or baby clothes or a cot or anything. We don't even have anywhere to live. I was living with my family before I came up here.'

'You'll find somewhere to live soon enough and as for the rest, an hour in a department store will fix all that. I don't see that you need to go rushing off quite so soon. It would be so helpful if you could stay.'

I shook my head and began to express doubts when he shut me up by resorting to bribery. 'I tell you what. If you stay and cook for us, then I can arrange for you and Eddie to take a vehicle home. You can have some days off on the way, go to Mission Beach or somewhere and have some time to yourselves. A romantic interlude, that's what you need. It will do you all the good in the world.'

Common sense flew straight out the window. *Romantic interlude*—the words brought an image to my mind of moonlit waves lapping on a beach lined with flickering palm trees. I imagined Eddie and I alone at a table at the waterfront eating exquisite food prepared by somebody else, free to converse with the spontaneity impossible when there is a crowd in the room next door. I agreed to stay till the end. In Blue Ridge where relations between the sexes swung between mutual incomprehension and raw lust, the idea of such an escape was very compelling. So there I remained until the very last moment.

* * *

One day during that final week, those of us left sat hunched over pizza and the miserable withered lettuce that was the best available.

'The topping is terrific Cynthia! Shame about the soggy base,' said Paul. This was typical of one of his remarks.

'Cynthia, did you have to put so much grated cheese on top? You know I've had hepatitis and my liver can't cope with all this fat,' said Sebastian as he crammed his sixth slice into his mouth.

I thought of Owen gasping at the thought of Stella's cooking and felt like a failure.

Jeremy sat at the head of the table, nibbling the food without interest. He had lost his zip and I hadn't seen a monkey act all week.

'Thargomindah. Why Thargomindah?' he muttered.

'Thargomindah's alright,' said Murray.

'To work with drillers? A man like me?'

'You've brought it on yourself, mate,' said James. 'You've been found out. You were seen. Seen cavorting about with naked women on a beach. When you were supposed to be here, working on the vehicles.'

'I wasn't cavorting with ...'

'You were seen. Frolicking about.'

'Look, I wasn't cavorting or frolicking with naked women. I simply stopped in Cairns for a break on my way through to Blue Ridge. Met a friend and we went to the beach. For a break. An hour or two. She was wearing a bikini. You people take a break at a road cutting, I take a break at a beach,' said Jeremy.

'Yeah, but a road cutting is work-related,' said James.

'Oh come on. To you guys it's fun. I took a break, that's all. And I don't know who saw me there, but it's somehow got about that I'm taking luxury holidays with a harem of females at the GIU's expense. It's ridiculous.'

'These rumours have nothing to do with the fact that we need a mechanic out at Thargomindah,' said Murray. 'It's a business matter.'

'Yes, but drillers? You know what happened in Burkes Hill yesterday when I did that run with the rock drums? Those men at the railway station were most unkind about my *Vogue for Men* shirt. I doubt the guys at Thargomindah will be any better.'

'Worse, probably,' said Paul.

'Just what I'm thinking,' said Jeremy. 'I need a change. Maybe the tourist industry is the thing for me. I could be a wine waiter at an island resort. Yes, that's an idea.'

'Want help to pack your bags?' Sebastian asked.

He was pissed off. There was Jeremy, in his opinion lacking the qualities required in the true man, frolicking with a bikini-clad woman on a beach, an attractive woman too by all accounts, while he and all the other field hands, oozing with rugged masculinity, were deprived of such pleasures. It was just another example of the gross unfairness of life. Besides, he had assumed Jeremy was gay and no competition at all.

After lunch Sebastian offered to assist with the dishes but he wasn't much help. He paced about the kitchen like a caged lion.

'I've got to get out of this place!' he shrieked abruptly and fled out the door.

Within seconds I heard him on his motorbike, screeching with freedom around the narrow streets of Blue Ridge. Paul was at the front of the house piling boxes into a trailer. He watched as Sebastian whizzed past: once, twice, three times. By the time Sebastian had completed his ninth circuit, Paul was leaping up and down on the footpath.

'Please! Stop!' he yelled. 'You've gotta let me have a go!'

Sebastian slowed to a halt. 'Sure,' he said.

And he loaded the trailer with renewed zest as Paul sped off with a wild cry of joy. But Paul did not get far. Soon after he had zoomed around the corner, we heard the motor putter, pause and then putter again. He reappeared—ignominiously, drooping and outraged.

'What's up?' asked Sebastian.

'It was the cop, standing there in the middle of the street with his arm up in the air. His hand out like this,' said Paul, raising both his arm and his vocal pitch in imitation of the policeman, who was apparently afflicted with a mincing soprano voice. *We like peace and quiet in this town, sonny. Pack it in.* I told him I had only just got on, but it was no use. He just laughed.'

Paul stomped into the kitchen.

'Life's shit,' he declared as he flung open the fridge and stared absently at the contents. 'It's this packing, it's so bloody monotonous.'

He poured himself a glass of milk and gulped it down.

'I'll die if I don't get some excitement in my life,' he muttered.

'Not long now and we'll all be gone,' I said.

'Not bloody soon enough,' he replied. 'You know I'm so bloody bored I'm even thinking of going to that thing that's on down at the community hall tonight. That'll be a change, won't it? Grasshopper and James can come too. They've been packing the office today. Must be bored out of their brains.'

'But that's a family slide show, Paul. Not your scene at all.'

'Yeah, it sounds pathetic, but you never know, it could be quite inspiring. People are showing their favourite holiday slides, that sort of thing. It'll give us a few ideas anyhow. Should take our minds off things for a bit, a sort of harmless diversion. That girl down at the grocery store told me all about it.'

If the girl from the grocery store had recommended it, I guessed they would all go. They would have cheerfully sung hymns at the weekly church service dressed in bunny costumes if she suggested it.

* * *

It was apparent the next morning that the community slide show had been a flop. Paul, Grasshopper, Sebastian and James sat quiet and blank-faced at the breakfast table. The impact of those slides on their already bored minds had slammed them into a state of hopeless mental vacancy.

'That slide show last night must have been terrible. You lot haven't woken up yet,' commented Eddie. 'I guess you were expecting to see images of the Iguassu Falls and the ski fields of Japan and you got little kiddies playing in the sand with buckets and spades instead.'

James turned dismal eyes on him. 'Huh,' he said, terminating the conversation.

But the subject came up again at lunchtime after Murray had been down to the post office. 'Weren't you fellas down at the community hall last night? I've just heard there was a brawl.'

Grasshopper, pink tinged, said casually, 'Not a brawl exactly, just a bit of a scuffle really. It was over that ...'

James broke in with quiet dignity, 'It broke out about that unfortunate woman from the grocery store. Those guys from the mine can get very wild.'

'You lot weren't involved, I hope?'

'What do you take us for, Murray?' asked James. 'Do we look like the types that would go brawling over women?'

'Priscilla always had doubts about those guys,' said Grasshopper reflectively.

The weather was just as hot that day, but they seemed to have lost their appetite for ice-creams. Not one of them went to the grocery store. Later in the afternoon a representative from the mine dropped by to see Murray. I put the kettle on, arranged biscuits on a plate, and took the afternoon tea into the dusty lounge room where they were sitting uncomfortably together on those rigid plastic chairs.

The man was saying, 'We'll be sorry to see you go. Such a small town here, a bit of fresh blood is always welcome. But, hey, boys will be boys. We have trouble with some of our lads too. Understandable in the circumstances. Not much happening. But we do try to provide a bit of entertainment.'

Murray nodded pleasantly, but said nothing, and the man continued. 'I understand Gerald Drake was interested in leasing these properties for the field season next year as well. We thought we'd give you some notice on that score. With the improvement in the economic climate, we'll be expanding our own operations. We'll be needing these houses ourselves. But you'll have several months to look about. I know the people over at *Three Trees* have a couple of shacks down on the riverbank. Perhaps you could do something with them.'

'Ah, well, thanks for letting us know. Actually, we've made pretty good progress here this year and it will probably be more convenient to move the program on. Gerald Drake has already been thinking of Burkes Hill as a base. Could be a good year coming up for all of us,' Murray replied.

'Terrific! Glad your program is progressing so well.'

Grasshopper had just walked into the house at that moment. He bolted into the kitchen and grabbed my arm.

'Did you hear that, Cynthia? Burkes Hill next year! Far out!' His eyes widened. 'Did you know that Burkes Hill has at least half a dozen pubs and a McDonalds? Hey, hey, hey. Bring it on. The good times.' And off he went with a skip in his step and a song in his heart.

The last day came. I sat on the rotting log beside the rambling bougainvillea vine and watched as they slammed the last box into a vehicle. I should have been excited; but I was only numb. A long tedious journey lay ahead, and there would be no romantic interlude on the way. That idea had vanished like a mirage on the road when Gerald sent Eddie an air ticket. Too bad about the cook. My contract was ending and there was no obligation to help me get anywhere.

I was now in my 36th week of pregnancy and no airline would take me, at least not without a doctors letter. As there was no doctor for hundreds of miles, there was not much I could do. In the end I travelled down to the Townsville Airport with Eddie, and Stella collected me there on her way south from Bogarilla.

The most romantic moment came when I washed down a greasy take-away with a tin of lemonade by the roadside and watched Eddie's plane pass overhead. He would be home in three hours. I would be home in two and a half days. The long road lay before me, but I had Stella with me, the cook who never failed, whose food had turned a sensible man like Owen into gibbering idiocy.

It was a journey of kitchen lore and recipes. As we glided down the bitumen on that headache-hot highway and I stared at the anthills and the gumtrees, I heard recipes for passionfruit mousse and mango chicken, beef wellington and chocolate mint cheesecake, and an unwelcome thought arose. Surely it wasn't inspiration, not this soon. But the niggling idea persisted, just when I was so relieved the whole thing was over.

I would try it all again sometime. How much better would it be, the second time around, if I could benefit from Stella's expertise. I thrust the thought aside. I was going home. But Stella kept right on talking.

Chapter 15

The house of the matriarch

'You're making a mistake, Craddock,' said Gerald Drake as he peered into the shadowy and deteriorated interior of a ramshackle dwelling in Burkes Hill. There were holes in the floor; the windows were cracked.

'It just needs a few repairs,' said Christopher.

'It's terrible,' said Gerald. 'And so filthy it's not fit for pigs, let alone a field party.'

'I don't know what we're going to do then. Believe it or not, this is the best of a bad bunch. And it's large enough. Must have been a grand place once.'

'It's not grand now! Lucky for you I've got a contact here. Give this lady a call and she'll fix you up with something much more appropriate.' Gerald scrawled a name and address on a scrap of paper and handed it over. 'You know Dennis O'Regan? It's his Mum. Mrs Wilma O'Regan. She's an old Burkes Hill girl from way back. Rents out a couple of places exclusively to geologists.'

'I was at uni with Dennis.'

'Good. Mention that and we'll get a discount. She's a domineering old biddy and you'll have to play by her rules or God help you. But that won't be your worry this year. The camp manager can attend to those details and you can concentrate purely on the mapping. I'm expecting great results. This should be a terrific season.'

Gerald slammed shut the door of the decrepit old house. They creaked down the worn steps and out through the thorny garden. There were many times in the months to come when Christopher would remember that moment and regret taking Gerald's advice. For surely that season would have been better if he had taken out the lease on that old ruin near the centre of town. But it was a new beginning and there was every reason for optimism in the thriving atmosphere of prosperity at large that year.

The GIU had taken on new staff. The first new recruit was Big Jill, a woman of statuesque proportions and wild hair, who looked like she would have been at home at the head of a rampaging barbarian army. She had established a reputation back in her university days as one who could drink all male companions under the table. It was said that Big Jill had told Gerald and the panel several inappropriate jokes at her interview, a strategy that would fail in this era, but back then was seen as a promising sign she would fit in well.

There were more doubts about the second appointment, at least from the general staff, if not from the management. His name was Malcolm Drake, and because he shared his surname with the boss, it was assumed he was a relative. In fact, there was no basis whatsoever to the rumour that Malcolm was Gerald's idiot son, unable to find work elsewhere.

Big Jill was joining the team at Bogarilla, but Malcolm was coming to Burkes Hill with us. Even though I now had a baby girl to consider, it had not taken me long to decide to join the camp for another season as cook. Unlike the previous year when I had no idea why I had said yes, or even if I had agreed to the proposal at all, this time round I had sound reasons for going north, reasons like keeping the family together and making some money at the same time. This decision may have been based on solid common sense, but there was also a tinge of idealism to it.

I could blame Stella for the starry-eyed sense of mission I harboured in the days before that second season actually began. During those two days we had spent driving down that long, hot, coastal road, she had imparted much about the motivations of her sterling soul. For Stella, cooking was more than a job; it was a mission. Well-fed people are happy people and happy people spread more happiness, and so good cooks are vital for the wellbeing of all human life. It was as simple as that. So, although I had no illusions that life as a cook with a small baby was going to be easy, and that it wouldn't be possible now to swan about in the wilderness or lie around in hammocks, I also thought that I would be making a small but positive contribution to humanity. Really, I should have known better.

What was it about the day before departure that brought strangers to the door? Last year it had been Paul's father with the crossbow, this year it was Malcolm Drake's girlfriend, Mia Wetherby, with a large box. Malcolm had left for Burkes Hill the week before. She stood on the doorstep in the gathering dusk looking like a hip librarian. Chic but quirky clothes, pulled back hair, serene blue eyes glinting at me through owlish spectacles. She asked if I could take the box to Malcolm and deliver it with a kiss. And looked at me with terrifying sympathy for being so unfortunate as to be going to a place as awful as Burkes Hill.

The accommodation was bad, she said. There was no furniture. There was nothing to do in Burkes Hill but walk around the park. Malcolm was so bored he had walked around the park seventy-six times already. I took this more as an indication of the defects in Malcolm's character than as a warning, smiled at her, and promised to deliver the box. I took it to the room where

Eddie was packing, hurling his field clothes into a large backpack.

'This Malcolm Drake guy must be a bore,' I said. 'No imagination. What does he mean—nothing to do in Burkes Hill but walk around the park?'

'Give the guy a chance!' said Eddie, stumbling as he took the box. The lid slipped off and we glimpsed the contents. They were unexpected. Comic books, packets of fluorescent bubblegum, a water pistol, a Gameboy, a rubber duck.

* * *

The next day we were back in the north. Christopher Craddock sent Sebastian to collect us at the airport. With the exchange of family news and GIU gossip, it was no time at all before we were amongst the ironbarks again. Sebastian flapped his arms about in his usual manner, but Eddie looked at him uneasily, as if he had never before noticed him fling his hands from the steering wheel as he drove along. We made good progress for a while, before we were held up by an old codger trundling along so slowly he could have been going to a Sunday School picnic in a horse and cart. He was probably just enjoying a relaxed day out, but for Eddie and Sebastian, his presence on the highway caused them to lose whatever cool they may have had at the start of the journey.

'You'll have to get round this jerk. He'll keep us here all day. C'mon you've got a chance now .... er no ... shit no! Why is the traffic so bad? Why are all these people on this road?'

Eddie was irritable. Sleep deprived and impatient.

Eventually Sebastian made a sharp decision, accelerated around the old feller, and slid back into the lane seconds before we would have been obliterated by a fresh pulse of oncoming traffic. He was congratulating himself on a slick manoeuvre when Eddie exploded.

'What the bloody hell do you think you were doing? We could have all been killed!'

A fiery exchange followed.

And suddenly we were stopped by the roadside. Eddie and Sebastian, back to childhood, were in the scrub throwing punches at each other. A nearby Brahman bull ignored them and went on searching for blades of grass. A couple of rusting beer cans and a demolished emu – such a sad sight – lay bleakly on the road's edge.

An unpromising start to a new season.

The baby and I stared out the window. The old codger drove past with a cheery wave. At the sight of him, Eddie and Sebastian came to their senses, leapt back into the car, overtook the old bloke again and sped along the road towards Burkes Hill. And we arrived, undamaged, at Mrs O'Regan's house—8 College Road, Burkes Hill. An unforgettable address.

From the outside it was an imposing place, dating from the goldrush days, a pristine, white, old Queenslander with an enclosed veranda, overshadowed by an enormous mango tree that pelted down fruit at any time of the year. The aroma of rotting mangoes drifted from the gutter as we emerged from the car although mangoes were not in season.

Jen, newly appointed as camp manager, came out to greet us. She escorted us into the house while Sebastian collected the bags and the paraphernalia needed for Emily Jane, the baby. Although the house was large, the living space was limited because the place had been divided and the field party only had access to half the house. Two geologists leased the other side but were rarely seen.

The veranda had a silvery timber floor with swags laid out at regular intervals. Next to one swag was a large trunk on which was propped a photograph of Mia Wetherby. Malcolm was probably out circumnavigating the park for the one hundred and eighty-ninth time. Stepping over these swags, we went through a doorway into a dingy room which lacked windows, and which served as a thoroughfare to the rest of the house. A rickety double bed was positioned in the centre, and swags and personal belongings were scattered with untidy abandon about the floor. Jen pointed to the double bed with the air of one about to impart a great favour.

'Youse two can have the double bed, seeing as you're married,' she said.

'Gee, thanks Jen!' said Eddie.

She grinned at us, apparently unaware that it was in any way unreasonable to expect a married couple with a baby to share a bedroom with a bunch of field hands. I had been so smug when Mia had tried to warn me about this place, thinking it came from the petulant waffling of an unimaginative man. But she had been right. This was truly awful.

I instantly felt that sinking feeling you get when it dawns on you that you have made a terrible mistake. It was all very well for Stella to talk of spreading happiness with food. She was not expected to share her bedroom at weekends with smelly and hungover field hands. I would not even be able to kiss my husband goodnight without it being a public spectacle.

Numb with horror, I followed Jen and Eddie into the dining room, a claustrophobic space cluttered with grubby trestle tables, and through into the kitchen, a room so tiny it could have served as the galley of a small boat. How was I supposed to cook for thirty people here? I started to laugh, for surely this was all just a bad dream—the fight by the roadside, the out-of-season mango tree, the creaky double bed in the centre of the field hands' room, and this tiny kitchen. None of it could be real. There's little point in getting too disturbed about a reality when it's likely to dissolve at any moment. I was probably still asleep in my bed in Brisbane.

'I've stuffed all your gear in the cupboards,' said Jen. Stuffed was the word for the doors were bulging. 'The food is stored outside in a little shed, but I don't know where to put those things.'

She pointed to boxes containing a food processor, a kitchen aid and a microwave oven. At least, in this dream, the GIU was providing some decent equipment even if there was no space in which to use it.

'I'll leave you folks to settle in. You'll have the place to yourselves this weekend. The rest of us are off to the Reedy Creek races. We're meeting up with the crew from Bogarilla. We didn't think you'd would want to come, seeing as you've only just arrived, and with little Emily Jane here. They say babies need lots of sleep. Hey Sebastian, move your arse! It's time we hit the road!'

She paced back through the house, patting the bed as she went through the bedroom, smiling at us as if she was thinking how lucky we were to score the only bed in the place.

'So long folks. Have fun. We'll all be back Sunday night for dinner.' And off she and Sebastian went.

We were alone now and I did not wake up. This wasn't a dream; this was what I had signed up for. The situation might have been absurd, but it wasn't funny. I stopped laughing. There was no point in us unpacking because there was nowhere to put anything. The floor was already strewn with the belongings of other people.

'It mightn't be as bad as it looks,' said Eddie.

'How? How could this possibly not be as bad as it looks?'

'Well, yes, I know it's not quite ideal, but it's early days yet. Things will sort themselves out. There are just some problems to solve, that's all.'

'Is that the way you see it? I don't see anything bright about this situation at all, except that they've all gone away for the weekend. I wonder why Sebastian didn't mention it. It would have cheered me up.'

'But look Cynthia. Look at the garden.'

Beyond the kitchen window was a vista of green. Although the town had an abundance of mango trees that must have tapped into some deeper source of water, at this time of the year the gardens were dry, featuring dust, thorns, and withered weeds. But here was a garden luxuriant, verdant, and useful. I could see Jen's tent out there among groves of pawpaw and banana trees. There were also mounds of parsley and mint, clumps of lemongrass, and bushes of chilli. This was a garden oblivious to the rules of water restriction that applied every-where else in Burkes Hill.

Once I had met Mrs O'Regan I realised that nobody would ever confront her about water use. She was a formidable woman, reminding me of one of those super-grannies they make cartoons about, the ones who whack all assailants with their handbags and reduce the toughest of adversaries to quavering wrecks. She had a particularly poor opinion of men, considering them so hopelessly inferior to women that gender equality was an unachievable goal. In her view, men were a bunch of blun-dering incompetents who stumbled through life only with the assistance of their more able female companions. Males were useful for breeding, provision of resources, and as a source of comic entertainment, but that was about it.

How she reconciled this view with the achievements of her son, who was the director of a mining company in Western Australia, I'm not sure. She probably attributed his success to the choice of a good wife and the efficiency of his secretary. Meanwhile, although she was obviously very fond of him, she regaled the people of Burkes Hill with tales of his bungling, and I was not at all surprised that Dennis O'Regan chose to pursue his business on the other side of the continent.

The weekend went by swiftly and on Sunday evening our housemates returned in the highest of spirits. The first person out of the vehicles was a tall, slender, young man with hibiscus flowers tucked behind his ears and a sarong tied about his waist. He slunk up the garden path like a model on a catwalk while the group behind roared with laughter. I was watching from the stairs when he flung a flower at me.

'You must be Cynthia. Why didn't you come to Reedy Creek? You would have had a ball,' he said, kissing me in an exuberant greeting. 'Lovely to meet you. I'm Malcolm Drake.'

Two things struck me at once. The first was that if Jeremy had ever tried mincing along dressed in a sarong he would have been derided, not applauded, so here was a particularly compelling personality. The second was that I would never prejudge anybody again, because whatever Malcolm was, he certainly was not an unimaginative bore.

While the newcomers settled in and squabbled over the shower, I laid some dishes of food on one of the trestle tables. These were clean now, so the space looked marginally more appealing. I had also discovered that it is quite possible to cook for a large party in the smallest of kitchens if there is no alternative.

'So how did the weekend go?' asked Eddie.

'So bloody marvellous I can't remember what happened,' replied Wally. 'Shed burnt down Saturday night. Must have been spectacular. Yeah. But I was so pissed I missed it.'

'Yeah, it was awesome!' said Grasshopper.

'But how did it happen?' I asked.

'Jimmy Keen was responsible,' said James. 'Should be kept away from these events.'

'Jimmy Keen? Wasn't he the guy who burnt his boots off in that paddock last year?' I asked.

'Yeah. That's the guy. The pyromaniac,' said Paul. 'Drinks so much whisky, he's flammable.'

'Just as well we had Big Jill,' said Priscilla.

'Thank God. Jimmy would have been burnt to a crisp if it weren't for her. Shook him to his senses and dragged him from the fire by the collar of his shirt,' said Christopher.

'Then she came back and put out the fire,' added Michelle.

'Hey, it wasn't just her,' Grasshopper protested.

The evening drifted on, not unpleasantly, until we heard the rustle of vegetation outside. Mrs O'Regan appeared in the doorway, bright eyes in a crinkled face. Her eyes missed nothing; perused the lot of us relaxing after dinner—Malcolm Drake with a flower wilting behind his ear, Christopher perched on a trestle table, Jen sitting cross-legged on the floor sipping coffee. A low murmur of conversation could be heard through the door as James and Grasshopper prepared their gear for the following week. Michelle and Priscilla were down in the laundry shed washing out some clothes.

'It's getting late. You should all be in bed,' croaked Mrs O'Regan.

'Sure Ma,' said Jen agreeably. 'We've had a heavy weekend and we're all tired. We'll be in bed directly.'

Mrs O'Regan went out to shift the hose across the garden before she retired for the night. One by one we fell into our beds. It was one of the most harmonious evenings we were to have that season.

Chapter 16

Click go the shears

GERALD DRAKE HAD BEEN FAR TOO optimistic about the prospects of that field season, which turned out to be not much more than a series of problems, all stacked up one behind the other, like cards in a deck. There wasn't even a honeymoon period in which everything glided along smoothly for a time. If there had been a moment when the team was enthused by the novelty of a fresh season, it didn't last long, because the problems were there right from the beginning and were apparent from the moment I first put my foot over the threshold of Mrs O'Regan's house. There were two fundamental problems right from the start – lack of space and lack of beds – and it made us all edgy. We didn't even have our full complement of staff yet. The mechanic and the draftsman were still to join our happy little band. It seemed as if things could only get worse.

One Sunday morning, after I had endured about a fortnight in that cramped house, I ducked behind a sack of potatoes in the shed out the back. At that moment Malcolm strolled past, seeking the seclusion of the garden for a quiet cigarette.

'What are you skulking about out here for?' he asked kindly, leaning against the shed wall and lighting his smoke. 'Hiding from an old admirer, are you?'

'No. Not exactly an admirer,' I replied.

We listened for a moment to the slow trickle of the hose amongst the plants and the whisper of the banana trees. From beyond these tranquil sounds came the low drone of voices. There was no doubt about it: Bill Sapshort was visiting.

Malcolm laughed. 'Cynthia! Surely you're not trying to hide from Bill?'

There was no time to explain. Already I could hear Bill clumping down the back stairs, probably making a beeline straight for me. I moved back further into the obscurity of the shed and upset a mound of pumpkins. It was useless trying to hide. There was Bill, barrelling towards me, with the attraction of an iron filing for a magnet, eyes agleam and mouth agape in a grotesque grin as he observed the mess in the shed.

'Remember that meal you cooked for us last year, Cynthia? That roast?' he laughed.

As if I could ever forget it with Bill hanging about the place.

'What roast?' asked Malcolm.

'I don't want to talk about it.'

I collapsed against the shed wall as Bill wandered further into the garden with Christopher and James, who had followed him down the stairs. Their words drifted back through the greenery.

'This place is getting me down already and the season's only just begun,' we could hear James say. 'No bloody privacy anywhere. I was getting changed yesterday and the bat that owns the place barged in and smirked at me while I was standing there in my jocks. Really, we shouldn't have to put up with it!'

'You can't do much about Ma O'Regan,' commented Bill. 'That lady's always been a law unto herself. She's known as the

Burkes Hill dragon. And this place of hers usually accommodates a team of six, not an entire mapping party. You're going to need more space.'

'You bet!' said James. 'And think about poor Cynthia. Did she look a bit strange to you, back in that shed, surrounded by falling pumpkins? She's probably cracking up already and I can't blame her. I mean she's sharing a room with Paul and Grasshopper.'

'And Wally!' said Christopher.

'Yes, and Wally. How the hell is that suitable? I can understand why she and Slanger have the bed. But field hands in the same room? I suppose Jen thought they'd be so boozed up they wouldn't notice the bub crying in the night. But it's not fair on any of them as far as I can see. We'll have a mad cook on our hands soon if this goes on.'

'Got any ideas Bill?' asked Christopher. 'You know Burkes Hill.'

'Actually, I do know about a place coming up for lease. Just up there on the corner. Walking distance. It would be ideal.'

It was impossible to hear any more of this conversation because Malcolm was overcome by mirth, apparently finding the bit about my declining mental health particularly amusing.

'Don't worry, Cynthia. I don't care if you are going nuts. Who wants to trudge down the narrow grooves of convention anyway? What we want around here is a wild adventurous cook, not the stable type opening the same tins day after day, and forever wiping down the benches.'

'Wearing a pathway around the circumference of the park, round and round, same direction, day after day,' I added, as I went back into the house to feed the baby. I wasn't sure why I made this comment because Malcolm had already given up walking around the park at weekends, preferring to drink gin and tonic with the female members of the local golf club, a far more appealing diversion.

The upshot of Bill's visit was promising. By the very next weekend Christopher and Jen congratulated themselves on solving the first and most glaring of their problems by acquiring the use of a house just up the street on the corner of College Road. We called this house the 'green house' due to the faded mould-green colour of its exterior and to differentiate it from the house at Number 8, Mrs O'Regan's establishment, which became known as the 'white house'.

On Friday afternoon, Eddie and I grabbed the mattress from our bed, transported it up the road and plonked it in the bedroom of choice up at the green house. The most attractive feature of this room was not its size, or the view out the window to the hill, but the fact that it was at the end of the corridor and possessed a door that could be shut any time we liked. And no room mates. A bright and airy room at the back served as a dining room and looked out upon the dry and neglected garden, which included a mango tree near the fence and a struggling custard apple tree. There was a veranda out the front, perfect for hanging a hammock, and the kitchen was large enough for all the equipment the GIU had supplied.

The green house even had a lounge room, nothing flash, but a room that could be devoted purely to relaxation. It had dirty lolly-pink walls, a nondescript linoleum floor and was furnished with a couple of brown vinyl-covered swivel chairs and a brown couch, dating from the early seventies. This furniture was unattractive but comfortable and I'm not sure whether it came with the house or if Jen had bought it from a charity store. There was also a coffee table, a television and a video player, so the room did offer an opportunity for rest and recreation despite the ghastly colour of the walls.

Nobody could say things hadn't improved. There was a

general rearrangement, and we all had a bit more wriggle room, a bit more ease. More space for sleeping opened up down at the white house, but there was always much coming and going up and down College Road on weekends as meals were served at the green house and there was more room for general relaxation there. But Christopher was still not satisfied.

There was not a bed to be had in either house, except for the rickety old wreck back at the white house, but that now lacked a mattress. Of course, everybody had swags, but Christopher felt this wasn't good enough. After all, they spent all week in swags. Surely it was only reasonable that they could look forward to the luxury of sliding between clean sheets in a real bed on their return to town. He pondered the problem. I can't say I had much faith in his ability to solve this one, remembering his inept attempt to provide me with a bed the year before, but he did try.

'Aha! I've got it!' he said eventually. 'Shearers stretchers!'

He beamed at Jen with an air of smug triumph.

'Shearers stretchers?' she echoed doubtfully.

'Just the thing!' he replied. 'Economical, readily available up here, and if you put in the order on Monday, they'll be here by the weekend. I've heard they're terrific.'

On Monday Jen ordered the stretchers as advised.

When Christopher moved up to the green house, Jen chose to remain at Mrs. O'Regan's to keep an eye on the field hands. Her canvas tent was roomy, like a second home, and she was happy amongst the banana trees in the garden. Even Michelle and Priscilla preferred to stay with her at weekends, sharing her tent in the quiet of that oasis, and forming a group that Malcolm always referred to rather rudely as the Hen Connection. This was probably just his idea of a joke, but he may also have picked up on the subtle power dynamic that had developed the previous year, but which at this point was causing nothing more disturbing than a vague unease.

During the week the white house was empty, and Jen came up to the green house for meals, for company, to work, or to take advantage of the lounge room. She was there with me on the afternoon that the shearers stretchers arrived. At first, I thought there had been a mistake. A man in overalls was unloading the truck with objects that resembled fencing material far more than anything that looked remotely useful as bedding.

When we approached him, he looked at us derisively and asked, 'Which clown ordered these?'

'I did, as a matter of fact,' said Jen. 'But it was Christopher's idea. Time we all had a bed he said.'

'Huh,' said the man, somehow managing to express a scathing analysis of Christopher's intelligence in that one syllable.

'What's wrong with them?' asked Jen.

The man laughed ghoulishly. 'You'll see. Or rather, you'll hear. You'll be calling me up next week asking if I can take these buggers away. Don't say you weren't warned.'

It was late afternoon and shafts of golden light slanted across the yard brightening the mango tree and lighting up the stretchers so they glowed with ruddy colour.

'So, do you want to come in for a meal tonight?' asked Jen.

'Nah, goin' to the pub,' the man replied hastily. He had looked briefly horrified by the suggestion and immediately galloped off as if we were a pair of sirens attempting to lure him to his death with song.

'Jeez, he's keen! Couldn't wait to get out of the place!' said Jen, watching him vanish. 'Sorry, forgot to introduce him. That was Cedric—GIU truck driver for the northern districts. He's actually entitled to eat a meal here, if he can stand it, which obviously he can't.'

'He didn't seem to think much of these shearers stretchers either,' I said. 'What do you suppose he meant?'

'Nothing, probably,' said Jen. 'The guy's a weirdo. Anyway, whatever he meant it's now beer o'clock and I don't think another night in a swag will do me any harm. I'll deal with this lot tomorrow.'

The next day she arrived to transport a bundle of these beds down to the white house.

'Can't say that I see much point in these myself,' she commented, as she stacked them into the back of a vehicle.

The shearers stretchers were like wire hammocks strung onto a rigid metal frame supported by short folding legs. When folded they looked much more like gates than beds. I could see at a glance that my mattress on the floor would be far more comfortable and I had no intention of trying one.

'Oh well, I guess they'll get us off the ground; I s'pose that's a good thing. With a swag mattress they might just do,' said Jen, shrugging as she slammed the door of the vehicle.

When Christopher arrived back on Friday afternoon he eagerly claimed two stretchers and bound them together in anticipation of the time when his wife would visit. How she responded to this act of devotion will be recounted later.

That night he went to bed in his new creation, slept soundly all night, and in the morning deemed the purchase of the stretchers a great success. But not everybody was so pleased.

We all know that some beds squeak and some beds creak. The shearers stretchers were capable of much more. They could squeal and shriek. This was no problem at all if, like Christopher, you slept like a lump of rock all night, sprawled out in the same position you started in. But if you were of a more restless disposition and wanted to flip over from time to time, or even just felt the urge to lift your little finger and scratch your nose, then it would begin, the orchestration of sounds that tormented not just the restless one, but all who shared that room and the one next door. Not exactly ideal.

Like most things in life the shearers stretchers were neither an unqualified success nor an abysmal failure. There were those who, on that very first night, flung out their new beds in exasperation and left them rusting under the mango tree until such a time as Jen saw fit to remove them. But there were others who thought the stretchers weren't all that bad and held onto them till the end of the season, tolerating the odd squeal and squeak just like they tolerated the neighbourhood cats having an occasional nocturnal scrap in the backyard.

Christopher and Jen, however, were satisfied that they had made reasonable progress in improving the living conditions of the field camp. The accommodation problem had been solved, and everybody who wanted a bed had one. The field camp was now ready for the new arrivals, the mechanic and the draftsman.

Chapter 17

Pig swill

THE TELEPHONE RANG.

'Hello. Do you smoke, drink, and have sex in peculiar positions in that house? Because if so ...' a chirpy voice was saying.

'I beg your pardon?'

What sort of weirdo was this on the end of the line?

There was a gush of laughter. 'Cynthia darling! It's me! Jeremy! Listen, I've just got into Burkes Hill. Groovy place hey? I just stopped to refuel and as there's a phone booth here, I thought I'd better call and let you know. Isn't it great that there's actually a phone in the place this year? So, what are the chances of a meal? Go to no trouble, just throw a few ingredients on the bench and I will assemble them myself.'

Jeremy must have been in an extremely elevated state of mind to describe Burkes Hill as 'groovy'. What had happened to make his mood soar like this? When I had last seen him at Blue Ridge months ago, he had been miserable, dreading a stint at Thargomindah and considering resignation. Perhaps his experience there had been so terrible he was simply pleased to be amongst us again.

We couldn't miss Jeremy's arrival at the green house. He

was driving a huge white truck, which he parked carefully next to the footpath. I could have assumed that his mood was due to pride at being in command of such an enormous vehicle, but he wasn't that kind of guy. He was more likely to be excited by a new brand of aftershave than by anything on wheels. Jen stood on the back landing, hands on hips, watching belligerently as he sauntered across the yard. She seemed affronted by the manner of his arrival.

'What the hell is that?' she asked, jabbing her finger at the truck.

'Oh that?' he remarked casually, 'That's just the recovery vehicle. Didn't Gerald tell you?'

'Recovery vehicle!' she snorted.

'Yeah, you know, you've got a breakdown out in the scrub. If it can't be fixed on the spot, I can retrieve the vehicle with this. That's the general idea anyway,' said Jeremy.

Jen scoffed with derision. 'If you do your job properly, there shouldn't be any breakdowns at all!' And she directed a look of withering scorn at him, as if he had dreamt this scheme up personally due to a pathetic, but grandiose, urge for heroics.

'I quite agree with you,' responded Jeremy mildly, holding two fingers up in a peace sign. 'Hey man, it's cool if Gerald wants to provide a recovery vehicle. Let it flow. You and I know the truck will never be needed. It's just a concept to make us feel safe. Just relax honey and get in the groove. The world is a crazy place. Ever been to Thargomindah? Go there and you'll find out all about it. Got any wine? I need a drink.'

Jeremy was tired of monkey acts that year and played the hippy instead. He shuffled across the kitchen to the wine cask, stumbling over the pigs' bucket on the way. Pigs' bucket? What was a pigs' bucket doing on the kitchen floor?

To explain I must backtrack a day or two to the moment when Mrs O'Regan charged into my life. She brought along gifts of parsley and pawpaws and began to organise my affairs. It was as if some ethical scruple had held her back while I was resident in her house, but now I was living up at the corner she could begin her program of education. She dropped by most days, accompanied by Ralph, her cattle dog, to instruct me in culinary matters, often reminding me that she had been cooking since before I was born. She knew how to roast bandicoots for dinner, how to convert cold beef into Burdekin duck, and how to manage the household scraps. To this end I was provided with a bucket and informed that a woman known only as the Pig Lady would be coming daily to collect the scraps, which she duly proceeded to do, day in and day out, through all the ups and downs of the season.

Jeremy may have started his stint in Burkes Hill by stumbling into the pigs' bucket, but he soon settled, finding a corner for himself down at the white house and pulling out his tan-through bathers. It wasn't long before he was back in the rhythm of maintaining his suntan as he worked on the vehicles.

* * *

We were still waiting for the draftsman. To my disappointment, Eric and Janey Smith were vanishing from my life and moving to Canberra. They had been such easy company the year before and I had been looking forward to seeing them again. Instead, I had been told to expect a man by the name of Rooster Sharmers. I can't say his nickname inspired much confidence and I was rather dreading his arrival. I know I said I would never prejudge anybody again, but there was something about the name *Rooster* that brought unfavourable images to mind. It was fine if applied to poultry, but when applied to a man it was hard not to picture a strutting over-confident, over-muscled guy crowing pointlessly from the top of a dunghill.

I don't know how Rooster came by his nickname, but I do
know he had only been in the place for a day before I stopped
regretting that the Smiths had gone to Canberra. On the first
morning after his arrival, quite early, he knocked tentatively at
my door, brought in a breakfast tray adorned with a pink hibiscus, and offered to hang out the nappies. After that, I probably
would have belly danced for his entertainment had he asked.
But all he asked for was coffee and cake in his caravan twice a
day. Rooster had a way of swaying the world to respond
favourably to him.

Donny Potts turned up to join the camp one Friday evening
about a week after Rooster's arrival. He had been engaged as a
field hand for the duration of the midyear uni break and had
driven an extra vehicle down from Bogarilla. He was up to date
with all the latest gossip, the juiciest of which concerned Big Jill
who had become involved with a field hand called Joe.

Priscilla and Michelle, stitching at tapestry in the brown
swivel chairs, shrieked with pleasurable horror. 'But isn't he the
one that looks like a cross between Gigantor and a gorilla?'
asked Priscilla.

'Yeah,' said Potts, 'That's the guy. Good description.'

'What can she possibly be thinking?' murmured Michelle.

And although Jeremy suggested that Joe was a really groovy
guy, Priscilla interrupted rudely and said that Big Jill may as
well be going out with a growth from an agar plate. They burst
into another shriek of laughter.

'Ah, you girls don't know what you're missing. Always
underestimating the fieldies. Should give us a chance!' said
Potts, winking at Priscilla who ignored him completely.

And then the phone rang.

As Jeremy pointed out, it was great there was a telephone in
the house at all, after the previous year when the only phone
available was the one in the booth by the post office. But it was

positioned right in the centre of the house where privacy was impossible, and the entire household got to hear whatever was said. In those days mobile phones looked like bricks and were only for the rich and famous.

The gossip paused for a moment as Malcolm was summoned, and the focus in the room changed. They all watched as he took the seat next to the phone, stretching out his legs with pleasure. Malcolm had few inhibitions and had no problem at all showering affection on his girlfriend while the household listened in.

'Hello darling. How marvellous to hear your voice. I've been thinking of you all week. Miss you ...' he began.

Pause. Mia's voice could be heard faintly murmuring.

'No, it's terrible here. And the week? Dirty, dusty, dry. You'd hate it!' And he was off with the usual drivel about how desolate he was feeling and how he would spend the weekend wandering lonely in the park, when everyone in that room knew he wouldn't even look at the park but would head straight to the golf club to laugh with the women and to drink gin and tonic.

And just at that moment when I heard Malcolm lying through his teeth to the girl he loved, telling her just what he thought she wanted to hear, just as my knife was poised above an onion, a wind blew through the house, ruffling some papers that had been left on the table and touching people so they could feel something on the back of their necks and through their hair. Some disturbance had arisen that was twitching at the ambience, just as if some mischievous spirit had entered the place along with the wind and was now crouched in a corner, eyes gleaming and smile mocking.

What? A goblin in Burkes Hill? Ridiculous. I just hadn't had enough sleep.

No wicked goblin would have hung around long in that house the next morning. Everybody was far too cheerful. Jeremy whistled the melody to *Magic Moments* while he buttered his toast and Potts came into the room with such a spring in his step he was practically skipping.

'Hey, great song! My mother's favourite,' he said, beginning to hum the tune himself. It was as contagious as the measles.

Grasshopper, slurping on porridge at the table, said, 'Jeez, you're cheery for a Monday morning.'

'Yep!' said Potts. 'Sunshine and daisies. That's how I feel this morning. Sunshine and daisies, mate.'

'Huh,' said Paul. 'Told you all that study would addle your brain.'

'Not at all. Just looking forward to getting into the field, that's all. You know—open space, fresh air, sun and stars and all that,' said Potts.

'Who are you with this week, then?' asked Paul. 'Ah yes, Priscilla, isn't it? Mmm ...'

But Potts had already gulped down his breakfast and was off to pack his vehicle, humming *Magic Moments* all the while.

Wally shook his head with amusement. 'Fella thinks he's goin' on a picnic,' he said. 'I shoulda warned him. It won't be a picnic. Not with her.'

'Ah well, he'll learn quick enough,' said Paul.

'Yeah, there'll be no pigs for him this week.' Wally glanced across at me as I cleared the breakfast plates from the table, and explained, 'That one, she's what you'd call a slave driver.'

Soon they had all gone off for the week and things were quiet in Burkes Hill. If that mischievous sprite was really there, then it wasn't up to much. We saw very little of Mrs O'Regan that week because her son was in town. Jeremy sang in the sunshine and tinkered with a couple of vehicles; Rooster got on with drafting and went for a run every afternoon. Only Jen was restless. It wasn't much fun being stuck in town with the paperwork week after week when everybody else was out in the field.

The tedium of the work barely compensated for whatever boost the 'manager' position may have originally given her. Besides she was concerned about Priscilla and Michelle. She thought they had been given a rough deal.

'What's with the gender balance around this place,' she asked. 'What do you suppose Gerald was thinking, shoving me into this job and not bothering to employ any other women as field hands? I mean where's his sensitivity? Just think of those poor girls forced to go into the field each week with nothing but ogling oafs for company. It's just not good enough!'

And once again a strange breeze blew in, stirring the dust and pricking the hairs on the nape of our necks.

'Hey, what was that?' asked Rooster, who had just come in for lunch.

'Nothin' That was nothin'. Just the wind,' said Jen.

Just the wind? Maybe. But something was brewing.

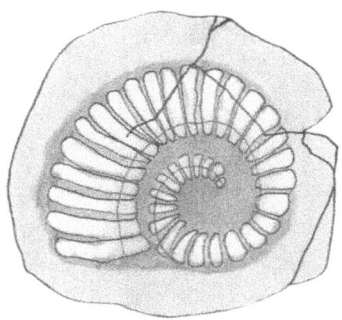

Chapter 18

Friday the thirteenth

THAT SAME WEEK, Friday the thirteenth rolled around. The superstitious call the day 'black' and associate it with bad luck and misfortunes. Interesting, when you consider what went on in the Burkes Hill camp that day. It was as if that goblin I had dreamt up really was there, stirring up a pot of trouble.

The day was deceptively calm at the beginning and events didn't crank up till later. In fact, the first thing I can remember was in the midafternoon when Christopher turned up with his wife, Suzanne, and baby son, Jack. I had been expecting them and went to greet them at the door. Christopher was looking pleased, Suzanne was looking exhausted, and Jack was asleep. Jack was encouraged to snooze on in Emily Jane's baby rocker as Christopher led Suzanne down the hall to his bedroom. I went into the kitchen to make tea.

I had just switched the kettle on when I heard a sound, a sort of querulous cry that you'd expect to hear from a female bird dissatisfied with its mate's nest-building abilities. Suzanne was probably looking at her accommodation in Christopher's room, with its dusty venetian blinds, tattered lino floor, and the shearers stretchers lovingly bound together.

'You've got to be joking! This is a joke, right?' she was asking hopefully. And when Christopher didn't burst out laughing and produce a more favourable alternative, she asked, 'And what's that thing supposed to be? A bed?'

I wasn't in the habit of peeking into Christopher's room and so had no idea whether he had made the bed up cosily with mattresses and sheets or she was looking at the shearers stretchers naked in all their wiry glory. Christopher replied that the stretchers were very comfortable, considering.

'Considering what?' Suzanne asked a little sharply. 'Hey Cynthia,' she called out, 'Do you sleep on one of these things?'

I glanced down the corridor and saw her hovering on the threshold of Christopher's room as if she couldn't quite commit herself by actually entering.

'No. I sleep on a mattress on the floor,' I said, deciding it was better to be frank than diplomatic. 'Apparently if you sleep like a rock they're pretty good, but they're very noisy.'

'Noisy?'

'Yep! They make a racket if you move. Even the slightest bit. It will keep you awake. You and everyone else!'

Suzanne cast a horrified glance at Christopher and tottered into the room, staring out through the blinds to the expanse of dust across the road that somebody called a park. And then I remembered that she had been travelling since before sunup to get here and would be in need of tea. I suggested she join me for a cup while Christopher went off to get the luggage.

We sat together on the brown swivel chairs. Suzanne sipped her tea and stared at the lolly-pink walls, and although we had some polite conversation about babies and sleep, I could tell her heart wasn't in it. She was really thinking how hideous the place was and wondering why she had imagined it was a good idea to come at all. The only time she smiled was when Jeremy rushed into the kitchen to gulp down some water and catching a glimpse of Jack still dozing on the rocker said enthusiastically: 'Hey. Groovy baby!' And then was gone.

I tried to tell Suzanne that life in Burkes Hill wasn't as bad as it looked, that I'd actually enjoyed myself the evening before. Paul had come in early with Christopher and we had all played Monopoly together. But she just looked at me bleakly and asked where the shower was.

She must have collapsed on the shearers stretchers for a nap because Christopher took care of Jack that afternoon and I didn't see her again until dinnertime. Christopher was already in the dining room feeding Jack the same veggie mush I gave to Emily Jane, when Suzanne trailed Wally and Potts into the dining room. Potts looked so dejected I could see that his week had not gone well.

'So how are the sunshine and daisies, mate?' Wally was asking.

Potts glanced about to see if Priscilla and her companions had yet arrived and said, 'Oh man! They faded pretty bloody quick, I can tell you.'

'Yeah,' said Wally, 'I rather thought they might.'

'She's good to look at, I'll grant you that. But Jeez, it's all so much easier with another bloke. You can relax more. You can say what you bloody like, you can be as filthy as you like, you can fart freely.'

'You can shoot pigs,' said Wally.

'And a bloke can't live on muesli bars and bean stews all week like she expects. Out on the rocks all day with nothing but muesli bars in the gut. It just isn't possible. What's wrong with bacon and eggs or a slab of steak? That's the stuff a man needs!'

'Yeah right!' said Wally, 'That, and pigs!'

The atmosphere at the meal table that evening was strangely sombre. The chirpy ambience of Monday breakfast had disappeared entirely. There was nobody cheerfully humming *Magic Moments* or any other song. What had changed in a week? It felt as if we were eating Christmas dinner with a quarrelling family, all trying their best to be civil to each other, but tense with the effort. As far as I knew there had been no quarrels, but something was going on. Potts politely tried to engage Priscilla in a conversation about the nutritional benefits of muesli bars, but she turned her back on him and asked Michelle about the craft market they planned to visit over the weekend. Jeremy didn't turn up at all and couldn't lend the gathering that infectious, rose-coloured glass attitude to life that had been dominating his mood.

'Hey, where's Jeremy?' asked Paul, as if he had only just realised how we had all taken Jeremy's more sterling qualities for granted, now that he wasn't present at the table to lighten the mood.

'Out to dinner with a lady friend probably,' suggested Sebastian, making a face.

'That'd be right, while the rest of us have to look at the same ugly mugs every weekend,' said James.

'But isn't Jeremy gay?' asked Bugsy.

'Nah,' replied Wally. 'He's a lady's man. Just the type of namby-pamby guy the sheilas go for. Hey Rooster?'

Suzanne looked quite ill, as if she had lost her appetite completely and was now not only struggling with how hideous the place was, but was also thinking how intolerable the people were, and was wondering how she would ever cope with the coming weeks. But if she thought things were unpromising at this point, she didn't realise how much worse they would be before the evening was through.

The group may have appeared crass to Suzanne, but they were sensitive enough to realise she would need some time and space with her husband. They all cleared out after dinner, most to one of the pubs, although Paul and Sebastian planned to go back to the white house to have a jamming session while everyone else was out. To his later regret, only James lingered. He was planning to join the others at the pub, but wanted a quick private word to Christopher, to ensure he never had to go out into the field with Sebastian again, because he didn't think his nervous system could stand it.

'Great guy, great guy,' he kept saying, 'he just gives me the jitters, that's all. And it gets me down.'

Eddie and I put Emily Jane to bed and went out the back to the shed where Jen had installed a ping-pong table amongst a store of tinned foods and some desks. Eddie used the space as an office, but this evening we slammed the ping-pong ball about while possums thumped about the rafters and stared at us with wide eyes. We were enjoying this rare moment of peace together when it was shattered by the sound of a car hurtling into the yard. The piercing tones of a horn echoed through the still night.

'Who the hell is that?' asked Eddie. He had been enjoying telling me about the bifurcating burrows he had seen in the rocks that week and didn't like the interruption. 'Ignore them and they might go away. Keep playing.'

'We can't ignore it,' I said. 'It's Mrs O'Regan. Something's wrong.'

'Damn!' said Eddie, flinging aside his ping-pong bat and striding out into the darkness.

Mrs O'Regan sat in her car. She was pale, her fingers gripping the steering wheel tightly, her thumb pressing the horn. She didn't bother with preliminary courtesies.

'Something dreadful has happened. My son has gone missing. You must organise a search party at once!'

'But where did he go? How long has he been missing for?' I asked.

'He went out for a hike this afternoon on his property, down along Cobblecundy Road, next to the river near Derry Downs. Said he'd back for dinner.'

'But Mrs O'Regan, Dennis will be fine. It's still early. He probably stayed out a bit longer to watch the sunset and is already on his way back. Why don't you come in and have a cup of tea, and when you get back home, he'll be there waiting for you,' suggested Eddie.

If Mrs O'Regan had been a dragon, she would have scorched him with her breath.

'Sunset!' she roared at him. 'Sunset! You know nothing!'

Eddie gaped back at her, astonished. There wasn't much he could reply to this.

'But of course, you don't understand. You don't know Dennis. He's accident-prone. Takes risks. Needs constant supervision. He nearly blew himself up in a tent when he was twelve. I tell you, something awful has happened to him.'

The misadventures of the child Dennis seemed so far in the past they were hardly worth bothering about, but we didn't dare quibble. In the back seat of her car, Ralph sat bored, nibbling on his fleas.

'It's that old taipan down by the riverbank. It's got him,' she said. 'And you'll be too late to help if you don't go soon. Please go and get Mr Craddock. He knows exactly where Dennis has gone. He's been there before.'

'But Mrs O'Regan, Eddie can go. Christopher's wife has only just arrived,' I said.

She looked at me severely. 'Cynthia! You're being frivolous! Mrs Craddock will be happy to wait, in the circumstances.'

Mrs O'Regan stayed in her car while we went reluctantly into the house to find Christopher.

'Of course Dennis hasn't been bitten by a snake!' said Christopher in exasperation when we delivered the message.

'It's too cool for snakes and anyway he's perfectly capable of looking after himself.'

'Just what I told her,' said Eddie, 'And she screamed at me. Look, I'd go myself, but the old lady doesn't seem to think I'm up to it. She wants you.'

Christopher looked as if he was about to explode in a string of expletives, strange for such a calm and well-mannered person. I felt sorry for the guy. He'd been looking forward to seeing his family for weeks. Now they were here, the afternoon had not gone at all as he had anticipated. And just as he was about to put things right, this imperious old dame turns up demanding that he, and nobody else, go out and rescue her son, when in all probability Dennis was right this moment driving back along Cobblecundy Road singing along to the radio. It was all too much.

Right then Mrs O'Regan wobbled into the house, having decided that Eddie and I were unreliable. Just one glimpse and we all knew it would be useless trying to persuade her that it was unreasonable to organise a search party when your son is only a few minutes late for dinner. James took one look at her, and probably regretting that he had ever had qualms about working with Sebastian and wasn't right now safely in a pub with a beer, said softly to Christopher, 'Sorry Buddy, but you're going to have to go. I'll come with you.'

I understood completely why he preferred to stumble along the riverbank in the dark on a fruitless errand than to remain behind to soothe Mrs O'Regan and Suzanne. He strode out of the house, Christopher trailing behind him with his head hanging down, like a man doomed to endure a whole month in the doghouse through no fault of his own. Eddie and I stayed to reassure Mrs O'Regan, but Suzanne just seemed to melt away. She could hardly be expected to stick around to placate the old woman who had sent her husband off on the first evening they had together for weeks.

We didn't have to soothe Mrs O'Regan for very long. She had been keeping a sharp lookout through the windows onto the road, and a few minutes after James and Christopher had left, she saw Dennis drive down College Road.

'Thank God for that!' she said, and without bothering to take so much as a sip of the tea we had made, she took off. Too bad for James and Christopher who continued driving along Cobblecundy Road to Derry Downs and the riverbank, unaware that Dennis had returned and was about to start gorging himself on his mother's dinner. These were the days before mobile phones solved these inconveniences.

Just as Eddie and I were thinking we could resume our ping-pong game out in the shed, we heard the sound of footsteps and Paul and Sebastian pitched up. Really it was one thing after another that evening.

'We thought you'd want to know,' said Paul, 'The mechanic has gone back to Bogarilla. Dunno why he forgot to mention it to you, too busy with all that "cool man" stuff I suppose. But his swag is rolled up and stashed in a corner and his bag has gone.'

'But how could he have gone to Bogarilla? His truck's still here! There are the keys, right there on the bench,' I said.

'Yeah, right! Jeez that's weird!' said Paul.

'He's done a runner,' said Sebastian. 'Always thought he would someday or other. Dunno why ... Hey, he was okay, wasn't he? Not depressed or anything like that?'

'Nah,' responded Paul, 'Couldn't have been depressed. He won Monopoly last night.'

'You know, I've never actually got on with the guy, but I'd hate to see him in trouble,' said Sebastian.

'He'll be fine!' Paul reassured us confidently. 'Probably just had an epiphany that's all!'

'A what?' asked Sebastian.

'It's probably just dawned on him that he's in the wrong job. I mean you don't look at Jeremy and instantly think—oh look there goes a bush mechanic. No. He's got airline steward written all over him. He should be on a plane greeting nervous customers with a corny joke, he should be propping pillows behind old ladies in the pointy section. Everyone would love him! But here, he's just like the Ugly Duckling, isn't he?'

'The what?' asked Sebastian, looking completely confused.

'Didn't anybody ever tell you that story? Jeremy will never be happy here because he's with us ducks, but he isn't a duck. He's really a swan. He needs to go join the swans,' said Paul.

'I didn't know Jeremy was into football,' said Sebastian, more confused than ever.

'This is shaping up to be quite an evening,' I said. 'First Dennis goes missing, but now he's found. Not that James and Christopher know that, so they're still out looking for him, and now you tell me Jeremy's disappeared.'

'Yep!' said Paul. 'Hey Sebastian, let's hang around for a while. Could be entertaining. There's some beer in the fridge outside.'

'So what you're saying,' said Paul after I had updated him on the evening's events, 'Is that James and Christopher are down at the river looking for Dennis who was not bitten by a snake but is eating dinner with his mother. Right. And Suzanne? Where's she? Did she go down to the river too?'

'Er, no. She's probably so fed up and exhausted that she's gone to bed. So we should try to be quiet'

'Ah,' said Paul thoughtfully.

Meanwhile down at the river, James and Christopher had not applied themselves to the search with much vigour. True, they did amble along the riverbank for a few yards, flashing the torch about and calling out, but they had no faith whatsoever that Dennis was there and so were not very thorough. They returned to Burkes Hill and drove straight to the O'Regan house where they found Dennis sitting in an armchair with his feet propped up, drinking coffee, eating cake, and watching the Friday evening movie on TV. Mrs O'Regan had already gone to bed with a novel, worn out with worry.

'All unnecessary!' Dennis laughed.

James and Christopher returned at last to the green house.

'Where's Suzanne?' asked Christopher.

'Gone to bed,' Eddie replied.

'Are you sure?' he asked, coming out of his bedroom. 'They're not there.'

'But they must be there,' I said. 'I didn't see them go out. I didn't hear anything.'

'Half the stuff is gone as well. How could you not have noticed? Where did she go? Didn't she say anything?'

Christopher had lost his cool and I couldn't blame him, and I didn't know what to say. I felt completely responsible. I should have been more attentive, more welcoming. I knew Suzanne was finding the place horrid, but I had just assumed she would adjust.

And then Sebastian made it all worse by saying, 'Well that's sus! I knew there was something wrong with that football story!'

'What?' asked Christopher irritably. 'You're not making any sense.'

'Well mate, I'm sure it's just an unfortunate coincidence, but the mechanic has vanished as well. Bag and all! We're not trying to insinuate that ...,' Paul began.

'God! That's awful!' said James. 'So sorry! Has she known him long?'

'Oh, for about three minutes,' replied Christopher, exasperated.

'That's all it takes, I've heard,' said James.

'Would you please stop this?' asked Christopher. He took a deep calming breath. 'Whatever this is about, I do not think they have run off together. That's a ridiculous suggestion!'

'But it's happened before, hasn't it?' Paul reminded him. 'Oh no, no it hasn't actually. No, it was the cook that time. The mechanic ran away with the cook.'

Fortunately for everybody, the phone rang, and we could all escape this painful conversation. I answered the phone.

'Hello.'

It was Suzanne. 'When Christopher's finished with his heroics, please tell him that I'm waiting for him across at the Parkview Motel, the one up the street with the garish sign. Can't miss it. You know, Cynthia, I've come here for a holiday and to spend some quality time with my husband and I realised it simply can't be done in that house. It's impossible.'

'Yes, I can see that. You haven't seen the mechanic over there by any chance?' I asked.

'Who is the mechanic?' she replied.

'You know the "groovy baby" guy.'

'Is he missing? Well, he's not here as far as I know. Tell Christopher it's Unit 5,' and she hung up.

'Parkview Motel, Unit 5!' I said to Christopher. 'I wish I had the sense to do that when I first arrived and was shoved in that room with all those field hands sleeping on the floor. Oh, and just for your information everybody, Jeremy isn't at the motel.'

'But where can he be?' asked Christopher, who had calmed down considerably. 'He's been okay, hasn't he? You don't think he's been depressed? He seems cheerful enough, but he does cop a lot of shit.'

'I keep telling everybody, Jeremy is not depressed!' said Paul, 'Not in the slightest! He won Monopoly last night, didn't he? He's on top of the world.'

'But where can he be?' repeated Christopher.

'He's probably just been inspired to go seek his fortune,' Paul suggested.

'No need for that,' commented James. 'He's already raking in the big bucks here. Hey Buddy, we'll find Jeremy tomorrow. Or maybe we're worrying about nothing and he'll just pitch up. You'd best be heading for that motel.'

The next day Jeremy did not appear for breakfast. Not that we really expected him to. Potts rang Micky Wren, his favourite contact at the Bogarilla Camp and asked if anybody knew anything about the disappearance of the mechanic. But Mickey was far more interested in telling Potts about Big Jill and Joe who had 'stacked it' last night. Their vehicle had rolled on the side of the road among the tobacco fields, probably, said Mickey, because Joe had groped her as she was driving. However, they were off the hook because the local cop had insisted the accident was caused by a large kangaroo. As for the mechanic, nothing to worry about. It wasn't the first time he had vanished. Remember the time last year when he'd been off chasing girls.

'How long do we wait before we declare him missing?' asked Eddie.

But right then the phone rang and there was Jeremy chirping on the other end: 'Cynthia darling, it's me. Are you missing me yet?'

'Yes. We've been worried out of our minds. Where have you gone?'

'So sorry. Meant to leave a note but I just ran out of time. I've done something romantic. You see, I'm in love. So naturally I've run away to get married. If you're going to take the plunge you may as well do it with flair.'

'I suppose so. Good luck with it then. I'll miss you.'

'I expect you will,' said Jeremy. 'I guess they'll send a replacement who'll be twice as good as me but nowhere near as entertaining. Never mind Cynthia. There's Rooster and Jen about to keep you amused. But seriously, this is no time for me to plod along till the end of the season. There comes a time when you've just got to seize the day at hand and go in a new direction and screw the inconvenience. You've no idea how stimulating it is! Better put me on to Christopher. It's been groovy knowing you. Be good Honey. Bye.'

Christopher took the phone.

'Jeremy's resigned,' he said, after a brief conversation. 'He's just posted a letter of resignation to Gerald. Apparently, he's getting married next week in Brisbane. Said we're all invited to the wedding but as he knows none of us can come, he's already refused on our behalf to save money with the catering.'

'Still a jerk,' said James.

'And I always thought he was gay,' said Bugsy with wonder. 'Hey, what about that truck out there? What do we do with it?'

'Good question,' replied Christopher. 'As far as I know, nobody else around here is licensed to drive the thing. It's completely useless. Nothing but a white elephant.'

I could have sworn I heard a tinkling sound. Was it that goblin giggling in the hallway?

What next? I wondered.

Chapter 19

Potato peelings and the call of nature

ANOTHER FRIDAY AFTERNOON HAD COME, and Jen, with a cigarette clamped between her teeth, was mopping the floors, complaining as she progressed through the house.

'What did I do wrong to deserve a bloody job like this? Mopping the bloody floors week after week, filling in all those bloody forms, buying supplies for everyone else to take in the field. Everyone but me, that is. This is a mug's job.'

She rammed the mop into a bucket of vile-smelling fluid and splattered it across the floor.

'I've had enough of this bloody town.'

Suzanne Craddock was in the kitchen helping with the pavlovas. The babies were on the floor in a corner tumbling amongst a mound of unsorted groceries. Life was trundling along in a mundane way and there was no sign at all of that mischievous goblin, probably because it had taken an excursion out into the field along with Priscilla and Sebastian that week and had been making trouble out there.

The first inkling I had of this was when Sebastian walked into the house. He was strangely silent, his arms rigid by his side. He did not bend over the kitchen bench and complain of starvation as he usually did on a Friday afternoon.

'How was your week?' I asked, although it was a stupid question because I already knew the answer.

He mumbled a depressed response and shuffled off down College Road to the other house. Priscilla appeared next. She, too, had no time for small talk or pleasantries. She looked at us as if we were kitchen machines and said, 'When Christopher comes in, tell him I need to see him immediately.'

She was followed by Jen, who showed no sign now of the bored humour with which she had mopped the floors only two hours ago. 'Christopher here yet?' she asked with the sort of frown you would expect from somebody who has just learnt of an Ebola outbreak in the local community.

Suzanne and I exchanged glances and shook our heads. Something very serious must have happened. What on earth had Sebastian done?

'Poor Christopher,' I said, 'He'll be barrelling down that ironbark highway right now looking forward to the weekend—a cold beer, a hot shower, some rest and recreation. But all he'll be getting is ...'

'Trouble,' said Suzanne, 'It certainly seems to be brewing.'

Everyone picked up on the atmosphere very fast that afternoon. There were no field hands lounging on the veranda, laughing, drinking beer and throwing cigarette butts out into the garden. Instead, Priscilla, Jen, and Michelle were perched on the veranda edge, waiting for Christopher. They had an air of such potent gloom they could have been the three witches from Macbeth. It was no wonder the field hands didn't want to go near them.

When Christopher finally turned up, he didn't even have time to get out of the vehicle. Suddenly they were there, jabbering at him through the window. He sat for a moment in stunned silence. He said later that his first impulse was to wind up the window and implore Paul to keep driving. He could see that they were distressed about something and he could hear that they were demanding that he instantly sack Sebastian Slanger. But he didn't want to know about it. Not then. Not when his body was still cramped from the journey and the filth of the week still clung to him. He needed time to take off his boots, wriggle his toes, feel the water of the shower stream down his back, sip a cold drink. Maybe then he could gather his faculties and face whatever the problem was.

'Give me a break!' he yelled, as he struggled out the door. 'Please, not now. Just fuck off!'

The words were out before a thought and he blinked with astonishment. Michelle, Priscilla and Jen were struck dumb for a moment, just as if their pet rabbit had suddenly grown fangs and injected them with venom. Christopher had always shown them support and no matter how much bad language was pitched about the GIU base camp at Burkes Hill, it had never before that evening emerged from his lips. Everyone thought him incapable of swearing. And yet here he was cursing the female members of the field party.

'Wonders never cease!' commented Wally afterwards.

'Yeah,' said Jen. 'Just look what marriage can do to a man. Why should he abuse us? We're only trying to promote social justice.'

Apart from these comments there was an unusual silence, loud and engulfing, as everyone wondered what the hell was going on. The three women, unable to air their grievances as soon as they wished, now clammed up completely and the potency of their gloom grew. That goblin had really gone to town this time. There was terrible tension in the house, but most of us didn't even know why.

We had to guess. It must be something bad, very bad.

Eventually Christopher and Eddie, realising this state of affairs couldn't go on much longer, walked down the road to see Sebastian. Perhaps he would tell them what was going on. They found him slumped on the veranda of the white house, strumming his guitar as the evening breeze slapped the banana leaves against the louvres.

'You don't even have to say anything,' he said, strumming a few gloom-ridden chords. 'I'll start packing in a minute, and then I'll be gone. I don't want to make trouble for you all. This has been the best job I've had in a long while, and I can't say I'm not sorry I stuffed it. And I was saving for some new front teeth, but it doesn't matter. One day I'll learn to keep my mouth shut.'

'But what happened?' asked Christopher.

Sebastian played a few more depressing chords and began the story.

'Wednesday evening and we'd just stopped for the night. Priscilla pulled some spuds out of the tuckerbox and directed me to peel them. That was all very well, but just then I had to go off into the bush. Just momentarily you understand. Call of nature and all that. Can't be helped. When I got back, she'd peeled those spuds herself and she screeched at me for failing to do as she asked.'

'Whoa there,' said Christopher. He had been expecting some squalid tale of lust and violence, and this waffling on about who peeled the potatoes seemed to be straying into irrelevance. 'If we get sidetracked we'll be here all night. Perhaps if we stick to the main issue.'

'What is the main issue? As I said, she screeched at me ... And then I lost it ... That's all. I mean I had every fucking intention of doing her bloody potatoes just like I'd done every other bloody thing she'd asked me all week.'

'Ah, so you lost it?' said Eddie.

'You could say that. Well, she made it clear right from the

start she hated me being there. Treated me like a mangy stinking animal she could barely tolerate. Picked holes in everything I did. And I tried. Man, did I try. But nothing was good enough. It gets at you after a while, that. So, come Wednesday, I lost it. I barked at her.'

'You barked at her ...' echoed Christopher faintly.

'If I remember correctly my precise words were: *I'm not your bloody slave, woman.*'

'Ah. What then?' asked Christopher.

'Nothing really. She just said I'd be punished for insubordination when we got back, and she barely talked to me again. Sort of froze me out of existence. Jeez, these have been the longest two days ever.'

'Is that all?' asked Christopher.

'What the hell were you expecting? What did she say?'

'She hasn't said anything to me at all. She's not talking to me either. I snapped at her too. And Jen and Michelle with her.'

'You?' asked Sebastian in disbelief.

'They hassled me as soon as I arrived. And I'm afraid I didn't handle it well. But look, forget about resigning and come up for dinner. We can sort this out. You can't lose your job over a squabble about who peels the vegetables.'

'I'm telling you, there'll be trouble. She wants me out of here,' said Sebastian.

'Maybe she does, but if we were all sacked every time we say things in the heat of the moment, there wouldn't be a workforce left.'

'It's a tough world when a man can't go off and have a quiet ...' began Eddie.

'All right,' Christopher interrupted, 'Let's go eat.'

It was a funny thing, but a spontaneous cheer broke out when Sebastian turned up at the green house for dinner with Christopher and Eddie on either side of him. Malcolm Drake, behaving as if he was at a party, uncorked a bottle of wine, slopped it into several glasses and handed them round the table.

'Hey, what's happened to the Hen Connection?' he asked, spinning round with the bottle.

'They're not here, mate,' said Grasshopper. 'They've gone downtown. Said they fancied a plate of chicken and chips tonight and made for *Red Rooster*.'

The gloom and tension lifted, and a feeling of friendship flooded the room as the wine and beer flowed. When Sebastian was encouraged to repeat his story, Potts slapped him on the back, as a mark of respect.

'You know I nearly said the same thing to her the other week, several times in fact. But every time the words were on my lips, she would smile at me and you know what? I'd run after her like a bloody puppy dog. Hated myself for it.'

'She smiled at you, did she?' said Wally. 'Well, aren't you the favoured one. But we gotta face it. What Sebastian said needed to be said.'

'Bossy, is she?' asked Malcolm, laughing with a deep throaty laugh. 'Oh dear, life is far too short to spend it bossing others about. She'll miss all the good things, poor girl. Oh well, she'll get some time out down at *Red Rooster* and can contemplate it all as she stares at the view over the car park. She'll soon get it in perspective and realise it's just an insignificant kerfuffle born of a grouchy moment. Not worth thinking of again. And they'll come home and laugh and the whole affair will be forgotten.'

'Yeah,' said Bugsy. 'By tomorrow morning they'll be smiling at this table, chatting about the hunks they saw at the take-away tonight.'

But what was that tinkling sound that came from behind the brown swivel chair? The goblin, probably, laughing at such foolish optimism.

Breakfast was awful. Jen, Michelle and Priscilla were back

in place, along with a dense black cloud of gloom that hovered over them. They weren't talking much, but the glares they directed towards Sebastian and Christopher were eloquent enough. They did, however, request an interview with Christopher. Everyone else shovelled down cereal and eggs as fast as possible in their haste to get out of the dining room.

After breakfast, Christopher had the look of a man who was wishing that many years earlier he had made a decision to pursue plumbing as a career. His eyes flickered nervously and his nose twitched, but he sat down to listen to the other side of the story. He began by apologising for his language the night before, but it didn't help matters much. Priscilla was a fluent speaker, but she was so upset that she let Jen speak for her. The message was simple: Sebastian Slanger must be instantly dismissed for intimidating a geologist and for sexual harassment.

'What was the nature of the harassment?' asked Christopher.

'Um ...' And then in a firmer voice, Jen said, 'It's the look in his eyes. You just know what he's after.'

Nobody could pretend that this was strong evidence for harassment, and realising this, Jen cranked up the stakes.

'Why should our geologists have to sleep each night in their tightest jeans because they're scared of being attacked by a toothless creep? You just think about that Craddock! Because if he doesn't go, I'll resign.'

'What?'

'You heard me. It's him or me. Make up your mind.'

Christopher was beginning to look really sick. He suggested there were other solutions. Sebastian need never go into the field with Priscilla again. It would be easy to arrange. But Jen's eyes bulged, her hair stood up on end, and she refused to compromise. Beside her, Priscilla's eyes were flashing. Michelle sat quietly, her face inscrutable. Perhaps she felt things were getting out of hand.

In the end Christopher shrugged, 'If that's the way you feel, let Gerald Drake know as soon as possible so he can start thinking of a replacement. You can try his home number.'

Carried away on a wave of passion, Jen rang Gerald, disturbing him as he mowed his lawn in the winter sunshine down in Brisbane, and resigned from the GIU. When she was through, she slammed the phone down and stormed out of the house.

The morning transactions had a most terrible effect on everybody at the Burkes Hill camp, with the exception of that household imp who was probably having the time of his life. Most people stayed right away from the house that day. Morning tea, afternoon tea, lunch were all non-events. Eddie had gone straight out to the shed at the back and lost himself amongst the maps. I don't know what everybody else did.

It occurred to me that I could create a gourmet feast, something so wonderful it would make us all forget the miseries of the day, but I wasn't equal to it. My spirit wasn't that generous. I pulled from the freezer a bag of large chops, which had come from some enormous animal the butcher called a lamb, and shoved it on the bench to defrost. I tore up a lettuce and rammed it in a bowl, then, uninspired, I gave up. It was likely nobody would even pitch up for a meal.

I tried to relax outside with Emily Jane but that was as unsuccessful as dinner preparations. I spread a rug over the prickles under the mango tree, but it wasn't comfortable, and we were disturbed by a bunch of smiling women waving red umbrellas against the afternoon sun. The leader spoke across the fence as if she had been specially commissioned by God. She admired the garden, which made me doubt her sincerity, and then abruptly changed the topic.

'We've come today to have a little chat about love. Do you ever think about love?' she asked in a honeyed tone.

This would have put me off at the best of times, but on that particular day I couldn't cope at all. Rudely, I snatched up the baby and fled into the house, leaving them to talk about God with the mango tree. Eddie took Emily Jane and, unmotivated, I went back to the kitchen. The house was empty. Depressing. The kitchen was buzzing with flies. And then Jen came in. She was alone and we stood together, enclosed by benches, silently staring out at the withered garden beyond the veranda.

'Bloody flies,' she said.

I could barely respond. I detested her at that moment. She had taken a bad situation and made it so much worse. She had been intolerant. And I was intolerant of her intolerance. Any light-hearted, civilised exchange was impossible.

'I'm so fed up,' I said stiffly. 'Why can't people make more of an effort to get on with each other?'

It was a pathetic attempt to express what I was really feeling, but it sure triggered a reaction.

'You're fucking fed up!' she screamed. 'What about me!'

She rammed her face right up close to mine until I was almost overwhelmed by her volcanic rage. But I also became aware that she was more miserable than the rest of us put together. All of us had been discomforted by this quarrel, but she alone had lost something that mattered. I stood rooted to the floor and listened as she poured forth anger and sorrow and confusion and anxiety. All my negative feelings about her had gone by the time she collapsed on the bench and sobbed to the microwave oven.

'What have I done? I didn't mean to resign. What am I going to do now?'

'Can't you change your mind? It's the weekend, nothing official ever happens till Monday.'

And I fled from the kitchen where emotions were swirling about the benches so powerfully, I felt I would be torn asunder if I stayed another second. I ran out to the fresh air and sat on the veranda steps at the front of the house. I bent my head and wept. Jen followed me out, sat beside me on the steps and she wept too. Then Grasshopper appeared and he sat on the steps with us, and I'm not sure if he wept or just kept us company, but it was comforting nonetheless. We began to feel much better, as if a great weight had just evaporated from the three of us. It was as if a wicked spell had been broken.

'Don't think I can do much more for Priscilla about this one,' said Jen sturdily. 'She'll have to manage it herself now. I mean it's not really about Sebastian and the potatoes, is it? It's the system that's wrong ... sending her out week after week with those pig-shooting blokes. Just causes stress for everyone.'

'How about I go get some beer?' asked Grasshopper.

Now that some of the day's tensions had dissipated it dawned on me that I had left the kitchen in a disgraceful state, with no meal preparation apart from defrosting a bundle of chops that were quite likely inedible, and that very soon a large group of hungry people would arrive expecting dinner. I would be sacked next, if I didn't do something quick. To make matters so much worse, right then I caught sight of a strangely familiar couple walking towards the house, across the dusty park, from the direction of the motel. I was expecting Christopher and Suzanne to come this way, but this wasn't them.

I must have been seeing things—stress playing games with my mind. Coming towards me were the most unlikely people I could possibly dream up to arrive on the doorstep at just that moment, when I was about to serve the worst meal of the season. Their outlines were clearer now and there was no mistake. Here were those specialists in gourmet eating, Owen and Stella. I had no idea why they were in Burkes Hill on this most inconvenient evening. Stella was supposed to be in Bogarilla, spreading joy with her food, and Owen was supposed to be in Bogarilla eating it.

'What are you two doing here?' asked Grasshopper.

But before they could respond Potts came through the gate and yelled, 'Turn back. Turn back, all ye who seek to enter. Get to bloody hell out of here. It's not fit for humankind. Go back to where you came from.'

'What's going on?' asked Owen.

'Oh, just some bloody bun fight about who peels the potatoes for dinner and everyone else sticking their beaks in as if it was a matter of great importance,' said Potts. 'Jeez, I'd rather have Jimmy Keen burning down a shed any day'.

'How sad,' said Stella. 'Oh well, I'm sure it's nothing that a good dinner can't fix, hey Cynthia?'

'Aah ...'

How very awkward.

'Stella needed a break,' said Owen, 'So we've taken a week off. We're on holidays. This is our first night. We're going down to the coast tomorrow.'

While all this had been going on, Eddie had been out in the shed, plotting the course of an ancient river, with Emily Jane on his lap. He had completely forgotten the weekend dramas. Trivial human problems, here today and gone tomorrow. The rivers of yesterday flowed for millions of years before humanity even existed. He wandered out of the shed, carrying the baby, and greeted Stella and Owen as if there was nothing at all unusual about their presence.

I escaped to the kitchen looking for a miracle, tossed the meat in a marinade, added some exotic ingredients to the salad, pulled a dessert from the freezer. It was an improvement but scarcely enough. And then, Christopher and Suzanne arrived, and bless their souls, they were armed with bags and boxes.

Christopher began to blow up balloons while Suzanne threw party hats and whistles on the table. She filled dishes with sweets and chips and put trays of sausage rolls and party pies in the oven. Christopher erected a *Pin the Tail on the Donkey* game on the wall. It was a miracle of sorts.

'We're holding a children's party for the babies tonight,' said Suzanne. 'We figure it will be a good stress buster.'

The house had slowly filled. Jen put a party hat on and blew a whistle until it drooped soggy from her mouth.

'I've been a dickhead,' she said to Christopher. 'I don't want to resign. I'd be miserable without this job.'

Christopher was relaxed in a party hat. 'It's okay. We can fix it. I'll call Gerald in the morning.'

Priscilla sat in a corner, pale and tight-lipped, reluctant to put a party hat on and join in the revelry. She was not friendless, but apart from Jen, there was nobody at the party who really understood that the whole affair was about more than an over-the-top reaction to a trivial disagreement and a misplaced allegation of sexual harassment.

As to the sexual harassment allegation, Sebastian had snorted with incredulity when told about it and proclaimed that he wasn't that bloody stupid. Tangled hair and missing teeth were not a sign that he was likely to ravish any female he found himself alone with. The glint of lust she thought she had seen in his eyes was actually a glint of resentment caused by her over-bearing approach to her own authority. The blunt reality was that they did not like each other, would never like each other, and that was that.

I doubt Priscilla would have disagreed with this point, but even so, she was probably unaware that evening of quite how demoralised and spirit-sapped she had become from venturing out week after week with blokes she had nothing in common with and no respect for, blokes she regarded as degenerate imbeciles. They had been relentlessly imposing on her personal space, and there hadn't been much she could do about it as it was all part of the job, but it was distorting her mind and soul.

'It's about being professional,' she tried to explain above the racket of the party, but nobody was interested in her explanation.

She slowly put a party hat on and accepted a party pie from Michelle, who smiled as she passed the plate about. Sebastian, blindfolded, stuck the donkey's tail on its ear and Potts blew a whistle for all he was worth. Malcolm collected the plate of chops and took them out to the barbecue.

'As if it matters who peels the potatoes. I mean who cares?' he said, as he flourished the tongs in the air and slapped the meat onto the hotplate.

Inside the house there was a knock at the door that could barely be heard. Grasshopper, party hat askew, opened the door.

'It's those women,' he said, coming back to the dining room. 'The ones I saw roaming the streets earlier with the red umbrellas. They want to come in and talk to us all about love.'

'Nah, tell them we're having a party instead,' said Wally. 'But you can invite them in if you like. They might like a beer.'

Chapter 20

A romantic dinner for three

THE VERY NEXT WEEKEND, Gerald Drake stood outside the green house in Burkes Hill and said, 'Marvellous country up here,' while pointing across the road to the barren and dusty park. 'And what about the stars at night! Aren't they something?'

After the debacle of the previous week he had been inspired to favour the field camps with a fleeting visit. Before heaving himself up the stairs he turned to address a girl waiting in the front seat of his vehicle.

'Come on Tiffany, come and meet the troops! They'll give you an idea of the work being done up here,' he called out. 'One of Oscar's students,' he muttered in explanation. 'Doing a training exercise in this vicinity; she's applied to do some holiday work with us in the summer.'

Pale and embarrassed, the girl emerged awkwardly. Jen, standing beside me, jammed her elbow in my ribs and winked at me with wicked delight, as if it was abundantly evident that Gerald was misconducting himself.

'Concubine!' she said in a piercing whisper.

But once she was out of the car, Gerald disregarded the girl, knowing there were others more qualified to show her about.

James McCracken appointed himself to the task and stepped from the waiting throng with a smile. He smoothly escorted her up the stairs, inviting her to morning tea and offering her a range of cakes that weren't on the menu at all. Morning tea was already laid out in the dining room—plates of scones with jam and cream, and pots of tea.

After the team shuffled in, Gerald smiled amiably. 'No one can pretend it's easy living in these field camps,' he began. 'It means living with people who might have bad habits, people with irritating ways. It means sharing a household with those, who, in other circumstances, would be the last people you would choose to live with.'

'You can say that again!' Wally muttered.

'But you people have certain advantages that perhaps you take for granted. You're not like the rest of us, trudging day after day into our airconditioned offices with our little bags of vegemite sandwiches. You have a much broader experience of life. Wide open spaces, splendid night skies. This is God's Own Country. You get to hear the birds call and the dingos howl. Dew on the grass and wind in the trees.'

Paul cast his eyes downwards, mouth twitching, and I read his mind clearly. *Not this bullshit again.* The words hung in the air more solidly than thoughts usually do and I couldn't bear to look at him. Wally, arms folded, had also averted his gaze, and was staring out the window at something nonexistent on the veranda. None of us wanted to give expression to that laughter that was bubbling up through Paul's being and which his mouth was furiously trying to suppress. It would have been dangerously infectious and completely inappropriate.

'Of course, personality conflicts will be inevitable,' Gerald continued. 'You'll get them everywhere you happen to be working. I'm not going to tell you to avoid them because you can't.

But what you can do is handle them in an intelligent manner and every single one of you is capable of that.'

He turned his attention to the tea and scones. 'I must say, these are the most delicious scones you've got here. Pumpkin scones ... my favourite. Have you put lemonade in these like Stella does up at Bogarilla?'

He finished the lecture by reminding everyone how fortunate they were not to have a cook who threw stews at people like the cook did regularly in the 1960 field season.

Once the pep talk was over, the forces scattered. Gerald asked an idle question about the progress of the mapping and Eddie dragged him out to the shed at the back to show him the course of the ancient river he was plotting, unaware that Gerald had ceased to be inspired by Devonian Rivers several years earlier. James took Tiffany out to the veranda and charmed her with a description of a phenomenal tectonic event, the record of which he had discovered in his rocks.

'Why don't you come down the road to the other house, and I'll show you some samples,' he suggested.

'Doesn't it just make you want to spew?' asked Paul.

I wasn't sure if he was talking about James's appropriation of the girl or the impressive display of industry going on in the front yard. Wally and Grasshopper were enthusiastically hosing down vehicles, while Sebastian cleared away the rubbish of the previous week. Jen cheerfully helped him cart the bags of garbage across to the bins.

'S'pose I'd better go and join the show,' said Paul as he glimpsed Gerald on his way back out.

Gerald stood in the corner of the yard, talking with Christopher and observing the camaraderie of the field hands. He avoided all mention of Jeremy's truck, the White Elephant, which was conspicuous on the footpath, but the absconding of the mechanic was certainly up for discussion.

'So, we've lost the mechanic. How inconvenient,' he said.

'It is a bit.'

'Still not as bad as the last time the mechanic absconded, that Jonesy fella, who ran off with the cook. That left us in a real pickle.'

'I remember.'

'Even so, I'm having no luck at all finding a replacement. You'll have to use the local services for a while, possibly for the rest of the field season,' said Gerald. 'Might be cheaper in the long run.'

'Quite possibly,' said Christopher. 'So, what will Jeremy do now I wonder?'

'Honeymooning right now I should imagine. He told me he's giving up mechanics altogether and has a job lined up with a children's television producer ... has to dress up in an animal costume and wave in a friendly way at kiddies.'

'He'll probably be very good at that,' Christopher laughed. 'We've been rather missing his sunny nature around here.'

'Yes, yes. So I've gathered. But things seem to have settled down here for now. At least these fellas are putting on a great show of unity. Time I got moving. It's a long drive to Bogarilla. And I've got to drop Tiffany back to the student group. Where did she get to?'

And off he went to become once more a voice at the end of the telephone and a name at the end of memoranda. Gerald's visit was not a waste of time, although he didn't seem to have done much apart from smile amiably, eat a plate of scones, and give a speech so similar to those he had given in the past the staff found it more comic than inspiring. And yet he had been like a catalyst affecting change by just being there. After Gerald left there was a realignment of resources. We tried to sharpen the edges of our lives, those edges that had grown dulled and blunt of late. There wasn't much we could do about that mischievous sprite in the house, if such a one existed at all, but we could all adjust our attitudes and try to improve our lives.

Jen, desperate for a break from Burkes Hill, headed out into the field with Priscilla for the week, a change that would give them both an opportunity to relax, refresh and de-stress. Jen and Christopher had decided, now the camp was well established, that it was feasible for her to go into the field more regularly to give some relief to Michelle and Priscilla, who had both been starved of understanding female company in the field so far that year.

The Craddocks were also heading out of town, going off for a week's holiday down to the coast. For me too there was a glimmer of hope on the horizon, a small spark of light to be sure, but for the first time in weeks I had something to look forward to. Eddie planned to return from the field a day early that week to enable Potts to drive the vehicle back to Bogarilla before his departure to Brisbane on the weekend. He was heading back to university life. This was the best news I had heard for ages. It meant that on Thursday evening Eddie and I would have the house to ourselves. Although this might seem nothing much to get excited about, when you've been living in a household full of people, and the only way to communicate freely and privately with your partner is to walk around the block, the prospect of an evening alone in a house is a big deal indeed.

Of course, Rooster would be about, but he always went to indoor cricket on Thursdays, so I wasn't expecting to see much of him. In fact, Rooster was particularly encouraging, perhaps appreciating those occasions over the last weeks when he had brought a girlfriend back to the house and I had kept a low profile, staying right out of their way.

'I know just what you need Cynthia,' he said. 'You need quality time alone with your husband. You've got to make this special. It could be weeks before you get another chance like this. You'll be wanting a good meal and a bottle of wine, maybe a movie. You can go rent a video, something different to the rubbish the field hands like to watch. Now you won't get any of that down at the Chinese. But if you do it here you can put Emily Jane to bed and relax together. I'll come back late. I can sleep in the caravan that night.'

The next day he went out for his afternoon run and came back with a magazine he had picked up at the newsagent on his way. It featured suggestions for romantic dinners for two and he pored over the recipes as enthusiastically as I did.

'I'd go the Italian one. This one here with the chicken breasts and tomatoes and garlic and mozzarella. Yum. I might even stay back from indoor cricket if you do that one ... Nah, just joking.'

'Good idea. Eddie'll have been eating steak all week with Potts.'

'You could always do the veggo one ... but no, nut loaf doesn't sound too exciting. Not my idea of a romantic dinner.'

Thursday afternoon arrived. I prepared the food. I swept the dust from the dining room and spread the table with a clean cloth. I placed a bottle of cabernet sauvignon and some pink hibiscus on the table, and I primed a cassette player with music. The only advice from the magazine I ignored was the bit about lighting. I knew in advance that Eddie would much prefer the glare from the electric bulb to candlelight.

'Yeah, you're right about that,' said Rooster. 'I don't know who spread all that stuff about candlelight being romantic. A bunch of old girls who don't want anyone noticing the wrinkles on their faces I reckon. But the rest of us don't want to be mucking about in the dark, hardly able to see the food on our plates.'

The afternoon opened before me, golden with possibilities. In due course Eddie and Potts arrived. Potts gulped down a coffee and was on his way. Rooster finished his work early that day, went out for his run and then left for the pub, where he intended to get a meal before indoor cricket. He instructed us to relax and enjoy ourselves and said he would be back late.

And there we were alone together for the first time since the mob had all gone to the Reedy Creek Races that first weekend. We took it simply and went out to the veranda to drink tea. We could hear the ping of insects, a thread of a breeze twitching the leaves of the mango tree. The afternoon and evening stretched out leisurely, luxuriantly before us. Eddie leant back in the rusty chair, sipped his tea, and watched Emily Jane on her rug bang a wooden spoon on an old pot. And then we heard a rumble in the distance.

The rumble was innocuous at first, undisturbing, like the sound of a faraway storm drifting away to somewhere else. But then it got louder, and louder still, until suddenly it was more personal, as if it was heading directly for us, while we tried our best to relax on the veranda. And then the truck materialised, slowing down as it came round the corner. It pulled up in the street right outside the house and Cedric emerged. He began to unload rock drums into the backyard.

'Oh, no, what's he doing here?' I asked.

'We do need those rock drums, Cynthia, you know,' replied Eddie.

'Well yes, but why now? He's entitled to a meal here, but I haven't catered for him and I don't want him, and he'll ruin all my plans,' I said uncharitably.

'I thought you told me he always refuses to come in.'

'That's true. He's never accepted so much as a cup of coffee in the place before. Can't wait to leave usually.'

'What are you worried about then? But even so we can't just sit here drinking tea and staring at him. We can hardly pretend we're not home. We'd better go and do the civil thing.'

Eddie wandered across the yard towards the truckdriver, and I scooped up the baby and followed, intending to get rid of him as soon as possible. Eddie propped himself against the fence and began to chat with him in the friendliest manner, although I hoped he was boring him witless with tedious details about fossilised wormy burrows in the rocks. Cedric, I noticed, was scarcely responding. His face was a complete blank. I sometimes wondered if he could string enough words together to form a sentence.

I interrupted the monologue by blasting him with the cheesiest and most off-putting grin I could muster. It was a smile designed to repel an antisocial character like Cedric, to make him flee in terror as he had done before. And then I invited him to dinner in the most unwelcoming and unattractive way I could think of.

'I don't suppose you'll want a meal here tonight? I didn't know you were coming, and I haven't catered for you. There's nobody else around here this week and stocks are low. There's certainly not enough chicken. All that's available is a hunk of old steak the boys brought back from the field. It might be all right.'

I injected extreme doubt into my voice so he couldn't miss the real message: *Your timing is rather awkward and we have other plans. I can't guarantee you won't get food poisoning so why don't you do yourself and us a favour and go off to the pub for dinner as usual.*

'Steak will be beaut, I'd like that,' Cedric replied with a thin smile.

What???

I knew that men are often stupid at picking up on subtle messages, but I didn't think this message had been all that subtle and I had not expected him to get it wrong. Eddie was silent. His brow shot up and his jaw hung down.

'Right ... fine! I'll just go and fish it out from the back of the vehicle, shall I? I do hope it hasn't gone off,' I said.

Cedric hauled the last load of rock drums into the shed and paused for a moment, hands on hips, sweating from the effort.

'I'll need to scrub up a bit first.'

'Yeah, sure,' said Eddie. 'Come back when you're ready.'

'Yes, what about dinner in about an hour and a bit?' I said pleasantly, all my dreams for the evening shattering into a million tinkling fragments.

'This is all your fault,' I said to Eddie as we watched Cedric climb back into his truck to go and clean up. 'You must have encouraged him.'

'Well you certainly didn't!'

'But what could have happened? He's always acted as if we'd suggested something shockingly horrible every other time we've invited him to dinner.'

'Who knows? There could be one hundred and one reasons why. Maybe he was in love with the barmaid, and she's just rejected him.'

'And I was so looking forward to the evening. I'd planned a romantic dinner, just for the two of us. The truck driver's going to ruin the atmosphere completely.'

Eddie shrugged, shook his head and said, 'Cynthia, I don't even know what a romantic dinner is. It would have been wasted on me. What is romance anyway? Really? Whatever it is, I'm pretty sure it can't be turned on and off like a tap with a scented candle and a plate of oysters ... I mean, when you think about it, our best times are always unplanned. They just spring up somehow from a moment or a spark or something. It can't be orchestrated. If you ask me, the real key is to enjoy what life offers up, at the time it's offered. And right now life's offering us a bloody good meal, a bottle of wine, and Cedric. That's not so bad.'

'I guess you're right. When has real life ever been reflected in the pages of a magazine anyway? It could have all gone flat; we might have squabbled, and now ...'

'We get to know Cedric. He seems an okay sort of guy.'

'He doesn't say much. There'll probably be long stretches of awkward silence.'

'No there won't. I'll tell him all about Queensland geology.'

'And by the time I bring out the chocolates, I'll feel like screaming.'

Our guest arrived within the hour, skin scrubbed and smelling of soap. He was wearing a fresh checked shirt and he had a six-pack of beer under his arm. I ushered him into the dining room, all set up for romance, but really, I wondered, as I pointed out a chair, what had I been thinking? Clean cloth, wine bottle, and flowers aside, it's impossible to maintain a romantic atmosphere when there's a baby in a highchair smearing vegetable puree over everything in reach.

I served zucchini soup and Emily Jane got into the spirit of the evening by grabbing Cedric's spectacles and smearing them with muck. He didn't appear to notice or care, and instead broke the ice by removing his watch and placing it on the table amongst the wilting flowers.

'How do you like my watch?' he asked.

'It's very nice Cedric,' I responded.

'Bought it on my holiday last year. In Hong Kong. Cheap,' he said.

'Really?' said Eddie, clearly wondering if it was too early yet to introduce the worms teeth theme.

'You gotta be careful with watches,' Cedric announced. 'You gotta look out. They can lead you to a bad end ...'

Eddie and I glanced at each other as we sipped the wine, wondering if he was mentally intact. On the other hand, perhaps he had hidden depths we hadn't expected. We waited for more.

'Take one of my mates now. He was a station hand, down Cracow way. I say was, because he's gone. Dead. Dead as a squashed cane toad splattered on the road. And guess what killed him?'

'His watch, I suppose,' I responded skeptically. It seemed an unlikely story.

'Right! His watch! Got entangled with the bridle when he fell off his horse and he was dragged along for miles. Real funny it looked, they say. We used to share the odd beer at the pub. Beyond beer he is now. Wrong watch you see.'

This was just the beginning. All my previous encounters with this truck driver had led me to believe that he was dour and taciturn, incapable of conversation, and yet here he was entertaining us with the most bizarre and ghoulish storytelling, an accomplished social animal. Eddie didn't have a hope, no chance to change the subject to worms teeth or ancient rivers or even oolites. Those yarns just kept spinning.

The steak was cooked, the chicken Milanese, the vegetables fresh from the market garden on the edge of town. And all the while we ate we heard about an axe-wielding maniac, a vengeful wife, a yowie sighting, and the vicious things drop bears do to unsuspecting tourists. I never suspected that this man could dominate dinner conversation with such spectacular flair.

I put the baby to bed. When I returned, I heard Cedric's voice still rambling on— 'Had a bust-up with his missus. Went to the railway track in time for the seven-thirty. Laid himself right down on the track. Head goes flying off. Body minced and I can tell you that's one train you don't want to catch. That's one ghost you don't want to see.'

I served dessert, chocolates, coffee. Time wore on. Eventually Cedric rose and said, 'Gee thanks. I enjoyed that. Didn't know what I've been missing.'

No. Neither did we.

The evening had been a bit disorienting. It was as if we had gone to the cinema expecting to see a rom com and had got the Dracula double feature instead. Not that it hadn't been diverting and a little comic. It was far too late now to enjoy the movie I had selected. There was nothing for it but to go to bed. At least the house was empty. There were no sounds of snoring and snorting; the bathroom and toilet were uncluttered. It had never been so peaceful.

For a short while ...

But then Emily Jane awoke and began to scream and would not settle whatever I did. Perhaps Cedric's stories had somehow penetrated her mind and she had nightmares. I don't know. I only know that it was after midnight when we all got into a vehicle and drove round and round the streets of Burkes Hill. It was silent, still and shadowed out there. We headed down a track leading out of town, avoiding the night creatures that scuttled across the road. But there were no yowies and no drop bears to be seen.

As the hum of the motor eventually lulled the baby back to sleep, Eddie said, 'Oh well, Cynthia, I'm sure some time in the next twenty years we'll get to spend an evening alone together.'

Chapter 21

Grilled cheese

As I said earlier, this field season was a series of problems, one after the other, although in truth there was respite following Gerald's visit, a week or two when the spirit of mischief seemed to have packed his bags and moved on. Things settled and we were all more relaxed. The conflict of the other week, and the underlying tensions that had caused it, had battered us about like a cyclone. Now the wind had subsided, the rain had ceased, and the sun had come out. But the storm had not gone, not yet. We were just in the eye and more heavy weather was on its way.

However, for all we knew right then, the conflicts were over, and the good times had come. The annual show came to town and we all went along. I made a mistake about the dress code, pitching up in shorts and a tee-shirt to an event in which every other woman was outfitted in her best dress and sloshed through the cattle manure in high heels. As an out-of-towner I could plead ignorance and enjoy the day in comfort. Michelle and Priscilla were more appropriately dressed, having put on the only finery they had brought north, and spent hours watching the showjumping or wandering around the craft exhibits, critically inspecting the knitting and needlework. Jen chose to hang out with the field hands, drinking beer at the bar and admiring the stud cattle, massive beasts of impressive composure. And Bugsy won a giant stuffed rabbit in a game at sideshow alley.

I collected recipes from the agricultural hall and wandered past mounds of tropical fruit, vegetables arranged in abstract patterns, an array of mineral ore, fake gold nuggets, and rows of gleaming jams. There were displays of children's art, shelves of decorated cakes and hand-knitted jumpers, tables of beautifully arranged flowers, walls of paintings and photos, cabinets of embroidery and painted china plates. A wealth of creativity from the beating heart of the Burkes Hill community. But the highlight I was told, would be the Sunday evening fireworks display. Not to be missed!

We drove up the hill to get the best view, bringing along Paul and Grasshopper as well. They had drunk far too much beer in the show bar that day to be safe driving themselves anywhere. Not that they were through with drinking beer yet; they had slipped a few tins in the car and planned to drink them as they watched the show. There were many other cars up on the hill, all with the same idea, but we found a space and we waited. And we waited.

'Jeez, they're taking their time about it, aren't they?' said Paul, after a while. 'This better be bloody good. Mind you, I've heard it is good. Heard it's bloody marvellous. Competition for Sydney New Year they said.'

And we waited.

'What's going on?' asked Grasshopper after another lengthy lapse of time. 'I've already drunk all the beer I brought along to drink while I was watching the thing. Shouldn't this have begun an hour ago?'

'No, no, not quite. It's about 45 minutes late,' said Eddie. 'Typical of Burkes Hill though, isn't it? I mean everything runs late here. It's part of the relaxed charm of the place ... if you've got the patience for it.'

Fortunately, Emily Jane was too young to know we were waiting for a fireworks show and was perfectly happy with the novelty of being in a car on a windy hill in the dark. She amused herself by poking faces at the men in the back.

'Hey, it's starting!' said Paul, eventually, as a firework burst into the sky. It sputtered and sank earthward almost immediately in a most dispirited manner, trailing a faded star or two, like a failing comet.

There was a pause and a second firework shot upwards, then dropped with a tired fizzle. A pause and then a third. A fourth, the same.

And then nothing at all.

The other cars were starting to leave.

'What!' said Paul, 'Is this it? Four duds and it's all over.'

We never knew what happened that night, whether it was just a typical Burkes Hill fireworks display and our expectations had been way too high, or if something had actually gone terribly wrong. But Grasshopper had his own theories. Nobody, he said, even the people of Burkes Hill, could possibly imagine that what we had just seen was a good fireworks show. His own family had done way better with fewer resources back in the good old days when cracker nights were still allowed in Queensland. No, this was the work of a jerk.

'There's always one about,' he said. 'And one is all it takes to ruin it for everyone else. They don't mean any harm, usually. Just a moment of inattention and the fireworks box is left out in the rain or put somewhere dumb and accidentally hosed. Next minute the whole town is assembled and all you've got is a washout. Not a functional firework left in the box.'

'Or maybe some dickhead tried to save money and bought them from some dodgy dudes,' suggested Paul.

'Same thing,' said Grasshopper, 'the work of a jerk. I can see it a mile off.'

* * *

The week after the show I went out into the field with Eddie. Like Jen, I needed a break from Burkes Hill. The streets and shops, the chook pens and mango trees were all very well, but I needed a glimpse of wider spaces. I wanted to see a wilder and more glorious world. So, we slept under the stars for a few days. I saw the black-headed rock python that sprawled across the outcrop, enjoying the sun so much it refused to move, even when Eddie politely nudged it so he could look at the rock in its entirety. I saw kangaroos drowsing in the noonday shadows, brolgas dancing on a sandbank in the river, and cockatoos shrieking high in the sky.

I was so refreshed by Friday that I didn't care that we needed to go directly to the supermarket on our return to Burkes Hill and were forced to appear in public like a family of tramps who hadn't bathed all week. People liked to dress up in Burkes Hill, even to go to the supermarket, so we were a pitiful sight. Emily Jane was grubby and lacked the clean white socks with frills about the ankles that all the other baby girls in the supermarket wore. Nobody was surprised; I had shown my true colours in terms of dress sense the previous weekend at the show.

We returned to the green house laden with boxes and bags of groceries that would have to be sorted before I could start the evening meal, but we had allowed plenty of time for this and had returned from the field particularly early. But not as early as James McCracken, who was already there, sitting out on the veranda drinking beer, with his feet propped on a box and a bowl of peanuts in his lap.

'You're back early,' said Eddie, staggering by with a box of bread and three heavy bags.

'Yeah, mate, yeah. There's a change coming. Can't you feel it? The humidity is rising. It'll be raining in a couple of hours. Thought it best to get back before it sets in. Don't want to be stuck out in the black soil country with a front of rain on the way.'

'You reckon?' replied Eddie.

There was not a cloud in the sky. The air was bone dry.

'Actually, I've been hassled all week. Needed a bloody break,' said James, as Eddie came back for another load.

'Weren't you camped out near that hut at Ten Mile Creek? What could possibly hassle you out there?'

'Possums, mate. Bloody possums. Plagued by possums, pestered by possums, pursued by possums, all bloody week. Found one in my swag one night nibbling on my toes. Must have taken a shine to the tinea powder.'

'Really?' I asked. This story sounded as far-fetched as his weather prediction.

'Yes really,' he said. 'Got back in the evening, took off my boots, washed my feet, dried my feet, put the tinea powder between my toes, and it would begin. Possums trickling from the trees, creeping after me, sniffing at my feet ... I reckon I had two hours sleep all week ... that ghastly noise they make at night. If I see another possum I think I might just lose a grip on my sanity.'

'You'd better lay off that tinea powder,' suggested Eddie.

'Hey, did you notice that girl who came here with Gerald Drake the other week? Her name was Tiffany,' James replied, lapsing into glassy-eyed silence as he munched thoughtfully on his peanuts.

We left him to his musings and went into the house. There were chores to be done and the afternoon progressed along sluggishly. When we'd dealt with all the groceries, Eddie took Emily

Jane off my hands and wandered off to the shed. Nobody else arrived at the house for a long time and James continued sitting in solitude on the veranda, gazing out at the prickly garden as if it was a sea view.

Eventually, Sebastian dropped Christopher off, but continued down to the white house for a shower. Christopher trudged in, dragging bag and swag which he dumped in his room, before plodding heavily back down the hallway to the kitchen for a cup of tea. Suzanne and Jack had recently returned to Brisbane and he could no longer look forward to weekends at the Parkview Motel.

'I'm beginning to dread the weekends,' he said with an anxious sigh. 'I'm not a morbid or anxious sort of person at all, but I spent the whole drive back wondering what's going to go wrong this weekend.'

'Why should anything go wrong?' I asked.

'I don't know, just the pattern of things I suppose.' He sipped his tea. 'I don't know why I'm telling you this, you'll probably think I'm going nuts, but I sometimes think there's a wicked spirit about this place that's playing games with us.'

'Really? Well, it's probably gone. Nothing's happened for the past two weeks at least.'

'Just what worries me,' he said.

'We've had troubles, but maybe they're all over.'

'No. No, they're not,' he said very definitely. He was looking towards the back and his eyes had widened. 'Mrs O'Regan has just driven in.'

'Oh well, she's probably come to give us some more garden produce. She's really very kind.' I said, stirring the soup.

But when Mrs O'Regan barged in without knocking, I could see she had not come to give us parsley and pawpaws. She was enveloped in emanating waves of disapproval. Christopher shot me a glance that plainly said: *I told you so.*

'Mr Craddock, I would like a few words with you,' she said crisply.

'Certainly, Mrs O'Regan. Would you like a cup of tea?'

'No thank you. Mr Craddock, are you aware that I rent out my properties exclusively to geologists?'

'Yes. Of course. A fine idea, very fine idea. We really appreciate the ...' Christopher gabbled nervously.

'Oh, be quiet man! And tell me then, please, why you have installed a mob of camp cowboys in my house.'

'Come now Mrs O'Regan. There may be a couple of geological assistants down there, but there are also several geologists— Michelle, Priscilla, Bugsy, Malcolm, James.'

'Camp cowboys, the lot of them. Don't think I don't know what they get up to at night.'

Christopher was silent. He had gone quite pale. I, too, was wondering with dread what scene of drunken debauchery she had stumbled upon, and how we were going to manage this situation.

'They make toasted sandwiches!' she exclaimed in the most accusing and judgmental voice you could imagine, as if she was announcing a particularly heinous crime.

'Is that a problem?' asked Christopher.

'They grill cheese!' she thundered, looking at him with disgust. You'd think he was the ringleader of a gang of thugs, just busted for drug trafficking.

'Oh,' he said in a dazed voice. 'I really don't know what to say.'

'No, I should think not, Mr Craddock! I was inspecting the place this week, and what do you think I found?'

'I really don't know.'

'I found burnt cheese caked on the griller! Filthy! Filthy! Filthy! What sort of establishment do you think you are running here Mr Craddock?'

'Just an oversight, I'm sure Mrs O'Regan. And your house is under the ... er ... the capable supervision of our camp manager. I'm sure she will ensure the grill gets cleaned properly next time.'

'Next time! There won't be a next time! As for your so-called manager, she's got a drinking problem. How can she possibly manage a mob of undisciplined camp cowboys if she can't even manage herself? Ralph there could manage the place with more efficiency.'

She pointed to the dog running in circles around the custard apple tree.

'I am far from impressed!' she continued in a shrill voice. 'In fact, so unimpressed that I am evicting them all.'

'I beg your pardon?' asked Christopher, and I began to laugh, for surely she was joking. I forgot for a moment that humour really wasn't one of Mrs O'Regan's finer points.

She glared in my direction for a moment, then snapped, 'They will leave my house. Every single one. Tonight. The contract is terminated.'

'Isn't that a bit unreasonable?' asked Christopher, quite mildly, considering the circumstances.

'No, it is not. I will be writing to Mr Drake to explain why.' And she swept out, whistling for Ralph.

The next moment Christopher had collapsed on the bench, all hunched up and trembling violently, covering his face with his hands, obviously in the grip of a monumental meltdown. I didn't blame the guy, but it was rather inconvenient, considering the complications of the evening. After all, there wasn't a smidgeon of a chance Mrs O'Regan would forget she had turfed out her tenants, and somebody would have to orchestrate the move.

Just as I wondered what best to do, the shaking subsided and he rose upright and wiped his eyes, and I saw that he hadn't been having a major nervous breakdown at all. He had, in fact, been overtaken by a paroxysm of laughter. What had just transpired had been awful, and would no doubt cause us all great stress, but it had also been absurd, utterly absurd.

'Dear, dear, dear,' he said, still chuckling, 'so we've been thrown out because somebody makes a toasted sandwich and forgets to clean the grill. That's marvellous. If you've seen what I've seen over the years, you'd find that funny.'

And he began to imitate segments of her speech, savouring certain words and phrases like *filthy, filthy, filthy* and *mob of undisciplined camp cowboys.*

Finally, he pulled himself together and said, 'Ah well, I'd better get on with it. Hey James ...'

Out on the veranda James looked up from his daydreams. 'Hi Christopher. How are you doing? Did you see that girl Gerald brought with him the other week? Tiffany? She's hoping to work with us in December ...'

'Forget about that right now. You'll have to finish that beer real quick and go back down to the white house to pack your things. You all have to move out tonight.'

'What?'

'I'm sorry but burnt cheese was found beneath the grill this week and Mrs O'Regan says you all have to move out.'

'But that's ridiculous. I mean you'd expect to find a bit of burnt cheese under the grill. So what? It's not as if she found we'd been grilling mice or rats or something. I'm not going anywhere. The old bat's suddenly gone mad.'

'Well, you could try grovelling to the woman. Apologise for daring to grill cheese at night. Agree to be supervised by Ralph from now on,' Christopher suggested.

'Who the hell is Ralph?'

'Her dog. She thinks he could manage the place better than Jen.'

'What did I say? I mean Jen might have an issue or two but she's better than a bloody dog. The old dame has gone senile, and the kind thing to do is not to pander to her whims, but to take her to the hospital for assessment and give Dennis a call.'

'You could be right about that, James, but who's going to take it on? You? There's not a person in this place she would pay any attention to, not even Michelle or Priscilla or Cynthia.'

'This is all Priscilla's fault in the first place. She's the one who stuffs herself with grilled cheese and hot chocolate in the middle of the night. How she keeps that figure of hers is beyond me,' said James.

Christopher went off to spread the news to all those who dwelt in the white house. 'We've got to move out. And fast! Apparently cheese has been found under the griller.'

There were some rude mutterings about Mrs O'Regan's sanity, but most of those concerned complied agreeably enough. At least it wasn't raining as James had predicted. By dinnertime they were all on the doorstep with bags and swags and sundry belongings. Eddie and I were compelled to move from the biggest bedroom in the house to the smallest, so our room could become a dormitory. Rooster abandoned his room and went to live in the drafting caravan. Malcolm moved in with Christopher, but at least nobody suggested sleeping in our new room as everyone crammed themselves into whatever space they could find. Jen erected her tent beside the custard-apple tree and Michelle and Priscilla stayed with her out there. It wasn't as beautiful as the banana grove at the back of the white house, but at least they had some privacy.

James alone remained unaccommodated. He prowled through the house staring into the bedrooms with resentment.

'There's no way I'll be shoving into one of these rooms,' he said belligerently, forgetting he had been sharing his bedroom in the white house for weeks. 'There's such a thing as personal space you know.'

Finally, he picked up his bundle and stomped off to the shed out the back. He stared at the ping-pong table, Eddie's desk and the store of tinned food. The place had potential. There was plenty of room. With a bit of ingenuity, the erection of a screen or two, he could claim a whole corner. Great idea. He could relax and dream in peace.

None of us were at ease that night when we retired to bed. The change had been far too abrupt for that. I was restless, tossing, turning, listening to the squeals of the shearers stretchers. At some hour in the depths of the night, I got out of bed and went to the kitchen to get a drink of water. There was somebody in the living room, huddled on the sofa, wrapped in a sleeping bag, staring at the walls with tormented eyes.

'James!' I said, 'What's wrong? Are you ill? Do you want a cup of milk or something?'

'Possums!' he whispered in a haunted voice. 'Bloody possums! Hundreds of the things, thumping and squealing and cavorting about.'

So the shed had not been such a great idea after all. But he only looked as if he was dissolving in a heap of apathetic misery. There was life in him yet. He suddenly sat bolt upright, eyes blazing with life.

'Hey, I've got it! I'm brilliant! Jeremy! The truck! The White Elephant!' And off he went to sleep in the truck.

It was midmorning before he pitched up again.

'Well,' he said, looking reasonably refreshed as he fixed himself some coffee and toast. 'Didn't I say a change was coming? Huh, all we need now is an extra bathroom or two and we might just cope till the end of the season.'

'Yeah, mate,' said Grasshopper who wandered into the

kitchen just then. 'You know what's going on here, don't you? It's the work of a jerk. There's always one.'

So, we were back to where we started. Not enough room, not enough beds, not enough bathrooms and still a few weeks to go before we were through.

Chapter 22

The incident on Cobblecundy Road

How DID we cope with these new cosy living arrangements? Endurance is the word that springs to mind. We endured the situation, sometimes with humour, sometimes without. It didn't help that the heat was cranking up again. It became hot, hellishly hot, and it made everything worse. There was no airconditioned comfort to be had in the green house. The best we could do was open the place up and hope the breeze blew in.

But even the breeze had its perils. Hadn't that troublemaking imp blown into the house on the breeze in the first place? The 'wicked spirit' that even Christopher had speculated about, despite his logical mind, was still at large, I was sure, sniggering in the shadows and orchestrating dramas. We may have been a raggedy-taggedy mismatched bunch with widely differing agendas and philosophies of life, but there was not one among us who truly harboured any ill will. We may have misunderstood each other, misinterpreted motives, got on each other's nerves, but there was nobody in that camp who preferred trouble to peace. And yet trouble we got, heading towards us as surely and as steadily as waves heading to the shore.

I didn't have a shred of idealism left about the value of good cooking in making the world a better place. I'd been dishing up wholesome meals for weeks and weeks now and although this physically nourished everyone there was no evidence at all that it made any other impact. There was no occasion when anybody had said, 'Hey, let's stop bickering and focus instead on the joy of eating this delicious meal.' Nothing like that happened and we all got fed up with each other towards the end of the season anyway.

I tried my best to whip up my flagging enthusiasm by choosing unconventional recipes to cook, adding chocolate to casseroles or a tin of tomato soup to cake batter (listed in the cookbook as *Mystery Cake*). But as the heat built up to an overwhelming wave and the flies buzzed about the pig swill, as the dust blew through the house and the humans quarrelled, my job degenerated into an uninspiring slog and I didn't care anymore. My primary consolation was to walk out each day, pushing the baby in her stroller to the highway that led out of town. I always paused for a moment or two to gaze down that bitumen strip until it disappeared into the heat haze. A day was coming when I would travel away from Burkes Hill down that road, and the way I was feeling right then, I didn't care if I ever came back.

The field hands, too, were trying their best to distract themselves, to push through the last weeks. One weekend they tried horse riding as a novelty. I forget how they came by this horse, who it belonged to or where it came from, although I know Priscilla had nothing to do with it. She and her companions spent as little time as possible around the camp at weekends, often hanging out at the milk bar at the end of the main street instead. I can recall, however, looking out the window and seeing a horse in the yard. The field hands were enthusiastically clustered about it as if it was their new best buddy. When I next looked out I could see Paul teetering on its saddleless back while the others cheered. The horse plodded past the mango tree as docile as a pony at a child's birthday party.

I had a meal to cook and no time to linger on the veranda watching the antics of the field hands, so I never saw what transpired later. But I was informed during the course of the afternoon that Sebastian had been carted off to hospital with a suspected broken arm after the horse, fed up, had tossed him from its back. He returned in the evening with his arm in a plaster cast and his ability to work as a field hand suddenly defunct. It was bad timing. He needed just one more instalment to pay for his new false teeth. And they were vital. Missing front teeth don't make a good impression in a job interview.

Eddie, aware of this problem, volunteered to take him on as a field hand just for the next week. Sure, Sebastian wouldn't be able to drive or be much help cooking meals, but he would be a companion, and it would be worth it if he had a better chance of getting another job later when his arm healed. And so off they went together for what was likely to be a very trying week.

* * *

The day they returned from the field turned out to be yet another of those memorable Fridays that marked that year. It was an extremely hot day, one of those days when dogs pant in dusty yards and horses huddle stoically beneath the trees, tails flickering, surrounded by heat shimmers. The people of Burkes Hill had all retreated away from the glare of the day into their shadowy houses. I was in the kitchen preparing a meal. The vegetables on the bench withered before my eyes. The flies cavorted around the pigs' bucket. The pig lady was late, and the swill was stinking in the heat. Nobody had arrived back yet, and I was wishing I was miles away from any kitchen, somewhere cool, swimming in the sea maybe, or walking through a rain-forest on a mountain.

The house filled quickly that afternoon as everybody, exhausted by the heat, came back early. When Eddie arrived, he stomped into the house with Sebastian two steps behind. Sebastian was waving his intact arm in the air and telling an unsavoury story about an unsavoury character he happened to know. He had a store of such stories, one for every occasion. Eddie ignored him, glared at the lolly-pink walls, and charged into the kitchen. He was prickling with irritation. I could almost detect the sparks arcing off his body.

'It's bloody hot,' he said. 'I need a drink.'

This was no homecoming to a welcoming house where he could relax and unwind after a difficult week. The atmosphere was far too hectic for that. The television was already blaring. Michelle was chatting on the phone. James was in the shower down the hallway, while Wally banged on the bathroom door and demanded that he hurry up. Out on the veranda people were downing drinks and yabbering together like a flock of overexcited cockatoos. There would be no quiet moment in which Eddie could settle his ruffled spirit. There was no refuge to be had in that house. And Sebastian was still trailing him, intent on finishing his story. They were heading out the back towards the drinks fridge, when Eddie stumbled on a bag of tinned food which had been left on the floor.

'What the hell's this doing here?'

'Oh, sorry. That's just some traverse food I picked up for Jen. She'll put it away soon.'

'You reckon?' He was right to be doubtful. There was a sound of building revelry in the place, as if nobody apart from the cook had any intention of doing any more work that day. 'What are you doing her shopping for anyway? Don't you have enough to do? Look at you slaving away in this bloody heat while everyone else is partying out there on the veranda.'

'I have to go to the supermarket. I may as well.'

'That's not the point,' said Eddie. 'The lazy cow ...'

I knew straight away that this comment had far less to do with Jen than it did with Sebastian and the difficulties of the past week. It wasn't Eddie's business to know how I chose to arrange my work with Jen, and in any case she had been out in the field that week with Michelle, and it was entirely reasonable that I picked up her shopping. Eddie would have been better off if he had just kicked the furniture instead of projecting his frustrations onto her, particularly as she overheard his remarks and couldn't help but take them personally.

Suddenly there she was in the kitchen between us, sizzling like a sausage on a barbecue, hair sticking on end, hands on hips, eyes glaring at Eddie as if he was a pile of dog poo she had blundered into on a footpath.

Another weekend was beginning badly.

Jen abused Eddie soundly, heaping up the insults and emphasising them with expletives before turning her attention to Sebastian, referring to him as a waste-of-space and listing his defects. Fortunately for all of us Sebastian wasn't in the kitchen right then to hear this. She then declared she wanted nothing further to do with either Eddie or Sebastian and commiserated with me for being involved with losers like them.

'Can't imagine what you see in such a know-it-all prick,' she said.

A bolt of lightning, a clap of thunder, and it was over. Jen went back to the party on the veranda, Eddie went off to have a shower, and I went back to cooking. It had been unpleasant, but everything was unpleasant then and it hardly seemed to matter. We were all hot and bothered. What the hell did anything matter?

The voices outside got louder and louder and then ebbed. I heard the sound of vehicles leaving and realised I was alone. Even Eddie had gone, walking off somewhere with Emily Jane. I went out to the veranda and sat down for a few moments. The heat was receding. The light had softened and there was a rosy glow over everything.

Just as I was taking in the peace, I heard the screech of a vehicle. The GIU troop carrier belted down the road and through the gates, circling the house three times, weaving between the custard apple and the mango tree. There was a tangle of faces in that vehicle as if all the field camp members were stuffed inside, and they were singing at the top of their voices. I thought I saw Jen waving cheerily out the window, but the vision was gone in a flash as the car whizzed by.

They'd all gone mad. I wasn't surprised and I didn't care. Then as swiftly as they had arrived, they were gone again, whizzing up the road with a trail of dust behind them.

Christopher was not around that evening to add his moderating influence to proceedings. He was still out in the field with Paul, hoping to catch up on some extra fieldwork before the season ended. Malcolm wasn't there either. Mia had come north for the weekend and he had gone off somewhere to meet her, well away from Burkes Hill and all its problems.

* * *

Our housemates were very late for dinner that evening. It wouldn't have surprised me if they didn't turn up at all, but they pitched up eventually, remarkably subdued after that wild ride. Jen, pink-eyed, stared at me for a moment like a midnight roo stunned by the headlights on a highway, and fled. Everyone seemed out of sorts all of a sudden. Were these the same people I had seen singing riotously not so long ago? They were now as dispirited as a bunch of puppets left drooping after the puppet master has dropped the strings.

Dinnertime was unusually quiet. Even Sebastian remained silent, at least at the beginning of the meal. James scowled at a sauce bottle; Grasshopper and Bugsy stared at their laps. Rooster, at the end of the table, struggled with his dinner; his right arm was wrapped in a bandage and bound in a sling, although he had been perfectly sound at coffee and cake time that afternoon.

'Rooster, what's happened to you?' I asked.

I had never seen Rooster embarrassed by anything before, but on that evening his face flushed till it shone like a traffic light, as if I had just asked him a completely inappropriate question concerning his private sexual practices. He squirmed in his chair and hung his head.

'Um ah um ah I um I ah,' he mumbled. He seemed to have completely lost his wits.

'What he's trying to say,' said Wally, 'Is that he came by an unfortunate ...'

'Indoor cricket,' interjected Priscilla sharply. 'He injured himself at indoor cricket. They gave him something for pain at the hospital, and just look at him. Poor guy. It's dulled his brain.'

'Indoor cricket, yeah ... yeah ... indoor cricket ...' repeated Rooster faintly.

'Yeah, sure. Indoor cricket. Just what I was going to say. Bloody dangerous game, indoor cricket,' Wally agreed.

They lapsed back into silence. Eddie, disregarding the peculiar atmosphere, took this opportunity to tell everybody about the Devonian fish fossils he had found that week. There wasn't much response to this topic, not even from Bugsy and James, but he went on anyway, filling up the silence with details of exactly which layer he had found them in, which species they belonged to, and the specific characteristics of those species.

'Would you just shut up!' yelled Sebastian eventually. 'The stress of having to listen to you constantly ramble on with long bloody extended explanations. I've never known anyone like you geos for bleating on in such boring bloody detail about matters of complete irrelevance.'

'Palaeontology isn't irrelevant,' Eddie protested.

'What! Some random fish dies a few million years ago. Big bloody deal. Nah, I've had enough. I'm getting out of here this week and when my arm's fixed I'm going to get a real job.'

'What's a real job, then?' asked Eddie.

'I want to be a garbo. Emptying the rubbish bins. That's a real job. An honourable job. Makes a real difference to peoples' lives. And the pay's good and it'll keep me fit.'

If I thought dinnertime was odd, the rest of the evening was odder still. I had turned the television off when they all went out, but nobody bothered switching it back on. Nobody inserted a video and settled into a swivel chair to watch a movie. Nobody went to the pub. Instead, a group huddled awkwardly on the veranda, whispering together. It was very strange to see Priscilla and Michelle, heads inclined towards Wally and Grasshopper, whispering tenderly.

By this time, I was well aware that something was going on, that they all shared a secret, and that Eddie and I were excluded from it. But did I care? Not at all. As for Eddie, he wasn't remotely interested in what anyone else was up to. Once Emily Jane was in bed, he was off to the shed to stare at his maps. I went out to the veranda briefly, not to pry, but to retrieve a book I had left on a chair. They clammed up immediately and Priscilla nudged Wally, who stumbled towards me grinning broadly.

'Hey Cynthia, I was hoping you could do me a favour. Yeah. You see, um … I have this dream … you could call it an ambition. I wanna be real good at my job. Yeah. And I wanna improve my cooking. You know, learn how to make scones for instance. Yeah. Then I could make Devonshire tea out in the scrub for the geos. Get a bit of jam, some long-life cream. Wouldn't that be a thrill for them? "Jeez Wally," they'd say, "You're not as dumb as you look." D'you reckon you can teach me?'

'What?' I asked. 'You want to learn how to make scones? Now?'

'No better time than now is there? For anything really. Hey, I've got an idea. How about I clean your oven while you explain it all to me and write out the recipe. Yeah, I like to keep myself busy.'

I already knew a mystery was afoot, but I didn't realise how BIG a mystery it was until Wally volunteered to clean the oven and learn how to make scones instead of shooting off to the pub. Even so, I had no curiosity about it and I didn't lie awake that night wondering what was going on. There are some things it's better not to know.

* * *

The knock at the door came very early the next morning. There was still a watermelon glow in the sky; the sun had barely risen. We were in our pyjamas, putting the second pin in the baby's nappy, when the door to our bedroom slid open. Jen stood in the doorway.

'I've come to apologise,' she said.

'It's okay Jen,' said Eddie. 'I didn't behave well either. Let's put it down to the heat and forget it.'

'Yeah, well, thanks. But look, I gotta come clean. There's something you don't know. There was an accident yesterday on Cobblecundy Road, after the radio skit with Christopher and Paul. I rolled the vehicle. It's a write off. Could have been killed. We all could have been killed. It's made me see things a bit differently. We shouldn't be going round making fusses about nothin'.'

'Yeah, I agree with you, Jen,' said Eddie. 'But Jeez, what happened? Where's the vehicle?'

'Out the back. Come and see.'

The sight of the crumpled wreck dumped behind the shed explained quite a lot about the previous evening. Eddie took one look and said, 'Oh my God. How the hell did this happen?'

'It was a nightmare,' Jen said. 'You know that time when the light fades? Lots of kangaroos and weird shadows about. You start to see things that aren't there. Logs start to look like dinosaurs. And the road ahead just seems to vanish or bend away, but it's still there going straight on. Suddenly you're driving right on the edge of the road, that slippery part where you sort of get sucked off.'

'Sucked off the road?' echoed Eddie.

'Yeah. Sucked off the road. Kind of. That's what happened to us. Next we were just rolled in the ditch.'

'Oh well. Cobblecundy Road. It's a bit tricky at the best of times,' said Eddie.

'Hey, what's Christopher going to say when he gets back today? This season's been one bloody thing after another. And now this ...,' said Jen.

But amazingly, Christopher was completely unfazed when he strolled back in later that day. This latest event, rather than pushing him over the edge, just seemed to nudge him towards a state of philosophic serenity. Nothing was going to bother him now. Accidents happen. Vehicles roll. It was fortunate there were no serious injuries. It was just a matter of following the protocol.

'We're not the first to roll a vehicle this season, anyway. They did one up at Bogarilla, weeks ago,' he said.

That mischief-making sprite must have been bitterly disappointed by this response. At that moment he probably packed his bags, evaporated back up into the breeze and wafted off to find another household to torment. It's clearly time to move on when your victims are no longer troubled by the troubles.

Not that the drama was over. As Christopher said, there was a protocol to be followed and Jen had not followed it. She and her passengers had been rescued from their predicament by a pub acquaintance who happened to be driving along Cobble-cundy Road at the time. This guy also organised some unorthodox means of getting the wreck back to the camp. The police were not involved and had not been contacted at all.

'You'll have to notify them,' said Christopher. 'It's not as if we can get away with calling this a minor ding. That vehicle will never drive again.'

When the policeman arrived, Jen and Christopher escorted him out the back to view the wreck. He wasn't as helpful as the Bogarilla cop, simplifying the whole thing by blaming a kanga-roo, but he seemed to find changing light conditions and a slip-pery road surface a reasonably plausible explanation for the incident. The paperwork was signed, and the wreck was towed away. And that should have been the end of it, but it wasn't, not quite.

A few doubts were fluttering about my mind, but they didn't settle on anything concrete.

'I saw that vehicle yesterday,' I said to Eddie. 'They were driving really crazy, round and round the house. But it wasn't Jen driving.'

'Which means precisely what?' asked Eddie. 'It doesn't mean she wasn't driving later.'

'No, but what was that whispering group all about? What were they trying to hide? Why didn't they just tell us what had happened?'

'They weren't thinking straight, I expect,' replied Eddie.

'And bonding with each other after a near-death experience. Understandable, I suppose.'

'And Wally cleaning the oven instead of going to the pub. Don't you find that strange?'

'About time the guy grew up,' replied Eddie.

And the season continued to grind on until a day came when we packed our bags and left Burkes Hill behind as we travelled south. None of us gave another thought to the incident on Cobblecundy Road. Not for several weeks at any rate.

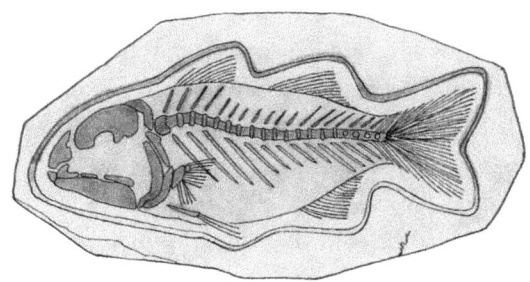

Chapter 23

Mr Silvertongue

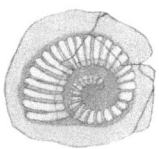

'THE CATS OUT OF THE BAG!' said Eddie with a grin.

He had just come home after a day at the GIU head office in Brisbane. I didn't have a clue what he was talking about. We had been back from Burkes Hill for several weeks now and well into the swing of a different life. As for the incident on Cobblecundy Road, it was over; best forgotten like the rest of the field season. But no, Eddie said that day, the incident wasn't over at all. Another version of the story had just come to light.

If it hadn't been James's birthday, it's likely that the real facts behind the accident would have been permanently obscured. But Malcolm Drake organised a birthday bash for him in a city hotel at lunchtime, and tongues were loosened. That morning Malcolm had passed around a hat for James, encouraging the staff to chuck in their spare change. He said he had a gift in mind that would be presented at the hotel bar during lunch. It would be well worth coming down to watch. At least, this is what he told the men. To the women, he spoke in a subtly insinuating voice that implied they would enjoy themselves much more in the downstairs café.

'No, I wouldn't advise going to that bar,' said Priscilla to

Tiffany, the student who had visited Burkes Hill with Gerald, and who was doing holiday work with the GIU. She was currently going out with James, a fact that surprised nobody. 'It's foul. It's noisy and stinks of beer and cigarettes. Can't imagine how anyone puts up with it. And all they serve to eat is pie and chips. Horrible. Come and eat with us downstairs. Then you can go somewhere classier with James after work.'

Eddie and Christopher, not usual lunchtime pub patrons, went along out of deference for Malcolm and James, although in truth they found the bar about as appealing as Priscilla did. However, they strolled into the place, ordered a beer and a steak sandwich (also on the menu), found a table, and waited.

Potts, who had come into the city for the occasion, was sitting at the bar with his friend Micky Wren. Micky worked as a lab assistant for the GIU over the summer. They were in tremendous spirits, bought James a birthday drink, and rowdily called for Malcolm to bring in the present.

At that moment a rather remarkable woman arrived at the pub. She was tall and plump and wore a maid's costume of the scantiest dimensions. Her face was brightly made up with splashes of red. She had red ribbons in her hair and a feather duster in her hand. Crowing with laughter, Malcolm greeted her and thrust her towards James, who paled with horror at the sight of this 'present'. She tickled his face and his crotch with the feather duster, sang him a rude song, then took a seat and pulled him on her lap.

Christopher groaned, 'What the hell was Malcolm thinking? This is appalling. Look at the poor guy, all slumped over. Looks dead.'

By this time the woman had removed her underwear and was cheerfully flapping it about. James, at the centre of this activity, was having the worst time of his life. Worse than possums in swags, worse than rain in black soil country, worse than driving with Sebastian. But if James was having a hideous time, Potts and Micky were having a ball.

Eddie said he thought the woman was a family connection of Micky's and that Malcolm had got mate's rates on the deal.

Fortunately, the swirl of embarrassment was quickly over. The over-inflated maid wished James a happy birthday, presented him with a bottle of whisky and planted a kiss upon his face, leaving behind an absurd crimson smudge across his mouth. And then she was gone. James slumped across the bar, breathing heavily.

'Wake up James,' said Malcolm cheerily. 'I'll buy you some lunch'

Potts and Micky, buoyed with laughter, caught sight of Christopher finishing his steak sandwich.

'Aha, look Micky. There he is. Mr Silvertongue himself,' said Potts.

This must have bewildered Christopher. Nobody had called him that before.

'Yeah, we reckon you're the best in the game,' continued Potts, pulling up a chair beside him. 'Bloody marvellous.'

'Yep,' said Micky. 'You sure pulled a swiftie.'

Christopher and Eddie had no idea what this was all about.

'Still, that cop must have been a bit of a twit, hey,' reflected Potts. 'I mean swallowing all that crap you told him about that vehicle getting sucked off the road. But you couldn't exactly have told him the truth. So ...'

'The truth ...' echoed Christopher faintly.

'Yeah, you could hardly tell him that Jen was as pissed as a fart and pulled the handbrake on Rooster just as he was taking that bend. Dunno what trouble Jen'd be in and as for the insurance ...' Micky blundered on, completely failing to observe the stunned expression on Christopher's face.

He only noticed something was wrong when Christopher suddenly bolted out of the hotel.

'What's wrong with him?'

'We've gone and done it this time Mick. Put our feet in it big time. He wasn't in on the scheme at all. Jen's going to be in the shit now. Jeez Micky, why didn't we just keep our mouths shut?' said Potts.

Eddie excused himself and raced out after Christopher, back up the hot footpath, catching him just as the doors to the GIU building swept open to swallow him. They walked together into the foyer, which was cool and impersonal, despite the smiling security man who stood guard at the entrance. Although it was soothing after the clamour of the public bar, Christopher was clearly agitated.

'Did you hear that conversation?' he asked. 'Apparently, it's common knowledge, gossiped about in the bars of Brisbane, how I signed a completely fraudulent insurance claim, knowingly and willingly, to save the skin of an utterly irresponsible ...'

'Well, I've not heard of it before this,' said Eddie.

'I really don't know what to do,' said Christopher. 'I'll have to go and see Gerald.'

Eddie went with him into a lift, straight up to the sixteenth floor. Gerald was bent over some paperwork, dozing off to the drone of the airconditioner.

'I can't say I share your concerns about this one, Craddock,' he said, after he'd woken up and heard Christopher's story. 'Pub gossip is never worth a pinch of ... I wouldn't give this story any credence at all.'

'But the implications ...'

'Are nonexistent. Look at it this way. Were Potts and Wren based at Burkes Hill when this event occurred?'

'Well no. No, they weren't.'

'And you? Were you based at Burkes Hill?'

'Yes, but ...'

'Then why are you paying any attention to their assessment of it?' asked Gerald.

'When you put it like that ...'

Eddie said Christopher was beginning to look like a prisoner in the dock who has suddenly heard a not guilty verdict when he was expecting life imprisonment, but he wasn't completely satisfied.

'It's still very disturbing to me that people are saying this, thinking this,' he said.

'Oh, people say and think all sorts of things,' remarked Gerald with a shrug. 'They say that dinosaur fossils are the work of the devil, that there are elves in the pantry, that bunnies lay eggs. Let them think it. Doesn't make any of it true.'

'Thanks Gerald. You've been really helpful,' said Christopher.

Actually, both he and Eddie were inclined to think that Micky Wren's story was closer to the truth than the version they had been told, but it was definitely more convenient to go along with Gerald on this one.

'But', said Gerald, 'We're kidding ourselves if we pretend that this season was an unqualified success. It wasn't all we'd hoped for, was it? Quite a few problems up at Burkes Hill. Take Jen, for example—great field hand, great technician, but perhaps not yet ready for leadership.'

'To be perfectly frank with you Gerald, Wilma O'Regan caused far more problems than Jen,' said Christopher.

'Oh yes. She was the troublemaker,' agreed Eddie. 'The old lady was a bit demanding, a wee bit unreasonable.'

'So I have discovered,' said Gerald. 'I had a letter of complaint from her. Look it up: it's on file. She wrote that Jen has an alcohol problem and can't control the filthy habits of the other staff.'

'Jen did seem to fall out of favour as the season went by,' Christopher commented.

'Yes, but when I looked into the matter, the worst Wilma could come up with was that there was some cheese caked on the griller. That doesn't seem very serious to me. In the light of that, I assume the alcohol problem means Jen has an occasional beer.'

'She's no worse than any of the other field hands,' said Christopher.

'Well, if that's all it was ... But there were other issues. There was that day she rang me in hysterics about that field hand. Slanger, that's right. Your brother, I think,' said Gerald, turning to Eddie.

'Yes, my brother Sebastian,' said Eddie. 'He's moved on, found a new niche collecting the garbage for the Cairns City Council.'

'A change, hey? I've heard it can do wonders. Maybe that's just what Jen needs. Perhaps she's been doing the same thing for too many years now. Probably getting her down. It's not the camp manager job she's needing, but something completely different. Look at that young mechanic fella ... I saw him on television the other night advertising cats' biscuits. He looked marvellous. He'll be in a soap opera next. Yes ... and come to think of it, we do need help out Thargomindah right now. She'd be a good fit, a real good fit.'

This is how the twist and turns of our lives can be determined, not by the force of our wills, but by a stray conversation or a random association of ideas. Suddenly the road ahead takes a sharp turn to the left when we were expecting to it to roll straight on for miles and miles.

The next day Jen was given a new opportunity at Thargomindah. Gerald might have been over-optimistic about the prospects of the field season just gone, but he was not mistaken about Jen fitting in at Thargomindah. Paul passed through the town a year later and called in to see her.

'She's kinda different,' he reported.

'Like how?' asked Grasshopper. 'You mean she wouldn't have a drink at the pub with you?'

'She still likes a beer. But she talks a lot about Buddhism. Grows veggies for a hobby. Gave me a jar of chutney. And she's got someone, a friend off one of the properties, comes into town to stay with her sometimes. Actually she seems real happy.'

Chapter 24

The Compound

I BLINKED A FEW TIMES, hoping the figure I had just seen would disappear; perhaps it was a trick of the light, nothing but a figment of my imagination. But the man kept on standing there, solid as a rock, clutching a plastic basket and surveying a wall of toothpaste.

What was Bill Sapshort doing here? In my supermarket? In Brisbane?

I backed out of that aisle as quick as I could. He had been so intent on the array of toothpaste before him that he couldn't possibly have noticed me. I would have been nothing but a blur of colour and movement. I pushed the trolley to the far corner of the building where the fridges were concealed by tall shelves containing plastic bags of bread. Here I could linger while Bill made his selection and went on his way doing whatever it was he was in Brisbane to do.

But apparently, Bill was in that supermarket specifically to remind me one more time of why I never wanted to be a cook again. Suddenly there he was beside me, reaching out for a packet of cheese slices, grinning at me in that ghastly way, delighted at the coincidence that had brought us together beside the cheese fridge, evidently under the impression that I would be equally as delighted to reminisce about 'that roast' in Blue Ridge. That meal must have been the highlight of his life, the way he went on about it whenever we met.

I never found out what Bill was doing in Brisbane. He was far too interested in dwelling on my culinary failures to tell me anything else, but I do know that he found time during his stay to visit GIU headquarters and to catch up with Gerald Drake. This was to be a serendipitous encounter, the meeting of minds that produced quite a spark, that moment when the concept of the Compound was born. 'The best working environment of the north' as Gerald foresaw, perhaps a little too optimistically.

It was no surprise that Bill and Gerald would have discussed the problems at Burkes Hill. Bill was a resident there and knew all about the issues. As they sipped their morning coffee, they would have commiserated with each other about the shortage of decent accommodation, particularly now Wilma O'Regan had banned the GIU from using any of her properties.

What was to be done?

As Bill contemplated the problem, it occurred to him to remind Gerald that the GIU had property in Burkes Hill, a large but barren tract of land on the other side of town from College Road, near the railway line. It was the site of an old gold mine, but all that remained was the trash. The place was littered with old mullock heaps and riddled with disused mine work-ings. Ah, but for Gerald it was so much more than this. Today's problems, yesterday's problems, were all forgotten, submerged by the joy of planning for a more brilliant and problem-free future as Bill and Gerald enthused each other with a new vision for this neglected old rubbish heap.

'We'll landscape it!'

'Fence it!'

'Put an ablutions block on it!'

'Bring in some caravans and dongas from the drill camps!'

With a vision of the completed compound gleaming in his mind's eye, Gerald said, 'It will be marvellous. This should be the best field season of all time!'

I suspect Bill later regretted mentioning that old gold mine to Gerald, no matter how much enthusiasm there had been at the beginning. He couldn't just fling the suggestion out and walk away, not once he was selected to personally supervise the development of the Compound project. He was also delegated to the role of party leader for the coming field season. Christopher would be too busy in the office writing reports to do any fieldwork that year. So, although Bill had looked so cheery when I saw him in the supermarket with his basket of toilet paper, toothpaste and cheese, that grin was soon to be replaced with a nervous smile and a careworn frown.

Bill was every bit as qualified as Christopher to oversee the mapping program, but his geological training had not equipped him in any way at all with the skills he needed to manage a construction project. It was a stretch. Perhaps not so extreme a stretch as Bugsy had to endure later on in his career, somewhere in the wilds of New Guinea, when he was expected to deliver a baby on the basis of his geological education, but bad enough. It's not that Bill didn't try his best to fulfil the vision that he and Gerald had dreamt of, it's just that he lacked the experience to know where the pitfalls lay. What had sounded so simple when discussed over a cup of coffee, turned out to be far more complicated.

He immediately organised for the Compound to be landscaped. Well, sort of. A man arrived with a machine, flattened a few of the mullock heaps, inadvertently severed the main water pipe on the property and left. Bill also arranged for unused dongas and caravans to be brought in from the drilling camps. These were plonked in military alignment on the flattened earth. The area was enclosed with an enormous fence topped with barbed wire, as if the place was intended to secure dangerous criminals. Security lights were installed and the ablutions block was brought in.

The ablutions block was amazing, or it should have been. It was a pre-constructed building featuring whole rows of toilets, showers and washing machines, everything that had been in short supply the previous year. But it was as much use as a mirage in the desert, just a fancy façade perched on a flattened mullock heap. The 'landscaper' was blamed for this disgrace but blaming him solved nothing and nobody in Burkes Hill knew how to correct the problem and connect the ablutions block with the water supply.

By the time the staff arrived in the north, the sparkling new work environment that Gerald imagined he was providing did not exist. Instead, the workers stood behind the great gates lined with barbed wire and surveyed a mess of upturned earth, gaping ditches and dusty caravans. There was no running water and the most basic of facilities were lacking.

'Looks bloody awful,' said Wally.

'Oh well, you'll have to make the best of it,' said Bill Sapshort, blinking out at his creation through his spectacles. 'See it as a work in progress. It could be worse. At least you've all got space.'

Priscilla took one look and knew straight away that she would not be living at the Compound. No way. She phoned Gerald and demanded alternative accommodation.

'A few teething problems, are there?' he asked indulgently, agreeing that she and Big Jill could rent a flat, at least initially.

Priscilla had lost her companions that year. Jen was already working out at Thargomindah and Michelle, in need of a lifestyle change, had gone to study education. Big Jill would join the Burkes Hill team that year instead. And James would go to

Bogarilla for the first couple of months of the season. Big Jill wasn't as bothered by the Compound as Priscilla was. She was inclined to shrug off inconveniences with a tin of beer and a crude joke, and she wasn't the type to object to urinating at night behind a mullock heap in the middle of a populated district, but if Gerald wanted to supply a flat, she wasn't going to refuse.

The green house in College Road was leased again, but was reserved for the use of the cook, the draftsman, and any temporary visitors. Even so, the place swarmed with people as all the other staff were obliged to drive across town to College Road if they wanted to eat a meal, wash their clothes, or use the bathroom. Driving across town to use a toilet becomes tiresome very quickly, and it wasn't long before everyone gave up and just stumbled out amongst the mullock heaps instead, hoping they were sufficiently hidden from the neighbours.

Yes. This was substandard. And yet I was planning to go there. Although at the end of the last season I had thought that I didn't care if I ever saw Burkes Hill again, I reconsidered when I heard that Gerald was planning extensive new field-camp accommodation up that way. If we weren't all going to be crammed in one smallish house and there was some other cook with the responsibility of feeding everybody, then Burkes Hill might be a different experience entirely. Something like a holiday.

So once again Emily Jane and I headed north, this time with a more carefree spirit. I can't recall if I was warned about the Compound. It's possible Eddie minimised the problems for fear I would cancel the trip. Nobody really wants to know that the facilities at their holiday destination are likely to be far worse than those they would encounter if they were going to be incarcerated for a few weeks at the Boggo Road Jail, where at least the prisoners had access to clean running water and flushing toilets. It's also possible that he tried to warn me, but I heard only what I wanted to hear and brushed the rest aside as gross exaggeration or some twisted idea of a joke.

Not that I could keep kidding myself that everything was fine once the plane had landed in Townsville and I saw Eddie heading towards us. There was something hesitant in his carriage and a distinct lack of jaunt. He stood silently for a few seconds before saying, 'Thank God you've arrived,' in a strangled voice.

This was not normal. Things became stranger still as we drove through the ironbarks towards Burkes Hill.

'You will be nice to Paul, won't you Cynthia?' he asked, a most peculiar question.

'Why wouldn't I be nice to Paul? I like the guy.'

'You see, he's done something ... noble ... Just for you, really,' Eddie continued.

'Oh, like what?'

'Well, he drove down here to Townsville a couple of days ago and hired a Port-a-loo.'

If I had thought things weren't right when I first saw Eddie, now the warning bells really rang out. 'Eddie, are you trying to tell me there are no toilets in this camp?'

'Oh no, no, no. Not at all. You needn't worry about that. There are toilets. Plenty of toilets. It's just that none of them work yet.'

'So, what you're saying is that there is a whole community living at this place, but not a functional toilet?'

'No, no, I just said. Paul fixed all that. Came down Thursday. But it was hot that day and those port-a-loo things aren't designed to be towed so far. Wheels melted on the bitumen on the way up. And it wobbles if you use it. He's a bit sensitive about it after going to all that trouble, so pretend it's all great and you don't notice it, okay?'

'But why should this be Paul's worry? I thought Bill was running the show this year.'

'Well, Bill's supervising the mapping, but as for the rest ... he's losing his grip. The Compound was supposed to be ready and it's nothing but a shambles. Not sure it's all his fault. I mean he's not a builder, is he? And then Gerald makes Paul camp manager. Absolute misfortune for the poor guy. I mean he'd much prefer to be coming out with us and shooting pigs. Instead, he's got a few problems on his hands. Well, more than a few. It's been rotten actually.'

'Aah.'

'Yeah, and the washing machine at the green house exploded last week. It was the last straw. I mean there's always the laundromat in town, but nothing seems to work. Even Malcolm broke down last week. Burst right into tears, and you know how upbeat he usually is.'

I knew from this conversation not to expect luxury, but even so, I was unprepared for how utterly squalid the Compound actually was—the expanse of dirt, the barbed wire, the port-a-loo precarious beside a dusty donga. Bugsy Burrell and Malcolm Drake emerged from this mess, unshaven and unkempt, looking just as if they had been shipwrecked in a sea of filth.

Malcolm waved a limp arm about. 'Welcome to the Compound Cynthia,' he said.

'Yeah, welcome,' said Bugsy. 'That's your donga over there, at the end of the row.'

'But it's not safe,' I said.

A deep trench had been dug directly beneath the doorsteps of the whole row of dongas. On the other side of the trench were huge mounds of red clay studded with rocks and other detritus. This was not a remotely suitable residence for a family with a toddler, even though the toddler in question was the only one of us viewing this spectacle with any degree of enthusiasm.

'Why are those trenches there?' I asked. 'It's a miracle you haven't all broken your necks just trying to get through the door.'

'Well, yes, it's a hazard all right,' said Malcolm. 'I assume it's all to do with the plumbing system—the nonexistent plumbing system, that is. It's said that once upon a time a man came to landscape this place, but he took fright and ran away. He's never been back, as you can see. And so here we all are. Sub-par I know.'

We climbed the huge mound of dirt and leapt over the trench into our donga, and so began my first sojourn at the Compound.

Chapter 25

Porridge

THE COMPOUND MAY HAVE BEEN SO abysmal that it made Mrs O'Regan's white house on College Road look like the Ritz, but at least the GIU had managed to appoint a decent cook. Sally was a woman neither young nor old, who had the first streaks of grey in her hair. She liked clothes of crumpled cotton from India and wore a string of beads about her left ankle. Sally was totally absorbed in her work and didn't say much, but her casual appearance gave the impression of a relaxed and easygoing soul.

Sally had spent the previous decade cooking in restaurants along the east coast from Byron Bay to Noosa, in quirky little places that got rave reviews from the Sunday papers. I guess she thought that a stint of cooking in the north with the GIU would make a pleasant change from the restaurant scene. In fact, she was far too qualified for the camp cook job, which called more for wholesome family fare and comfort food than exquisitely plated cuisine nouvelle, and some of the field hands weren't so impressed with her sensational cooking, preferring large plates of meat and potatoes 'served plain'. But almost everybody else saw her as a treasure, a sort of magical being sent along by fate to cheer them up in their misery.

Not that she wasn't watched rather carefully at the beginning of the season. After all, she was a cook and they all knew how troublesome cooks could be. Even though there had been no issues with troublesome cooks over the last couple of years, that old myth that all cooks were bad news had not entirely faded away. It was possible she was too good to be true and that sooner or later a crack would appear. But when Grasshopper suggested that he suspected Sally had fallen in love with Bill Sapshort everybody scoffed.

'Don't talk rubbish!' interrupted Malcolm. 'No woman could possibly be in love with Bill. I mean he's practically a geriatric, almost nursing home material.'

'I heard Sally telling him a dirty joke yesterday,' said Grasshopper, as if this was reasonable evidence of a love affair.

'Yeah? Well Sally told me that joke too and she's not in love with me. That's obvious. No, Sally is probably the victim of a tragic romance and now just devotes herself to her art.'

'Yeah, but he laughed,' said Grasshopper, although this was more an indication of how rare it was for Bill to laugh nowadays. He hadn't even smirked at me when I arrived, hadn't even so much as mentioned that roast. In the bigger scheme, a raw roast is a fleeting thing of just one moment, one day, and pales into insignificance beside the catastrophe of the uncompleted Compound, that non-functional eyesore that the staff had to cope with week after week.

Like everybody else, Sally had her flaws. She thought her responsibility ended at the plate and seemed unaware of the pig-trough conditions in which her gourmet treats were eaten. She never looked in the dining room and ate her meals alone on the veranda, where she sucked furiously on cigarettes and gazed out into the distance. But the dining room had not been cleaned for weeks and the table was thick with spilt tomato sauce, jam, mustard and melted butter. There were ashtrays full of cigarette butts and weeks of old newspapers, some glued to the table with remnants of food left behind from previous meals. And into this trash heap arrived plates, all delicately arranged with a variety of taste sensations. I can only imagine that the dining room looked fine to people accustomed to the view of mullock heaps and barbed wire at the Compound, and it hadn't occurred to them that it was in any way inappropriate to eat such fine food in such a lousy environment.

In the mornings Sally pottered about the kitchen in bare feet, a cotton smock popped over her dress, and all may have appeared well at the green house, but Sally wasn't as relaxed as she seemed. This became apparent on the day Emily Jane inserted a pencil into the video player just moments before the field hands planned to watch a movie. A momentary lapse of attention on my part, just a few seconds of distraction, and the cook was short a pencil and the field hands set for disappointment.

This awkward moment was made much worse when Sally took the whole thing poorly, making us all aware that her temperament wasn't as serene as had been supposed. She exploded with rage, treating me with a severity out of all proportion to the circumstances. You'd have thought a precious jewel had been lost to the oceanic abyss because of my irresponsibility, and she went on at me about how it shouldn't have happened with as much tenacity as Bill Sapshort carrying on about the raw roast, minus his humour. I feared that mothers and babies were going to be forever banished from the premises, and we would be forced to eat meals in isolation at the Compound.

It wasn't as if she was going to miss the opportunity to view some great classic film either. The movie appeared to have been fished from a bin of cheap discards at the local roadhouse. The cover displayed a cheesy drawing of an unnaturally busty blonde woman in a cavewoman costume, wielding a cobra like a weapon. It was the type of movie Wally wouldn't have dared to bring near the place if Priscilla was likely to visit.

As it turned out, Rooster fixed the machine in five minutes with a screwdriver and a pair of tweezers, so there was nothing to prevent the field hands' excursion into mindless oblivion after all, and Sally got her pencil back.

'Don't worry, Cynthia,' Rooster had whispered as he bent over the player, 'Poor Sally has been working too hard. Even on her days off, she sits out on the veranda reading *Gourmet* magazines. Besides, I don't reckon anything Wally picked is likely to be much chop. Complete rubbish probably.'

The whole incident was scarcely worth the discharge of emotion it had caused, but it was evident that Sally was desperately in need of a break. It was fortunate that she would be able to get some time out the next weekend when a fund-raising dance at the local football club was scheduled. This occasion promised to be a great night out for everybody, including Sally. There were bands coming up from Townsville and food available all evening. This was the chance for her to have an evening off and for the GIU to support the local community by buying their dinners at the football club and attending the dance.

When the night of the dance finally arrived, we all got to the club early and sat around the tables in the stiff, polite manner of people who know they'll be letting their hair down some time soon but aren't quite ready yet. Bugsy offered to buy a round of drinks and blinked a few times when Sally ordered a triple scotch. Malcolm leant towards her and said with encouragement, 'That's the spirit!'

When the drinks came, Sally threw hers down her throat as

if it was lemonade and went to order another, and then another. A few uneasy glances were cast about the table, but the music started and soon enough nobody noticed what the cook was up to anymore. By the time Eddie and I left with our drooping child, they were all bouncing about the dance floor in an uninhibited way and Malcolm was swaying to the music in the grip of one of the local girls who had been dancing next to him.

* * *

'Just another day in paradise.'

It was morning, and these words came lilting across the dirt and ditches. I stuck my head out the door and saw Malcolm sitting on the doorstep of his donga, right next to ours. He was lacing his boots and looking out cheerfully at the sun shining on the mullock heaps. I doubted if he could remember either the name or the face of the girl with whom he had been clasped the night before, but even so the experience had evidently done him the world of good.

'It's a fine morning!' he called out.

Malcolm rarely suffered hangovers, not like Grasshopper who right at that moment stumbled out sleepily from behind a mullock heap.

'Hey, what you lot doin' up so early?' he muttered. 'I need another ten hours sleep at least.'

'Feeling a bit poorly, are we?' asked Malcolm. 'Not going to join us for breakfast?'

'Jeez no ... ah dunno ... maybe. Yeah, nah, yeah ... okay.'

We piled into a vehicle and drove across town to College Road for breakfast.

'I wonder what delights Sally has in store for us this morning?' asked Malcolm on the way. 'Croissants stuffed with bacon and herbs? Eggs benedict? I'm starving. What a treasure Sally is. Good to see her loosening up a bit last night.'

'Huh!' muttered Grasshopper, but Malcolm took this not as a comment that might have warned him to lower his expectations, but as a complaint about hangover and headache.

The green house was silent. There was no fragrance of cooking drifting out and no breakfast clatter could be heard. Nevertheless, Malcolm went striding eagerly into the house. Sally could not be seen, but she had left a pot and a pile of bowls on the bench.

'Mmmmm, I wonder what's in here,' said Malcolm, lifting the lid with a hand that trembled in anticipation. 'Oh yuk! Porridge!'

'Yum! Porridge! Just what I feel like,' said Grasshopper. 'I get sick of all this fancy stuff that Sally cooks. I love porridge.' He too lifted the lid, then rammed it shut again. 'That's not porridge! That's some kind of glue!'

'What's going on?' asked Malcolm, thrusting his hands on his hips and peering into the empty kitchen.

'Jeez mate, what were you expecting?' asked Grasshopper. 'I mean, I feel pretty crook myself and I just drank beer, not triple scotches ... and then there was that other business. Sally must be feeling terrible right now—body and soul.'

'Body and soul? What are you waffling about? What other business?'

'If you hadn't been slobbering over that girl, you might have seen for yourself. I tried to tell you Sally was in love with someone.'

'But Bill wasn't at the dance last night,' said Eddie.

Bill, who had suggested everybody attend the function, failed to turn up himself.

'It's not Bill,' said Grasshopper. 'You won't believe this, but Sally has the hots for... She has the hots for ...'

'Spit it out,' said Malcolm impatiently. 'For who?'

'For Big Jill. They were dancing side by side. Sally suddenly rammed her hand fair between Big Jill's legs.'

'What? Are you trying to tell me the cook has the hots for Big Jill? God help us. It's hopeless. Big Jill goes for great big brawny men like Joe what's-his-name at Bogarilla, not lady cooks. What the hell next? No wonder there's nothing but porridge on the bench this morning,' said Malcolm.

'Yeah, and Big Jill doesn't know her own strength. Dunno, quite what she did, whether she punched her or what, but next thing poor Sally's flying across the dance floor.'

'Not the most subtle of overtures perhaps,' murmured Eddie, making an attempt on a bowl of porridge.

'What are you eating that muck for? Let's give Sally a break. Give her a chance to get over it. We can go to McDonalds for breakfast,' said Malcolm.

Malcolm hoped that if we all gave Sally some space, she could get over her frustrations and embarrassments, pull herself together, and be back in top form for dinner. But he was disappointed. Dinner was more revolting than breakfast had been. Sally slammed two pots on the bench and fled to her room. One revealed a foul mixture of cold browned mince and tomato sauce, the other a mass of carelessly cooked pasta. Silently we began to devour this mess.

Malcolm nearly choked, pushed his plate aside and stared accusingly at Big Jill. 'I hear you're responsible for this. Sally's cooking was all I was living for in this ghastly hole and you have to go and resort to violence. It was completely uncalled for. You don't have to publicly humiliate a person to say 'no'. There's such a thing as tact.'

'Cool it, Malcolm. I didn't mean to hurt her feelings; it was just a reflex action, that's all. I've already apologised. Anyway, don't know what you're complaining about. There's nothing wrong with this tucker. Tastes all right to me,' said Big Jill.

She scraped her plate clean and went back for a second helping. 'Sally just partied a bit too hard, that's all. She'll be right by tomorrow.'

But the next morning, Sally served porridge again.

Chapter 26

Three field hands

ON SUNDAY AFTERNOON, three shabby men swaggered into the Compound to meet Paul. They were the field hands employed directly from Burkes Hill to simplify accommodation. As the afternoon breeze blew the dust across the Compound, one of them slumped with Wally on the heap of dirt near our donga. There really wasn't any place more suitable to sit.

'Hey, hey, hey,' I heard him say unpleasantly, 'I'm in luck.'

'Yeah?' said Wally.

'Yeah, it's my turn out with that cute little sheila this week.'

'Really? And exactly what kind of luck do you call that?' Wally replied.

'Aw mate, you know!' and the bloke chuckled suggestively in a most revolting manner.

'Nah, mate. Can't say I do know. At least not where she's concerned. She might look like a pussycat, but she's more of the sabre-tooth tiger variety. Not to be messed with. And the only creature she lets near is her pet bloody dog. You'll have that fleabag along for the week, and if you'd take my advice, you won't want to get on the wrong side of it.'

'Stop your bullshit, Wally. I know how to handle a dog, and I know how to handle a bloody woman.'

This guy may have imagined he was Brad Pitt, but he can't have looked in a mirror anytime recently. He had a bulging beer gut, lank greasy hair and a bad skin. I know looks aren't everything, but in this case there were no other obvious redeeming features like sweet nature or sharp wit. Although Priscilla was clearly shining like a beacon for him, his hopes cast a sad reflection on his intelligence and his grasp of reality. It seemed he and Priscilla were both headed for a rough week.

* * *

Monday morning saw the lethargy of Sunday gone. There was a hurry-scurry at the Compound as everybody prepared to go back into the field. Paul wandered about the vehicles, helping with this and that, while Malcolm secreted a bottle of whisky and a bag of chocolate bars into his tuckerbox, supplies he considered to be necessary consolations for a life of misery.

The three field hands I had seen the day before turned up, dragging canvas bags and dressed alike in checked flannel shirts, stubbies and work boots. Big Jill and Priscilla arrived soon after, fresh and ready for a week of fieldwork. Priscilla, dog at her heels, looked less than delighted as she contemplated her assigned field hand. She refused to return his cocky grin and issued him instead with a series of sharp directives. That luck he thought he had was already ebbing away. Paul grabbed one of his companions and propelled him across to where I sat perched on the brim of the plumbing trench.

'Cynthia, meet Shane. He'll be taking you and Eddie out this week.'

Shane was young, long and lean. His straggling blond hair was tied back in a ponytail and a shark's tooth dangled from his neck. He carried a moth-eaten black hat, which featured more sharks' teeth gleaming in a string about the brim.

'She'll be right,' he said in an encouraging voice as he went off to get the vehicle ready.

'Great guy. One of the best we've got this year, terrific with the pigs. A real killer!' said Paul in an encouraging voice.

A few minutes later this guy who had just been described as a *real killer* knocked politely on our donga door and said, 'She's filled with water, fuel and food. Give me your gear, and I'll whack it in, and we can be on our way.'

Eddie strapped the infant seat into the vehicle. We put Emily Jane in the seat, climbed in ourselves, and had not yet shut the door when the vehicle shot off with a screech through the Compound. Before we reached the edge of town, I had concluded that those other two field hands must be woeful, if this guy was the best of the bunch. He may have been friendly, personable, helpful, but he was also insane, cackling with wild laughter and driving in a crazed fashion that made Sebastian look like a conservative and over-cautious old man. The drive was like one of those horrible rides you wish you had never got on at a fun park, the type that flings your body this way and that with nauseating regularity, while the outside world spins by in a hideous blur. Ironbarks, cattle yards and dry creeks whizzed by.

When we finally arrived at our first stop, I reeled from the vehicle, giddy and disturbed. Shane leapt out and went down to the creek to get firewood to put the billy on.

'What are the others like, if this guy's the best?' I asked Eddie, who was looking remarkably composed after such a journey.

'Oh, Shane's all right. He just goes bonkers whenever he gets a steering wheel between his hands, that's all,' said Eddie complacently, as if he had never punched into his brother by the roadside the previous year for what he thought was dangerous driving.

'A bit risky, isn't it? We didn't buy tickets for a thrill ride.'

'It probably seemed worse from the back ... now somewhere down this creek is a site where we can find articulated bony fish fossils. We'll check it out when we've had our tea.'

Within a few minutes the gum leaves were crackling and snapping on the fire and the billy was boiling. There are times when a mug of billy tea is far more effective in inducing relaxation than a glass of wine would be. We were back in the bush again and the concerns of town and highway dropped right away, as if they belonged to a different world. Here there was more to be found than fish fossils. The place resounded with the rustles of life and a family of rollicking dingo pups played in the sunlight on the far bank of the creek. The thought of Burkes Hill and the Compound disappeared completely, just like a bad dream does with the coming of daylight.

I came to realise that week that Shane wasn't nearly as mad as he had first appeared, although he was undoubtedly an eccentric. Fortunately, he had the grace to restrain himself from those particular eccentricities that he figured might be problematic for me. If Paul hadn't called him a killer, I doubt I would have guessed it, so tenderly did he search out creatures show us —an echidna shuffling through the undergrowth, dingos on patrol, grazing kangaroos, basking lizards, spiders hanging from monstrous webs.

'Just as well he's not killing pigs this week,' Eddie said. 'You'd never cope.'

He told me that when Shane shot a boar, he hacked off the head with an axe and secured it to the front of the vehicle like a war trophy. 'You'd think he was an ancient warrior, chopping the heads off his enemies and dangling them from his bridle. Stinks something rotten.'

'Can't you stop him?'

'No, not really. He's way too keen. When he gets home, he boils those heads up in a ten-gallon drum and when they're clean he sticks them in the garden.'

'What for?'

'Some people like gnomes. Some people like rubber tyres shaped to look like swans—a few of those in Burkes Hill. But Shane, he prefers rows of boar skulls, the bigger the better.'

* * *

The week turned out to be quite different from what I had imagined during that wild drive on Monday morning. By the time Friday swung around, I was so relaxed that I scarcely noticed as we flew across the cattle grids on our way back to Burkes Hill.

'Hey look, you can tell we're getting close to civilisation,' said Shane, pointing to a strand of toilet paper rippling across the road like a snake.

A large piece of corrugated iron, nailed haphazardly to the trunk of an ironbark, bore the words *Bong On* in large, dripping, red letters.

'Ah', said Shane, 'The pleasures of life.'

He could afford to be appreciative. He was going home, back to his garden of boar skulls where the dandelions pushed through empty eye sockets. But we were returning to the Compound and would be obliged to hang out at the green house in College Road for meals. My mood was dropping by the minute. Two crows conferred on the fence at Dismal Bridge on the edge of town, cawing mournfully like portents of doom. My mood dropped further.

Crows are prolific birds, squawking raucously from the trees, swooping through the sky, strutting down highways, raiding rubbish bins and generally carrying on their crow lives. If we all read signs of the future into crow behaviour, we would all be in a constant state of confusion and anxiety. And, as it turned out, those sadly cawing crows were not foreshadowing anything at all. Things were not nearly as bad back in Burkes Hill as I was expecting.

The Compound was still a barely habitable wasteland with no prospect of a hot shower any time soon, but things had improved on other fronts. Sally had got over the last weekend with such a burst of energy she had gone to the trouble of spring-cleaning the green house. The place positively glowed and there were flowers on the table in the now impeccable dining room. The aroma of exquisite food drifted once more from the kitchen. Malcolm was so relieved that he went to the Phoenix Hotel to buy a carton of Spanish sparkling wine. He gave a bottle to Sally, keeping the remainder for more general celebrating. Grasshopper questioned him about the wisdom of giving alcohol in any form to the cook, but he just laughed.

'Really Grasshopper, you're becoming as gloomy as James. There's nothing wrong with a few sparkles. It's mostly bubbles anyway. They can't do any harm.'

Spirits were high in the green house that night. Big Jill and Sally joked together about the misunderstanding of the previous week and the tensions dissolved. The only person out of sorts that evening was the field hand with the beer gut who had spent the week with Priscilla, but he fled almost as soon as he reached the Compound and showed no interest in hanging out for a beer with the other field hands. No, he did not want to talk football with Wally that day, and neither did he want to reflect on the week that had just been. Nobody likes to hear the words *I told you so.*

Priscilla wasn't at the green house either. She showed little interest in the goings on at the camp, catering for herself at the flat and keeping company with her dog. She rarely came to the green house and was probably lonely, but everybody was struggling that year, so nobody gave her much thought. The next week I got a glimpse of what it was like to be sent out into the field with an uncongenial field hand, when the third of the new town-based field hands was given the job of assisting Eddie.

After I met Hobson, it astounded me that he had a job at all as he seemed entirely unsuited to any form of employment, with drug dealing a possible exception.

Hobson must have been caught in that immature phase of brain development that afflicts young men, when the prefrontal cortex isn't functioning well, and civilised behaviour is difficult to maintain. I guess it's possible that it all settled down with time. For all I know he eventually became a fine upstanding citizen, helping old ladies across the road, contributing to charities and going in for local politics. But if that did happen in some rosy future, there was certainly no glimmer of it the week he came out with us.

Hobson was an uncooperative character, refusing to come to the Compound on Monday morning to prepare the vehicle. It wasn't his job to cater for family visitors, he said. Eddie would have to organise it all himself. Hobson asked to be collected from his house on our way out of town. He lived in a typical Burkes Hill house, small and shadowy, overhung by mango trees. There were no gnomes or rubber swans or even boar skulls in this garden, just poultry pecking about old car parts scattered amongst the weeds.

When we pulled up, a dishevelled woman in a pink satin nightdress stomped out onto the porch brandishing a rifle. Seeing the GIU insignia on the vehicle, she bellowed into the house. Hobson appeared at the front door, a stocky young man with an inscrutable face and close-cropped hair. To our astonishment the woman proceeded to slap him about the head, yelling insults. She reminded me of an enraged Tasmanian devil I'd once seen in a film, viciously attacking her partner following copulation. Hobson responded to this abuse with a creepy quiet smile, as if such behaviour was a turn on for him, a sign of his good taste in selecting a woman of attitude and spirit, nothing to be embarrassed about.

After this peculiar farewell ritual, he came down the stairs towards us, a gun slung over his shoulder, bag in one hand, swag in the other. After stowing his baggage, he slid into the driver's seat, placing the gun beside him with a menacing swagger, as if he wanted us to know that it defined him in some fundamental way, as did his relationship with that wild woman, who had disappeared back into the darkness of the house. Hobson greeted Eddie in a cool fashion, ignored me completely, and began to drive steadily down the road in silence.

Hobson's driving was so steady that he saw no necessity to pull over for a moment or two when a cattle train approached like most drivers do, allowing the truck to keep to the tar. Instead, he belted towards it, grinning like a ghoul. When collision seemed inevitable, he averted the steering wheel with one hand, and skimmed along the edge of the ensuing whirlwind. This was unnerving and far worse than driving with Shane the previous week. It was a great relief when we left the highway.

We crossed the Black Bream River. There were screeching cockatoos in the treetops. A flock of galahs flew overhead. I caught the colour of a king parrot as it flashed through the trees and we saw a black-headed rock python basking in the sun. But the atmosphere inside the car was morose and oppressive. When the track we were following diverged, Eddie glanced at the air photo and said, 'Go left here, Hobson. We're heading for that rise in the landscape. There should be a mass of outcrop that way.'

'Nah mate. We're goin' to the fuckin' right,' Hobson replied.

'No, the outcrop lies to the left,' said Eddie with a patient sigh, under the impression he was addressing an imbecile with no comprehension of basic geology.

'Nah mate. The bloody outcrop is better to the fuckin' right. I want you to bloody see it,' said Hobson.

He drove down the right-hand track. We were speechless. Yes, we could have said this, or we could have said that. But who is ever prepared with a response when somebody behaves with such a surprising and blatant disregard for the usual codes of behaviour?

Hobson continued to drive in a smouldering silence. He was simmering with suppressed aggression, the gun resting beside him on the seat, and I could understand why Eddie sat quietly without more protest. I guess he was hoping that despite Hobson's appalling manners, he might actually be familiar with the terrain and have something of interest to show him. We drove along without a word being spoken by anyone for a few more kilometres, until the vehicle suddenly halted.

'The Missus has to get out now,' Hobson announced, not bothering to look at either of us, but staring straight ahead.

Eddie's jaw dropped. He turned to stare at Hobson. He was clearly gobsmacked.

'Why?' I asked.

'Track's too rough.'

'Well, I don't care. I've been on rough roads before.'

'Track's fuckin' rough. Get out!' he said.

I can't say now what went through our minds right then, but a few seconds later I was standing by the roadside with Emily Jane, while the vehicle chugged on along the track without us.

Worst case scenario: Eddie was in the hands of a crazy psychopath and we were stuck here in this remote place with little chance of rescue.

Best case scenario: Hobson was a poorly understood social

incompetent who meant well but couldn't express himself properly.

The truth lay somewhere in the middle. When they returned an hour later, Hobson was in a better temper although his language hadn't improved.

'I reckon you was right,' he said in a conciliatory voice. 'The outcrop is fuckin' better down the other track. Let's take a gawk at it now. That track should be okay for the missus.'

I saw a paper bag stuffed with leaves in his shirt pocket and realised that he had been inspecting some hidden cannabis plants and picking what he could from them, while he directed Eddie towards some nearby scrappy bit of rock.

* * *

'Whatever inspired the GIU to employ him?' I asked Eddie at the end of the day.

The afternoon was golden. We sat with Emily Jane in the shallows of the river, watching a pair of brolgas on a sandbank downstream. It would have been idyllic if Hobson hadn't been hunched on the riverbank like a brooding vampire.

'I don't have a say in the matter,' said Eddie. 'I've just got to cop what I get given. Bill Sapshort appointed those guys, claimed they were already trained.'

'Trained in what? Thuggery and drug dealing? Don't you know what he was up to this morning?'

'Of course I do. But what can I do about it? We've been lucky. Bugsy was forced to have dope plants drying out on the vehicle motor last week. Wasn't comfortable about it, but thought he'd get a bullet through the brain if he didn't agree.'

'Gerald Drake would freak if he knew this creep was using the GIU as a convenience for his drug growing activities.'

'Gerald Drake would prefer to know nothing about it.

Anyway, these guys probably won't stick around long. According to Paul, they're not impressed with the GIU. I don't know what company they worked for last, but apparently, they were given a carton of grog, a bag of dope, and a visit to the brothel at the end of every traverse. The GIU can't compete with that.'

We made an awkward group that evening, sitting around the fire in silence, eating the usual Monday spaghetti bolognaise meal.

'Well Hobson,' said Eddie, trying his best to ease the tension a bit, 'Have you seen any good films lately? Anything you can recommend?'

'Nah.'

'What sort of films do you like?'

'Violence. Yeah. I like violence ...'

The conversation fizzled out. We lapsed back into silence, hearing only the crackle of the flames and the quiet rustle of nocturnal creatures beyond the firelight. Emily Jane was already asleep in the portable cot next to our swags.

After the meal was over and we'd cleaned up, Hobson glanced at us with bored disgust and walked across to the back of the vehicle where he rummaged amongst his gear. He returned a minute or so later holding a clear plastic kangaroo, a sort of bottle that was available in those days at corner stores, filled with red or green frozen cordial. They were usually sold to children who liked to suck on them in hot weather. Hobson had recycled this object and was now using it as a bong. For the remainder of that evening, he sat by the fire sucking greedily at this plastic kangaroo, inhaling the dope fumes and ignoring us completely.

When we woke in the early morning light, the fire had already been rekindled. Hobson was hunched beside it with the plastic kangaroo pressed to his lips. The day had scarcely begun, and the man employed to drive was already half off his head. But if I thought this was a problem, Eddie was not overly fazed.

'He can't cause too much trouble today. There's nobody about out here and we've no choice but to go slow in this terrain.'

Hobson, stiff and silent, drove us from outcrop to outcrop like a vacant robot, but it was far less unpleasant than the previous day when he had been taut with aggression. By the afternoon we had travelled downstream to a place where the river formed a long, deep pool, bordered by a wide, sandy bank rimmed with paperbark trees. Hobson stopped the car.

'There's fish in this pool,' he announced. 'Hey, I can lend you a line. You could catch us some dinner.'

These words were addressed to me and he had turned about to look at me as he spoke. Surprised by his sudden geniality, I found myself agreeing with his suggestion. He may have wanted to get rid of me from the vehicle again, but it would be far more pleasant sitting on the sand by the river than jolting about in the back of the vehicle as Eddie went about the outcrops. I took the baby, a water bottle, a packet of biscuits and Hobson's fishing gear and went down to the water's edge as they drove on. Emily Jane played in the sand as I dangled the fishing line into the pool. The green water was still; behind us the paperbarks were motionless. The air was heavy but thin wisps of high-level cloud scudded overhead.

When Hobson and Eddie returned, we were sitting beside the river, mesmerised by the silence and heavy calm of the afternoon. I had caught no fish. Not even a ripple had disturbed the surface of that pool. Was it my imagination, or was there a flash of disappointment flickering on Hobson's face? Had he been that keen on fish for dinner?

'You didn't see old Snappers then, hey?' he asked.

'I beg your pardon?'

'Old Snappers ... Bloody great croc that lives in this pool. All the locals know about Snappers.'

'Are you telling me that you recommended we fish in a pool you knew was inhabited by a large crocodile?'

'Fuckin' oath, I did. Thought it'd be a bit of a thrill for youse ... Ah, he's fuckin' harmless, never eaten anybody yet. People come and swim here on weekends and he goes off and hides. Yeah, it's just fish and turtles he wants.'

'Did you know this creature lived here?' I asked Eddie.

'I'd heard something about it,' said Eddie vaguely. 'But Cynthia, you would have to be very fortunate to see an animal like that, like seeing sharks when you snorkel. Never mind, you might catch a glimpse of him next time ...'

* * *

The next day we woke to lowering clouds rolling across the sky, casting a softened light over the landscape. By midday the sky was dark, we could scent rain on dry earth and an occasional raindrop fell, bouncing in the dust. An hour later rain had set in, falling steadily in sheets.

The rain did not disturb Eddie and it disrupted his work schedule no more than the fire had on a previous occasion. He put on a shabby waterproof coat and kept going. He had found a wall of rock exposed on the riverbank, full of ripple marks and worm burrows, and nothing was going to prevent him recording each feature in painstaking detail, rain or no rain. After all, rainfall is just a transient piece of weather, a small part of the vaster and more interesting panorama of climate and the changes that can occur over millennia. Eddie put forward his hand and traced on the wet rock the trail marks of an ancient and long extinct animal. Hobson, with a curse on his lips, threw a fishing line into the nearby river.

Emily Jane and I huddled in raincoats and looked out upon a wet world.

That night, the four of us were forced to shelter beneath the limited dimensions of a small tarpaulin. There was no fire, and the small space was pervaded by the smell of Hobson's dope. We lay down together to sleep in unwanted intimacy. Hobson was so close I could hear the breath whistle in and out of his lungs, could hear his teeth grind, and all the while the rain continued to fall, belting down on the tarp and dribbling down the sides.

The tarp failed in the night, dumping a swimming pool of water on us as we slept. We awoke to the gloom of morning in a sodden misery. But the light of worm trails was still shining in Eddie's eyes and there was no point in suggesting we return to town. Hobson sucked upon his plastic kangaroo as if it was a baby's bottle and muttered a long string of expletives as he looked upon the weather.

By midday, Eddie was coughing, feverish, and pale. He ignored these signs of illness, brushing them aside as if it they were just another inconvenience like the rain and continued to gaze at the outcrop and to scribble into his damp notebook.

'This is ridiculous! You're getting pneumonia, and the rest of us will have it before the day's out if we don't get out of the rain. We need to go back to Burkes Hill,' I said.

'But this is my job,' Eddie protested feebly, pointing a shaking finger towards a ripple mark.

'Rubbish! No one works when they are ill, and no one works in this weather. I bet everybody else went home yesterday.'

'But Hobson's enjoying himself,' Eddie said in a quavering voice, scraping for an excuse to stay at the rock.

Hobson was humming to himself, leaning against the outcrop a few metres away, his fishing line dangling into the swirling black water below.

'Well, he can stop enjoying himself,' I said in a low voice.

'And I promised him we could drop in on his friend on the way back tomorrow, the hydroponic watermelon farmer up at the crossroads.'

'Hydroponic watermelon farmer? Huh! The local drug dealer more likely. He can visit him next week. Hobson's going to do what I say for a change and if he doesn't want to go back to Burkes Hill, we can always leave him behind. I wouldn't feel the slightest twinge of guilt if we did.'

And as Eddie succumbed to the barrage of rain and encroaching fatigue, I clambered across the slippery rocks towards Hobson. 'Eddie is sick, if you haven't noticed. We're going back to Burkes Hill.'

'Fish aren't fuckin' biting anyway,' he replied.

* * *

It wasn't long before we were sliding our way across the wet roads towards town. The way back was mildly terrifying due to slippery surfaces and poor visibility but there was some relief in knowing we would soon get rid of Hobson to his witch of a woman and drive off without him. We had forgotten for a moment that we were not going back to the luxury of our own private existence but were heading straight for the Compound.

At the barbed wire gates, we paused and surveyed an utterly dismal scene. The last twenty-four hours had transformed the Compound into a huge quagmire. The dongas were afloat in a lake of mud. It was here that Eddie reached breaking point. He got out of the vehicle and stared at the scene before him, as if in the hope it might suddenly dissolve as a nightmare might, then he lifted his face to the glowering sky and yelled as loud as I had ever heard him yell.

'I hate this bloody place! I hate it, I hate it, I hate it ...'

But the sky was relentless and insensitive, and the rain kept pouring down with a gentle roar that drowned out his words. He got back into the vehicle and we drove through the slosh into the gloom of the Compound. We did not know, as we approached our donga, despondent, demoralised and soaked to the skin, that a miracle of sorts had occurred during the past week.

Paul had discovered the strings that needed pulling to get anything moving in this slow-going town and had finally arranged for the connection of the ablutions block. Bill could take no credit for this achievement; he was visiting distant gold mines. We now had access to as many hot showers as we desired, but a river flowed in the trench outside our door and to walk anywhere within the Compound meant sinking knee deep in mud. Paul placed planks across the trenches and arranged chunks of limestone over the earth mounds. We needed to drive twenty metres to the ablutions block and wobble over the limestone if there was even a remote chance of returning from a shower cleaner than we started, but it was a definite improvement.

The deluge lasted several days. During this time Eddie lay ill, irritated that he could not continue his work with the ripple marks and worm burrows. The donga smelled damp and sprouted fungal growths. But a morning came when the sun was back in place in the eastern sky, sending rays of light glittering on the puddles and shining on the mud. The rain was over. It wasn't long before the mud crusted and cracked, the dust settled back into the dongas, and the weather was hot.

The week after the rain stopped, Priscilla went out into the field with Hobson, came back early, and left Burkes Hill for good. She neither complained about him nor demanded the termination of his employment. She just said that enough was enough. She had been defeated that year through isolation from the rest of the party and the constant companionship of unsuitable assistants.

'Couldn't hack the pace!' said Paul, failing to understand, after he delivered her to the airport.

Big Jill moved to the Compound and made no comment.

Priscilla might have been finished with the field camps, but she was not yet finished with the GIU, not by a long shot.

Chapter 27

Smoke and steam

'WHAT THE HELL is going on, Cynthia? What's the story with this cook of yours?' asked James McCracken.

He had completed his stint in Bogarilla and was back in town. Not too happy about it either, by the look of him. He perched on a stool in our donga, while Emily Jane took an afternoon nap. Eddie was working across in the office, a flimsy, prefabricated building which had been plonked near the gates.

'It's nothing to do with me. She's not my cook. I'm a guest here. I came up to see Eddie, for a sort of holiday.'

'A holiday! To this dump? You'd have to be crazy wouldn't you? I mean, what the hell was going on with Gerald when he figured this was the best place for us all. It's a disgrace. All this cracked mud and barbed wire. You couldn't even put prisoners up here. There'd be an outcry. Riots.'

'Yeah, it's awful. Something went wrong with the planning.'

'That's an understatement. You probably won't believe this, but I'd been looking forward to getting back here for this mining conference next week. Thought it would be the highlight of the field season. My girlfriend's come up. We were planning to go to the conference together. You know, Tiffany, the girl who visited last year with Gerald. Remember?'

'Yes, I do.'

'Yeah, well, you know what they say about best laid plans ... What do I get for my trouble? The bloody Compound and the bloody cook and all my plans in ruins.'

'Well, I guess the Compound is the worst place possible to spend a romantic week, but look on the bright side. At least the ablutions block is functioning,' I said. 'Or you could go to the Parkview Motel'.

'But we weren't supposed to be staying at the Compound at all. Paul promised us a room in the green house. Tiffany came up a couple of days ago, but when I arrived at College Road this morning bearing gifts and joy, what did I find? Do you think she was pleased to see me? Nope! She was packing her bags hell bent on getting out of the place on the midday bus. Wouldn't listen to reason. Nothing I said made any difference.'

'But why?'

'I told you. It's the bloody cook's fault. Behaved abominably! She's read the book all right.'

'What book?'

'The one called *All the worst habits of GIU cooks*. She's a specialist! And Malcolm told me the woman's brilliant. Can cook up a storm he says! Sure can! But I thought he meant a culinary storm.'

'That's what he did mean. She's an amazing cook.'

'So I've heard. It astounds me. That woman could sour milk with a glance. She put the hard word on my girlfriend. Can you believe that? And that cook can't handle rejection. Apparently never learned it's just part of bloody life. Happens to us all. But she's made life so unpleasant over there that Tiffany refused to stay another minute. I suggested we move to the motel, but she wouldn't have a bar of it. Nah, turned her back on me, the conference, the whole bloody lot! Thanks to your brilliant cook!'

He gazed across the Compound, at the dried mud, the ditches and the mullock heaps.

'Now Paul has given our room to Owen and Stella and I've been sent down here to wallow with you lot. No wonder Priscilla left! She's got more brains than the rest of you put together.'

James sighed miserably.

* * *

Many from the GIU were coming to Burkes Hill for the mining conference, some to try out the accommodation at the Compound, some to the motel, and some had rooms reserved at the Phoenix Hotel. Even Gerald Drake was on his way, although he had no intention of sampling Compound life, and had booked a suite at the Parkview Motel instead. He did, however, intend to visit the Compound to see for himself how the best working environment in the north was coming along.

I daresay Bill Sapshort had explained to him that the whole project was behind schedule, but I don't believe that Gerald had a clue what this really meant, not until the moment he stood at the gates, his jaw hanging slack as if he'd been punched and an aghast expression on his face. The mess before his eyes bore no relationship to the vision that had been in his mind. Not Bill's finest hour, as he stood next to Gerald gabbling about how slowly the cogs move in a town like Burkes Hill. Nothing to be done about it. Rome wasn't built in a day, you know. And there stood Gerald, stunned to silence, dazzled by the pure incompetence of it all.

'It seems to have escaped your notice, Sapshort, that this is not an imperial city. It is a field camp and, as far as I can see, an uninhabitable one. Why haven't the trenches in front of the dongas been filled in?'

'They're waiting for the pipes to be laid, of course. Landscaping guy left it like this. He seemed to know what it was all about.'

'Did he indeed? I doubt that. This landscaping he did isn't at all what I had in mind.'

It must have been an excruciating moment for Bill. But Gerald would have been aware that he, too, had to take some responsibility for this mess. It had been his judgement to burden Bill with this project, for no better reason than he happened to live close by, while Bill carried on with his usual duties and managed the field mapping as well. And although Gerald did not for a moment lose sight of the potential for the place, despite the sorry spectacle before him, it also dawned on him that his vision would never be realised as long as Bill was in charge.

But there was nothing he could do about it right then. He couldn't reach into his pocket for a wand and convert the bleak landscape of mullock heaps and haphazard dongas into a five-star resort with the flick of a wrist. Everybody would have to keep on coping, for the time being at any rate. In the meantime, there was a mining conference to attend.

And how was Sally going to cope with this mass arrival of GIU personnel on this particular week? I'd heard that she had been moody since her fancy for Tiffany had not been reciprocated. What if this translated into a stream of dismal meals as it had done on the earlier occasion? Fortunately, Gerald considerately declared that the GIU staff would not impose on Sally for most of the week. It was her usual time off and she was entitled to it. He did request, however, that she serve a special dinner on Wednesday evening to the GIU staff and to a few specially invited dignitaries from the conference. Could she please collaborate with Paul who would manage the logistics?

Paul's brow wrinkled. Sensing a looming debacle, he wished he was way off yonder hunting pigs. But Sally took a different tack. Malcolm had said she could cook up a storm. She fully intended to. She would cook a meal to be remembered for years, a meal that could not be remotely matched by any other Burkes Hill establishment.

On Wednesday morning, the day of the dinner, I went to College Road to visit Stella. Paul was creeping about on tiptoe, assembling trestle tables and throwing cloths over them. He had assembled stacks of chairs, piles of white china plates, teacups, cutlery and paper serviettes. The aroma of simmering garlic and wine drifted through the house.

'That smells glorious, Sally,' said Stella, noting Sally's clenched mouth and tense brow. 'Cynthia and I know just what it's like. If you want a hand, give a yell. We both know how difficult it is when extra guests are coming for dinner.'

Today's cook looked up into the eyes of another GIU cook and one ex-cook, but was not soothed. Her frown furrowed deeper. Her eyes darkened.

'There is something you can do,' she said. 'Piss off out of here! I need to concentrate.'

We bundled Emily Jane into the stroller and walked to town. We lingered over morning tea at the milk-bar, wandered up and down the streets gazing into shop windows, visited the town park with its rotunda and its enclosure of pet kangaroos and emus. But we couldn't wander around forever and eventually we returned to the green house. The Compound was way too unattractive an option. We sat in the far corner of the veranda, speaking in whispers and noting that dinner was shaping up to be something very good indeed if the fragrances drifting from the kitchen were any indication.

Meanwhile the geologists were at the conference, sitting through an afternoon session devoted to the economic aspects of geology. They arrived back at the green house as afternoon drifted into evening with all the enthusiasm and relief you would expect from a bunch of kids let out of school for the day. They went straight to the drinks fridge, and I noticed several familiar faces.

Christopher Craddock, in town just for the week, took one look at the haggard expression on Bill's face and realised that he was very fortunate not to be involved in the field camp that year. I had never seen him quite so relaxed at the green house before. It was no business of his if this dinner worked out or not. All he had to do was to eat it and be sociable. Murray Crow sat in a swivel chair with Emily Jane on his lap, squeaking and spinning, as exuberant as a boy. In the centre of the room Dennis O'Regan conversed with Gerald Drake.

Even Jimmy Keen was there. He was the guy I'd heard stories about, who had burnt down a shed at the Reedy Creek races and had set a paddock on fire the previous year. But either those stories were inaccurate or appearances are deceptive. Jimmy was a middle-aged, respectable-looking man in a crisp shirt. He looked much more like the guy who volunteered to address school children on the dangers of alcohol than the guy with a reputation for whisky and reckless pyromania.

Sally's first course was a sensation. Two soups of contrasting colour and flavour were served together in the same bowl, meeting in the centre where they blended in an arty swirl. But if Sally was expecting the same acclaim she had attracted previously when she had served this dish in her restaurant days, things did not go quite to plan. There was certainly no lack of enthusiasm when the bowls were served, but these diners did not gasp over the beauty of the colours or the care Sally had taken to etch each swirl. They did not savour each drop. In fact, at first, they didn't bother tasting the soup at all, they just gaped at it for a moment or two before bursting into an excited cacophony of observations. To Sally's horror, these spectacular bowls of soup rapidly became the subjects of debate and experimentation.

This wasn't soup. This was a perfect example of how liquids of different densities behave when meeting. The cutlery which Paul had laid out with such care became tools with which they could replicate various physical forces. Jimmy Keen poured water from the jug on the table into his soup to illustrate a point, while Murray tipped beer into his. By the time they all got around to eating it, the colours had muddied and the soup had gone cold. Sally looked fit to explode as she witnessed this behaviour but only Stella and I noticed.

'Marvellous, marvellous, Sally,' said Gerald. 'How clever of you. And is there a geological theme to the next course as well?'

But nobody could find any hidden geological themes in the simple Coq au Vin with vegetable sides that was served next. It was, however, done so perfectly that they all forgot about geology for a moment or two. Madness transformed to quiet appreciation. Malcolm's eyes glazed over and even James smiled at the pink hibiscus that adorned the tablecloth. He forgot that he had dozed off at the conference that afternoon and told his neighbour how much he had profited from his talk about economics. Gerald smacked his lips and waved a paper serviette about with the satisfied complacence of the man who had organised such a fine dinner.

As soon as the banana and rum crepes were served for dessert, Sally fled to her bedroom, slammed shut the door, and in need of instant relaxation, began to feverishly smoke a joint. By the time Gerald's guests were rising from their chairs, the smell of marihuana smoke seeped from under her door and curled along the corridor. Paul took a sharp sniff of the air.

'It's such a lovely evening. Let's have our coffee out on the veranda,' he suggested.

He led the guests outside to stand amongst the rusting chairs. The withered garden didn't look so bad under the cover of darkness.

Dennis O'Regan took Gerald by the arm, 'That was truly a superb meal. How fortunate to have found such a capable cook in these parts.'

'Ah yes. Excellent. Excellent. Where is she by the way? We should all give her a round of applause for such a fine effort. It was marvellous. Paul would you find Sally please and bring her out here so we can all express our appreciation.'

Paul was cluttering about with coffee cups. He looked up with a distracted frown and nodded feebly. Eddie found him peering nervously through the keyhole of Sally's door.

'What's up?' asked Eddie.

'Who's that out there? Piss off,' drawled Sally, from behind the door.

'Gerald wants me to bring out Sally so he can thank the excellent little woman himself. And she's in there smoking reefers like they're going out of fashion, stoned out of her bloody brain. Can't you smell it?'

'We can all smell it, Paul. In fact, Jimmy just accused me of smoking dope, just because he found me stashing a used nappy in a bag in the bathroom. But look, tell Gerald that Sally's so exhausted she's gone straight to bed and is too shy to appear in her pyjamas,' Eddie suggested.

Paul delivered this message back to Gerald, handing him a cup of coffee, and kicking shut the door to prevent the fumes from Sally's bedroom drifting out onto the veranda and assailing the guests. Possession of cannabis was illegal, and this could be very awkward for Gerald, who right at that moment took a deep breath and peered out into the darkness.

'Somebody must be burning off somewhere tonight. Peculiar smell. Reminiscent of ....' he murmured.

Eddie interrupted. 'Hey, Dennis, how's your mum? And Ralph? How's Ralph getting on?'

'Ah yes!' said Gerald, forgetting the peculiar smell in the drift of conversation. 'Your mother, you must give her our regards.'

James, standing nearby, could not suppress a snort. 'Regards! Huh! Hey, who's got the gall to smoke dope around here?'

'Shut up, James,' said Paul. 'It's just some local burning off.'

'Smells like dope to me.'

'Shut up, James.'

But James had no particular interest in concealing the cook's bad habits from Gerald. Even so, the conference came to an end without the boss detecting any of Sally's issues and she remained for him, always, the most brilliant and flawless cook the GIU had ever engaged. She was certainly the most brilliant.

* * *

Before he left, Gerald visited the dust and ditches of the Compound once more. He addressed the staff with a speech that was part apology and part pep talk, and which, remarkably, did not involve wind in the trees, dew on the grass, or dingos howling in the night. He spoke about the rewards of patience and outlined his vision for a productive work environment, for gardens and recreational facilities. He had great plans. Things might be challenging now but stick it out a while longer and improvements were on their way. It would be the best field camp ever.

But who believed him then? Certainly not James, who now the distraction of the conference was over, slumped into a depressed state every time he thought of the girlfriend who had so unceremoniously abandoned him.

'There's no need for gloom, James,' said Malcolm, strolling across the Compound with his swag in tow, after their first week back in the field. 'You get accustomed to the squalor after a while. Just look across to the horizon and focus on other things. Anyway, it's improved this week. Gerald must have given them all a kick up the arse.'

The trenches had been filled in, all the dongas now had running water, and some of the mounds of earth were flattened.

'It's not that. I can put up with this dump like I've put up with the dumps of the past …. I mean, I've been dreaming of that bloody woman for weeks and she runs off as if I'm of no account at all. I know she was being pestered by the cook, but I could have put a stop to that real quick,' said James.

Malcolm heaved his swag onto the ground, and sat upon it, reaching for his cigarettes from his top pocket.

'A bit of a drama queen, is she? But James, you're taking it all too seriously. There are other women in the world besides Tiffany, right here in Burkes Hill.'

'What?'

'Look James, this loyalty in relationships is a fine thing, as far as it goes, but let's not put ourselves under undue pressure. Take Mia for example, a wonderful woman with a generous spirit. None better! I don't imagine for a moment that she expects me to eke out a miserable monkish existence up here. Not with all the problems we've had to cop this season. We all need cheering up, so I say we have a night out on the town. We'll go down to the Federal Hotel. There's a band playing there tonight. And we can meet a few girls—Bugsy will be in on it. And Rooster.'

I suspect he had no idea I was within earshot when he expressed this point of view. But at least I had some warning of what was to come later. The disturbance woke us up well after midnight. There was a racket going on outside.

'What the hell is that?' asked Eddie, sitting up in bed.

'Probably those people who live on the corner. Brawling again,' I replied sleepily. They usually did on a Friday night.

'That's not brawling. It's singing. Sort of. And it sounds like Malcolm.'

We listened and the sound began to make a semblance of sense. 'When you're with the Flintstones have a yabba dabba doo time, yabba dabba doo time, yabba dabba doo time ...'

Malcolm was singing with hearty exuberance and slurred voices were echoing. 'Yabba dabba doo time, yabba dabba doo time, yabba dabba doo time ...'

'I hope this isn't going to go on all night,' said Eddie.

'They wanted to meet some girls tonight,' I said, peering out the window.

A nearby caravan trembled in the darkness. Somebody from within chucked an empty rum bottle from the door and four shadowy figures tumbled out after it.

'There aren't any girls,' I said.

'Evidently not!' replied Eddie. 'I wish to hell they'd shut up.'

Malcolm and his mates had begun an uncoordinated attempt to knock the caravan over, with such mismatched screams of 'One two three' and 'heave ho', that the whole enterprise was obviously hopeless. When it dawned on them that they lacked the strength to topple the caravan, they all clambered onto its roof instead.

For a moment the four of them stood there like kings surveying their lands. They gazed across the mullock heaps vanishing off in the distant darkness and to the fringe of dozing houses beyond the security fence. They gazed up at the stars and saw something beneath that brilliant, glittering, endless sky that spoke of loss and sadness. James murmured something indistinguishable and suddenly they broke into a wail that took flight across the Compound. It was almost a primal scream.

Lights flickered on in the surrounding houses. The neighbours were awake. This was not the usual Friday night brawl up at the corner. Something different was going on.

Emotions are fluid, transforming with expression. The wailing soon changed into a screech which rent the heavens and resonated across the Compound to the surrounding district. And somewhere in that screech James and his companions found the root cause of their disturbance. It was clear and simple. They wanted somebody to fuck. I put it crudely because these were the exact words they used to express their dilemma to the midnight sky, in a relentless chant that swept the neighbourhood and seemed set to go on with hideous monotony for some time.

'Embarrassing,' said Eddie.

By this time, the neighbours were spilling out of their houses into their front yards, looking with bewilderment across to the Compound. How to make this awful chanting stop? Ring the police? The ambulance? Who were these lunatics anyway? Escapees from that institution on the other side of town? Or were they out-of-control mates of Bill Sapshort's? What was going on?

Fortunately, Rooster distracted everyone just seconds before the neighbours went to call the police. He stopped chanting and leapt from the roof of the caravan, landing on his feet like a cat. And although he briefly vanished, he was back within seconds, as naked as the day he was born, carrying Bugsy's running shoes and a tube of toothpaste. This was such unusual behaviour that his mates stopped their chant and fell silent for a moment while he sat on the doorstep of the caravan and put on Bugsy's shoes. The neighbours, assembled on the footpath, stared at Rooster in horrified fascination. Even the Friday night brawlers were there watching.

Rooster ignored them all as he carefully smeared toothpaste

all over those shoes. When he had finished, he stood erect, unashamed of his nudity, and commenced to run a marathon around the perimeter of the Compound, to the wild cheers of his drunken companions, as described right at the start of this book.

Many of us who witnessed this affair could understand why these guys had yelled their personal desires to the night wind. After all they were lonesome and fed up, in need of some comfort. But nobody had a clue as to why Rooster was motivated to cover those shoes in toothpaste and go running naked into the night. Rooster himself was at a loss to explain it when he had returned to his senses, except to comment that it had seemed a good idea at the time, and it was in fact a very liberating thing to do. He would recommend it to anybody in need of stress relief.

This run was the finale of the night's proceedings. Rooster stumbled over the mullock heaps, and Malcolm, James and Bugsy cheered him on until they were all exhausted and collapsed in a drunken heap. None of them surfaced until quite late the next day, by which time Bill had already received a barrage of unpleasant phone calls from neighbouring households.

'Just a few of the lads letting off a bit of steam,' he replied each time.

Towards lunchtime, I saw Malcolm wander out of the ablutions block. He walked towards me, shaking his head sadly.

'Poor old Bill's lost the plot. Must be having a nervous breakdown or something. He just bowled up to me and demanded that I pull my head in and start behaving myself. And to stop disrupting the whole neighbourhood. He can't be right in the head. What the hell's he talking about?'

'Don't you remember last night, Malcolm?'

'Last night? Sure do. Went down to the Federal with James

and Bugsy and Rooster. Thought it would do them good. You know, meet some local women. Have a bit of fun. But it was a flop actually. That Bill Sapshort doesn't have a leg to stand on, coming up and abusing me. He and Gerald between them have turned us all into social pariahs.'

'Pariahs?'

'Yes. Pariahs. Those poor guys don't have a hope this season. No girl wants to come near us when they know we're from the Compound. They look at us funny and make excuses to go to the bathroom, never to be seen again. And we were getting on real well with some of them, until the Compound came up. We gave up in the end. Came back here and consoled ourselves with a quiet rum in that caravan and evidently went to sleep there. Surely there's no problem with any of that?'

'So, you don't remember singing the Flintstone song last night, trying to topple the caravan, bellowing from the rooftop? Rooster streaking through the Compound?'

'Streaking? You mean he was naked? That's possible I guess; he was starkers when he woke up. Stank of toothpaste too. Flintstone song you say? Mmm, maybe that rings a bell somewhere.'

'The truth is Malcolm, you lot all made an atrocious racket in the night. You woke us all up and the whole neighbourhood was out there gathered on the footpath, looking in. And you four were bellowing from the rooftop.'

'You're not kidding are you, Cynthia? So, what were we bellowing to have attracted such a response?'

'You might prefer not to know.'

'Come on. I'm entitled to know how I conduct myself, if my own memory is such a blur.'

When, under pressure, I outlined the gist of what had been echoing across the Compound the previous night, Malcolm stared at me with horror, then crumpled in a heap upon the ground, covering his face with his hands. He was clearly shocked.

'Good God. You mean to say the neighbours were out there with their little kiddies all tucked into bed listening to us screaming that ... I'll just have to give up the grog, that's all. I've been told that I'm a rather charming, lovable drunk, but in fact it sounds as if I shouldn't be let loose in the community at all in that state ...'

James was loping towards us, across the Compound. I wouldn't say there was a spring in his step exactly, and he wore his dark glasses like a shield against the brilliance of the day, but there was a marked lightness in his being which had not been in evidence recently, as if the activities of last night had somehow unburdened him.

'Good morning, good morning,' he said reasonably brightly. 'Or is it afternoon? I've been looking for you, Cynthia. I've come to apologise. Big Jill tells me I was screaming obscenely from the roof of that caravan last night. Can't say I recall doing any such thing, but if it's true, I'm most frightfully sorry. I imagine I was just letting off a bit of steam.'

'Yes, that's it,' said Malcolm, 'Letting off steam, that's all we were doing. Has to be done sometimes, doesn't it? Just like a pressure cooker.'

'By the way,' James continued. 'Anyone seen Bugsy's running shoes? They've gone missing.'

Chapter 28

Malcolm's mistake

Have you ever made a wish, and discovered later that the wish was fulfilled, but in such a vastly different way to how you imagined it, that it almost escaped your notice? This happened to Malcolm and his mates after they screeched their desires to the night sky. It was as if the sky had listened and sent them Cheryl in response to their plea. The cosmos works in mysterious ways. Of course, it's possible that Cheryl was in the vicinity of the Compound that night, heard the racket, and appointed herself to the task of helping these guys out. Whatever the mechanism, she materialised in their lives soon after they sent their request to the heavens.

Not that she was ever known as Cheryl at the GIU camp. She was always called Rollerball, an unkind name invented by Malcolm and James, who were both inclined to snigger about Cheryl, at least in the beginning. She was a girl of generous proportions and flamboyant dress, with a no-nonsense zest for life. Apparently she had been to school with Shane, although these days she worked as a nurse at the local hospital.

'Poor patients!' commented Malcolm, without justification, because Cheryl actually had an earthy kindness and the sort of coarse humour that was probably appreciated by the ill and injured.

Rooster recognised her qualities right from the start, but then he had benefited from that liberating midnight streak about the mullock heaps and had evidently gained insight into the deeper stirrings of his soul. He realised that he was wasting his time with those girls he occasionally brought back to the green house. It was all so awkward, so much hard work, offering them cups of tea or glasses of wine as he cast about for a topic to engage them—the taste of the new burger on the McDonald's menu, for example, or the latest video releases, or their yearning to escape Burkes Hill for good. But deep inside he knew that he was not remotely interested in their opinions on these matters and to pretend otherwise was to mislead them. He was interested in something more basic, like a lizard in the springtime in the grip of a powerful biological urge.

Rollerball was a revelation to him, another springtime lizard whose attitude reflected his. She had a simple no frills approach. Life was for living and living well. There were pleasures to be enjoyed, but she felt no need to string herself up over them. She expected nothing in return for her favours apart from the pleasure of the passing moment, not money, commitment, love or romance. Certainly not marriage. Even conversation was not strictly necessary.

By this time the field season was plodding along sluggishly towards the end. Everybody had been over it weeks ago, but this year there was none of the restless irritability that had marked the end of previous seasons. Conditions had been so bad that spirits had degenerated into dull passivity. Everybody had gone numb and they were now just trudging wearily along with the slow-moving clock. Everybody except Rooster, who, in contrast, radiated a serene contentment. His face held a ruddy glow as each afternoon he went for his run, on some days returning much later than usual. When they were in town, Bugsy, James and Malcolm looked on in horror.

'Rooster's gone mad!' said Malcolm. 'The woman looks like a cross between an old cow and an ironbark tree.'

'Yeah ... Rollerball ...' sniggered James.

It never occurred to them that Cheryl was the 'somebody' they'd all been calling for on that memorable night, a generous being who could give them exactly what they had asked for. But then I'm not sure they actually recalled asking for anything. Even if they did recognise a genuine private desire in the words they'd been told they were yelling, the 'somebody' they yearned for would be far more discriminating in her choice of lover than the woman they called Rollerball.

'Really Rooster, are you sure you know what you're doing?' asked Malcolm one afternoon. 'You'd want to be careful. I mean you don't know where she's been.'

They were sitting on the veranda of the Green House and Malcolm wrinkled his nose with fastidious concern as he tapped the ash from his cigarette into the barren garden bed.

'As far as that goes, Malcolm, who knows where you've been? Or what you were up to last year with those golfing types?' replied Rooster.

'But you don't think she's treating you like a ... well, like a sex object? A toy boy?'

'Suits me,' said Rooster, and he laced up his shoes and plunged off into the afternoon sun.

When Rooster disappeared around the corner, Malcolm collapsed onto the rusty chair, helpless with laughter.

'Poor Rooster. Lost the plot.'

'Would you fellas zip it!' said Wally, stomping out onto the veranda. 'I get sick and tired of hearing about it. That Rooster, he's no fool, and as for her, she's a good sort.'

'What, you know her then?' asked James.

'You could say that. Met her last year. At the pub. Like I said, she's a good sort, so shut up.'

* * *

When the field season had just about run its course and there was only a week left to go, Bill organised a celebration to mark the end. It was likely that he, too, was counting down the days till this nightmare field season was over and the field party had all left town. He booked the function room at the Phoenix Hotel, and on the last Saturday evening of the season everybody assembled there.

Bugsy, Malcolm and James had no intention of letting their hair down quite to the same extent they had done several weeks ago. This time there would be no surprises when they awoke in the morning, no descriptions of behaviour they couldn't remember. Malcolm had been very careful with alcohol since that occasion. Not that he had given it away completely. Something was needed to ameliorate the miserable conditions they were living in, but he was very moderate and refused to overindulge. On the evening of the party, he selected a bottle of red wine, poured himself a glass, sniffed the aroma and held the glass to the light so he could admire the ruby glint.

'Nothing wrong with a glass or two of wine,' he murmured.

'God no. It's been a bummer of a season, even worse than usual,' said James, helping himself to a glass.

A smiling girl arrived with a tray of sausage rolls. She offered them one each and wandered off to where Hobson and his partner stood scowling in the corner.

'Yes,' said Malcolm, raising his glass of wine. 'I propose a toast to the end of the worst season ever.'

'I'll drink to that!' said James.

Bugsy and Eddie raised their drinks.

'The worst season ever.'

Grasshopper and Wally pushed their pots of beer forward, 'Yeah! Worst season ever.'

Even Bill raised his beer glass, 'To the end of the season. And yes ... it was pretty bad.'

'Don't think we're blaming you, mate,' said James. 'We all know there's forces beyond your control and you've got your own job up here, apart from keeping us on our toes. And as for the Compound, jeez what a headache that must have been. Whose idea was it anyway?'

'Ah well. No need to go into that right now,' said Bill. 'Yes, let's drink to the end of the season. May better days be coming for all!'

Right at that moment Shane arrived with Cheryl in tow.

'Look out! Here comes Rollerball! What the hell! What sort of getup is that?' said James rudely.

Cheryl rolled into the room like a beachball, dressed in a bright yellow boilersuit, hair dyed purple and gelled into spikes, hot pink lipstick splashed across her mouth. Gaudy discs hung from her ears, so large it was a miracle her ear lobes weren't shredded. She must have been the brightest object for miles. Malcolm's eyes were riveted on her with the same appalled admiration you would give to a tiger if it was focussed right on you and heading steadily your way. He quivered with nervous laughter, spilling his wine until it dribbled down his shirt.

'What's the joke?' she asked, finding an empty glass and holding it out towards him.

'James just told me a story about an idiot field hand,' lied Malcolm, pouring her a glass of wine. 'I guess you're looking for Rooster.'

'Oh, not particularly,' she replied, glancing at him bright eyed.

The next morning Sally made gluggy porridge for breakfast

and disappeared back into her bedroom. She had once more wiped herself out with a bottle of whisky and partied too hard, celebrating her impending departure from Burkes Hill.

'No, I won't be back for another season,' she had said. 'Burkes Hill is a hole. Not my scene. Can't wait to leave. Might go south. Melbourne maybe ...'

She wasn't the only one who had partied too hard. There were several sore and sorry faces at breakfast; the atmosphere was subdued. Wally was sitting with his head in his hands, massaging his forehead and temples.

'Oh jeez,' he said. 'I think I'm getting too old for this.'

'No you're not, Wal,' said Grasshopper, and he looked thoughtfully at the porridge pot that Paul had just placed in the centre of the table. 'Has anybody seen Malcolm? He's not in his donga this morning.'

'Nah, he didn't come home with us as far as I recall,' said Wally. 'So, what was he up to, hey? Yeah, I wonder.'

Big Jill was ladling out porridge, pushing the bowls about the table to unenthusiastic recipients. 'Well, if you ask me,' she said, 'Malcolm was getting very friendly with that mate of Rooster's, that nurse. Probably went home with her.'

James spluttered into his coffee cup and Rooster winked at him. And although nobody really knew how Malcolm had spent the night, his reputation as a discerning man of style was torn to shreds at that moment. It was just too tempting not to imagine that he had awoken wedged against Cheryl's ample bosom.

Malcolm crept into the dining room as everybody was finishing their porridge and silently helped himself to a bowl.

'Where've you been?' demanded Grasshopper.

Malcolm ignored him.

'Hey mate, I'm feeling pretty crook this morning. Brought it on myself of course,' said Wally, as he contemplated Malcolm absently shovelling porridge in his mouth. 'But you look worse. Made a mistake, hey? Sometime in the night?'

Malcolm looked across at him.

'Shut up,' he said.

And kept eating porridge.

Chapter 29

No hand starts

A YEAR later I was back at the GIU field camp in Burkes Hill. It would have been more sensible to stay right away, given my most recent experiences at the Compound, but I wanted to see Eddie and I craved a break from routine life. Time spent at the Compound would be sure to make everyday tedium seem like a luxury. Besides, I wanted to visit the rock wallabies and bee-eaters and to take in that God's Own Country vibe that Gerald liked to go on about.

The field season had been in operation for several weeks when I arrived. Burkes Hill never changed much, although the Police Station in the main street had been damaged by a fire started by aggrieved cattle rustlers. Willy-willies still swirled their dust across the mullock heaps on the edge of town and over on College Road, Ralph the dog still sat panting on the footpath outside Mrs O'Regan's house.

But the Compound was so transformed, it was unrecognisable. There were cement paths and struggling lawns, garden beds and a volleyball court. Most of the mullock heaps had disappeared, replaced by landscaping and buildings. There was a new street of dongas beyond the ablutions block, and in the centre of the Compound, near where the port-a-loo had teetered, there was a large building containing a kitchen, dining hall, office space, and recreation area. The whole place still had the look of a penitentiary, largely due to those blasting security lights and the massive wire fencing that nobody could possibly scale, but there had been an attempt to soften this impression with a few vines planted about the fence.

Most astonishing of all was the atmosphere of contented tranquillity I detected in the dining room on my first morning there. The new catering-size kitchen glittered with stainless steel. And in this kitchen, behind the gleaming benches, stood a man dressed in clothes of such dazzling white he could have made an income advertising washing powder. This angel-in-cook's form was doling out the most enormous breakfasts with such a smile it was impossible to quibble over the size of the portion. I had great trouble convincing him that pregnant women do not need to eat twice as much as everybody else.

Christopher, back as party leader, sat at a table contentedly consuming his breakfast, a plate piled high with a smorgasbord of breakfast foods.

'I see you've met Robbo,' he said. 'Isn't he terrific? He's an ex-army cook.'

If the cook's cheer and the general vibe of satisfaction pervading the room wasn't enough to make me think that the golden age had finally arrived at the GIU, I only had to glance at Malcolm to be utterly convinced. He sat in a corner, away from the others, sipping coffee and nibbling on his breakfast, while a young woman stood behind him massaging his shoulders.

'Who's that?' I whispered to Eddie, confused by the cosy intimacy of the scene.

'Lindy. That's Lindy. Nice girl.'

'Yes, but who is she?'

'Oh, some friend of Malcolm's. Perhaps she's his sister ...

now these caves we found a fortnight ago have the most amazing fossils in them. We must arrange to visit them one weekend ...'

'Sister?'

Grasshopper leant across the table and said in a low voice, 'She's not his sister. She's part of Malcolm's policy never to suffer through another field season like last year. Lindy is another one of his comforts like the bottle of whisky and the chocolate bars. And she's going along with it because she's enjoying the game.'

'But what about Mia?'

'Mia, apparently, is a tolerant, liberated woman, or so I've been told. And Eddie here is too nice a guy to grasp what's going on and claims it's all innocent.'

I glanced across at them. Lindy had stopped massaging Malcolm's shoulders now, and they sat whispering together in the corner, until she suddenly lunged forward and dabbed her tongue on his ear.

'Doesn't look innocent,' I said quietly.

'Doesn't look it because it isn't,' Grasshopper replied.

Then I noticed that there was somebody missing from the breakfast table. 'Hey, where's Wally?'

'Gone,' said Eddie.

'Gone where?'

'Wally's given up on us all. He's moved to greener pastures,' said Grasshopper.

'Yep, it seems that shooting pigs isn't such a thrill for him anymore. Must have met a girl,' said James.

'Yeah, when he told me that painting houses is a more reliable way to make a living than fieldwork, I couldn't believe my ears,' said Paul in disgust. 'Painting houses better than shooting pigs? You'd have thought the guy's gone and got married or something. Never would have thought it; not from a guy like Wal.'

'Wait till you meet his replacement,' said Bugsy.

'Oh God,' said James, 'It's just as well Priscilla's not here this year. The guy would have been mutilated by now.'

Behind the kitchen bench, Robbo waved his tongs in the air. 'Hey, you lot, are you done with the food? Can I clear this stuff away?'

The leftovers of what had been an excellent breakfast were rapidly losing their appeal, sitting neglected on the bench cooling and congealing unpleasantly. A couple of flies that had miraculously teleported themselves through the insect screens buzzed about the trays.

'I think you can get rid of it,' said Christopher. 'There's only Hendo left and we're not likely to see him in a hurry.'

'Nope' said James. 'He'll have a hangover for sure. That guy's worse than Wally.'

'Sick is he? Better send him in some breakfast in bed,' said Robbo, piling a plate with the breakfast remains and garnishing it with flakes of congealed grease and a generous squirt of tomato sauce. 'Here Grasshopper, send this along. Should wake him up a bit.'

'Jeez, Robbo, this looks bloody revolting,' Grasshopper observed as he took the plate, 'If Hendo's not sick now, he will be when he sees this. There's even a drowned fly in it.'

'Hate to waste good food,' Robbo replied.

But Hendo was not sickened at the sight of his breakfast at all. Within a few minutes Grasshopper returned with an empty plate that appeared to have been licked clean.

'He was real appreciative actually.'

In fact, Hendo, unaccustomed to breakfast in bed, was so impressed by the gesture that he dragged himself out of his lair and into the dining room. Having just emerged from bed, he stunk like a walking pub and was completely dishevelled. He had a wild mop of dark curls and an irregular stubble across his face that gave him the appearance of somebody dangerous from a 'Wanted' poster. Despite this, Emily-Jane almost immediately regarded him favourably, taking him for some sort of furred critter, like one of those mildly belligerent, but lovable, monsters escaped from Sesame Street straight to the Burkes Hill Compound.

'Hey Robbo! Thanks mate. That was bloody delicious. I'm touched, real touched. You're a king amongst men.'

His eyes roamed the room and fell upon me. He had an arresting gaze that had challenge in it as well as a sort of contemplative intensity as if he had long ago discovered the absurdity in his own being and in the human world at large and was now intent on a reckless course of stirring the pot. It was not comfortable being the subject of Hendo's attention.

'Hey, what have we got here?' he asked. 'I've got to see this—the woman who can put up with Slanger.' And he began to inspect me in the rudest manner, circling about and staring from all angles as if I was a poultry exhibit on display at an agricultural show.

'Just ignore him,' said Eddie. 'It's really the best way. He comes from the town of Banana. Maybe that explains it. But he's probably just spent so long at the drillers' camps he's forgotten how to be civilised.'

'Slanger's just intimidated by the calibre of my intellect,' responded Hendo. 'I should be advising the government I get such brilliant ideas about reforming society. They might be a bit controversial, but they sure would solve a bloody lot of problems.'

I knew this man was going to subject me to his theories whether I wanted to hear them or not, that they were likely to be unedifying and that they would be out of his mouth before I could flee the room.

'Here's one you'll be impressed by. My plan for creating the ideal society,' he began, 'You know, what they call a utopia. The first thing to do is to deposit all women in banks.'

His gleaming eyes gripped mine with that contemplative gaze and it felt as if he had thrown out invisible ropes that restrained me from escape, forcing me to listen to this bilge. 'Yeah ... to be withdrawn only when necessary,' he continued, barely repressing his glee, like a fisherman watching a large fish swim towards the bait. But I responded with nothing more than a bored nod as if he had been droning on with tedious details about the drought down in the Banana Shire.

'No one cares for your ideas, Hendo,' said Big Jill. 'Why don't you stop trying to annoy everyone. Are you coming down to the Footie Club tonight? There's a dance on'.

'So, I've heard,' said Hendo. 'I might just cruise on down and check out the local talent.'

'The local talent in this town might be more than you bargain for, mate,' commented James.

'Do you reckon Rollerball will be there?' asked Bugsy with some anxiety.

'I think it's highly likely, and on that account I'm not so sure I want to come along myself. When I think what happened that night to ...' and James shuddered. 'Just like a fly in a spider's web.'

'Who's this Rollerball? What are you fellas talking about?' asked Hendo.

'We're talking about a voracious, rapacious female called Rollerball,' said James.

'Sounds interesting. Never met a voracious, rapacious female before. Better put her in a bank,' said Hendo.

'It's no joking matter,' said Bugsy. 'She's terrifying! I mean we're all here to do some serious geology, but she thinks we're here just for her personal use, a sort of specialised stable of stud men she can toy with at will, and pick off slowly, one by one.'

'For God's sake, Bugsy. Where did this all come from? Stop being a wuss,' said Big Jill. 'Cheryl's just a girl after a good time. Ask Rooster when he's back from Bogarilla next week. He'll tell you the same.'

'Yeah, don't be such wusses you two, and come along to the Footie Club tonight. As for this Rollerball, can't wait to meet her,' said Hendo.

* * *

That evening the group from the GIU gathered awkwardly around a table beneath the lights of the football club, sipping drinks and eating peanuts, while the first band set up and the Burkes Hill crowd slowly dribbled in. A ripple of unease was darting about the table, and apprehensive glances were exchanged from time to time between the men, as if they were reluctantly attending a magic show and were all nervously hoping that somebody else would be selected to participate when the magician wanted to saw a victim in half. But nobody could articulate these fears, not with Lindy sitting there next to Malcolm. She was probably wondering why everybody seemed so strange and uptight when this was supposed to be a fun evening out.

And then Cheryl arrived. She bounced into the club with the same vibrant flair she had shown last time, although her colour scheme had changed. Her short hair was now crimson, and she had on a purple outfit that involved a tight-fitting zippered top. James and Malcolm did not laugh at her appearance on this occasion, but they quivered along with the other guys at the table, and they all fixed their eyes somewhere else, willing her not to notice their group and pick it out for any special attentions. But their determination not to be noticed only worked as an attractor, and as soon her eyes fell upon them, she headed in their direction, beaming with wicked pleasure.

The GIU guys looked just like a bunch of cowardly cowboys back in the days of the Wild West, trembling in a saloon at the approach of a temperamental gunslinger in a bad mood. Malcolm slithered to the floor, muttering to Lindy that he had lost a coin. James and Grasshopper leapt into each other's arms and clutched at one another in a failed attempt to appear homosexual. Only Hendo seemed to be enjoying himself.

When Cheryl reached the table, she paused for moment, half a smile on her lips. Then she raised her finger and pointed it directly at James. In a hooting voice she loudly announced, 'I'm going to fuck you ...'

There was a horrified silence for a second or two. James had gone very pale and grabbed convulsively at Grasshopper. He had been dreading an encounter with this woman, but this onslaught was more immediate and even more hideous than he had been expecting. The band had not yet begun, and her voice had reverberated across the club. Everybody in the place was probably staring at him. Somebody was laughing uproariously near the bar, almost certainly at him and this ghastly predicament.

But then her finger slid along and pointed to Grasshopper, 'And you.'

Then to Bugsy, 'And you.'

'And you, you and you ...' finger pointing slowly and surely at each man.

The glasses rattled as Malcolm shuddered underneath the table. Big Jill nearly choked on a gulp of beer. Bugsy's face was as crimson as Cheryl's hair and Lindy's mouth had dropped open with shock. But Cheryl wasn't finished.

'And no hand starts!' she yelled.

I think it's fair to say the only person in the group undisturbed by this behaviour was Hendo, who rammed a handful of peanuts into his mouth and chewed on them noisily while directing his gaze towards her, eyeball to eyeball.

'Interesting offer,' he said at length. 'Better show me your credentials so I can think it over.'

They stared intently at one another for a moment or two and there seemed to be a buzz in the air as if they were a couple of Jedi knights about to pull out their light sabres to engage in a duel. Cheryl was clearly up for the challenge. Barely hesitating, she unzipped that purple top, exposing voluminous breasts swelling out from an inadequate lacy black bra. Her flesh gleamed beneath the fluorescent lights. A moment of excruciating entertainment just for the GIU table. A shudder of extreme discomfort swept over everybody forced to view this spectacle, with the sole exception of Hendo, who sipped calmly at his beer and slowly looked her up and down.

'Sorry love, seen better on a cow,' he remarked, waving her away with a shrug.

Mercifully, right at that moment the band cranked up and nobody could hear a word more. Cheryl did not appear to be remotely demoralised by this encounter, if anything she looked pleased that she had at last met a worthy opponent. Giggling, she made her way to the bar where the person who had been laughing uproariously applauded her enthusiastically. This turned out to be her old school mate Shane, who had been employed as a field hand by the GIU the previous year. He had probably put her up to it.

Eddie and I left soon after that; we had a child to get to bed. By the time we were leaving, Hendo had already gone from the table across to the bar, where it looked like he was striking up a thriving friendship with Cheryl.

'Oh my God,' I said to Eddie. 'He's recognised a kindred spirit. And God help everyone if those two join forces.'

'I don't even want to imagine it,' said Eddie.

When we got to the Compound Robbo was mopping out the dining room.

'You're back already,' he said. 'I was just about to head over to the Footie Club myself. Any good?'

'The band was just getting going when we left, but it sounded okay. There's certainly plenty of entertainment going on over there tonight,' said Eddie.

'Good ... good. Ah Cynthia, before I go, I've been saving something for you,' and Robbo gave me a tray laden with twelve portions of dessert. 'Look, put these in the fridge in your donga and then if you get one of those cravings I've heard about, you know, in the middle of the night or something, just help yourself.'

Chapter 30

Venus and Mars

ROMANCE SPROUTED that year like the grass that Paul watered at the Compound each week. At least it did for James and Malcolm, if you could call what went on romance. But these affairs also brought complications, as I began to discover one Sunday morning when I wandered into the office, not expecting much in the way of revelation or entertainment.

Only a few weeks ago this place had been brand new, pristine and shining, but the gloss was fading now, giving way under an untidy scattering of papers and maps and a thin layer of dust. Nobody was working, but Hendo was hunched over a computer screen in the corner, playing Pac-Man and frowning at a disturbance going on across the room near the whiteboard on which was scrawled the roster for the coming week.

'No Bazz! No way! I forbid it!' screeched a small, round woman with frizzy blond hair.

'Aggie, it's my job. See!' protested her companion, pointing at the whiteboard.

I'd heard about this guy, a new field hand who resided in town, like Shane and Hobson had the previous year.

'I'll be having a word with Christopher, then, won't I,' said

Aggie. 'If he doesn't know what's going on, then it's high time he found out.'

'But Aggie ...'

'Nobody's coming between me and my new pergola. You're not to buy so much as a chocolate bar at the moment.'

Bazz was a man of such enormous dimensions he could easily have picked Aggie up between his forefinger and his thumb and hurled her over the security fence. But he just looked bewildered.

'Won't it be nice when we can entertain your friends at home?' she asked.

Bazz looked blank. 'I dunno, Aggie,' was all he said.

'Cut the domestic. I'll go with Malcolm next week. You can go with Slanger. We'll swap. Anything to shut the Missus up,' yelled Hendo, jamming his thumb down on the keyboard.

Bazz shrugged. Aggie glared. Hendo rejected the computer as a companion and galloped out of the office, leaving Aggie and Bazz to plan their pergola, and I followed him, curious.

'You gotta feel sorry for Bazz,' muttered Hendo, treading heavily on the earth of the volleyball court. 'Forever bound to a sheila like that.'

'She's probably got a heart of gold,' I said.

'She's bloody bossy with it,' he replied. 'You know, I once thought of getting married. Trouble is, any woman silly enough to marry me, is possibly too silly to marry if you see what I mean. Well, I look at Bazz and I thank God.'

'Why doesn't Aggie want Bazz to go in the field with Malcolm?'

'Because Malcolm's having some kind of early-onset mid-life crisis, that's why. His brain's gone bloody walk-about. Dunno where it is, but it's definitely not in his head. It's been kicked out by another part of him, if you know what I mean. It happens. Seen it before.'

'Yes, but that shouldn't impact Bazz and Aggie.'

'Shouldn't and doesn't are two different things. It impacts us all. You see Malcolm's field area is to the east of here, down on the escarpment, and it's not too much of a stretch to drive into Townsville at the end of the working day to visit his girlfriend, who happens to work in some therapy centre down there. Malcolm thinks it's great fun for all, if we go and meet up with the bloody sheila in the Breakwater Casino or somewhere. Yeah, but we expect to swag it all week and live on spag bog and barbecued steak provided by the GIU, and you can't swag it in the streets of Townsville. We end up having to buy take-away and paying for a spot in the caravan park, while he's dining in a restaurant and sleeping with her. But we're all here to make a crust, not to aid and abet the bloody ill-advised love affairs of the geos at our own expense.'

'Well, it's good of you to get Bazz out of it.'

'Bazz is a good fella. He does what he's told. But me? I can tell Malcolm where to stick it. On the other hand, if I happen to feel like a night out at the casino, well I might just cooperate.'

'But what can Malcolm be thinking? He's already got a girl-friend at home, and from what I've seen she means the world to him.'

'Yeah, so I've heard,' said Hendo. 'But like I said, you can't think when you've got no brain. It's a curse. Can strike the best of us. And he'd better bloody hope that his brain turns up soon or he'll lose the girlfriend and the job. Yeah, he's heading for big trouble. But I told you, didn't I, Cynthia —if all women were shoved in banks, none of this drama would be going on.'

Hendo dangled this bait at me any chance he got, but there was a woman he didn't think should be shoved in a bank and to whom he would never dream of voicing such an outrageous opinion. This was Shona, a teacher from the local school, with whom James was developing a new and beautiful friendship.

The relationship had blossomed on the night of the football club dance and I suspect that James now thought that going to that event had been the best thing he'd ever done in his life, and worth every excruciating second of his encounter with Cheryl.

Shona had dark hair that rippled way down her back and a face so lovely that even the cynical and coarse Hendo was stricken with dumb tenderness whenever he looked at her. Any cracks about women he may have had in him died on his lips when Shona was in the room. It wasn't that he considered James a rival or that he desired Shona for himself. Whatever his past experiences had been, he was well aware that such an approach would only lead to hopelessness and heartbreak. Instead, his attitude towards her was more that of a troubadour of old, composing songs for an unattainable, but beloved queen, a woman who inspired his spirit in a way that was beyond the mundanities of life.

Hendo hovered over Shona like a doting father, critically assessing suitors for their worth, although his concept of 'worth' was rather different from a typical father's. In his opinion, Shona deserved the best, but as the best was unavailable in Burkes Hill, then contenders should at least be capable of showing her a good time.

One Friday evening I saw him sprawled on the doorstep of James's donga. His legs were stretched out in a leisurely way as if he was settling in for the evening and he was surveying the sky where the first stars were glimmering. James appeared at the window and shouted at him in an irate voice. 'What the hell are you sitting here for? I'm not going out with you lot tonight. I've got better things to do.'

'Yeah, I know you have. I'm just looking at the stars; there's a great view of them from your doorstep. I just saw a satellite go by, and look, Mars is shining over the Compound tonight. See right there, that droopy one with the red glow. That's Mars,' said Hendo.

'Piss off. We're not interested in planets right now.'

'What? An intelligent couple like yourselves not interested in planets?'

'No, not at this minute. Would you please go away. Go to the pub and get pissed or go visit Rollerball or whatever it is you like to amuse yourself with on a Friday night. Just do it. Drive up the hill and count the shooting stars if you want. Just not here!'

At breakfast the next morning Hendo raked James with his blue gaze, 'Initiative, that's all you need! I sat on those steps on purpose, to measure the vibrations, and I can tell you I was bloody disappointed.'

But James just shrugged and laughed as he poured himself coffee. I had never seen him so relaxed and happy. This was a different James to the one who had become so jittery over the girl from the grocery store at Blue Ridge. And different again from the glassy-eyed man musing over Tiffany the following year. I wasn't entirely sure, and didn't want to ask, if his relationship with Tiffany had actually ended, although it was clear enough that his fascination for her had been subsiding ever since she had fled from him before the gold conference.

Christopher plonked a plate of scrambled eggs, grilled tomatoes, mushrooms and toast on the table and went to get a cup of tea. 'Hey Eddie,' he said, 'Do you reckon you could stick around after lunch for a bit. There's a student in town who wants a bit of background on her project area, which is out where you've been working. She'll be heading up to Oscar's field camp on the Black Bream River tomorrow. I thought you'd be able to give her a hand.'

'For God's sake, Christopher. Give the man a break,' James interjected, with all the benevolence of a contented soul. 'Cynthia hasn't come all this way to sit bored in the Compound on weekends while Slanger hangs around to advise the student population. No Eddie, take your family for that picnic by the river this afternoon, as you'd planned, and I will take care of it. I'm as familiar with those rocks as you are.'

'Thanks James,' I said. 'Robbo's already packed that picnic. I was really looking forward to it.'

'No problem. No problem at all. We've got to help each other out. You know, flow of life and all that. You enjoy your picnic,' he replied. And he wandered off, whistling to himself.

We spent the afternoon on the riverbank, beneath the green light of the paperbarks, listening to the sound of rippling water as the river flowed by, blissfully unaware of the difficulties that James had brought upon himself with his generous impulse. But on our return, when we saw him, red, flustered, and trembling in the recreation area out on the porch of the communal building, we realised that something had gone wrong. He was pleading with Grasshopper and Hendo.

'Come on guys. You gotta help me out. Please. I don't know what to do.'

'Hey James, what's up?' asked Eddie. 'That was a great gesture of yours. Lovely down by the river today. We really appreciated it.'

'Yeah, I bet. But if I'd known what I was letting myself in for I would have got to hell out of here myself and left you to it. I can't get rid of her. She refuses to leave and she's creeping me out. Reminds me of that randy emu that chased me that time .... She even put her finger through the hole in my jeans for god's sake ...'

'Some people complain about nothing,' said Grasshopper, who was trying to finish a game of darts with Hendo. 'Whinge, whinge, whinge ...'

'But you don't understand. Shona's coming here soon. We're

going out for dinner at the Chinese, and then for some ... coffee ... back at her place. And the last thing I need right now is an amorous girl hanging off me. It could all get a bit awkward. I want her off the premises before Shona turns up. We were done going through the data well over an hour ago, and she still won't bloody leave. Keeps asking questions about the Burkes Hill nightlife. Nightlife? Where the hell does she think we are? Surfers bloody Paradise?'

'Yeah, but what are you expecting us to do about it?' asked Hendo, hurling a dart at the bullseye. 'It's easy. Just tell her to piss off. There are times in life when you've just gotta be blunt.'

'But I don't want to be rude. I don't want to alienate the woman; might have to work with her someday. I just want her gone. I've dropped hints. I've even told her I'm expecting my girlfriend to visit. But it's not getting through. I need a Plan B.'

'Oh yeah?' said Hendo in a bored voice.

'Yeah. I reckon you two could easily scare her off if you go into the office and carry on like a pair of crude pigs ....'

'Shouldn't be too hard,' I couldn't help saying, although I didn't think very much of this scheme at all.

'Shut up, Cynthia!' said Hendo.

'Come on, you've got the talent Hendo. You know you have. Revolt her, disgust her, slouch, swear, pick your nose, spit on the floor, tell her you think women should be locked in a bank, aren't fit to be educated. Use your imagination. Have fun with it. Just get rid of her ... I've got to get ready. Shona will be here any minute now.'

But right at that moment Shona arrived. She drove through the gates, pulled up beside the field vehicles, and emerged from her car, walking along the cement path in the golden afternoon light, dressed in white cotton and flicking her hair back behind her shoulders. The men were silent for a moment, watching as she approached.

'That girl will just have to get the bloody message,' said James. 'I'd better go and get a quick shower. Won't be long.'

'We can't do much about the girl, but we'll look after Shona all right,' Hendo volunteered.

He invited her to sit on the dusty bench near the ping-pong table and tossed her a can of beer. Grasshopper sat beside her and entertained her with embarrassing stories about James, most of them involving possums. Meanwhile, the student was still wandering about the office, peering at maps and air photos. Eventually, she settled herself behind a computer and switched on the games. She was apparently not planning on going anywhere.

James had showered in double quick time and was still threading his belt through the loopholes of his jeans as he crept quietly into the building through the kitchen door, trying to avoid the girl who was still lurking in the office. And right at that moment the telephone rang and echoed out across the Compound.

'James!' yelled Robbo, after a few seconds had gone by. 'Phone call for you. Local call, some lady called Tiffany.'

'Tiffany? Tiffany ...' repeated James in a pale remote voice as if Tiffany was a distant memory he was trying to recall. 'Oh God.'

He wobbled to the telephone and after a minute or two, replaced the receiver and wobbled away with an ashen face. You'd have thought he had just heard news of an impending death in the family.

'You okay?' I asked him. 'You don't look so well.'

'It's Tiffany,' he whispered. 'She's waiting for me down at the Phoenix Hotel. Calls it a special surprise. What am I going to do?'

But Tiffany wasn't his only problem. That enthusiastic student had heard his voice and came out from the office.

'Hey, what's been keeping you?' she asked, ignoring the stunned-mullet expression on his face, and clasping his arm. 'What say we go down to one of the pubs in town and have a couple of drinks to finish off with. Anywhere we can go bopping tonight?'

Something snapped in him at her touch. He snatched up her books, thrust them into her arms, and bundled her out through the kitchen door. 'I'm sorry but you'll have to go bopping another time ... I've just been called up by a colleague. Need to get to Julia Creek immediately. Can't waste another minute ... goodbye ... Nice meeting you and all that.'

And then with great effort, he propelled himself robotically towards the recreation area.

'Shona ... Shona my darling ... something terrible has happened ...' he stuttered in an anguished voice, face contorting as he struggled to find the words to deal with his predicament.

To think he'd been on top of the world that morning, and now he was feeling like a besieged worm. Behind his back, Hendo had the grin of an amused orang-utan as he watched proceedings.

'Craddock has just sent me out into the field. Told me to leave immediately. Says there's an anomaly with my data and I've got to check it out right away ... I'm so sorry. I'm devastated. But he just won't listen to reason.'

At this speech, Grasshopper's dart flew way off the mark, missed the board entirely and plummeted earthward. Hendo was now looking like a confused orang-utan. 'What the hell?' he muttered.

Even Shona looked as if she couldn't believe her ears. 'Christopher said that? But he's such a sweet man.'

'Yes, well he can be sweet,' said James, rubbing his head as if the effort of lying was making it ache. 'But he's a perfectionist. And he has impossibly high standards. When you don't quite meet his expectations, he suddenly becomes ... er ... irrational and demanding. Ask Eddie about it; he'll tell you.'

'Surely he doesn't mean you to go right away?' asked Shona in disbelief.

'Immediately,' replied James sadly.

'But it'll be dark in an hour,' she said. 'There doesn't seem any point.'

'I know; I know. We all know. But like I said irrational and demanding.'

It was just as well Christopher did not appear during this exchange or things could have become very awkward indeed. Perhaps anxious about that very possibility, James, overwrought with emotion, grasped her around the waist and kissed her. 'I'll return on Thursday. We'll postpone our dinner until then ... Come on Grasshopper, you're leaving for the field in five minutes. Get your act together!'

'What?'

'I said we're leaving for the field in five minutes.' He lowered his voice and muttered, 'Look, I'll buy you a carton of beer and we'll be back a day early. I'll explain later, just get ready. We can't waste any more time. We'll be swagging in the old shack at Ten Mile Creek tonight.'

'What? Don't be bloody ridiculous,' said Hendo. 'You've all gone mad. There's something bloody fishy going on here and I don't like it.'

But James just clasped Shona closer and caressed her head into his shoulder so she couldn't see a thing and mouthed the words *carton of beer* at him. Things were getting costly for James that weekend. Hendo shrugged and stomped off in disgust while Grasshopper, eyes still bulging with astonishment, found himself in a whirlwind flurry of pre-field preparation. Before he had any real idea of what was actually going on, he was reversing a vehicle out of the Compound with James a trembling wreck beside him, waving at Shona as she made her way back to her car.

'It's either a drought or a raging bloody torrent,' he complained.

'Yeah, this is the land of droughts and flooding rains alright. Always has been,' Grasshopper commented unhelpfully. 'You know that poem we learnt at school, *I love a sunburnt country* …'

I expect they dropped by the Phoenix Hotel on their way out of town, and I don't know what story James told Tiffany, although I doubt it was the truth. I imagine she was as bitterly disappointed as he had been by her desertion the previous year and she may have thought it was payback. In any case, it was a relationship not destined to endure for much longer.

Grasshopper reported that they ended up that night at the shack by the creek as James had said they would, and that James, it seemed, had at last learned to appreciate the possums. At any rate, he found their nocturnal trampling a pleasant alternative to the web of romantic entanglements ensnaring him back in Burkes Hill.

'Nah,' said Hendo the next week. 'James is just a wimp. Can't face his own problems without running away with his tail between his legs.' And he ripped open a tin of beer. 'But he buys a good carton, I'll grant him that.'

As for Malcolm, he continued on with Lindy, heart as light as a feather, oblivious to all predictions of troubles and disaster. There was no field season he ever enjoyed quite so much. 'Consequences. What consequences?' he would have replied if anybody had asked if this fling would impact his home life. 'My life with Mia? Certainly not. Not in the least. Why should it?'

At the end of the season, Malcolm cheerfully parted ways with Lindy. It was as if they had been partners in a folk dance, partners who had danced with each other for a few moments, then bowed and moved on. And it was Mia who waited for Malcolm, as usual, at the Brisbane airport on his return. She held a gift wrapped in bright purple, tied with a green ribbon. Malcolm hurled himself at her, fell to his knees, and before his on-looking, pink-eared colleagues begged her to marry him.

Chapter 31

Out of the frying pan

THE YEAR in which the Compound building was brand new, and Robbo cooked behind the benches, was the best field season we ever had at the GIU. Robbo's only flaw was that he served such generous portions of delicious food we all risked getting fat. Those old stories about defective cooks wrecking field seasons were forgotten. But not for long. When Robbo was snapped up by a more permanent concern, the GIU was once more minus a cook. It was the moment for Priscilla to step in. When she recommended the appointment of Morris all those memories of just how bad field cooks can be came flooding back.

Priscilla had been forging a career for herself in administration back at Head Office these last years. This change of direction made good use of her organisational skills, improved her lifestyle, and got her away from that pig-shooting, leering, wild crew up north. Nobody would ever have suggested that she lacked the skills for management, but even so, her rise in the GIU was far more rapid than anybody would have anticipated, being largely due to an unfortunate circumstance that afflicted her immediate superior, the immaculate Lenora Worthington.

Lenora was cool, disciplined and just a little dictatorial,

qualities that made it all the more extraordinary that she was recorded by the the security cameras one evening cavorting half-naked with the personnel manager on the cement floor of the basement. She would never be viewed with the same fear-tinged respect at the GIU again. One couldn't expect the security staff to keep an episode like that to themselves; it was the most interesting thing that had happened in years of dreary toil. There was generally nothing to be seen in the basement security film footage but empty rows of dusty archived files. But now, there it was for all to see, each moment of Lenora's abandoned encounter with a man known as the most boring member of staff.

When she left the building on that remarkable evening, smiling softly to herself, she was met by a bunch of smirking security men.

'A bit dishevelled are you, love?' one of them reported asking her, winking in a particularly hideous manner.

She would have known immediately that she would have to leave if she didn't want to be the butt of teatime jokes for the rest of her GIU career, a person who triggered stifled whispers and giggles down every corridor and in every office.

Lenora and the personnel manager moved to South Australia together and Priscilla was promoted. Consequently, she was empowered to wield her influence over the next field season by recommending Morris.

Priscilla knew he was a friend of Wally's, but she couldn't have known that Wally's yarns had confused him. Morris thought that a cook and a field hand were one and the same, and if he took on the cook's job he would be plunged into the life of wild adventure he yearned for. Morris might have been okay as a field hand, but as a cook he was woeful. Not that Priscilla could possibly have detected that, not when he brought her a slice of exquisite chocolate cake as a sample of his skills. She never guessed till long afterwards that it had been purchased at his local bakery.

* * *

That year my mood plummeted the moment I first glimpsed the Compound. Strange, because the place looked physically the same, the upbeat arrangement of lawns, garden beds, volleyball courts and dongas. But despite the sunshine, the atmosphere was dull and heavy as if a toxic mist hovered over the paths and seeped into the donga windows. Mood can be as infectious as a virus.

When we collected Grasshopper outside the barbershop on our way through town, he recommended I stay right away from the Compound. 'It'll just get you down,' he said.

'But I need a couple of days to get organised, I can't come out into the field straight away. I've got to think about Mary-Lou as well as Emily Jane. Nappies and things ... Is there anybody at the Compound at the moment?'

'Sure, there's people there. There's the cook, but you may as well hang out with a cockroach. There's Brett, a field hand from Canberra waiting for his crew to arrive—an absolute jerk. And there's Tracy,' said Grasshopper, pronouncing this last name with a drawled inflection that implied he had measured Tracy against his usual expectations for humanity and found her some-what lacking.

'Who's Tracy?'

'A uni friend of Potts. They're both up here to do a project,' said Eddie.

'Yeah, but Potts is in the field and she's here, for some reason I can't figure out. Potts claims she's his girl, but that's not how it looks to me,' said Grasshopper.

'What about Paul?' I asked.

'He's taken a break,' replied Eddie. 'Gone off pig-shooting for a few days.'

'He can't stand the Compound at the moment either,' said Grasshopper.

'Well, I'll just have to manage,' I said, hoping they were exaggerating.

Grasshopper dragged our gear to the donga while Eddie took us to meet the cook, who was slumped over the pool table. He was a small, nondescript man with shaggy brown hair and depressed eyes, dressed entirely in black.

'Cynthia, this is Morris. Perhaps you can give him a hand while you're here,' said Eddie. It was only later I realised how hopeful he sounded.

Morris gave no response at all; he didn't even look up. He just slammed the ball across the table.

Eddie shrugged and we walked away. 'There's something seriously wrong with that guy,' he said. 'But look, I have to go now. Why don't you take the kids inside and switch on *Playschool*?' And he kissed us goodbye.

We sauntered into the recreation area to find the television already monopolised by a slouching creep with a pink sarong tied loosely about his middle. This was Brett, the field hand from Canberra. He was shovelling sardines into his mouth from a tin in his lap while a graphically lurid piece of pornography beamed out at him from the screen. I knew instantly it was a waste of time asking to switch the channel across to *Playschool*.

I rushed outside with the children, not wanting to stay at the Compound a moment longer, hoping to catch Eddie and Grasshopper before they drove off. Grasshopper was right. There are times when it's not worth trying to be sensible and this was one of them. But they were already beyond recall, disappearing in a swirl of dust, and we were alone, staring vacantly at the bottle tops and cigarette butts that littered the Compound grounds. I couldn't say I hadn't been warned.

That evening Morris told me to choose a tin from the store cupboard and heat it up myself. He didn't bother eating anything, but as the sun set, he lit a fire in the barbecue place out on the porch, and hunched before the flames as the light dimmed, swigging from a rum bottle he shared with Tracy. Brett was still watching porn and was perfectly happy eating tinned sardines.

As the evening progressed, Morris complained at length about his life in a dull, droning voice. He said that he was over-worked and under-appreciated, that the GIU was awful, and everyone treated him badly, particularly Hendo. I wondered that Tracy could stand all this whingeing, but to my astonish-ment, she drew her chair close, patted his hand in sympathy and enlaced her fingers with his. Morris seemed way too self-absorbed to be attractive, but she evidently saw some appeal to which I was blind. When I came out of the ablutions block that night, I noticed Morris follow her into her donga, staggering like an aged tomcat. She held the door open for him, so I guess he was welcome, whatever her relationship with Potts was supposed to be.

Over the next two days I did whatever I could think of to stay away from the Compound for as long as possible. I roamed the streets of Burkes Hill, pushing Emily Jane in her stroller, the baby strapped to my back. I gate-crashed local playgroups, visited Mrs O'Regan and Ralph, and bought clothes I didn't need from the shops in the main street. My distaste for Compound life was so great that when Eddie returned on Friday evening, I insisted that he take us out for dinner to the Phoenix Hotel. We escaped out of a side entrance after our meal to avoid being incorporated into a group of boozing field hands, but it gave us a break.

It was Saturday before I had the chance to sample any of Morris's cuisine. He wasn't too bad in the porridge and muesli department, but lunch was, to borrow a phrase from James McCracken, bloody awful. A large tin dish had been slopped full of burnt sausages, onions, gravy and mashed potatoes. The whole lot was so thickly adorned with lumps that the entire meal had the unwholesome appearance of being covered with warts. I looked around for some bread and vegemite to eat instead, but nothing else was on offer.

The meal wasn't good, but I didn't think it warranted quite the horrified, ominous hush that it was received with by the other partakers, not until I realised that this was the meal served up week after week, with relentless repetition.

'Not a-bloody-gain!' groaned James.

Bugsy had gone pale. 'I'm starting to have nightmares about sausages,' he said.

'He's playing with our heads,' said Hendo. 'Bangers and mash used to be my favourite, but now I gag at the thought. Hey, mate,' he said to Morris, 'You've brought shame and disrepute to a good, decent plate of bangers and mash, now hated and rejected by all. Bloody hell, man, is there nothing else you know how to cook?'

But it was Malcolm who was most badly affected. He quivered at the head of the table, staring at the sausages on his plate in an agonised way. Suddenly, a strangled primeval growl emerged from deep within him. He thrust his chair out, took up his plate and strode into the kitchen. Slamming his lunch on the bench, he grabbed Morris by the neck of his tee-shirt.

'This is what I think of your meal, Bozo!' With a spectacular flourish he scraped the meal into the garbage bin. 'Think twice before you serve that crap again.'

Tracy glared about the room. She was the only one present at all outraged by this insult to Morris and his terrible cooking.

Love had evidently obscured all her senses. Potts, munching on a sausage, glanced at her with a look of disgust. Whatever fantasies he had ever entertained about this girl had proved as empty as the contents of an over-inflated balloon that pops and falls deflated and limp to the ground.

There was an awkward silence.

And then Paul said, 'Hey, Morris, could you vary the menu a bit? I mean sausages and gravy is all right in itself, but maybe you could try something different, like ... um, quiche for example.'

'Real men don't eat quiche,' said Hendo.

'Well pizza then ... or a pie ... or toasted sandwiches.'

'Tacos or ham and salad rolls or ...' began Bugsy.

'Even salmon mousse would be okay,' said Grasshopper.

It amazed me that Morris was not completely demoralised by this negativity, but it actually seemed to spur him to action, at least for a short time. That same afternoon I heard his voice hiss at me from the back door of the kitchen when I was taking down nappies from the lines that had been erected along the fence.

'Hey Cynthia, do you know anything about bread-and-butter pudding? Mine's gone funny.'

I trailed him into the kitchen and stared at a mess of milk and bread. 'Did you put eggs in it?'

'Eggs?'

I refrained from laughter. Anybody who has ever served a raw roast to guests is scarcely qualified to make fun of the defects of another cook. I whipped up another pudding and put it in the oven. That evening Christopher said, 'Hey look, Morris is turning over a new leaf. Hooray. There's some bread-and-butter pudding.'

His assessment was premature, although the next day at lunchtime, Morris varied the menu as instructed and did not serve sausages and mash. Instead, he swaggered into the kitchen at twelve noon, carrying enormous packages wrapped in greasy newspaper. He rang the bell and waited for the throng to assemble. When all were present, he unwrapped the packages with the air of a famous chef displaying a very difficult and spectacular culinary technique, as he awaited the murmurs of appreciation he expected as hungry geologists surveyed their fish and chips. The fact that he was standing in front of a catering-quality deep-fryer appeared to escape him.

Eddie piled his plate with fish and chips, then said in the politest of tones, 'Hey, Morris, do you have any salad?

'What?' yelled Morris with a belligerent glare, as if Eddie had requested *Lobster Thermidor* as an alternative meal.

'I was after a bit of salad, please,' repeated Eddie.

'It's a reasonable request, isn't it?' asked Hendo. 'You do know what salad is? Tomatoes, lettuce, cucumbers, carrot. That sort of thing.'

But Morris remained outraged. His face puckered. He'd gone to all the trouble to get these fish and chips from the takeaway, expecting everyone to be pleased, and still they weren't satisfied.

'I'm not a fucking gourmet chef!' he screamed. 'You geologists make me sick! You ponce in here demanding all these bloody frills as if you're in some five-star joint on the harbour in Sydney, but all I'm paid for is to provide youse all with some basic bloody chow!' He folded his arms together and refused to move a muscle.

But Eddie contributed to the mess fund like everybody else and he wanted salad, not anything fancy with carrots carved into roses and shavings of truffle, just plain salad. He stared across at Morris with an expression on his face similar to the one I had seen on that horse, back in Blue Ridge, when the animal had sized me up next to the rubbish bin, a sort of speculative contempt. Evidently concluding that Morris was not a force worth bothering with, he barged into the kitchen and thrust him aside as he would thrust aside any other useless obstacle standing in his way. Eddie scrounged through a box of rotting vegetables lying untouched out the back and salvaged enough to construct a rough salad, while Morris looked on, glowering and foolish.

'Come and get it; come and get it,' called Hendo. 'Any of you lot who think you might have a touch of scurvy. You know: if your eyeballs are falling out, or your skin's peeling off, or whatever else happens with vitamin deficiency.'

No wonder there were all those stories about cooks ruining field seasons. I was watching it happen right before my eyes. One discontented individual and the whole ambience of the place had transformed. The cheery atmosphere that had stemmed from Robbo's good will the year before had evaporated completely, replaced by one of sombre irritability.

Even the conversation topics had changed. I didn't hear any gossip about the amorous activities of others. The field hands never mentioned pigs. Even the woman they called Rollerball didn't excite much interest anymore; she was just a mate of Hendo's with an off sense of humour. But, hey, anyone who could make them laugh in a season dominated by an endless succession of badly cooked bangers and mash was appreciated, no matter how distasteful the jokes. Everybody much preferred to talk about food, obsessively dwelling on pumpkin soup, chicken broth, roast lamb, crisp potatoes, pavlova and lemon meringue pie. When they tired of that they moved on to Morris, describing him with a series of imaginative expletives, and when they ran out of bad words, they wondered what the bloody hell Tracy saw in him.

In a way, I felt sorry for Morris. He was a misfit for the job, clearly miserable, stuck behind the security fences of the Burkes Hill Compound without so much as a recipe book. This was vastly different from what Wally's stories had led him to expect. He had imagined he was coming north to a wilderness where he could shoot feral pigs and struggle with crocodiles, while he whipped up the odd stew over the campfire on the odd evening. It was a terrible mistake, but he did nothing about it. He just stayed on at the Compound, wallowing in disappointment, resenting the freedoms of the rest of the field party, and failing. But a day came when I lost all sympathy for Morris.

It was a Friday, and Eddie, Potts and Paul spent the day at the Compound, packing rock samples. Tracy was supposed to be working with them, but she hadn't lifted a finger to help, preferring to slump over the pool table with the cook, who also would have been better off if he had spent his time organising an evening meal. As the day wore on, I became more frustrated at the sight of him. I remembered Robbo, the year before, preparing trays of lasagne or pots of curry on Fridays. I remembered Sally, apart from a lapse here and there, bending tenderly over the morsels she assembled each Friday afternoon. Even I had put in effort on Fridays. But this sort of diligence wasn't for Morris. It would be more than enough exertion for him if he lifted his hand to the telephone to order in some pizza.

The sun was setting before he drew himself up, glanced at the dimming light and said, 'It's nearly dinner time. What the hell am I going to do? Do you reckon we could order Chinese?'

'Oh, for God's sake,' I said. 'Haven't you got any plan at all?'

'Yeah, I have. Ordering Chinese.'

'You do get paid for this job don't you Morris? You're not here as a volunteer? Seems to me you do bugger all to earn your wages.'

'Hey, I thought you were on my side!'

'Don't see why. I used to do this job. And look, I wasn't the most brilliant cook they've ever had, but I put in a lot more effort than you do, and for a lot less pay, from what I've heard.'

'You were just a fool,' he sneered. 'These guys aren't worth the trouble.'

It didn't seem to occur to him that there was a moral dimension to this, that he was paid to provide a service whatever his opinion of the rest of the staff and that it was wrong to take wages for services not rendered. I thought for a moment of Stella, indulging the staff up at Bogarilla with her favourite comfort food. The contrast between Stella and this smirking sleazebag was so great that I burst into tears and fled to the mullock heaps, where Eddie and his companions were still working in the gathering dusk. I crouched on a mullock heap and wept for a world afflicted with small-minded and ungenerous souls, while Emily-Jane clambered through the dirt and the baby found a discarded bottle top.

'What's up?' asked Potts.

'It's Morris ...'

'Ah, it's no wonder you're upset then. Anybody would cry at the bloody thought of bloody Morris. Man should have been shown the door the first time he cooked those bloody foul sausages,' said Potts. 'Paul, you're supposed to be the bloody camp manager. What the hell are you up to with a useless piece of shit like him on the payroll? Should be booted out by the seat of his pants. There must be someone in Burkes Hill who wants a job.'

At that moment a vehicle swept into the Compound and pulled up in the dust. James flung himself out the door, opened the back and yanked out his swag with such violent haste he lost his grip. The swag hurtled down the sloping ground towards us, threatening the order of the freshly packed rocks.

'Hey! Watch it!' yelled Potts.

'Shut up!' yelled James.

'What's your bloody problem?' Potts demanded.

James stared at us clustered amongst the earth mounds and

flung his hands in the air. 'I'm finished! Finished! I've had it! Give me another week or two and I'm gone! Gone from this lousy hole forever! Dennis O'Regan is looking for a mine geologist over in the Hamersley somewhere. You're looking at him chum. It's me.'

'What? But what about Shona?' asked Paul.

'She can come with me. They must need teachers in Western Australia.'

'Ah, no, you're nuts,' said Paul. 'You'll be stuck in some hot pokey town with nowhere to go. You ask Murray Crow about it. He got a job in some ghastly God-forsaken hole of a town once and got so bored he joined the women's sewing circle. You better learn cross stitch .... And there won't be any pigs!'

'Don't talk to me about feral animals,' yelled James. 'I've had just about as much of feral animals as I can stand.'

'Where've you been to make you so jumpy?' asked Eddie.

James didn't answer, but Hendo, who had been driving James that week, and had just wandered down to join us, said, 'We've been down at that abandoned homestead at Snaky Creek. You know the one. Pretty place, all covered in bougainvillea. Brumbies running wild ...'

'Huh... a mistake. Wish I'd never laid eyes on the place,' said James.

'Yeah, I know the one,' said Eddie, 'Lots of brumbies down there .... and feral goats.'

'Don't talk to me about goats!' thundered James.

'Sure, if you'd rather not,' said Eddie. 'But what's up? That animal magnetism problem hit you again? Been sexually abused by a goat this time?'

'Nah, bloody mongrel thing jumped in the window while we were looking at the creek,' said Hendo. 'Shat all over the passenger seat and ate his notebook.'

'What?' said Eddie.

'Bloody goat ate my notebook,' said James.

'You mean, all your data? Gone?'

'Yep. Goat ate the lot! Most of it anyway. I may as well have been down at Magnetic Island bathing in the sea for the last six weeks, for any results I'm going to get from all this slavery. I tell you mate, we gotta get out of this place. It's a mug's game! Not worth the bloody effort!' said James.

The stars were beginning to gleam in a slowly darkening sky and a dry breeze brushed against my cheeks, whispering of faraway things, a hint of a wider world, far beyond the Compound and Burkes Hill. We stumbled our way back up the stony slope towards the row of dongas to face yet another shambolic evening managed by Morris. But there was something different in the air that weekend, as if a wind of change was blowing through the place. There was a restlessness, a recognition that things could not keep going quite the way they had been.

* * *

On Saturday evening, Bazz and Aggie held a party to christen their new pergola. This was a special occasion, because it meant Morris didn't have to cook. The guests huddled beneath the structure and pretended to admire Aggie's pot-plants, but what really grabbed their attention was the food table. There was a tray of baked potatoes and a dish of sour cream. There was a mound of sweet corn and a rainbow salad. There was pavlova slathered with tropical fruit and a cheesecake dribbled with chocolate. And whatever was sizzling on the barbecue smelled fantastic and wasn't sausages.

The good food affected us all like too much champagne and the party was going with a real swing when Eddie and I left early to put our girls to bed. Even Morris had flung off his depressive mood, and was suddenly in the highest of spirits, leaping exultantly on Bazz and Aggie's bed with Tracy. Bazz, disturbed, lurked in the corridor. When Aggie had suggested it would be a fine thing to entertain his friends under the pergola, he had not bargained for guests who would take liberties of this kind in his bedroom.

We hadn't been back at the Compound for long when Potts turned up. The girls had only just been settled to bed and we had gone across to the dining room for a cup of tea. Potts burst into the room and flung himself on a chair, red-faced and gasping for breath.

'What are you doing back so early?' asked Eddie. 'I would have thought you'd still be swigging beer.'

'So did I mate. So did I!' said Potts. 'But circumstances changed. Hey Cynthia, can you do me a favour? Look outside and check there's no great hulking shape heading this way.'

'Nobody out here at all,' I said, glancing outside.

'Good, good, that's good,' said Potts, relaxed for a moment. 'What a bloody week it's been, hey? I might have known it would be a mistake to come and do my project with you guys.'

'But it's a terrific project,' said Eddie.

'Yeah, I know,' said Potts. 'Took me long enough to organise. But then I have to go and bring Tracy along. What kind of idiot does that? Contributed bugger all and probably expects a free ride on my work to get a decent grade. Well, she can get stuffed. I won't be sharing a thing with her. Not a thing! Not even a ride back to Brisbane. She can catch the bus.'

'You're better off without her,' I said.

'Yeah, lucky escape is how I see it—Hey what's that noise?'

I couldn't hear anything, but Potts was on the edge of his chair again, trembling as if a zombie army had marked him out for deletion and was closing in on him right now.

'Cynthia,' he gasped. 'Lock the door. Lock the windows. Turn out the lights.'

'What are you so afraid of?' asked Eddie.

'Bazz!' said Potts.

'Bazz?'

'Yeah. He might be under the mistaken impression that I was messing with his missus,' said Potts.

'Messing with his missus? Surely not,' said Eddie.

'Well of course I had no intention of messing with his bloody missus. I mean why would I? Only intention I had was for the next beer. But that Aggie, she lost the plot. I blame all those daytime cooking shows on TV. You know how those cooks are always quaffing wine as they stir the pot. Well look at all the cooking Aggie did. That'd be a lot of wine. She was already pie-eyed when we arrived,' said Potts.

'She seemed alright to me,' I said.

'Well, she wasn't! Can't have been! She leapt at me as I was coming down the corridor after taking a piss. Hurled me against the wall and rammed her tongue so far down my throat I thought I'd be sick. Never knew I was so bloody irresistible. I mean I've only just been rejected for the most pathetic loser the planet's ever seen.'

'Unaccountable,' said Eddie.

'Ironic I know. Then I saw this shadow on the wall, like something out of a horror movie. Bazz! I know I'm big, but Bazz is bloody bigger. He could shatter all my bones before I had time to explain.'

'Oh, Bazz is just a gentle giant,' said Eddie.

'Is that what you think?' asked Potts. 'Haven't you ever noticed that box he carries around? Made it himself? Of matchsticks? Have you never asked yourself where a guy would get all the spare time to make such a thing? I can tell you, because I asked him myself. It was when he was doing time for assault and battery of the last guy that tried messing with his missus.'

The next morning Potts poked his head out of his caravan and took a cautious survey of the Compound.

'I'm still in one piece,' he said as he trickled from the door. 'He mustn't have seen anything. Good. I can breathe freely again.'

With our girls in tow, we headed to the dining room for a cup of tea and a bowl of cereal. But everything seemed to have changed. There was a cheerful clattering of crockery, an aroma of appetising food, a glimpse of a broad bosom, a frilly apron with bright red spots. Were we dreaming?

Christopher stood in the doorway with a smug smile on his face, as self-satisfied as a tyrannosaurus rex about to feast on a triceratops.

'Hey, what's going on?' asked Eddie.

'The sun is shining, the birds are singing, and Morris is gone,' replied Christopher.

'Gone?'

'Run away. Oh, thank the Lord.'

'Where's he run to?' asked Potts. 'Or do I care?'

'Look, this is a bit embarrassing, but it looks like he's run off with Tracy. Both gone! Sorry Potts. I know she came up here with you,' said Christopher.

'Nah, it's okay. They deserve one another.'

'I must confess I'm happy to see the back of them both,' said Christopher. 'That girl wasn't cut out for geology, and it's good she's realised it. As for Morris, he's saved me a lot of trouble. I was going to have to let him go anyway. Serving an unimaginative menu is one thing, but using the food budget to buy takeaway? That's never going to fly. What did he think we employed him for? We don't need a cook to drive to the take-away.'

'He seems to think they can run a pub in the outback somewhere,' said Big Jill. 'Heard him say so last night.'

'Yeah, well I'd like to see that. Takes hard work. Those places don't run themselves,' said Hendo.

'When you find out which pub, let me know so I can avoid it,' said Malcolm. 'At any rate you seem to have found a replacement quick enough. Breakfast smells awesome.'

'Ah, yes, well, it was all so fortunate,' said Christopher. 'There was a bit of a scene last night when Bazz got upset with Morris and Tracy for bouncing on his bed like a pair of kids. But when they explained they were just happy because they had decided to run away together, Bazz cheered up and instantly recommended Aggie take over as cook. Well ... after that terrific spread she put on last night— Good God Potts, are you alright? You look awfully pale.'

A greenish tinge had spread across Potts's face. His words echoed across the Compound.

'Out of the frying pan into the fucking fire.'

Chapter 32

A pizza delivery

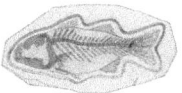

THERE WAS a time when I thought that Burkes Hill and the Compound would periodically disturb my life like a recurring nightmare. But the year Morris cooked those sausages turned out to be my last visit for a long time. To my surprise, the earth kept spinning and time moved on. Life changed.

A few years later, Eddie convinced me, one more time, to cook for an expedition going north, an expedition which also involved Wally and Grasshopper. But that's another story, for another time. Things were already quite different by then, but not as different as they were on my most recent visit to Burkes Hill.

The main street had retained its slow quaint air of belonging to a previous century, but the Compound had been obliterated off the face of the earth. That place where we had all struggled had become the car yard on the edge of town, not a mullock heap in sight, just rows of gleaming new utes shining in the sun. Even the green house on College Road was transformed out of all recognition, freshly painted and well cared for. Baskets of ferns hung from the veranda and the garden beds were no longer barren. The dried-out prickled yard had gone, along with the rusting swing set. Only the mango tree remained, standing by the fence surrounded by grass. There were birds singing in the shrubs in what had been that empty expanse of dust across the road. It looked like a real park.

Did I imagine it all?

* * *

At the GIU, staff shuffled in and shuffled back out, some moved on to careers elsewhere, and some remained to form new mapping parties in other localities. Gerald Drake eventually retired from the GIU to pursue his fascination with the reproductive habits of Queensland butterflies, proving it's never too late to pursue your real passions. As for James and Malcolm, yesterday's Casanovas became today's stable family men, weekend swing pushers, fully acquainted with the mysteries of Bananas in Pyjamas. Many of the field hands moved on too, like Wally had done, and found new arenas for their energies, losing their enthusiasm for culling feral pigs and baking dampers. Paul left the GIU a couple of years after Eddie, moving to Sydney and working on the Sydney Harbour Ferries. Last we heard, he had taken up dealing in art and antiques. And so over time, that team we got to know during those eighties field seasons dispersed.

But on special occasions of particular geological interest some of the old troops mingled together again. These meetings took place in a large buzzing airconditioned seminar room in Brisbane. A couple of tables were usually pushed against the wall at the back of the room waiting for the delivery of pizza, timed to coincide with the end of formalities. And although there were Eskies of ice and cold drinks alongside, the attendees typically ignored these refreshments at the beginning of the meeting and sat in rows as they waited for the day's speaker.

On one of the most memorable of these occasions, James McCracken, visiting from Western Australia, sauntered out to the front of the crowd, beaming upon the audience as the noise levels slowly diminished.

'It's an honour for me, on this visit to Queensland, to be asked to introduce the speaker for this year's *Gerald Drake Memorial Lecture ...*' he began.

'But I'm still alive!' croaked a voice from the audience.

Surprised at the interruption, James glanced down and saw Gerald, older, greyer, but not dead, seated in a prominent position and wearing an eye-catching tee-shirt decorated with a large image of a Ulysses butterfly.

'And great to have you with us tonight Gerald!' continued James, smoothly ignoring his error. 'Those of us here who shared in the ah ... special magic of those GIU field seasons organised by Gerald in days gone by, will have first-hand knowledge of the great contribution he made towards our development as geologists. In recognition of his contributions towards the Earth Sciences, I wish to introduce tonight's speaker, a man who could not have got where he is today without his early years of training in the GIU. Please welcome Dr Donald Potts.'

There was a round of applause and an almost unrecognisably respectable Potts strode confidently out to the front. There was an air of prosperity and success about him. His hair was short, and he wore a shirt with a collar. A debonair linen jacket had been flung on at the last minute against the icy blast from the airconditioner and added to the casual assurance with which he proceeded to enthral the audience. His talk was accompanied by what would appear to an outsider as a series of thoroughly uninteresting images depicting a camera lens cap against a barely changing background of a sand dune, and yet everybody was gripped enough by this material to ask a series of questions at the end, delaying the gravitation towards the drinks and pizza boxes.

After the formalities, James observed Priscilla who was standing by the table reaching for a slice of pizza. 'Hi Priscilla. It's been a long time ...' he said.

Priscilla, like Potts, had been transformed by the years, and there was barely a resemblance now to the girl with the long blonde plait who had tormented the miners at Blue Ridge years before. This woman was clipped, curled and smart.

'I hear you hit it good at the GIU, Priscilla. I knew you would, knew years ago. As for me, I was glad to get out of the place. I still shudder when I think of that Compound. Took me years before I could bring myself to eat a sausage after that last field season.'

'Well then James, you'll be pleased to know that the Compound is gone, sold off to the highest bidder. It was one of the first things I did after I became Director.'

'What? And you actually found a buyer for that heap of shit?'

'We did really well out of it. There were many people keen to purchase the land. And as for the fixtures, the Prison Service snapped them up.'

'Prison Service! That'd be right!' James turned. 'Hey Big Jill, great to see you. So, you're across from WA too?'

'Yep. Hi Priscilla. How are you doing? Heard on the grapevine you married that driller. Congratulations.'

But Gerald Drake disrupted the conversation and incorporated them into a group standing about the Esky. These were familiar faces, Christopher Craddock, Murray Crow, Bugsy Burrell, Malcolm Drake, Tiffany and Eddie. Gerald gulped down beer with the same enthusiasm he used to display at past Christmas parties.

'Those were the days,' he said. 'God's Own Country, hey?

Wind in the trees, dew on the grass, starry skies, dingoes howling in the night ... I remember back in 1961, paddling down a river to get to the outcrop. Crocodiles lurking on the riverbank—I tell you they don't come that big these days. That was the year the cook went mad ...'

Acknowledgments

Firstly, I must acknowledge that this book would not exist at all if not for my husband, Simon Lang, who habitually challenges me in such a way that I find myself in unexpected places doing unexpected things. This story reflects an early example. Simon has never stopped luring me out from the bookshelves to travel down rough and surprising roads, and I rarely regret these experiences in retrospect. Both his enthusiasm for the wonders of this ancient and ever-changing earth and his ability to spin a good yarn have found their way into this book. I am grateful for his never-failing support, encouragement and geological advice.

I am thankful to all those people who shall remain nameless, but who shared in those early field camp experiences. The colour of their personalities and daily lives inspired me to attempt to recreate their unique ambience in writing. I particularly thank those 'informants' who entertained me with yarns of bad cooks, wild women and other field camp eccentrics. I have harvested much from these stories, accurate or not.

Thanks to Ian Withnall and John Kaldi who both provided early encouragement and helpful comments. I am grateful to my sister-in-law, Christine Maine, whose enthusiasm for an early draft encouraged me through multiple revisions. I am sorry she's no longer here to see the finished product.

The contribution of Annie Smith is gratefully acknowledged. Her intelligent engagement with the text and insightful comments and suggestions inspired me to proceed with the project when I was tempted to throw the whole thing away.

My most appreciative reader is my mother, Daphne Butler, and I thank her for her ongoing encouragement and support. She can be relied upon for honest, common-sense feedback and her sharp eyes are terrific at detecting errors otherwise overlooked. More importantly, it was she who asserted that a manuscript eventually needs to be converted to a book. It should not be sitting in a corner gathering dust nor should it be subjected to eternal revisions. 'Just get it out there,' she said. Thanks Mum.

My neighbour, Gweneth Binks, who has published her own beautiful children's book, 'Winston', provided much encouragement and advice about the publishing process. She also, in a moment of inspiration, put me in touch with the talented Alice Taylor who has illustrated this book so wonderfully. Alice was inspired by her own experiences as a jillaroo in Queensland and as a field hand elsewhere, and her drawings complement this book beautifully. My thanks to both Gweneth and Alice.